HEROES
OF THE
BLOOD CURSE

J.N. JACOBS

Jacobs, J.N. (author)

Heroes of the Blood Curse

ISBN: 979-8-89694-426-3 - Ebook
ISBN: 979-8-89694-427-0 - Paperback

Fiction
Fantasy

Typeset Calluna 11/16

Cover photo by Adobe Stock

For Kaylee & Bliss.
My babies that are the light and love of my life

ONE

Callum Peterson sat bolt upright, gasping for air. Cold sweat poured down his face as his heart pounded so violently it threatened to burst open his ribcage.

He shuddered, no longer in his bed but on the floor. The small bedroom with its peeling white paint that had been home for years, seemed foreign somehow. Callum forced himself to fixate on the wooden ceiling fan hanging precariously from its wires, creaking in its circular path, not daring to close his eyes again. His heart rate slowed with the hypnotic spins.

It's just a nightmare. Shake it off and get ready for work.

But each nightmare left him more drained, taking longer for him to recover come morning. The ten minutes he spent lying there felt like hours until he could muster the will to move. He lifted his arms but they fell limply back to the floor. It took all his strength to lift his leaded body off the floor.

He stumbled toward his broken wardrobe, where one door hung diagonally on a single hinge and raked his fingers through his messy brown hair—a habitual gesture to self-soothe. He tugged the crinkled grey shirt off his gaunt frame and replaced it with a clean one, then pulled his jeans over his long skinny legs and walked to the mirror. The reflection sniggered, chilling his limbs to a freeze.

A figure with charcoal, scarred skin and red eye sockets glared back at him. Callum staggered back. Blood oozed from exposed bone and muscles along a side of its face as the demonic creature bared its decaying teeth into a grotesque grin.

With a cry between terror and disbelief, Callum shuffled back further on his bottom and jammed his eyes. There was no way he'd let that hideous thing take hold of his mind. But the harder he tried, the stronger the unseen force that held his eyes open became.

The monster was clad in a warrior's garb —brown leather covered its upper body, with a silver breastplate, brown pants, and black leather boots lined with metal plates. It twisted its bony face into a snarl, its hollow eye sockets flashed red, then black, as it raised an arm and pointed a leather-gloved finger at him.

You, the creature mouthed.

Callum's eyes darted from the rumpled single bed to the uneven bedside table, then back to the wardrobe, searching desperately for something, anything, to defend himself with.

This isn't real. This isn't real. That thing is just an illusion that will be gone any second.

The grey figure etched the corner of its mouth up in a sneer, and shook its head in mockery.

Callum swallowed the rising lump in his throat. As far as he was concerned, he was still trapped in his dream world, but the gnawing twist in his gut told him otherwise.

A loud voice from outside the window broke his trance.

'Oi! Don't you throw that garbage by my dumpster,' a woman yelled from the next apartment block. 'Put it on your side.'

A dog barked, and a cat hissed in response to her shrill voice.

'Oh, shut up, you old hag,' a man countered.

'Get your drugs and homeless rags out of here!'

A loud thud, wafted up the smell of rotten eggs that made him gag. He pulled on his jeans and leaned out of the open window, curiosity piqued by the commotion below.

Grey clouds made the alleyway darker than usual. The cigarette smoke that drifted up, teased his nostrils and triggered a sneezing fit. The clatter of smashing glass drew his attention to the resident homeless men below. They lounged languidly in rags by the bins, drinking from bottles, seemingly oblivious to the arguments above.

'Him! The screams came from his room,' the woman pointed as soon as she spotted him.

Callum froze, his inhale halted mid-breath. He had lived alone in the same cramped third-floor apartment for ten years, no one had ever spoken to him. Until now.

'Yeah, what gives?' a young man hollered. 'You've been screaming every night for months.'

Beep, beep, beep.

The sound jerked his attention back to his room. The clock read 5.00 am, 28 March. It was his twenty-first birthday, but the significance barely registered.

'Sorry, must go. Have to be at the hospital by six,' Callum called out hastily before slamming his window shut.

He risked a glance back at the mirror and breathed a sigh of relief when his own tired brown eyes gazed back at him. It was just a remnant of the nightmare. He'd panicked over nothing.

Nightmares, figments of the subconscious. He should've known better than to panic over a hallucination. He slung the backpack that contained his cleaners uniform over his shoulder, while his stomach grumbled. He ignored it and searched for his hospital ID badge, which was next to his petty cash box on the kitchen bench. Pocketing the badge, he opened the box, dismayed to find it empty.

In his wallet was a grand total of ten dollars—just enough for the weekly train ticket. He opened the fridge door in the hope there was something left. There was nothing.

Callum sizzled out a disheartened breath—he would have to scrounge for leftovers on the hospital food trays to tide him over for the day. The unpalatable, leftover hospital food had saved him from hunger many times.

As he rushed out the door to catch his train, he stepped on two white envelopes. After a glance at his watch. He jammed the envelopes into his bag and sprinted towards the train station. Only ten minutes left.

'Wait,' he shouted as he flew down the platform steps.

The whistle blew. The train doors beeped and began to close.

Callum squeezed into the nearest carriage before the double doors snapped shut. Puffing, he collapsed onto the nearest seat.

Once he'd caught his breath, he pulled out the two envelopes from his bag. One was an eviction notice. He was four weeks overdue on his rent payment. The other was from Garland Tech University, informing him he wouldn't be able to enrol in his next year of Biomedical Engineering if he didn't make the upcoming payment. His chest tightened into a dull ache, and his stomach knotted. Being an engineer was his dream.

In despair, he pulled a photo from his wallet. It was dog-eared and crumpled, a tangible link to a happier time. He touched the picture of the smiling young woman hugging her ten-year-old son. She had long, wavy brown hair, an elegant, oval-shaped face, bright eyes, and heart-shaped lips. It was the most cherished face in his memory.

'Mum,' he whispered, his eyes wet. 'I wish you were still here.'

He steeled himself against the tears—the picture of his mother always gave him strength. He took one last look and carefully tucked the photo back into his wallet. It was the last picture he had of her.

The window with its moving scenery passed the familiar sight of Sam's bakery, the single-storey houses, the Eagles soccer stadium, and then the string of garish billboards. The images moved like scenes in a movie, swirling and blurring into each other, so fast, he had to shut his eyes.

A hand gripped his shoulder and jostled him. He held up his arms, to fend off his attacker.

'Wake up!' a woman called out.

'Next stop, Dabury City Station,' a female voice announced through the speakers.

Callum wiped the saliva from his cheek, and a plump, middle-aged Hispanic woman came into focus, her eyes full of concern.

'Are you alright?' she asked. 'Did you have a nightmare?'

'You were thrashing so loud some passengers moved to the next carriage,' said an old man sitting across from them.

'Sorry,' Callum mumbled and propped himself up.

The train rumbled and screeched to a stop. Three beeps sounded before the metal doors swung open. The signs confirmed it was his stop. He swung his backpack on and darted out the train doors to escape further questioning.

As he made his way along the platform, a white-hot stab through his temples flashed the memory of razor-sharp teeth and burning green liquid against his neck. He clung to the station rails as busy commuters swarmed past him. Tentatively, he touched his tender neck and held up his hands. Nothing.

He massaged his neck in circles and worked to slow his breathing, while he focused on the Dabury City Station sign, not moving until he was sure he was fully lucid. Forcing the horrific creatures into a corner of his mind, Callum made his way out of the station.

Night time nightmares were one thing, but now, daytime nightmares too? His stomach clenched threatening to release bile from his gut. But they weren't just bad dreams. Every slice, every claw, every bite in his mind triggered his pain centres into overdrive. No, they were more than just nightmares. They were real. It felt *real*.

He swallowed the rising lump at the back of his throat, the ghastly images would have to take a back burner until work was over. Callum strode down the bustling streets of the city, crossed the road past the coffee shop, the fruit vendor, and the newsstand—the same sights he'd encountered every day on his way to work at Dabury hospital. After he turned onto Bentley Avenue, the hospital was only ten minutes ahead.

He moved slowly down the familiar street and looked up—same blue skies, same high-rise buildings, and the same taxis lined up in the rank on the curb.

I must not have had enough sleep, that's why the nightmares came. Maybe it came because I've been so stressed. Maybe I need to work less. Maybe I need to eat more. Maybe...

Before Callum could take another step, a sharp pain lanced through his brain. His vision flickered from streets filled with towering buildings to scenes of twisted scrap metal and flaming rubble. He shook his head, desperate to clear it.

Before him, dozens of people crossed the road, each absorbed in their own world. Cars honked incessantly in heavy traffic that clogged the streets.

The images that flickered back and forth in his mind, intensified. It was like having his scalp slowly ripped apart. An anguished cry escaped him as he doubled over.

'Hey man, you okay?' a passerby asked, his voice cutting through the haze.

Callum turned away, the passerby's voice faded into the background.

The images flickered again until his vision settled on the apocalyptic scene of deserted streets.

This can't be happening, I'm not asleep!

He slapped his cheeks in a desperate attempt to wake himself. But even with his cheeks stinging raw, the streets before him remained unchanged.

Every twitch in his muscles urged him to flee, but something invisible held him firmly in place. A decaying stench hit his nostrils. He turned to locate its source and immediately regretted it. Human body parts lay strewn across the street, a grotesque scene of an unimaginable horror.

He forced himself to breathe through the reek of decomposing flesh. A hot breeze grazed his cheek, while swirls of red dust danced through the air. It rose towards the sky, turning the yellow sun and once-blue heavens into a blanket of sickly crimson.

Desperate, he scanned the desolate street for signs of life—of anyone still alive. He stumbled forward but tripped, landing face-first into a pile of decaying flesh.

His stomach contracted again and again, emptying out every last drop of acidic juice, taking out any energy he had left to scream.

Callum scrambled to his feet and stumbled aimlessly down the street. The red dust thickened with every step—dust he inexplicably knew was the blood of millions.

Taunting laughter filled his ears. 'Run, run, run, but you will never escape.'

'Who are you?' Callum cried.

Faint voices echoed in the distance. Hope surged as he turned toward the sound. He strained to make out their words, but there was no one in sight.

The cacophony grew louder, filling the air with screams of terror, desperate cries for mercy, and the ghastly sounds of flesh being torn asunder. Each shriek sent waves of agony rippling through him.

He crashed to his knees, clutching his head. 'Stop, stop, please stop! I'm begging you.'

But the sounds looped through his mind in an endless, brutal replay. He couldn't breathe. He couldn't move.

Then everything went black.

Two

Voices from above tore through Callum's consciousness. He tried to open his eyes, but they were glued shut. His hand brushed against the hard concrete and a pair of shoes.

'Oh my God, someone call an ambulance,' said a female voice.

'Is he still breathing?'

'Check his pulse.'

'Does anyone know CPR?'

'I do,' a man replied. 'Everyone, move back and give this poor guy some air.'

Two cold fingers dug into Callum's neck, and a big hand pressed down on his chest.

I'm fine. You don't need to give me CPR.

'He's breathing, and he has a pulse,' a man said. 'Give me a hand; we need to roll him into the recovery position.'

With concentrated effort, Callum flung his eyes and waved his arms. 'I'm good. Don't roll me.'

The onlookers took a step back.

Callum crawled to his knees only to buckle back down onto his hands.

'I don't think you should get up,' the man said, placing a supportive arm around him. 'Let's get you to the hospital. It's right up ahead.'

'No, I'm fine,' Callum insisted and forced himself to stand. 'I need to go. I'm late.'

Despite the protests of the onlookers, Callum elbowed his way through the crowd and charged toward the hospital.

Ignoring his spinning head, he hurried through the glass entrance of the hospital and up the six flights of stairs to the cleaner's locker room. A quick glance at his watch revealed his misadventure had cost him four hours of pay.

Quickly, he changed into his dark-grey overalls and grabbed his pager. Three missed calls—all from the same number: 5681. David Grant's extension—his boss. Worried, Callum found the nearest phone, dialled, then braced himself for the verbal onslaught that was sure to come.

'Where in God's name have you been?' David said, his voice crackling with indignation. 'I'm understaffed and had to clean up two bloody spills myself. Do you know how angry that makes me?'

David's rant continued, each word making the room spin faster. Exhaustion seeped through every pore and the day hadn't even started yet. Callum bit the inside of his cheek to keep seething remarks from escaping. He couldn't afford to lose his job.

'I'm sorry, David,' Callum said in a flat tone. 'It won't happen again.'

'Guys like you are a dime a dozen. Now get your arse to the surgical ward,' David barked. 'The nursing manager has been calling for hours.'

Callum suppressed a groan. So much for leftover breakfast.

***

Callum wheeled the creaky cleaning cart out of the elevator and followed a trail of bloody footprints down to the surgical ward. He poured detergent into the bucket, then searched for a pair of rubber gloves in the trolley.

Without warning, a body barrelled into him. Unable to keep his footing, he skidded and fell face down on the dirty floor.

'Oh my God, I'm so sorry. Are you okay?' A woman took his arm and helped him to his feet.

His brows shot up when he found himself face-to-face with Paige Corlee, the pretty, ginger-haired assistant nurse.

'Are you okay?' she asked again, her big hazel eyes full of concern.

'Yes,' Callum mumbled.

Paige glanced at his hospital ID. 'Callum Peterson, I have an emergency call in the next room, but I'll make it up to you. I'm here until ten tonight. Come find me.'

'Paige!' a senior nurse barked from the room. 'In here. Now!'

'Coming, coming,' Paige disappeared among the crowd of medics into room B25.

Curious, Callum pushed his cleaning cart closer to view the resuscitation. He loved watching—their skills always fascinated him.

At the head of the bed, the anaesthetist secured a tube in the patient's throat and attached the airbag. The monitor by the old man's bedside beeped loudly, the irregular green line dancing wildly across the black screen.

'He's in asystole. CPR, now!' the doctor barked from the top of the patient's bed.

Paige stepped onto the stool, placing both hands on the old man's chest, and delivered rhythmic chest compressions with the strength and ease of an expert.

'Julie, prepare the defibrillator,' the doctor called out to another nurse. 'Deliver the shock as soon as we get a rhythm.'

Callum distractedly mopped the floors. How amazing would it to be a doctor—with all that respect and authority. Being a nurse would be good too. Most people liked nurses.

He was still mopping when the team burst out of B25 with the patient, the heart monitor now beeping at a regular rate. The patient was being transferred to the intensive care unit, the team moved so fast, Callum had to press himself against the corridor walls to make room.

Moments later, Paige stepped into the hallway, her red hair dishevelled and her pink scrubs tucked messily into her matching pants. She looked tired, but the relief on her face was evident. She walked into the nurses' station and collapsed onto the nearest chair.

A young doctor glanced up from writing his notes. 'Great work on that resus, Paige. How about we go downstairs, and I shout you a well-deserved coffee?'

At that moment, another doctor appeared at the bench with two cups. 'She already has her coffee, Martin,' he said, grinning.

Dr. Martin's charming smile evaporated into a scowl, just as a buzzer went off. 'Grr, Patel.'

A look of relief washed over Paige's face as she rushed off. 'I'm sorry, doctors, duty calls. I'll talk to you another time.'

Dr. Patel pointed an index finger at Martin's nose. 'She's mine,'

'Sure.' Martin smirked, grabbing the coffee meant for Paige and taking a long sip. 'It's called delusions. I can write you up for some olanzapine if you like.'

'Ha. The children's ward needs another clown doctor. You might want to apply,' Patel huffed out and stalked off.

Callum ducked his head, stifling a laugh. He was often a silent witness to Paige being endlessly hit on by hospital staff. If it wasn't someone flirting with her, then it was gossip about who she was going out with.

Paige Corlee was the most talked-about assistant nurse on the ward. Everybody—her colleagues, her patients, the doctors, even her superiors—liked her. There was something magnetic about her. Anyone who spoke to her seemed to walk away happy. There were times Callum could have sworn he saw a pink glow emanating from her. He, too, felt a pull toward Paige, but unlike the others, it had nothing to do with attraction.

THREE

In Luigi's quaint Italian restaurant, Stacey Langcastor waited at her table. She pushed her silver-rimmed glasses closer to her eyes to check her watch again. Her date was thirty-six minutes late. She twirled her blonde ponytail through her fingers in impatience. She prided herself on being reliable and punctual, and expected the same from others.

It was Kate Henshaw, her best friend, who had insisted she go on the date, ignoring her numerous objections to the set up. Kate was like a trusted sister ever since they met in university and very difficult to say 'no' to.

Stacey adjusted her white blouse, loosening it from the tight rolls by her hips. Kate, with her pretty face and model-like physique, could never understand the impact of carrying stubborn extra kilos to a blind date. Being four years older, Kate did not seem to notice the disparity between their looks. She had taken her under her wing when Stacey had been awarded the University Science Scholarship at age fourteen and had become her best friend ever since.

Though lately, Kate had become an annoying matchmaker, setting her up on an endless series of blind dates to get her to 'go out more.' As if eighteen was some magic age to hook up or become the next socialite.

Stacey was as enthused about meeting new people as she was about chewing on whiteboard chalk. Strangers were unpredictable, volatile, and that was frightening. She much preferred working at Micro Labs, with variables that she could understand and control. But deep down it was lonely, although, she would cut an arm off first before she would admit to wanting love like everyone else.

That evening, her blind date was Liam Michaels, an eighteen-year-old amateur athlete who Kate met at her gym while he was trying out for the Eagles' soccer team.

'He's a sweet guy,' Kate had said. 'Same age as you. You'll have lots to talk about.'

Stacey checked her watch again, unsure if she was relieved or offended that she'd been stood-up. Idly, she stared at the candle flame on the table. It rose out of the glass cup, briefly formed the head of a dragon, and then disappeared, leaving behind a smoky trail.

Stacey jerked back, slamming into the back of her chair. Her blink rate increased ten-fold.

As if taunting her, the flame rose out of the glass cup again; this time it formed a smiley face.

Stacey furtively turned her head around to see if anyone had noticed. The other patrons chatted away, completely oblivious.

She stared at it. There had to be some kind of logical explanation. Flames don't just spring up and form pictures.

She picked up the glass cup and brought it close to her face. It was like any ordinary drinking glass—round with a thick bottom. There were no oils or chemicals in the glass, just a small white candle the size of a fifty-cent coin attached to a grey metal base. The flame flickered from side to side as Stacey moved the cup back and forth in her hands.

She placed it back in the middle of the table and closed her eyes, tired from looking down a microscope all day. That must be it.

She rubbed her temples, longing for her couch and a Hawaiian pizza.

When a warm rush of air pressed against her face, her eyes snapped open. The flame had risen out of the cup again to form an angry face.

Stacey shot out of her chair straight into a tall guy by her elbow. The impact knocked her back into her seat. When she steadied herself, he took the opposite seat. The guy wore a rumpled white shirt, a dark brown jacket and a navy cap pulled low over his forehead. His face was strong, well defined with a straight nose, and stubble covered his square jaw.

'I'm Liam Michaels. Sorry I'm late.' His grey eyes looked fatigued. 'Didn't mean to knock you over. Are you okay?'

Scathing remarks crossed her mind as her left arm throbbed, but she bit her tongue, remembering Kate's request for her to 'be nice'.

'I'm fine,' she said after a moment of silence.

'You must be Stacey Langcastor.'

'I must be.'

'I like that you're dressed so casually.'

Stacey looked down at her white blouse and grey skirt suit in disbelief. It was the best outfit she owned.

'You're better looking than I imagined,' Liam said, smiling. 'A little chubby, but hey, still cute. It works for you. And you're blonde. I thought only clever people can be scientists.'

Stunned, many biting comebacks swirled through her mind, she didn't know which one to say first. All that came out was a disgusted grunt.

'Oh, hey Stace, it's okay to be nervous,' he said. 'I can assure you I'm just a regular guy, nothing to be nervous about. So, what do you want to know about first? My ambition is to be a great soccer star. You know my father owns a big sports agency. We recruit …'

And on and on, he droned about soccer. Stacey rolled her eyes—it was going to be a long night.

'Why don't we order?' Stacey asked when Liam finally took a breath after a thirty-nine-minute recount of his favourite game.

'Of course, yes, I almost forgot,' Liam said. He waved to the waiter. 'I'll have a bottle of the 1984 Cabernet.'

The waiter eyed Liam's appearance. 'That Cabernet is eight hundred dollars a bottle, sir.'

'Yes,' Liam said brightly. 'My girl and I will have it on ice.'

'Uh, no. I don't drink—' Stacey began.

'That's nonsense,' Liam replied with a snort. 'Everyone drinks. My dad and I have it after long games. Trust me, you'll like it.'

Stacey arched an eyebrow, embracing a new level of annoyance. She hated people making decisions for her.

Liam turned back to the waiter. 'I'll have the salmon, and the lady here will have the veal.'

'I'm allergic.' *Was this guy incapable of hearing her?*

'Oh, sorry. You know, if you ate more protein, it would be easier for you to tone up.' Liam beckoned the waiter over again for an order change, missing the wide-open scowl Stacey made no attempt to hide.

Stacey's legs twitched, and she moved one leg out from the table, itching to leave, but she didn't want to risk causing a scene or appearing rude. She could just imagine Kate saying, 'Give the guy a chance, don't judge someone from first impressions, you can't keep rejecting all your first dates.'

Reluctantly, she pulled her foot back in.

After Liam had recounted his last three favourite soccer games, Stacey decided it was time to change the subject, if only to preserve her mental state.

'You know, I'm working with the renowned microbiologist Professor Leanne Hamilton on the Cytoplon bacteria,' she said, doing her best to turn her gritted teeth into a smile. 'It's a huge honour. I get to be second author on her research paper.'

'Got it, really smart chick. Go on.'

Stacey pressed her lips together to keep a rude remark from escaping. But at least they had moved off the topic of soccer.

'The Cytoplon bacteria was discovered twenty years ago but poorly understood. It can mutate and adapt to its environment at ten times the speed of any other micro-organism.'

Stacey, caught up in the passion of her explanation, barely noticed the glazed-over look in Liam's eyes. The free flow of her knowledge on Cytoplon escaped her like water from a broken dam. 'Our theory is that if we could harness that mutative ability, then we could use biotechnology to encode repair sequences.'

'Mmmm,' Liam mumbled. His head bobbed as he pulled his cap down over his eyes.

She droned on.

A snore from Liam made her stop.

This was the worst date ever.

The flame from the candle shot up and formed a picture of another angry face, then swirled again to form flaming arrows pointing at Liam. Stacey took the candle cup and furiously blew on it. The candle flared as if mocking her, continuing to dance and flicker sideways like a cheeky toddler.

Panicked, Stacey blew harder onto the flames. It formed a laughing face and blew out 'zzz' from its flaming mouth. Then heart-shaped fires floated towards her, dissipating into smoke, centimetres from her nose.

She lifted her wine glass and poured its contents on the flame. Her shoulders relaxed with relief, as it fizzled out.

Her date let out another snore.

'Are you asleep?' Stacey asked loudly, putting the candle cup under the table.

'What?' Liam asked groggily, wiping the drool from the corner of his mouth. 'No, no, of course not. I am very interested in your Cyclopoop... thingy. Um, let's have dessert.'

Stacey wanted desperately for the date to end. Liam stared at her as she inhaled her dessert.

'Are you in a hurry?' he asked with a look of confusion.

'I realised I left my little brother on his own for too long. I need to go.'

'Oh, okay,' Liam said, looking put out.

'Thank you for a lovely evening.' She picked up her purse.

'Oh no, don't worry,' Liam said. 'I'm paying. What kind of guy would I be if I let you pay?'

'I would prefer to pay for my own meal.'

'Nonsense.'

Liam reached into his pants, and a look of dread formed across his face. He dug his hand into the side pocket of his left jacket, then his right. His face turned shades of white, then red.

'Are you okay?' she asked.

Liam cleared his throat. 'Um, I think I left my wallet in my locker. Would you mind getting the bill this time?'

**

Stacey left the restaurant and power-walked to her car. She flicked on her Bluetooth to dial Kate's number. Her irritation rose like a shaken fizzy drink in need of release. Kate picked up after two rings, and without bothering with greetings, Stacey launched into a rapid recount of the dinner date.

'It was a disaster. I don't think I have ever been so insulted. He thinks that scientists can't be blonde. And that I'm fat and need to eat more protein.'

Kate chuckled. 'Surely he didn't say that.'

'He did,' Stacey said fuming. 'All he talked about was soccer, and more soccer. Then he dozed off.'

'Oh no,' Kate said between laughs. 'That's awful. I'm sorry.'

Stacey waited for her to stop laughing. Her best friend should be dating alongside her. It seemed unfair for her to endure a string of bad dates on her own. She coughed down the boils of hopelessness that bubbled up. Love seemed to drift further away with every unsuccessful date.

'Anyway, I don't want to talk about it anymore,' Stacey huffed. 'Tell me about your day at the legal aid office.'

'It was pretty boring. Only minor theft cases. A couple of pre-teens got caught stealing computer games and a phone. They're probably going to be let off with two hundred hours of community service.'

'I still can't believe that for someone who graduated top of their law class last year, you've chosen to work at the legal aid office. You had a ton of offers from big firms.'

'I know,' Kate sighed. 'I'm just more passionate about fighting for the less fortunate. It's not about the money for me, you know that.'

'Yes, you've been telling me that since we first met,' Stacey said.

'To this day, I'm still amazed you were able to finish a university science degree at eighteen,' Kate shot back. 'Most people don't get in till they're eighteen.'

'I got lucky with the scholarship. Anyway, you seem so unfulfilled when you work on these minor cases. Is there anything else you can do?'

'It would be nice to get a real case,' Kate said. 'You know, something really challenging, where I'd need to fight for a man who has been wrongfully accused of murder or something like that.'

Stacey laughed. Her friend's passion for justice was much like hers for science. 'How cliché of you. Be careful what you wish for, Kate.'

Four

At ten-thirty in the evening, Callum's shift finally ended. After finishing the unexpected dinner Paige had left for him in the ward, he packed up and changed out of his work clothes. As he walked out of the hospital, he welcomed the familiar rush of cold night air that often signalled a welcomed end to a long work shift.

He had twenty minutes to make his train. He usually ran the entire ten blocks to the station, but this time would good to spend figuring out how to overcome the hurdles in his life. There had to be a better way. He intended to spend his day off seeing the university finance officer to ask for a payment extension, but that still left his unyielding landlord who'd wanted to evict him for years, despite all the repairs and renovations Callum had made to the apartment.

When Callum turned the corner onto Baxter Street, a loud crash made him turn. He hurried toward the alleyway, where a large boy with a pregnant-like belly pinning a skinny, sandy-haired boy against rectangular metal industrial bins. Two other boys took turns kicking him.

'Stop. Please, stop!' the boy yelped.

'Shut up, you fag,' snarled the big one. He grabbed the boy's shirt, yanking him closer. 'Freaks like you shouldn't be allowed to exist.'

Blood trickled from his lip and the boy raised his thin arms to push off his attackers.

A burning rage erupted in Callum's chest charging him into the alleyway. 'Get away from him, now!'

'Who the hell are you?' The bullies snarled.

'Hey, Butch, it might be another fag from down the club,' the curly-haired one smirked.

'Let that boy go, or—'

'Or what?' Butch countered.

Before he could utter another word, Callum slammed a fist into his nose. His hand throbbed, but he ignored it and threw another one into Butch's stomach.

Butch howled and doubled over. 'Get him!' he bellowed at the other two. 'Make him pay.'

Having spent years weaving his way out of attacks from bullies, Callum was adept at dodging punches. He gave one of them a side kick, then rolled over him to kick the other in the crotch.

The boy shrank into the shadows, readying to run.

A sudden blast of wind hit Callum squarely in the chest. The sky darkened in an instant and the sun swallowed by a thick, churning mass of clouds. A rumble rippled through the street, and the ground beneath them trembled as if something massive was stirring below.

Without warning, the asphalt cracked open with a deafening grate. Cracks spiderwebbed across the surface, converging at the centre of the street and a gaping vortex appeared. It was as if the earth itself had been torn apart, revealing a hungry void beneath.

The wind howled and pulled everything towards the swirling hole as the very air twisted and writhed in its grip.

When the boy didn't move, Callum climbed to his feet and lunged forward. He grasped his arm and pulled him backward.

As the strong winds swirled around them, the terrified boy clung to his arm. 'What's happening?' he squeaked, the pupils in his widening eyes reflecting the growing portal.

He flung his small trembling body into Callum, who gripped the side of the metal bins with one arm and the boy with the other. Horror spread through him like weeds on steroids, as the vortex drew the bullies nearer.

The wind knocked them facedown, and they dug their fingers into the ground.

They screeched for help and clawed their finger nails in deeper. Despite their efforts, the wormhole dragged them closer to its opening,

Just when Butch's feet along with his two mates were dangling over the opening, a medium built man in a black suit, with a wide brimmed straw hat shadowing half his face, stepped out of the shadows. He strode toward them, and he raised an open hand. A familiar white hospital plastic ID badge materialized in his palm. 'Callum Peterson, Cleaner,' he read.

'Hey, that's my hospital access card.' Callum lunged to snatch it back, but the man swivelled out of his way.

'Finders keepers,' the man sneered, pocketing the badge.

Butch screamed as the vortex pulled him in further.

It took a couple of attempts before Callum found the courage to speak. 'Make it stop.'

The man laughed and crouched down low to meet his eyeline. From under the wide hat, a grey face with black eyes blinked at him. Callum jerked back, banging his head against the metal bin.

'S-stop the vortex,' Callum said, less bravely.

'I'm afraid I can't do that,' the man said, reaching out to squeeze the small boy's face. 'Only he can.'

Whimpering, the boy wriggled like a worm caught out of its hiding place.

'What do you mean, 'only he can'?' Callum asked.

'Only the boy can close the vortex,' the man drawled, 'he's the one who opened it.'

'What?' the kid gasped.

The man flexed his legs and towered over the kid cowering at his feet. With a flick of his wrist, the bullies projected out of the vortex. Butch crashed to the ground and landed awkwardly on his leg. His howls escalated to an intolerable frequency that could shatter glass.

'They will no longer be a problem,' the man said. Black crackling energy rays burst from his eyes, landing on the trio. The dark rays wrapped around them in a dark halo, then ejected them onto the adjacent street by the alley.

'I'll see you soon.' And with that, he faded into the darkness.

'My leg is broken,' Butch whined and dragged his bent leg forward to hobble with the other bullies across the street, out of sight.

The vortex snapped disappeared and Callum turned to the boy. 'Are you okay?'

'Thanks to you, I am. I'm going home now.'

'It's better if I take you to the Emergency Room. You're injured.'

'No, no, I'm okay. My home isn't far, and my sister is waiting for me—'

'You're hurt.' Callum took his arm and steered him toward Dabury hospital. He stopped when the boy shook.

'Look, I'm not going to hurt you,' Callum said in a soothing voice. 'We can call your sister at the hospital.'

'Okay,' he said, less agitated now. 'Who are you?'

'My name is Callum Peterson. What's yours?'

'Ryan Langcastor.'

FIVE

Callum sat beside Ryan on the uncomfortably hard plastic chairs in the hospital emergency waiting room. His gaze wandered over posters of vaccinations, hand hygiene, and basic resuscitation, before it settled on the red entrance doors by the reception desk. He willed the doors to open, but they remained stubbornly closed for over an hour. Too late for him to catch the next train home.

To distract himself from thoughts of missed trains, Callum decided to find out as much as he could about Ryan. If he really was the one who created that vortex, the kid must have some extraordinary powers.

'So, Ryan, how old are you?'

Ryan rubbed his hands up and down his arms. 'Fourteen.'

'What were you doing out so late at night?' Callum asked.

Ryan stared at the TV in the reception area, ignoring him.

'Isn't it a school night?'

'So?'

'Don't high school students have to stay home and do homework or something?'

Ryan shifted in his chair and folded his arms. 'Or something. It's none of your business.'

'Sure.' Callum shrugged.

'I mean, don't get me wrong,' Ryan said. 'It's cool that you came to help, but I don't really know you.'

'Fair point,' Callum admitted. 'Why were those guys beating you up?'

Ryan looked away; his expression closed off.

'Hey, I was bullied in school too,' Callum said gently. 'They used to throw me into the dumpsters behind the school gym.'

'At least your bullies didn't beat you up for liking boys,' Ryan blurted out, then slapped a hand over his mouth.

Callum arched a brow. 'Are you saying those guys beat you up because you're gay?'

'Shush! Not so loud,' Ryan hissed with darted eyes around the room.

'Being gay is nothing to be ashamed of, Ryan,' Callum said firmly.

'It is where I go to school. You get shamed for being different.'

Callum clenched his teeth, old memories resurfacing like an infusion of poison. Images of his teenage self being shoved and spat on by his older schoolmates appeared before his eyes, followed by flashes of his foster father striking him. A burning sensation gnawed at his chest, making it difficult to breathe. He became light-headed, and the waiting room began to sway. The chairs and TV blurred with blotches of red, as if someone had splashed paint across the room.

Crap. No, not again!

A strong tug at his arm dissipated the images. The room was still again, and the TV news reporter droned on.

'Hey Callum, if I tell you something, you have to promise not to tell my sister, okay?' Ryan's voice cut through the fog.

Callum drew in a much-needed breath, blinking as he tried to remember why he was sitting in the emergency room.

Ryan scanned his face. 'You look kind of pale. Did you hear what I just said?'

Callum shrugged, trying to appear nonchalant. 'Tell me. I don't know your sister.'

Ryan hesitated, then sighed. 'My sister was out, so I went down to The Diamond Rainbow.'

'The Diamond Rainbow?'

'It's a gay bar. The best one in Dabury City. It's awesome.'

Callum eyebrows shot up again. 'You're underage. You didn't sneak in, did you?'

'No,' Ryan said quickly. 'I wanted to see it from the outside. But then I saw Butch and his friends come out. And that's when they chased me into the alleyway. As if it wasn't enough that they beat me up in school, they have to do it outside too.'

'I see,' Callum said, dots connecting in his mind.

'See what?' Ryan asked sitting up straighter.

'Their problem with you. You're a reminder of what they're trying to hide in themselves.'

Ryan frowned. 'When you put it that way… Oh my God, wow,' his eyes widen with what must be realisation.

The red door swung open, and a nurse stepped through with a clipboard in her hands. 'Ryan Langcastor?' she called.

'Present,' Ryan answered, raising his arm with enthusiasm.

'Come on. This isn't rollcall at school.' He pulled Ryan to his feet.

Callum involuntary took a step back. The ED nurse waiting for them was Paige Corlee. She must be working a double shift for extra pay.

'Come on in,' she said warmly, beckoning them into the assessment room. 'We're a bit understaffed, so I'll be starting the assessment, and the triage nurse will be in shortly.'

The bags around Paige's eyes affirmed her exhaustion.

'Hello. It's Callum, right?' Paige asked once they were seated by the consultation table.

'Yes,' Callum replied. She remembered him, he couldn't imagine why.

'Is this your brother?'

Before Callum could respond, the door burst open, and a plump, blonde-haired girl in her late teens with silver-rimmed glasses hurried to Ryan's side.

'No, he's mine,' the girl cried, wrapping her arms around Ryan. 'What happened? Oh God, Ryan, are you okay?'

'I'm fine. Nothing happened,' Ryan mumbled, his cheeks blushed with pink as he tried to push his sister away.

'It does not look like nothing.' She cupped her brother's face and studied it intently. 'Was it Butch again?'

'Stop that. I'm okay,' Ryan said, slapping her hands away. 'Let's drop it and go home, okay?'

'I'll get the doctor,' Paige said and left the room.

Stacey's voice trembled. 'Butch and his bullies did this to you didn't they? Why didn't you tell a teacher!'

'I'm fourteen, Stace, not four. A teacher is not going to do anything,' Frowning, Ryan crossed his arms. 'Stop fussing. You're not Mum. It's embarrassing.'

Stacey drew back and bit her lip looking hurt, but quickly composed herself. 'What were you doing out so late? This didn't happen in school, did it?'

Ryan stared at the wall, avoiding her gaze.

'No, they attacked him in the Baxter Street alleyway,' Callum interjected.

'Callum helped me fight them off,' Ryan said.

Stacey turned and acknowledged Callum's presence for the first time. 'Thank you so much for helping my brother.' She stepped over and hugged him.

Callum tried to pull away, but this only made Stacey hold him more firmly. He cringed, and politely excused himself to catch the next train.

By the time Callum made it through his front door, the blurry lopsided clock in his living room read 3 am.

He stumbled over the hole in his floorboards and landed on his grey L-shaped couch, on top of scattered dirty laundry. Who cared about dirty laundry, when sleep was the only thing that mattered.

The dream came immediately.

Six

Seconds passed and his consciousness slipped deeper into sleep. Callum floated into a desert, where a tall, bare-chested man with wavy grey hair and black leather pants stood with a battle axe thrust high in the air. He was poised to charge.

His golden crown glistened in the sunlight.

Thousands of bare-chested soldiers, armed with spears, stood in disciplined rows behind him. Opposite them, about a kilometre away, hundreds of thousands of men clad in red leather and silver-breasted armour advanced, their raised swords and shields ready to attack.

'King Argos, the Lyarian army outnumbers us ten to one,' a general said, his voice tense.

'Don't worry, Ezra,' the king replied, his deep voice unbending. 'We are mighty warriors of Ceres. I won't let my kingdom be taken over by these barbarians. With our ancestors' powers on our side, we will fight and we will win.'

King Argos's mouth twisted into a snarl and he clutched a round diamond hanging on his chest. His eyes glowed black, and his face morphed into something grey and bony as he unleashed an ominous boom, 'Let them come.'

With eyes blazing, he lifted his colossal battle axe with its blade pulsing with dark energy, and slammed it down.

The ground shuddered beneath his feet. The earth split open, a jagged chasm tore through the sand, and from its depths came guttural howls. The air grew cold as shadowy tendrils of smoke spiralled upward and twisted into monstrous forms.

Out of the abyss, mummified wolves emerged—hulking beasts with eyes like molten embers, their skin blackened and cracked as if forged in fire. Their claws scraped the desert floor, leaving deep gashes in the sand, and their breaths were searing winds that scorched the air. The chasm continued to widen at the king's feet, vomiting forth thousands of the wolves.

In that moment, King Argos was not just a man, but a demonic beast. The creatures bowed to him, then at his command, they tore into the advancing Lyarian army like they were made of paper.

Horror seized Callum's throat as the creatures devoured the soldiers in minutes. Shrieks of terror reverberated, as fountains of blood whipped high into the air by desert winds and turned the once-blue sky into a terrifying shade of crimson.

Then the scene before him wavered into an image of a village with burning straw huts.

King Argos loomed into view, his hollow red eyes flashed, his face a spectre of ash. He appeared more demon than human. As he raised his arms, dozens of mummies in silver armour surged to attack the villagers.

Cries of panic filled the air as the people fled, but the mummies slew them without mercy. The screams of the dying echoed in Callum's ears.

The diamond around King Argos's neck, housed in its round, brown stone casing, shone brightly. With every life taken, his eyes glowed brighter, and his face contorted further, becoming more monstrous. Callum expected to feel terror staring at the king, but instead, a puzzling connection warmed him which defied understanding.

The image of the king faded, replaced by an elegant woman. Her slender form was hugged by a flowing white gown. Callum shifted to catch her face, but was blinded by the diamonds nestled in her intricately styled hair.

He floated after her into a vast hall with marble walls and floors. Three green-white columns lined each side of the vast rotunda. At it's centre a pair of golden thrones perched at the top of a stair led dais. Down the centre, a red velvet carpet stretched to where four warriors stood waiting.

The woman Callum floated after exuded grace and authority. She stopped at the base of the stairs, hidden from the warriors' sight. A man in a white robe, with short grey hair and moustache framing a dignified face, approached her.

She tilted her long neck then shook it, her voice a whisper. 'How can I to approach them with such a request, Vizier?'

'You must, my queen. It is the only way.' The Vizier handed her a wooden box.

The queen, squared her shoulders, sniffed, and wiped her eyes. She clutched the box tightly to her chest and stepped forward. She watched the four generals argued amicably on the red carpet and sighed.

'Lang,' a general clad in a gold-plated cuirass barked, turning to a woman behind him, 'must you wear that God-forsaken animal head every time we present at court?'

He doubled over in a sneezing fit and his bronze helmet toppled off and rolled down the scarlet walkway.

Lang scowled, flicking her emerald mail coat over her shoulder and methodically stroked the wolf head draped across her aqua hauberk. She shifted a spear back behind her belt to reveal a horn and lasso. 'General Castor, we have more pressing matters than your nasal ailments.'

Castor growled, rubbing his red watering eyes.

The bare-chested warrior in blue leather pants standing opposite Lang, threw his head back and chuckled heartily, then thumped his bare muscular chest with a fist. 'You should follow my lead and do away with cumbersome armour.'

Lang's hands flew to her tunic chest armour. 'Sir Mye-kols, I am a dignified noblewoman.'

Mye-kols guffawed, the axe and sword hanging by his side swinging as his body shook.

Lang narrowed her eyes and pointed the head of her silver spear at him. 'You dare laugh at me, general?'

General Corlee slung the lasso and bow over her metal shoulder plate, the arrows in her quiver rattling as she stepped between the squabbling duo. The spearhead nicked her breastplate, running down the large, embroidered azalea on its front.

She stretched out her leather-plated arms. 'Stop it, generals. Queen Enactra will be here any moment. We must show her a united front against the growing threat of King Argos.'

Castor let out a thunderous sneeze and stomped his gold-plated boots across the carpet to reclaim his position. 'General Corlee is right. King Argos has now invaded more than half the land across the united seas.'

Corlee reached behind her belt buckle, retrieving two scrolls of tattered paper. 'I received these from the carrier pidgeons. My soldiers at the border speak of the many horrors wrought by the blood-thirsty king.' She unrolled the parchment and scanned its contents. 'They say he raised armies of earth creatures with black eyes and hollow bones that swallowed soldiers and villagers in the blink of an eye.'

'Surely that's not our king,' Mye-kols said, disbelief in his voice.

Queen Enactra approached her generals, the Vizier trailing closely behind. Her subjects bowed low as she neared. 'It is all true.' She motioned for them to rise. 'The king has lost his humanity and is conquering kingdoms at an alarming speed.'

Her eyes glistened with unshed tears, but her voice was steady and resolute. 'Thank you for coming. Each of you has served my family for many seasons. I am grateful you are willing to stand with me against the king.'

'Of course,' Lang said, bowing her head once more. 'We will die to protect your Majesty and the Kingdom of Ceres.'

The other warriors mirrored Lang's gesture, crossing their right arms over their chests in unison. 'We salute you, Queen Enactra.'

'Noble warriors, I am forever in your debt.' Her voice cracked with emotion. 'I cannot reach my king. His bloodlust is too strong. I'm afraid he won't stop until he massacres every living being.'

In a swift movement, the queen dropped to her knees. The warriors gasped and quickly followed suit.

'Your Majesty, you cannot do that,' Castor protested, concern etched across his face.

'Yes, I must,' Queen Enactra replied. 'For what I am about to ask is more than your lives. It will also affect the lives of your descendants. Should you fail in your mission, your bloodline will be cursed to continue what you have started until peace is restored.'

The warriors stared at her, their unblinking expressions shifting from astonishment to confusion.

Corlee swallowed hard. 'What is your plan, majesty?'

The queen held out the old wooden box and opened it, revealing its contents. They gaped at the legendary treasure.

'By the animal gods, that is the life stone,' Mye-kols murmured. 'How did you get it away from the king, ma'am?'

Queen Enactra shifted her gaze but remained silent. She tossed the stone into the air and directed an energy beam at it. Her eyes glowed brilliantly as she chanted a spell. The warriors cried out in unison as the life stone shattered into pieces. The fragments landed back into the box, each glowing in a different vibrant color: blue, yellow, pink, white, green, purple, red, and black.

The golden double doors to the throne room exploded open with a boom, shaking the marbled walls, threatening to shatter the glass dome of the rotunda. King Argos stormed in, two generals trailing behind him, their faces shadowed by the twisted fury of their enraged sovereign. Every step Argos took, echoed like a drumbeat against the polished floor. The air rippled with the power radiating from him.

'Where is my life stone?' Argos's voice thundered through the hall.

All generals leapt to their feet, and drew their weapons, their faces a mask of resolve as they prepared to confront the oncoming storm.

Queen Enactra placed herself between them. 'Argos, please,' she pleaded and gripped his shoulder, locking her eyes onto him, as if searching for the man she once loved beneath a monstrous facade. 'I know this isn't you speaking. You can fight the evil curse. Give me a chance, let me help—'

King Argos let out a guttural sound that shook the foundations of the palace. With a violent shove, he pushed the queen backward. A surge of energy crackled from his fingertips, manifesting as a bolt of lightning that he hurled at the wooden box. It splintered apart and scattered the precious stone fragments across the floor.

With determination, the queen's warriors launched themselves at the king and his generals. In the ensuring chaos, the queen crawled across the floor, gathering up the stones. The Vizier aided her in retrieving them, then pulled her away from the battle.

Mye-kols and Castor charged at Argos, their determination as fierce as the storm that raged around them. With weapons held high they launched at the corrupted king. He retaliated with a wave of his hand and sent the warriors flying, like ragdolls against the marble columns with bone-jarring force.

'What have you done to my life stone?' Argos bellowed. He seized Enactra by the throat and lifted her into the air. Her breath became laboured as she clawed at his fingers, but his grip only tightened.

'Please, think of our son,' she choked out her lips turning blue. 'He needs his father.'

'I have no son!' Argos's eyes flashed with unbridled fury as he dropped her to the floor.

Enactra crumpled, pain and fear etched into her face. She drew her knees to her chest, her voice barely a whisper. 'Our baby boy, Calister. He is only three months old. If you don't stop, our son will be cursed to pay the price for your crimes. Argos, please. I am begging you. Stop the killings.'

'Traitor. Liar!' Argos spat out. 'You will pay with your life.' He raised his axe high, the blade gleaming as he poised to deliver the fatal blow.

In a swift manoeuvre, Generals Lang and Corlee hurled their lassos through the air with precision. As soon as the ropes coiled around the king's waist, they pulled him back with a sharp tug. Argos struggled, his muscles straining against the bindings.

'Run, Majesty, run!' Lang and Corlee shouted, sweat rolled from their foreheads, as they strained to hold the enraged king at bay. 'We can't hold him long.'

The king's generals charged, their swords raised high, grim determination etched on every part of their faces. Castor and Mye-kols rose to intercept them. They planted themselves in the path of Argos's warriors, and became as immovable as the marble columns that surrounded them.

The Vizier, with what seemed like courage from desperation, pushed Enactra aside and launched himself at Argos. He tackled the king with such force that they both sprawled onto the ground. Lang and Corlee seized the opportunity, dragging Argos further away, their every muscle straining under the Herculean effort to contain the king's wrath.

Argos bellowed, his fury echoing through the hall as he writhed and struggled.

Queen Enactra gazed at her warriors with a sorrowful expression. 'Please forgive me,' she whispered, her voice only audible to Callum in the clamour of battle.

With renewed urgency, she gathered the scattered stone pieces, her lips moving in a chant that resonated with ancient power. The earth trembled in response, the low rumble grew into a mighty quake.

The fighters were frozen by a magical force. They began to rise, suspended in the air as if held by invisible threads, then drifted backward through the room.

The stone fragments leapt from Enactra's hands and shot upward to the floating warriors. Each fragment glowed with vibrant colour, matching the hues of the warriors' clothing, and flew unerringly to its intended bearer.

King Argos broke free of his bonds and bull-dozed toward Enactra. But the earth beneath them shuddered violently, opening a chasm at their feet. Argos stumbled, falling to the ground just beyond reach of the queen.

In a brilliant flash of rainbow light, everything came to an abrupt halt. Each hovering warrior absorbed their respective coloured stone, their forms glowing momentarily before they vanished, whisked away by the power of the enchanted gem fragments.

SEVEN

Callum woke with a jolt, his skin slick with cold sweat. The remnants of the dream clung to him like a shroud.

Another nightmare, always another nightmare.

But this one was different; not the usual torn body parts and deserted streets. Was this nightmare trying to show him something before that apocalypse? Was the demonic King Argos the one responsible for the catastrophes in his recurring nightmares?

He swung his legs over the side of the bed, intending to get a drink to calm his racing heart. But his gaze fell on an unexpected figure standing at the edge of his room.

An old man, with hair as white as freshly fallen snow and a beard that stretched past his navel. He regarded him with a serene expression. His multi-coloured robes fluttered around him like the vibrant wings of a butterfly, and the moonlight caught the gleam of a clear pyramid crystal atop the staff he held which cast prismatic reflections across the room.

Callum gulped, his mind scrambling to make sense of the unusual vision before him. He seized the new baseball bat from beneath his bed, his hands shaking as he brandished it in front of him. But after the second swing, he lost his balance and crashed to the floor.

He scrambled back up, pointing the bat at the old man, whose eyes twinkled with sympathetic amusement.

'It's okay,' the stranger said, his voice calm and reassuring. 'I'm not here to hurt you.'

'W-w-who the hell are you?' Callum's voice trembled as much as his hands. 'And h-how did you get in here? What do you want?'

The old man closed his eyes, and when he opened them again, they shone with an ethereal white light. A peculiar pressure on his wrist made him fling the bat, and it landed harmlessly on the other side of the room.

Callum pressed against the wall, his arms raised, his mind whirling.

The old man tilted his head slightly, eyeing him with cat-like curiosity.

'My name is Hubert Waltor. I am the Grand Vizer. There's no need to be afraid.'

'Grand what?' Callum croaked above the hammering of his heart.

'Grand Vizer,' the old man repeated, his tone patient and soothing. 'An adviser. A mentor. I am a warrior trainer and can see the past, present, and sometimes the future. I am here to start you on your mission.'

'M-my what?' Callum shook his head, trying to dislodge the surreal words from his mind. He had stepped into a waking nightmare. *Wake up. Wake up. Wake up. This is just another hallucination.*

'This is not a hallucination, Callum,' Hubert said with an unwavering smile and a voice filled with gentle assurance. 'And you aren't sick. Far from it.'

Callum sank to the floor. He pulled his knees to his chest and searched the room for an escape or some semblance of reality. 'Wait, how did you...?' *This was madness. How does he even know my name and what I said?*

'Those dreams you've been having—' Hubert began, his voice steady.

Callum's mind spun, his grip on reality slipping like sand through his fingers. 'How do you know I've been having dreams?'

'They're not dreams,' Hubert explained, his eyes glowing with an otherworldly certainty. 'They're visions. Everything you have seen either has happened or will happen.'

Callum gagged as if invisible hands were squeezing his throat. His head pounded with an intense pain that made him dizzy. Every instinct screamed at him to flee. 'That's... that's... you're nuts.'

Hubert nodded calmly as though he had heard these things countless times before. 'It is part of your awakening.'

'Awakening?' Callum echoed, the word foreign and terrifying.

'A war is coming,' Hubert said heavily. 'It is prophesised that billions of lives will be lost if we do not unite the stone-bearing warriors.'

Callum rubbed his face with shaking hands, trying to dispel his panic. Surely the old man's words were the ravings of a delusional mind.

Great, a whack-job burglar with grand delusions.

'A whack job, eh?' Hubert chuckled. 'I am telling you the truth.'

Callum's jaw dropped. 'How did you... I didn't mean... but I didn't say anything!'

'I'm a telepath. I can hear your thoughts,' Hubert said, the twinkle in his eyes grew brighter.

'Great, you're a mind reader, too,' Callum muttered, then climbed onto his bed. There was no such thing as a telepath. Was this a psychotic neighbour? Maybe he'd leave if he played along. 'But I'm only a cleaner. What can I do about it?'

Smiling, Hubert stroked his beard slowly. 'You are so much more than that. You are at the centre of it all.'

'How?' Callum desperation seeping in to his voice.

Hubert waved a hand dismissively, as if brushing away details that cluttered a larger picture. 'All you need to know is you hold the key to bring them all together.'

'Key?' Callum repeated.

'The life amulet on your chest,' Hubert said.

A sudden weight around Callum's neck made him glance down in surprise. Resting against his chest was a circular rock, its surface etched with intricate patterns that glowed with an inner light. When he tried to tear it off, a searing pain shot through his wrist., Forced to let it go, the alien rock clunked back onto his shirt.

'You need the life amulet to guide you to the stone bearers and bring out their powers,' Hubert said firmly.

'Why me?' Callum cried, teetering on the edge of hysteria. 'Why are you giving this to me?'

The air around Hubert shimmered like a desert mirage. 'I'm not giving it to you,' Hubert said. 'I am returning it.'

Then his form blurred and dissolved into a cloud of white light, 'You will find yourself drawn to certain people and situations. Follow it,' he said before he disappeared.

'Wait! Come back. What is this?' Callum reached out toward the vanishing figure, but Hubert was already gone. Only a fading trail of luminescence was left in his wake.

***

Callum awoke in bed, his heart racing as the beep of his alarm clock pierced the morning air. Just another dream.

Sighing with relief as he sat up, the remnants of the bizarre encounter faded like mist in the sunlight.

But the cold weight on his chest told a different story.

He glanced down, and there it was—the life amulet, resting heavily against his shirt, its surface glinting with an otherworldly sheen. He stared at it, numb, and held up the circular ornament to make sense of it.

Life amulet? Life amulet. He let the words roll around in his mind, wondering why Hubert had called it that and what he was expected to do with it.

Callum slapped the side of his face to wake up. But the stone amulet still sat cold and heavy in his palm. It seemed ludicrous to consider that a figment of his imagination could be real enough to give him anything. Yet he had no idea how to explain the coffee-coloured stone hanging from its cord around his neck.

The irregular indents at the centre of the amulet grazed his fingertips. It looked as if something had once been attached to it. There were gold symbols in a random smashing of shapes, engraved around its edges that reflected the morning light. Was this supposed to be some ancient writings?

The phone by his bedside buzzed, breaking his trance.

'Where in God's name have you been for the past two days?' David blasted through.

'Sorry? I don't understand what you mean.' He wasn't due for work till the next day.

'Don't try my patience, Peterson. I warned you. You think you can pull a no-show like that and expect to get away with it?'

Callum's head hammered. Was he in another one of his ranting moods again? 'But I was there for my shift yesterday.'

'No, that was Friday,' David said. 'Today is Tuesday. Don't you know what day it is?'

Callum looked down at his phone screen and gasped. It read Tuesday, 10:20 am. Shit. He'd been asleep for two days. How did that happen?

'I—I'm sorry, David. It won't happen again, I promise. I'll come in straight away. I'll do extra hours. I'll—'

'Don't bother. If you want the last of your pay, hand in your uniform and access card,' David said. 'You're fired.'

Callum stared at the concrete under the curled-up portions of dried paint. The phone had gone silent, but his hand still clutched it tightly against his ear. He wasn't ready to let go.

The room spun. His body rocked. All he could do was stare at the wall, willing the dizziness to subside. Why couldn't the universe give him a break! He'd had enough. This curse—or whatever was happening to him—needed to end.

An intense heat exploded inside, and his vision turned red. A surge of energy coursed through him, making him stand taller, strengthening the power in his limbs. The force expanded so rapidly that it threatened to burst him wide open.

Callum let out an animal roar he'd never heard before. He bent over and lifted his couch and tore it apart with his bare hands. When the heat vanished, he collapsed from exhaustion and shut his eyes.

***

In the afternoon, Callum trudged down the streets of Dabury city, his mind a swirling fog of confusion and his body numb. He had replayed the morning's events a thousand times, but nothing could explain what had happened to him, or why his three-seater lounge was now shredded in pieces across his living room floor.

He glanced down at his arms—still the same scrawny limbs that struggled to move the lounge last year. His eyes landed on the pay check sticking out from the edge of his fist, the one he had retrieved from David in his hospital office. There was no use trying to make sense of the inexplicable. He had more urgent matters to attend to.

Stuffing the check into his jean pocket, he forced his unsteady legs to keep moving. Was there any point in returning to an apartment he could no longer afford? With a frustrated sigh, Callum ran his fingers through his hair to calm himself.

An itch in his fingers made him pull the cheque back out, hoping for a better number. The harsh digits, one-five-eight, stared back at him coldly, as if to say, 'That's it, suck it up, loser.'

Suddenly, a body slammed into him, and the check fluttered to the ground. Callum dived for it, scraping his cheek and nose painfully against the concrete. What the hell was wrong with people, did he have a 'hit me' sign on his back?

'Are you okay?' a female voice echoed above him.

Callum shoved the cheque deep into his front pocket before allowing himself to be pulled to his feet. Blinking, he stared into the face of a vaguely familiar blonde girl with silver-rimmed glasses. His mind swirled, trying to connect the round face to a name.

The girl took a step back, tilting her head to study him. 'You're the guy from the emergency room who helped my brother the other night. Cal... Callum, right?'

Callum averted his eyes. Being recognised by someone he had trouble remembering was unsettling.

His mind flickered back to Baxter Alley two nights before. 'Uh, you're the boy's sister. Spacey, right?'

She smiled. 'Stacey.' Her brows knitted together as she touched the side of his cheek. 'That's a nasty scrape. Your face is bleeding.'

Callum pulled back, now aware of his throbbing face.

'My apartment is just a few meters ahead. Let me clean you up.'

Callum winced. He didn't want help or pity, least of all from a girl he barely knew. He needed to find a job, immediately. He strode away. 'No thanks.'

'Hey, wait, please,' Stacey said when she caught up to him. 'You helped my brother, Ryan. Let me do the same for you. I don't want that wound to get infected.'

'No, I'm—'

A sudden hot pain pierced his head and stopped him in his tracks.

'It won't take long, I promise,' Stacey's voice called from a distance.

'*You will find yourself drawn to certain people. Follow it.*' Hubert's voice blared so loudly it doubled him over. The pain intensified, threatening to split his head open. He banged his fists against his temples, willing it to stop.

Stacey shook his arm. 'Callum. Oh my God. Callum, what's going on? Let me take you to the hospital.'

'No!' Callum shouted. 'Head...ache. It's nothing.'

'Then come to my place. I'll give you something for the pain.'

'*Follow her. Say yes,*' Hubert's voice echoed from nowhere.

The excruciating headache escalated the urge to vomit. 'Okay,' he wheezed.

Hubert's voice faded, and Callum was able to relax. Suppressing a groan, he allowed Stacey to escort him up the steps of her apartment building.

At apartment eight she plugged in a key, and when the door swung open, Ryan's grinning face greeted them. He engulfed Callum in bear hug. 'Wow, it's you.'

Callum frowned. *What was it with this family and all the hugging?* He kept his arms by his sides until it was over.

'Ryan, Callum had a fall. Give him some space. You act like we've never had a guest over.'

'We haven't for ages,' Ryan said but let him go.

When Stacey guided him inside to the two bedroom flat: a combined kitchen and a lounge living area, and at the end a door to a bedroom. Callum took a seat on the U-shaped couch opposite a large TV unit, while Stacey disappeared into the bedroom.

Ryan bounced over and sat next to him. 'Awesome, you're by the games console. We can play Ninja Flips.'

Callum stared at him, still trying to clear his mind's haze. 'Ninja Flips?'

'Yeah. It's the best game ever.' Ryan dived into the compartment below the black TV unit and tossed out its contents. Within minutes, the floor was scattered with games. He grunted in frustration until he finally found what he was looking for.

'Ah, here it is.' He held up a CD and popped it into his game console. 'This is so cool.'

Stacey reappeared with a white first-aid box.

Callum tried not to flinch while she gently wiped alcohol swabs across his face. To distract himself from the sting, he focused on the screen behind her. It displayed brightly animated images of two ninjas flipping in combat. Ryan was engrossed in the game, moving his body in sync with his character.

Callum couldn't help but smile. Ryan was so carefree, the pure joy from something as simple as winning a game was infectious.

Stacey held his chin with her free hand and applied a cold cream. 'Ryan would get scrapes and bruises all the time.' She paused for a moment to inspect her handiwork. 'There, all done,' she said and smoothed a bandage onto his cheek then handed him two small white pills and a glass of water. 'Take these.'

Callum lifted himself off the couch, about to refuse, when the blazing determination in Stacey's eyes made him accept the medication. It was almost as if she would set him alight if he didn't comply. With her hands on her hips, Stacey nodded in satisfaction when he swallowed the pills.

'Good. I'm going to make dinner. Callum, would you like to stay?'

Callum would have said no, but feared triggering another bout of splitting headaches. A garbled response escaped his throat.

'I'll take that as a yes,' Stacey said and headed towards the kitchen.

As soon as Stacey had gone, Ryan shifted closer to him and dumped a set of controls into his lap. 'She's like a dragon, isn't she?'

'Ryan,' Stacey called from behind the kitchen bench, 'turn the game off and help with the chopping, please.'

'But—'

'Now.' Stacey commanded.

Ryan groaned and made his way quickly to the stools by the island bench.

Callum, unsure of what else to do, followed and settled into the seat next to him. 'I'd like to help, too.'

Stacey smiled. 'In that case, would you mind chopping the carrots?'

She handed Callum a bowl of vegetables, and Ryan a mixed-fruit bowl.

While peeling and chopping, Ryan chatted about computer games, soccer, and the latest celebrity gossip. An unfamiliar warmth filled Callum's chest, and he found it difficult to stop smiling.

His stomach gave an approving growl at the smell of the freshly cooked meal. It wasn't takeaway, hospital leftovers, or frozen food, but a real, home-cooked meal. It was like the meals his mother used to cook for him. A small tear trickled down his cheek.

'Hey, you okay?' Ryan asked.

'Uh, yes,' he said, looking away.

Stacey was a perfectionist, everything had to be well-cooked and presented. Plates of food covered the dining room table—pot roast, potato bake, Greek salad, a cheese platter with cold meats, stir-fried noodles with prawns and chicken, calamari rings with fried fish cutlets, and a large plate of mixed fruit. Callum had never seen so much food in his life. It was enough to last him a fortnight.

He savoured every bite. Stacey seemed pleased as she piled more food onto his plate. 'Do you have family here, Callum?'

'My mother died when I was ten, and my father left when I was five.'

'That must've been tough,' Stacey's tone soft with sympathy. 'Were your foster parents good to you?'

A sharp twist in his chest made him wince. He had spent years trying to forget his foster experience. 'I've been living on my own since I was fourteen,' Callum swallowed the rising tirade of guilt.

'Why?' Ryan asked.

Callum wasn't ready to delve into his past, but it was hard to avoid their questions with both of them staring so intently at him. 'Um, my foster parents got sick.'

'I'm sorry,' Stacey said. 'They must've put you in another home.'

'Yes, three.'

'Then why would you be on your own at fourteen?'

Callum's voice cracked. 'They all became seriously ill.'

'That's so odd,' Stacey said. 'For all three foster parents to fall ill like that. Were they really old?'

Callum shifted in his chair. Stacey's questions were like an excavator digging up wounds he had spent years burying. How could he explain to her that he was the cause of their sickness? Anyone who tried to care for him either died or became severely ill. The doctors had no explanation, but in his gut, he knew he was the reason, even if he had no idea why.

'I might have cursed them.'

Stacey frowned. 'How can that be true?'

'It felt like it at the time. It didn't feel right living with sick people. So, I left.'

Stacey changed the subject as if the tragedy was too much for her to handle. It was a welcomed change and Callum found himself opening up about his life and his aspirations to become a medical science engineer.

Her eyes lit up, and she offered to lend him her old textbooks.

'Do you plan on moving closer to work?' Stacey asked. 'There are plenty of apartments to rent near the hospital.'

'I can't afford it here,' Callum said. 'I've lost my job. But I'll probably be looking for another place anyway. I'm being evicted.'

'Come and stay here,' Ryan piped up.

Callum blinked rapidly at him. 'No, that wouldn't be fair to you.'

'I don't mind,' Ryan said. 'You can have my room.'

'No, Ryan.' Stacey said sternly

'Why not?' Ryan asked. 'You're an orphan. We're orphans too.'

'Ryan!' Stacey snapped.

Ryan ignored his sister. 'Come live with us, we can support each other,'

Stacey scraped her food across the plate. Callum should have changed the subject to something less contentious, but curiosity got the better of him.' What happened to your parents?'

'They died ten years ago when Stacey was eight, and I was four. Our foster parents were awful to us, so we left after a few years. My sister worked two jobs supporting us ever since.' Ryan beamed at his sister.

Callum stared at Stacey with newfound respect. 'How were you able to afford your degree?'

'I won a science scholarship at our school. Our parents left us each a trust account, but our foster parents hid it from us.'

Callum nodded. 'But they gave your money back in the end?'

'Not until my best friend Kate threatened to sue them. We were her first clients while she was still studying. Speaking of which, she might be able to help you with your eviction. She's a lawyer.'

Callum raised his eyebrows. 'Really? Why would she want to help me?'

Stacey's face brightened. 'She likes doing things like that. I'll get her to give you a call if you're okay with it.'

'Uh, yes, of course. But I wouldn't be able to afford her.'

'Kate works at the legal aid office,' Stacey said. 'She won't take a fee.'

Callum's mind spun for the umpteenth time that week. But now it was from the light giddiness of hope.

EIGHT

At Dabury Hospital, Paige sat alone at the nurses' station that morning, enjoying a rare moment of peace.

She stared at the messy pile of patient notes on the workbench, tired of having to put everyone's files away. Not this time. As she checked to see if there were any outstanding tasks from her hand over sheet, the buzzer to room C20 went off, summoning her down the hall to answer the call.

At the doorway of room C20, a young man about her age with short brown hair, grey eyes, and a strong square jaw, stared expectantly at her. Clean-shaven, she could see how the other nurses might find him attractive.

She studied his chart. 'Is everything okay?'

'That thing above me keeps beeping every time I move.'

Paige shifted to check his heart rate monitor. One of the leads had fallen off.

'I'll replace this lead, and that should fix the problem,' Paige said. 'Liam Michaels, right?'

'The one and only,' Liam said, smiling brightly. 'Are you a nurse? You're the prettiest one in here.'

His face dropped when a doctor walked through the door.

'Hello, Mr. Michaels. I'm Dr. Leslie Parker, your anaesthetist. The plastics team will be repairing the torn tendon in your hand today.'

Dr. Parker dragged a chair to Liam's bedside and began unpacking the cannulation set.

'I'll insert this plastic needle in to deliver the medication that puts you to sleep during your surgery,' she said. 'Do you have any questions?'

Liam's face paled. Paige gave Liam a reassuring smile and turned to leave.

'Wait,' Liam called out with a hint of desperation. 'Nurse, can you stay?'

Taken aback, Paige looked to Dr. Parker, who had the needle ready. Before she could answer, Liam gasped and thrashed at its touch. Blood spurted into the air. The doctor tore off the tourniquet and applied pressure to the wound.

'Come here, nurse' Dr. Parker said, motioning for her to hold a wad of gauze on his wrist. 'I'm going to get another set.'

Beads of sweat appeared on Liam's forehead. Paige was about to deliver her usual patient-soothing speech when her throat tightened. No sound came out. Her eyes widened, astounded to find sweat dripping from her face onto her work pants. Her heart thudded, and her hands shook.

What was happening? She wasn't scared, how could she be? For some reason, Liam's terrified expression seemed to mirror the winding in her gut. She could always empathise with patients, but nothing like this.

'I hate needles.' Liam cried out when Dr. Parker re-entered the room.

Paige was going to tell him that it would be okay, that she would be here and it would all be over soon. The childish utterances that tumbled out made her flush with the glowing intensity of ten neon lights.

'No needles. Hate them!' Tears streamed down her face, like a broken tap.

Liam gave her a bewildered look.

'Paige, are you alright?' Dr. Parker asked with facial lines etched with concern. 'This isn't like you.'

Paige tightened her lips together, refusing to let another word escape. She'd never lost control of her emotions before. When the drop in oxygen levels burned her lungs, she allowed herself a shallow inhale and a meek smile. 'Sorry,' she said, then caught sight of two of her colleagues looking through the window and dreaded the gossip that would soon circulate.

Dr. Parker sat down on the opposite side of Liam's bed. 'Can you hold him? I'm going to try again.'

Paige nodded. Liam's face grew paler than the bed sheets as he clutched her hand. Her fingers tingled and began to lose feeling.

'Wait,' Liam said. 'Maybe you could do it later. My surgery isn't due yet.'

'No, I was paged,' Dr. Parker replied. 'Your surgery was bumped up. You're going in next.'

'What?' More colour drained from Liam's face and he turned an extra shade of white.

Paige's body shook like she was having a seizure, and the twisting of her stomach threatened to encore that morning's breakfast. Before she could comprehend what was happening, a loud crack sounded from behind. The pipe under the wash basin burst open. Water spurted up in a thick stream and crashed over them. She and Liam screamed, while Dr. Parker's calm demeanour turned to horror as the room flooded.

Paige shot up from her chair in a panic and slammed the emergency call buzzer.

***

That evening, Paige stood at the nurses' station writing notes into the patients' files. It was difficult to focus as memories of the morning's events came back. She cringed, remembering what a colleague had said to her. 'What's with the jock having a panic attack? Couldn't you calm him down?'

Paige's intestines knotted. She had let the team down. It was imperative she made a good impression if she was going to work here after completing her nursing degree. Dabury was the most prestigious hospital in the country.

She wheeled the blood pressure trolley stand around the ward, making her last round of observation recordings before handover. When she entered Liam Michaels' new room, he was asleep. The white basket that held the blood pressure machine rocked at the top of the stand as she wheeled it into the dimly lit room.

The sweat scent of perfume filled her nose. The floor was covered with flower baskets. She weaved through them to Liam's bedside, as he opened his eyes.

'How are you feeling?' Paige asked.

'Tired and nauseated,' Liam said groggily, trying to wriggle to a sitting position.

Paige quickly lifted his hand. 'Don't put pressure on that arm. You might burst open the stitches.' Once she was satisfied that he wasn't going to move it, she wrapped the blood pressure cuff around his upper arm.

'My hand's throbbing,' said Liam in a subdued tone.

She gave him a reassuring smile. 'The night nurse will come with your pain medication soon.'

'You're leaving?'

'Yes, I finish in fifteen minutes.'

'Oh, I see,' Liam mumbled, looking disappointed.

'Don't worry. You're doing well.' Paige wrote down the readings on the machine without looking up. 'That's a lot of flowers you've got there. Did your family visit today?'

Paige was stunned when Liam's face fell. But before she could stop herself, a tear rolled down her cheek. *Oh no, it's happening again. Quick, think of something else.*

'I don't have a father or a mother. They died,' Liam said is a childish tone and began to cry. 'I really want Mum here.'

Paige reached for the nearest box of tissues. She blew her nose loudly and sat down next to her patient. She willed herself to think of something else, combat training with Uncle Rob, her puppy, her new cocktail dress, but despite her efforts, she continued to be as sad as Liam. She shifted to get away, but was stuck in place, perturbed by the disconnection between her mind and body's reactions.

A creak from across the room drew her attention to the spurts of water that spouted out of the basin taps, landing on the flower baskets. It was happening again. She looked at Liam, the water spurts seemed to be in sync with his sobs.

'Stop crying,' Paige choked out.

Liam hiccupped, grabbed some tissues, and blew his nose. This sent another wave of water into the room.

'Please, stop crying,' she begged.

'Okay,' Liam sucked in a breath and wiped the last of his tears from his face.

In awe, Paige watched as the water in the room flew back into the taps as if it were a video on rewind. 'Did you see that?'

'See what?'

'The water from the basin. It came out of the tap while you were crying.'

'Really? That's bizarre.' Liam rubbed the back of his neck.

Paige fixated on his gestures. 'It stopped when you stopped crying.'

'Why are you looking at me like that?'

She averted her gaze. He couldn't have caused that. She was just tired and imagined it.

'Can you stay a little longer?' Liam asked, his tone almost pleading.

Paige pushed aside her weariness and sighed. She made it to the end of her shift, she should be looking forward to a relaxing hot bath at home. Instead, she focused her thoughts on being kind. Liam seemed to need someone to talk to. 'What happened to your family?'

Liam sucked in a quavering breath before replying. 'They died in a car accident ten years ago.'

'That's awful. I'm so sorry,' Paige said, fighting back tears.

'My dad's best friend Jeff became my foster father. He gives me everything I need, but never shows much affection. He makes me train all the time. I'm not allowed to eat until I complete my regime.'

'That's really harsh.'

'I mean, he's not abusive or anything, he's just serious all the time. Like he's afraid of something. When I try to ask him why he shuts me out, he just orders me to continue training.'

Paige's vision was misty from tears that mirrored Liam's. This time it was her own sadness. Their stories were so strangely similar. 'My parents died too in a car accident, ten years ago, when I was nine,' she said. 'My father's brother, Rob, became my foster father.'

'Wow. We have the same story.'

'Uncle Rob gets me to train too,' Paige said. 'He's a judo and boxing instructor at his own gym. We do all sorts of training—cardio, weights, jujitsu, boxing. Everything.'

Even as kind as Rob was to her, her chest still ached from her parents' absence. A wave of despair washed through her, threatening another floodgate of tears. Not wanting to cry in front of Liam again, she changed the subject.

'What happened to your hand?'

'I tripped trying to chase after my date. My foot caught, and I crashed into a waiter carrying wine glasses,' Liam replied with a hopeless look.

'Oh no.'

'She didn't even look back. She was already out the door, like she couldn't wait to leave,' Liam said miserably.

'What went wrong?'

'I have no idea. That's never happened to me before. I mean, girls usually like me.'

'What did you talk about?'

Liam thought a bit, then said, 'Soccer games.'

'Anything else?'

'Her science-y work.'

'What kind of scientific work?'

'I can't remember,' Liam said, turning pink. 'Something nerdy in a lab.'

Paige was beginning to understand why the girl had left. She was unsure whether his ignorance was due to arrogance or simply immaturity.

'Did you at least try to show some interest?'

'Yes, I mean, I tried,' he said, sounding defensive. 'I was exhausted and dozed for a bit. Do you think she got offended by that? She didn't say anything.'

How could he be so clueless? Liam made all of her bad dates look like Prince Charming.

'So, why do you like this girl so much?'

Liam looked up and scratched his chin. 'I mean, I don't usually go for her type. But... I don't know, she's kind of cute. Any advice on what I should do? I can't stop thinking about her.'

Paige wasn't in the business of giving dating advice, but Liam looked so forlorn she felt sorry for him.

'Maybe call her and apologize, be sincere, and ask for a do-over.'

'Apologize and ask for a do-over,' Liam echoed.

'And this time, actually listen and show some interest. Ask questions about her. And whatever you do, don't talk about soccer.'

A colleague poked her head through the door. 'Paige, have you finished with the observation chart? The doctors need it for their ward round.'

'Coming.' She stood up from her chair, relieved to be able to move again. She turned back to Liam. 'Good luck. It was nice talking to you.'

'Yeah, right back at you,' Liam said with a disappointed look.

NINE

The following morning, Callum paced around his lounge room, phone pressed against his ear. He hung on Kate Henshaw's every word, barely able to contain his excitement.

'So, you're saying I have a right to claim back the money I spent fixing the apartment?' By his calculations, not only would that cover his arrears, but there would also be enough left over for him to rent in the city for six months.

'Yes, we can get a tradesman to look at the parts you've replaced to give a price listing of the repairs. We can use that to make a claim,' Kate said. 'I'm surprised you didn't ask for reimbursement years ago. It's within your rights as a tenant.'

'I didn't know. Are you sure I can make a claim?'

'Yes, absolutely.'

He closed his eyes, a smile spread across his face. Finally, a break.

Kate chuckled. 'It'll take me a couple of days to do the paperwork for the tenancy tribunal, but in the meantime, Stacey and Ryan said they are going to help you look for a place.'

'They did? Why would they go to so much trouble for a stranger?'

'Stacey may be a little neurotic, but she has a good heart. The Langcastors must see you as their friend now.'

Callum's throat tightened with an unfamiliar feeling as he let out a garbled thank you. He hadn't been this emotional since his mother died; not even when he'd left his foster parents or when the bullies tortured him.

'No problem,' Kate said. 'You might want to start packing, though.'

'Why?'

'You've passed your eviction date. The Langcastors will come pick you up.'

***

Later that afternoon, Callum hurriedly threw the contents of his wardrobe into a large open suitcase on his bed. He had finished boxing up everything in the kitchen and lounge room, all that remained was his bedroom.

A bedroom without much in it anyway. A dozen pieces of clothing and a few personal items. As he debated whether he should bring the lopsided mushroom lamp he'd fished out of a dumpster two years ago, a voice echoed behind him.

'Why aren't you wearing the life amulet?'

Callum spun around to Hubert standing in the middle of his room, in his blinding techno-coloured robe, stroking his long white beard, with a disapproving look.

'You must wear the amulet at all times,' Hubert said sternly.

'Was that you in my head the other day?' Callum asked, still trying to process his appearance from nowhere.

'The stone bearers don't know who they really are. You need the life amulet to identify them,'

Callum shook his head; not this stone mumbo-jumbo again.

'No, Callum, this is not a dream,' Hubert was reading his thoughts again. He waved his hand, and the round amulet appeared against Callum's chest again. 'Take it off one more time, and I will permanently attach it to your flesh,' he said, then vanished.

'Great. How am I supposed to find these so-called stone bearers?' Callum mumbled to the empty room. 'Crazy old jerk.'

He zipped his suitcase shut and pondered whether he should report the strange intruder to the authorities. Maybe Hubert was just an old man suffering from dementia or a delusional disorder and forgotten to take his meds. At that last thought, a piercing pain shot through Callum's mind.

'*I am not a demented old man in need of medication!*' Hubert's voice roared in his ears.

Callum clutched his head. 'Okay, I'm sorry.'

'*Stay alert. Your amulet will glow when you're near a stone bearer. They will come to you. You need not chase them.*'

A loud knock on the door made him jump, and the sharp pain immediately ceased.

'Coming, coming,' he said while he swapped his dirty shirt for a clean one.

He opened the door to the smiling faces of the Langcastor siblings.

'Hey. Langcastor Removalists at your service,' Stacey said with a playful salute.

With a nervous laugh, Callum beckoned them inside. 'Come in. I'm almost done.'

'Wow, this place is tiny... and it smells,' Ryan said, pinching his nose. 'And what happened to your couch? It looks like a bomb hit your lounge room.'

'Ryan, manners,' Stacey said sternly.

Callum's cracked a smile, it was amusing how the Langcastors seemed more like mother and son than siblings. 'There was an... accident with the couch. The place is crappy, but it's been home for ten years and got me off the streets.'

Ryan cocked his head. 'Some accident.'

'Things will get better.' Stacey gave Callum a warm hug. 'You've got us now.'

A heated sensation spread across Callum's chest and he jerked backward. Bright yellow light shone through his shirt. He gasped, slapped a hand on his chest, and spun away.

'Are you okay?' Stacey asked. 'Did I hurt you?'

'Uh, no, no,' Callum muttered. He sprinted into the bathroom and slammed the door shut.

With his back against the door, he pulled the amulet out of his white shirt and studied it. It glowed golden and then faded back to brown. He turned it over in his hands, and ran his fingers along the irregular grooves in the centre.

Did he imagine it? But Hubert was just a loony old man. Maybe his nightmares caused him to see things. After a few deep breaths, he took a final look at the amulet, satisfied it was just an ordinary inanimate object, he stepped back into the lounge room.

'Is everything okay?' Stacey asked.

'Yes, sorry. I must've eaten some bad food.'

Ryan appeared with the candlesticks in his hand. 'Hey Cal, do you want these packed away too?'

A red-hot sensation radiated across Callum's chest again, but this time the amulet gave an emerald glow. 'Arrgh-oww.'

Ryan stared at him. 'Cal, are you okay?'

In another fit of panic, Callum fled back into the bathroom. He tightened his fingers around the amulet again, it continued to glow bright green. His mind raced. *Stacey and Ryan couldn't be stone bearers—this is madness.*

Hubert. What am I supposed to do now?

He leaned back against the door, looked up at the ceiling, and waited for a response. But there was only silence.

A loud knock brought his attention back to the door.

'Hey Callum, you nearly done?' Ryan called. 'I need to pee.'

'Sure, one second.' Callum shook his head to clear it. Whatever was happening would have to wait.

He left the bathroom and headed straight for his bedroom, ignoring Stacey's worried glances. He ripped open his suitcase and rummaged until he found his brown jacket. It was the only piece of clothing thick enough to conceal the glow from the amulet. Despite the hot weather, he put it on and zipped it up to his neck.

Stacey eyed the jacket with a perplexed expression. 'Are you sure you want to wear that? It's boiling.'

'Yes, I'm feeling... cold,' Callum replied, well aware of how ridiculous he sounded.

'Are you sick? Let me feel your forehead.'

Callum waved her away. 'No, it's okay. Let's get on with the move.' He picked up the biggest box he could find, eager to put some distance between her and the amulet.

With a bewildered expression, Stacey looked over at Ryan, who shrugged.

***

At Stacey's apartment, the trio collapsed, exhausted, onto the lounge. There were only three boxes stacked in the corner, but carting them up four flights of stairs had been harder than he'd imagined.

'I don't know how to thank you for helping me,' he said.

'Glad to,' said Stacey. 'We'd better get some sleep, it's getting late. You take the couch. I'll bring you a pillow and blanket.'

After Stacey and Ryan retired to their bedroom, he stretched out on the soft three-seater sofa and dropped off to sleep.

A sudden shock of ice-cold water jolted him awake and almost immediately, he heard Stacey scream. Behind him, a dark-cloaked figure loomed over Stacey in the back corner of the living room.

Ryan charged at the intruder with a gargled battle cry. Driven by instinct, Callum clenched his hands and did the same.

The figure swivelled and sidestepped Callum's swinging fist. In a blur of motion, the intruder reached and latched their curling fingers around both boys' throats. Callum's lungs burned as the pressure around his neck increased. He clawed at the hand to pry it loose, but the fingers only squeezed tighter. The cloaked figure lifted them both effortlessly higher, feet dangling, flailing in the air.

Ryan let off a series of raspy gasps which grew fainter as Callum's vision blurred from the intense pressure on his windpipe. Gasping for air, he kicked one last time, and though his boot connected with the enemy's shin, it had no effect.

The stranger tilted their head, their fiendish purple sockets flashing under that dark hood, as if savouring their struggles with bemused delight. When they tightened their grip by another fraction, the room faded and the amulet slipped out of Callum's jacket. It glowed with the brightness of burning coals. Callum's arm tingled, and instinctively, he raised his hand at the hooded face. To his astonishment, a blast of flame shot out from his palm.

The intruder jerked back with a hiss, released them and vanished.

The boys sprawled on the floor, gulping for air as Stacey rushed to their side.

Ryan's eyes darted continuously around the room. 'Is he gone?'

Callum shrugged and climbed to his feet, while Stacey fixated on him as if he had grown an extra limb.

'How did you do that?' she asked with narrowing eyes.

Before he could answer the hooded figure re-appeared. It raised a hand and crackling violet energy shot at them. Callum dove the Langcastor siblings out of the beam's trajectory. The energy blast flew over their heads and shattered the overhead cupboards and island bench, covering them with splintered shards.

The figure approached them again, with energy crackling from both hands ready to fire. Callum pushed in front of the siblings, making his best effort to protect them with his body. 'Who are you, what do you want?'

The figure advanced with gleaming eyes, hands charged with a brighter energy. A thunderous blast came at them, Callum rolled them to the side, the violet beam sizzled passed them, this time creating sprays of shattered china.

'Get out,' Callum said shoving the siblings towards the front door. 'I'll hold him off.' He touched the stone at his chest.

Before they could exit the flat, the intruder fired another beam, and the front door slammed shut.

Callum took the only option to protect them. He stepped directly in front of the stranger, until he was a hairbreadth away from their nose. He did his best not to shudder at the faceless figure with violaceus glowing eyes. The intruder was a wraith but somehow solid enough to be kicked.

Callum held up both hands. 'You can fire at me, but let them go.'

The words barely left his mouth when Hubert materialised through a flash of white light behind the wraith.

It spun away with a hiss.

No longer in the firing line, Callum ran to the pair huddling behind the long lounge chair, daring only a few peeks when curiosity got the better of him.

The air crackled with tension as the two magical beings faced off.

Hubert raised his hands, summoning blinding arcs of white lightning. The cloaked figure unleashed a swift wave of dark purple energy at him.

White magic flared again, forming a shield of energy. The purple energy collided with it, creating a boom that shook the walls. Hubert retaliated with a focused light beam, but the purple wraith deflected it, sending sparks flying.

The intruder motioned to the floor beneath Hubert's feet which erupted in a burst of lavender flames. He barely managed to leap aside, countering with a hail of sharp, glowing shards. The shards sliced through the air, but with a flicker of the intruder's hand a violet swirl sucked them in.

A burst of white light from Hubert extinguished the remaining flames. The two magicians weaved across the room, no longer solid beings but a spectacular array of white and purple flashing lights.

Then, all was still for a brief moment. The room was thrown into darkness when the duo disappeared, only to reappear just as quickly.

Hubert's eyes glowed white, his arms open wide. Rapid successions of energy emanated from his body and hurled forward in thunderous blasts. Callum's jaw dropped as their attacker dodged and deflected them, somersaulting through air like an acrobat, unaffected by gravity.

Callum didn't understand what the dark figure was doing until he looked at Hubert again. The more blasts he sent, the more drained he looked. The assailant was trying to wear him out. Something inside Callum took over. Something instinctive. He took Stacey's hand, dragged her to Hubert, and interlocked his other arm with Hubert's. This time, when the warrior trainer threw a wall of energy against the enemy, their combined golden-white blast sent their attacker crashing into the kitchen wall.

The wraith rolled up, fading into the walls, their glowing eyes giving a final ominous flash before disappearing.

Callum's shoulders lightened and a profound sigh of relief escaped him.

Frowning, Hubert ran his eye over them. 'Are you alright?'

'Who was that?' Ryan whimpered from behind the couch.

'That,' Hubert said gravely, 'was the Destroyer's deadliest assassin.'

TEN

Stacey sank into the couch and rubbed her hands together to stop herself from shaking.

She twitched when an arm wrapped around her shoulders. 'It's okay,' Callum said softly. 'He's gone.'

'They can come back,' Hubert said.

Callum glared up at him, while her own vocal cords were too paralysed to produce any coherent sound. What she had seen defied everything she knew about the laws of physics. It wasn't possible for a physical being to enter the apartment without using a door. Nor was it possible for a human body to project energy blasts like that. Blasts so strong that nothing was left of her kitchen but blackened walls. The stove and all her utensils were in a melted heap on the floor, the wooden bench ash-black and splintered.

Her gaze locked onto Hubert, with his snow-white hair, long beard, and rainbow cloak, he was like a wizard out of a children's storybook.

'Here,' he said, handing her a warm mug, 'perhaps some tea would help. I made it myself.'

Stacey took the cup and sipped it, not bothering to ask where he got it. She welcomed the warmth passing through her, and her heartbeat began to slow.

'Who *are* you?' she asked, finding her voice again.

'I am Hubert Waltor, the Grand Vizer and warrior trainer.'

'Like Merlin and Dumbledore?' asked Ryan. 'Or Gandalf?'

Hubert's eyebrows climbed. 'I am your guide.'

'Guide to what?' Stacey asked.

'Why, a guide to you coming into your powers, of course. But you will need to find your life stone first to control them. Stacey—'

'Wait, how do you know my name?'

'Stacey,' Hubert began again, 'you are the bearer of the yellow life stone, the commander of fire. Ryan, you are the bearer of the green life stone. You have the power to move through space and time.'

'I can teleport?' Ryan's eyes widened with child-like glee. 'Cool. I'll fly us somewhere out of danger.' Then he collapsed onto the couch giggling uncontrollably.

'Yes, exactly,' Hubert said with an unflinching smile.

'I think he's serious,' Callum said.

Stacey gave Callum an incredulous stare. *Not you too.*

***

Stacey spent all of Monday ordering her kitchen. Callum insisted on helping, but the replacement materials were still costly. Callum was a comfort to have around, like the big brother she never had.

Every morning flashes of the hooded figure haunted her, making the weekend's events impossible to forget.

On Tuesday, she decided to take the bus to work. It was oddly comforting standing in the middle of a crowded bus for the first time. As she held on to the bus's monkey bar, an old man got on, swiped his card, and sat in the front row. A young mum dragged her fussy toddler out the door, followed by a middle-aged lady with a large handbag. Her heart rate slowed and the churns in her gut eased. These were ordinary, *normal* people going about their everyday lives. Normal was what she wanted, what she needed.

There was a sense of disappointment when she arrived at her stop. She comforted herself by ordering coffee at her favourite cafe, The Morning Cup.

She was greeted warmly by the shop owner. 'Here you go, Stace. Large cap, no sugar and a toasted ham croissant.'

She left the shop more settled as she continued her walk to work.

Stacey arrived at her workstation at Advanced Micro Labs at 9:00 a.m. on the dot. She sat on her work chair, sipping her coffee. Her workbench occupied the far corner of the lab and was exactly as she had left it last Friday. The three fifteen-inch monitors hadn't moved or been blasted into oblivion; they were still attached to a keyboard and mouse next to the metre-high cylinder electron microscope.

On the opposite side of the room, two of her colleagues were working on knee replacement designs and arguing loudly over which instruments to use. Ordinarily, that would have annoyed her, but the familiarity was comforting today.

She found her Petri dishes of Cytoplon bacteria and carried them back to her bench. She inserted the first dish into its holding under the electron scope and flicked the dial to one hundred times magnification. She liked observing the whole colony before zoning in on each under two thousand. The bean shaped organism flapped their pili through the medium, such mundane movements but so incredibly cathartic to watch.

Stacey loved her work. It gave her a sense of purpose. She could lose herself here, no matter how much the outside world disturbed her. And after the terror of the attack, she needed that sense of calm.

She was engrossed in her observations when her supervisor Lyanne entered the lab. 'Stacey, there's a young man downstairs who says his family wants to donate to our research lab. They'll be attending our fundraising event next month.'

'Who are they?' she asked, eyes still glued to her screen.

'They're from Prestige Sports,' Leanne said. 'The owner's son wants a tour of our facilities and specifically asked to see you.'

'Why me?' Stacey asked as she continued to type, only half-listening.

'He says his name is Liam Michaels. Ring any bells?'

Stacey's elbow slipped forward, knocking her coffee cup off the table. 'I thought I was done with him.'

'Clearly not, because he's waiting for you in the lobby,' Leanne said. 'He seems very insistent on speaking with you.'

All the frustration of her date came flooding back. Talking to Liam was a variable in her day she was unprepared for and she hated being taken off guard. 'Don't you discourage social meetings at work?'

'You're right, I do. But if that guest is willing to make a large donation to our division, I'm happy to make an exception.'

'But, I'm in the middle of my analysis,' she said a hint of irritation creeping into her voice.

'I can see you don't want to go, but his donation would be more than enough for us to buy more Cytoplon colonies,' Leanne said gently, moving her chair away from her desk. 'Might be worth talking to him.'

Stacey stifled a groan and gave a grudging nod.

She made her way to the marbled lobby, where she found Liam talking to the front desk staff. He smiled when she approached. 'Hey, Stacey.'

Her heart did an unwanted backflip. He looked handsome in his white shirt and dark blue suit, his face clean-shaven, and his dark brown hair combed neatly back.

'Nice to see you,' Stacey said looking down at her feet to hide her blush.

'Yeah, you too.' He shuffled his feet.

Stacey searched for something to say, when a bandage on Liam's right hand caught her attention. 'You're injured.'

'Oh, this is nothing,' Liam said and lightly waved his injured hand. 'I fell onto some broken glass and tore a tendon. Just got out of surgery yesterday.'

'That's terrible. What happened?'

'I was chasing after a great girl who left in a hurry.'

'She must've been some girl.'

Liam leaned in; his face so close she could smell his cologne. 'She is. I'm hoping she'll give me another chance.'

Stacey's ability to respond escaped her in that moment. She banished the thought that the girl he referred to might be her. Their date had been a disaster, and good-looking guys like Liam don't go chasing after frumpy science nerds. She had plenty of evidence from her high school experience to attest to that.

'So, this is where you work?' Liam asked. 'It's… nice.'

'What are you doing here?'

'I would love to know more about your work.' Liam tugged at his wrist cuffs, cheeks flushed. He ran his fingers through his hair a few times before they returned to fidget with his cuffs again. How odd of him to act so fidgety. She couldn't imagine why.

'You want to see my lab?' *You weren't so interested the other night.*

'Cytoplon bacteria,' Liam cleared his throat. 'You are studying how it replicates so you can engineer it in a vaccine that can mutate according to the host's repair signals, right?'

Goodness, is this the same guy from our date?

Unable to think of a response Stacey gave a slight nod then turned to the lifts and led him in.

They stood quietly until Liam broke the silence. 'So, we're going to see your lab? How…exciting.'

Was he being sarcastic? Why he would even consider donating to her research lab? Her mind raced with questions but was too tongue-tied to speak. Instead, she took him to Leanne's office, her boss would know what to do with him. Stacey couldn't deal with any more awkwardness.

'Who is Professor Leanne Hamilton?' Liam asked, reading the name on the office door.

'My research supervisor.'

Leanne was on the phone but immediately hung up when she saw them. 'Mr Michaels, what a pleasant surprise. Welcome,' she said extending a hand.

'Thank you,' Liam said returning the hand shake. 'I am so honoured to be in this renowned facility.'

Stacey had never seen Leanne smile so much; Liam must be making quite a big donation. 'Our institute does world-leading research into knee replacements, microbiology, and genetic engineering,' Leanne continued.

As the boss started her media pitch, Stacey slipped out to return to the sanctuary of her workbench.

She hummed her favourite tune as she gathered her Petri dishes and slides again from the specimen fridge. While deciding which specimen to study first, the lab door squeaked open, and two familiar voices floated in.

Stacey crouched lower, if she stayed there long enough, and didn't move, there was a good chance they would leave without bothering her.

'Hey, Stacey,' Liam said, looking over the fridge door. 'Whatcha doing down there?'

Stacey banged her head on the edge of a protruding shelf on her way up. Through gritted teeth she slammed the fridge door shut and plastered on a polite smile. 'Collecting samples.' With her slides she strode to her workbench.

He moved to her elbow, trying to look at the slides.

'Enjoy yourself, Liam. Stacey is the most promising young scientist in her field. She's my favourite prodigy. She can answer any of your questions,' Leanne said cheerfully, then left.

Stacey glanced at him, expecting a smirk, but only saw a genuine interest as he bent down further to the bench. Trying to ignore how close he was, she put her first slide under the microscope. When she looked down the barrel, Liam inched in until his breath was against her ear.

She raised her head, about to ask him to give her room, when two Bunsen burners on the end of the bench sprang to life. Yellow-blue flames flickered high into the air. They formed the shape of dragon heads, swirled briefly, and then died into a smoke trail.

'Wow,' Liam breathed. 'That is some experiment. How do you get the flames to do that?'

Stacey's stomach knotted. It was happening again. 'I don't know. That's not my experiment.'

She led him to the reconstruction table. 'I share the lab with four other scientists. Burton and Larry are working on new material for knee reconstructions for sports players like yourself. They are also designing a smaller probe to introduce the material via keyhole surgery. You might want to have a look.'

When Liam bent down to examine the equipment, she returned to her workbench to continue typing her observations into her computer.

'Are you avoiding me?' Liam called out. 'Is it because I dozed off and left you with the bill at dinner?'

'It's over now. Don't worry about it.'

'But I don't want it to be over,' Liam said. 'Can we start again?'

He took large steps towards her, tripping over a stool but managed to clutch the edge of the chemical bench to stop his fall.

'Careful,' Stacey yelled.

It was too late. With his unsteady balance and wildly flapping arms, flasks and test tubes rolled across the table and shattered onto the floor. Pink- and blue-coloured solutions splashed in every direction.

Liam's eyes widened. 'Shit. Sorry.'

'Did any of the chemicals splash on you?' Stacey asked, running over to put his arm under the tap. 'They can burn.'

'I'm fine.' He yanked it free and fell backwards into another workbench. Papers flew into the Bunsen burner. The spilled chemicals ignited and spewed out a cloud of silver smoke.

Panicked, Stacey pulled him up and tried to find the fire extinguisher in the thick smoke.

'Liam. Get out,' she shouted as the flames licked higher.

Before Stacey could think of what to do next, a loud rumble sounded. Water burst from pipes under the sinks and doused the flames. Smoke alarms wailed from above, and water poured down from the ceiling sprinklers.

Her joy was short-lived when sharp stings grazed her head from a shower of ice. Water from the sprinklers danced through the air in waves, then clumped together forming cubes and tiny spheres strangely reminiscent of soccer balls.

Liam stared at them, his lower jaw sagged. 'Is that part of the science experiment, too?'

'No,' she said, glaring at him.

ELEVEN

Callum was glad he had the kitchen to fix, to occupy his time since leaving work. It made imposing on the Langcastors less uncomfortable, even though they kept insisting they were happy to have him.

Knowing how much Stacy loved to cook, he'd installed a new island bench with a cream laminated top over the past week and picked out stylish cone-shaped downlights. Along the back wall, he'd put the oven, rangehood, and marble-grey cupboards with silver handles.

He took a crinkled magazine picture from his pocket to check that the kitchen was installed correctly.

Now for the pipes, and he was done.

He was under the sink with a wrench when the front creaked open and clunking footsteps approached.

'That looks awesome,' Ryan said. 'Stacey's been wanting a new kitchen for years. You're making her MasterChef dreams come true.'

Callum laughed. 'How was school?'

'The same,' Ryan leaned on the kitchen bench, pensive. 'How do you know how to do all this?'

'My old apartment always needed repairs,' Callum said. 'I had to do them myself because I could never afford to get anyone to do it.'

Ryan seemed lost in thought, then asked, 'Hey Cal, do you believe that Hubert guy?'

'I don't know.' Discussing Hubert and the life stones was the last thing on his mind.

'How do you teleport?'

'I have no idea.'

'So, if we're the stone bearers, what does that make you?' Ryan asked. 'You threw that fireball.'

While Callum and Stacey were keen to forget their magical encounter, Ryan seemed fascinated by it.

'Maybe you can ask Hubert next time,' Callum said with a slight edge.

'Are there others?'

'Probably.'

'Aren't you going to find them?'

Callum was tired of Ryan's rapid-fire questions and wanted nothing to do with stones or powers. He just needed life to return to normal and to finish the kitchen before Stacey got home. He eyed the lounge room clock, willing it to move faster to bring her home from work. She was the only one who could get Ryan to stop.

'Why does that rock around your neck always glow when Stacey and I come near you?'

Callum let out a frustrated cry when the U-shaped pipe sprung out of place and hung ajar from its connection. He crawled out from under the sink, Ryan wasn't going to stop until his questions were answered.

'All I know is that the life amulet glows whenever I'm near a stone bearer, and I can tap into their powers.'

'Like a syndicate?' Ryan asked.

Callum rubbed his chin as he considered the concept. 'Yeah, like a syndicate.'

'So, could you teleport too if I held your hand?'

'I'm not keen to try.'

'We need to find the other stone bearers, then.' Ryan's eyes lit up with excitement.

Callum cringed at the thought. 'I don't know how. It's not like they'll come knocking at the door.'

'We did, didn't we?'

'You and your sister were a coincidence.'

The sound of the front door unlocking ended their conversation. Stacey came with three bags of groceries.

'We're going to have fresh food tonight.' She dropped the bags on the nearest couch. 'The kitchen looks amazing.'

'Sorry I couldn't get the sink connected in time,' Callum said, happy Stacey approved.

Before they could answer, a loud knock echoed from the door.

Stacey froze, whitening. 'We're not expecting anyone, are we?'

'I'll see who it is,' Callum said. 'You two stay back.'

He opened the door to a young man with a bouquet of roses in the corridor. 'Hello, I'm here to see Stacey.'

'Is she expecting you?'

'No, but before she tells you to say she's not here,' the young man said, 'tell her I'm sorry. I want to make it up to her.'

Callum was about to ask how he knew Stacey when his chest grew warm, and the amulet began to pulse brightly under his shirt. His jaw involuntarily dropped as he took in the tall muscular guy who looked barely out of high school.

'It's okay, I've got this.' Stacey appeared and pulled Callum back into the apartment. 'Liam, I just got home from work and am really tired. How did you know where I lived?'

'I met Kate at the gym again and begged her to tell me.'

'She's going to get it when I see her,' Stacey muttered and began to close the door. 'I'm busy, not tonight.'

Liam wedged his foot in the doorway. 'I'm sorry about what happened at your lab today. Let me take you out tonight. I'll make it up to you, I promise.'

Callum held his breath as the amulet glowed an increasingly brighter blue as Liam pushed further inside. Ryan's eyes grew wide as saucers.

'It's fine, you really don't have—' Stacey attempted to push Liam back out.

The blue heat emanating from Callum's chest became so intense it forced him to cry out.

'Stacey, let him in.'

'Why?'

'Because your Liam is the blue stone bearer.'

TWELVE

Stacey stared at Callum, as if sulphuric acid had dissolved his skin off. Was he making a joke? But Callum didn't seem like the laughing type, and his pained expression supported it. He pulled the glowing blue amulet away from his chest as if it were burning him.

'Liam is the blue stone bearer,' Callum repeated in a mechanical tone.

Liam narrowed his eyes at Callum. 'You're not Stacey's boyfriend, are you?'

'No,' Callum muttered.

'You're Stacey's date from the other night, right?' Ryan asked. 'You're beefier, and taller than I imagined.'

Liam grinned. 'She told you about me. That's a good thing, right?'

'She said it was the worst date she'd ever been on, period,' Ryan replied.

Liam's face fell. She wished the earth would open up and her swallow her in, at that moment. Anything to spare her from Liam's forlorn expression. She could strangle Ryan for being so tactless. She may not like dealing with people but hurting their feelings was far worse. How did things get complicated so quickly?

'Hey, now that you're here, why don't you stay for dinner?' Ryan said, bubbling with excitement. 'Stacey's a mad cook. She's never brought a guy home before. Let's celebrate.'

Liam's smile reappeared. 'Sounds good.'

Any hope of a quite evening was gone. Stacey curbed the urge to smack her brother, but gave a slight nod not trusting herself to speak. It would be a good opportunity to find out what all the blue stone bearer business was about.

'Great.' Liam peered at Callum. 'Hey, that's a nice blue necklace.'

'It's glowing more now,' Ryan said in awe.

Callum nodded and moved closer to the cerulean stone bearer. The amulet glowed a brighter blue, as did his own vision. He raised a hand, and water from the jug on the dining room table rose into the air, danced, then splashed back into the jug.

'What's going on?' Liam jumped away. 'How did you do that?'

'You're a stone bearer,' Callum said. 'I'm accessing your powers.'

Liam burst out laughing. 'What?'

'You're the blue stone bearer,' Ryan repeated.

Liam blinked. 'Stone bearer? What powers?'

'Hubert said that this evil force will destroy the world in the future, and only the stone bearers of the life stone can stop it. I'm the green stone bearer, and Stacey is yellow,' Ryan continued, oblivious to the sceptical look on Liam's face.

Stacey groaned. Liam was bound to think they were all crazy. She wished Ryan would stop talking but had no idea how to explain what she barely understood. Why wasn't Callum saying anything? At least, coming from him it might sound less idiotic.

'That all sounds like a fantasy movie,' Liam said.

'Nope. It's real,' Ryan said. 'We were attacked last week by an assassin because of it.'

'Attacked?' Liam looked at Stacey with concern. 'Was anyone hurt?'

'Yeah, we're fine. Old Hubert came in time to fend them off,' Ryan replied.

'Who's Hubert?'

'Some old guy who looks like Dumbledore,' Ryan said.

'Is he seeing a shrink?' Liam whispered to Stacey out of the corner of his mouth.

All she could manage was a sigh and motioned for Callum to explain.

'I know it's hard to take in,' Callum said, 'but you seem to have powers. Have weird things happened to you in the past when you were near water? Things you couldn't explain?'

Liam scratched his chin. 'I don't think so. I'm just a regular guy.' He lifted his hand and waved it across the room, imitating Callum's earlier movement. 'See? No powers.'

As soon as the words left his mouth, water from the jug bounced high into the air. It formed into a large round ball of ice that shattered on the tiled floor. Liam reared back and waved wildly through the air. Water burst from the sink through the open pipe into the lounge room.

Liam's arms shook. Horror snaked through her as water spurted from every tap in her apartment. They would be flooded in minutes.

She grasped Liam's hands, he had to stop shaking. 'It's okay. I know it's hard to take in, but try to relax.'

'Is that me? Did I just—? Is that my p-p-power?'

Callum gave a rueful smile. 'Yes, that's your magic at work,'

'It looks like you have hydrokinetic abilities. Take some deep breaths. Calm down,' Stacey said keeping a firm hold over Liam's hands.

'Hydro what?' Liam cried.

'The power to move and manipulate liquids,' Callum said.

Liam's eyes narrowed again. 'Who *are* you people?'

'Ah, crap. My sneakers are wet,' Ryan shouted, hopping up onto a dining room chair. 'Guys, do something or we'll be swimming in our apartment.'

'Callum, can you reverse this?' Stacey asked, frantically looking around for a bag for Liam to breathe into.

'I'll try.' Callum stepped over and grasped Liam's arm. His eyes glowed blue again when he made an anticlockwise motion with his right arm. To Stacey's relief, the water from the pipes and taps regressed like a rewind.

Liam jerked his arm back from Callum. 'What are you?'

'A syndicate I suppose. I can momentarily use your powers if I'm near you.'

'I don't want to be involved in this crazy shit,' Liam huffed and stalked out of the apartment.

'Liam, wait,' Stacy dashed after him. 'Come back.'

She ran, and though she pushed herself to go faster down the fire exit, she couldn't close the gap.

It was moments like these that she wished she were fitter. It wasn't until Liam slowed halfway down the street that she nearly caught up with him. Before she had a chance to say anything, the dreaded figure from her nightmares reappeared in front of her.

The assassin whipped around, and back-handed her in the face. With a scream, she slammed against the side of the brick building and fell to the ground. Liam drew the attacker away from her, balled his hands into fists and moved rapidly at the assassin with a flurry of punches. His height and strength worked to his advantage, effectively blocking him from her.

Unable to breach his defences, the assassin stepped back and threw a purple firebolt at him. Liam arched sideways, and it hit the wall, gouging a hole in the bricks. As he raised his hand to throw another, a siren wailed in the distance, and Hubert appeared in a blinding flash of white light.

The assassin took one look at him, and the approaching police car down the street, then disappeared.

'Who was that?' Liam asked. 'And who the hell are you?'

'Come on, let's get you two off the streets,' Hubert said, holding out his hand to help them both up. 'I'll explain when we're all safe.'

***

Back in her lounge room apartment, Stacey stood by the couch with Liam by her side and watched in disbelief as Hubert stood in the middle of the room, with his eyes glowing white, rocking on his heels, making low screeching sounds.

'What on earth are you doing Hubert?'

'We can't stay here long.' His eyes now a brilliant white. 'It would be safer for me to take you to my manor and start your training immediately.'

Liam shoved his shaking hands in his pockets and leaned on Stacey. 'Who… *what* are you people?'

Not wanting another burst pipe, Stacey locked onto his arms to ensure they remained firmly in his pockets. But all that did was make her shake in sync with him. She had no idea how to comfort Liam while trying to manage her own grip on fear.

Her spine chilled at the realisation that the assassin could easily attack a third and fourth time. Hubert was right—her apartment was no longer safe. She had to get Ryan to safety. 'We need to get out of here before that hooded menace attacks again.'

'Are you sure?' Callum asked concern knitting his pressed eyebrows.

Stacey nodded as tingling numbness spread to her feet. 'I don't want to stay here if it means Ryan could get hurt, too.'

'C'mon Stace, it's not that bad. How can things change in an hour?' Ryan asked with a bewildered expression.

Hubert banged his staff louder on the floor repeatedly, as if growing impatient with the conversation. He pointed the staff at an open space. The air in front of him shimmered and thickened like quicksilver, a hole appeared in the middle forming a bright white cloud.

'Walk through the portal. It will take you to Waltor Manor.'

Liam went pale again.

Ryan leapt up from his seat. He clapped his hands and made his way towards the portal. 'That was so awesome.'

Stacey lunged to pull her brother back and gripped him tightly by the hand.

'Wait.' She looked at Hubert. 'Why are you taking us to Waltor Manor?'

'It's where I live and train warriors like yourselves,' Hubert replied.

Liam gazed upon her as if looking at a stranger. 'Warriors? What are you involved in?'

'There isn't much time, Liam,' Hubert bellowed. 'I can't keep this portal open forever. Come now.'

'How do you know my name?' Liam asked.

Callum came to her brows crossed in a solemn expression. 'This could be dangerous.'

Stacey wriggled out of Liam's grip to reach for Callum's hand. 'Come with us.'

'Yes, of course,' Callum said. 'But—'

'Please? I would feel safer with you around.'

Callum nodded, placing a hand on her shoulder. 'We'll find a way to keep you both safe.'

Liam tugged Stacey's arm back. 'Then I'm coming. I can keep her safe, too.'

Stacey nodded, drew a deep breath and looked at the three boys, then stepped through Hubert's white cloud.

THIRTEEN

Stacey, still huddled next to the boys, found Hubert waiting on the other side of the white portal.

The cloud cleared, replaced by blinding light. She jammed her eyes shut as the others pulled away. She stumbled forward, searching for Ryan's hand, but all she caught was air.

Her pulse and breath quickened as an invisible force slammed her against a hard object and bound her arms together behind it.

'Ryan!' she called out frantically, trying to open her eyes, but the intense light forced them shut again. 'Where are you?'

'Stacey, what's going on?' Ryan's whimpering response floated back to her. 'I can't see a thing.'

'Let me go,' came Liam's voice.

When the light dimmed, Stacey opened her eyes and looked. Her legs were bound to a wooden chair floating a couple of metres off the ground. She let out a scream as her heart thudded against her ribcage.

She drew in a slow, deep breath and summoned the courage to peer down again. Below her was an empty room with shiny white walls that crackled with electric energy. The guys were floating in a circle and bound to similar-looking chairs.

'Hubert!' Callum called out, wriggling in his floating chair. 'Let us go. What kind of game are you playing?'

Hubert floated in a lotus position in a corner of the room. He had a peaceful look that made Stacey want to punch him on the nose. He softly hummed a tune, oblivious to their panic.

'Let us down,' Stacey begged. 'Why are you doing this to us? You said you'd bring us here to protect us.'

'And I have.' Hubert nodded in time with his humming. 'This is my magnifier room. It is spelled to tap into your emotions and thus your powers, to show you what you can do out there. Let's begin your training.'

'What, now?' Callum said. 'Don't you want to let them settle in first?'

Hubert cocked his head to one side. 'I did say that I would start your training immediately, did I not?'

'Yes, but not immediately, immediately,' Callum shot back. 'They've barely recovered from the shock of the last attack.'

'Hm. What did you think immediately meant?' Hubert asked with a stroke of his beard.

'I don't see how making us play musical chairs in the air is training us,' Liam growled. He twisted his wrists, but the invisible binds remained. Blue rays shot from his eyes as his chair continued its circular path.

Stacey and Ryan reared back as the ray passed between them. It bounced off the wall then fell in a clump of ice and shattered on the floor.

'Ah, yes,' Hubert said, his eyes lighting up. He waved his hand in their direction. 'These are fear-bound chairs. The stronger your fear, the more tightly it holds and the higher you will float up.'

'How do we get out of them?' Callum asked.

'Yeah, 'cos this—this ain't cool anymore.' Ryan made a clumsy attempt to wriggle his way out of the chair. He managed to free an arm briefly before they were pulled back to his chair.

'How is this meant to train us?' Stacey cried as her chair ascended.

'As you learn to embrace your fears, the chair will loosen its grip and you will eventually descend.'

Stacey flinched as she crept further to the ceiling. 'Eventually? How long are you going to suspend us up here?'

'As long as it takes for you to embrace your fears and control them,' Hubert replied.

Stacey's head spun so quickly that dizziness blurred her vision. She fought to control her breathing, which raced in sync with her pounding heart. 'I'm afraid of heights. Please, please let me down. I'm not the yellow stone warrior you're looking for. Please let us go.'

Hubert shook his head. 'Tsk, tsk. Unfortunately, I cannot. Only you can unlock that hold.'

The room whirled faster and Stacey lost track of all direction. 'What do you mean you 'cannot'? You're the one who put us here!'

'Ah, true. But I did not activate your fears. You did. So only you can reduce the intensity of your own terror. I am merely a trigger,' Hubert said in a faraway voice.

His words were like static background noise that made no sense to her.

Anger swelled inside her chest. 'Let me down from here!' Flames burst from her mouth when she shouted at the top of her lungs.

Callum and Liam let out cries as the flames grazed past them.

'I always thought you were a dragon,' Ryan said. 'Now, this proves it.'

'You're not helping!' Stacey barked.

'Okay sis, stop freaking out. You want me to sing for you like Mum did?'

'No!' Flames shot out from her eyes this time. 'I'm the eldest. I'm not a child. I can control my own fear.'

The back of her chair rammed into the ceiling and whacked her bound wrists against it.

'Yeah, try not to go through the ceiling there,' Ryan retorted, then fell back into an open green-black portal.

'Ryan!' Stacey shrieked. 'I'm sorry, come back!'

'Hubert, they're scared out of their minds,' Callum said. 'Can't we do this on the ground?'

'This is the fastest way to learn,' Hubert said calmly 'As warriors, you will be thrown into unexpected and disorientating situations. You must master your fear in order to control your powers. Only then will you become true warriors.'

'I don't want to be a warrior!' Liam and Stacey hollered at the same time. Water and fire shot out from their eyes and bounced off the opposite wall. Callum leaned to the side to avoid them.

Liam pulled hard at his chair. 'Why are these rays shooting out from me?'

Ryan tumbled out of his vortex. 'Dude, what have we been trying to tell you all this time? You're the blue stone bearer with super-cool water powers.'

Stacey breathed a loud sigh of relief.

Ryan's chair continued to gain momentum. It somersaulted through the air and knocked Callum into the open vortex. 'I can't stop this. Watch out!'

Ryan thrashed in his chair and collided with Stacey. It knocked her off the ceiling and sent her flying head-on into Liam.

A chorus of screams echoed between the crackling walls. Fire rays that shot from Stacey's mouth were neutralised by ice rays from Liam's. The momentum of the blasts knocked Ryan back into his vortex right before it snapped shut.

'This is not quite how I pictured our first intimate moment, but okay,' Liam said with raspy breathing.

Another bout of screams escaped Stacey's lips along with another continuous ray of fire.

Liam exhaled heavily to form an ice shield that deflected her fire.

Stacey made the mistake of looking down at the floor. Her stomach heaved and she projectile vomited fireballs that swept across the room. The motion pressed her back against the ceiling once again.

'Ryan's gone. Callum's gone,' Stacey choked out. 'Bring them back Hubert, please.'

Hubert smiled 'Not to worry, my dear. They are perfectly safe. I have sealed this training room; your brother will only be able to teleport within the confines of this room. They will come out when they're ready.'

Stacey could not believe the nerve of the old man. She took a deep breath and her arms were released. She lunged forward, arms raised towards the smug warrior trainer. This time she gladly allowed fire rays to shoot from her eyes.

The rays bounced off Hubert who floated in a protective bubble. When his eyes twinkled in amusement, she shot out more flames.

Hubert chuckled. 'Attacking me won't help you control your fear of heights, nor your powers.'

Stacey closed her eyes and forced herself to take slow deep breaths as she counted to ten. 'Fine then, what will?'

'Lean into the fear; gradually turn towards it. Feel it,' Hubert said.

'What do you think I've been doing this whole time?' Stacey said through clenched teeth.

'I said lean into it, not scream at it.'

Stacey let out an exasperated cry and jammed her eyes shut. 'Fine, leeeaaan into it. I am now leaning into it. What else do I do now, wise old warrior trainer?'

'Acknowledge its presence and allow the thoughts and feelings to pass through you without judgement. Feel it, hear its message.'

Stacey pointed an index finger at him. 'What kind of crappy training is this?'

The fire ray from her finger bounced off Hubert's bubble, ricocheted off the wall, and grazed Liam's shoulder on its way down.

'Hey!' he cried. 'What was that for?'

Liam was settled with both feet planted on the ground throwing ice cubes and rods against the wall. How was it possible that he was on the ground and she was still suspended?

'How did you learn to do that?' Stacey called out.

'I dunno. I think of the object and it appears in my hands. It's kind of nifty when you get over the craziness of it all,' Liam grinned up at her. He tilted his head as if an afterthought came to him. 'Hey Hubert, was that bad headache you in my head telling me what to do?'

Hubert gave a slight nod.

'Come down so I can show you some of this stuff. It's fascinating.'

Stacey resented that he found it sound so simple when she could barely budge from the ceiling. She had never been so overwhelmed.

'Hubert, why did you let Liam off his chair when you're forcing me to stay in mine?' she yelled.

Hubert shook his head. 'I didn't. He let himself off. He made his choice. What is yours?'

Stacey narrowed her eyes and twin turrets of heat swirled around her chest like a pair of dancing dragons. She blew the flames towards Hubert again. 'Then I choose to run, to get out of here. Stop this nonsense. Hubert, please let me down.'

Hubert arched a brow. 'And when running away is not an option?'

Stacey chewed on her bottom lip. It didn't seem like she was getting anywhere with the old man. Below her, Liam was throwing water bombs against the wall. She wondered how a sports freak like Liam could figure out something so complex when she was terrified out of her mind. She'd always prided herself on her ability to analyse and problem-solve. Now, stupidity was taking a fast hold in parallel with her escalating fears. She debated fiercely with her wounded pride about asking Liam for help.

Just swallow it. What good is preserving your ego when it's keeping you in this damn chair?

She gritted her teeth. 'Liam, could you please tell me how to get off this chair?'

Hubert smiled. 'Asking for help is a good alternative to running.'

Liam grinned up at her with a small wave. Water arched through the air and drenched her. Stacey coughed and choked as the water shot into her mouth. Fireballs sizzled out from her eyes and landed centimetres from Liam's feet.

Liam danced his way around them. 'I guess that makes us even.'

'Tell me what to do!'

'Er, okay. I dunno exactly. But while I was floating, I thought back to my last social soccer game. With fifteen minutes left, I had an opening and shot the ball. I missed and the other player intercepted it. So, I was like, 'oh crap that sucks'. I mean, I was pissed it didn't go into the goal like I wanted, but hey—'

Stacey's mind whirled and it seemed to be picking up speed by the second. Her body tingled and her head lightened. Something else took over—a new level of rage. Flashes of their first date, the explosion in her science lab, his uninvited appearance at her apartment, and now the biggest challenge of her life and she had to endure yet another one of Liam's soccer recounts.

'Really? You want to tell me about another one of your dumb games at a time like this!' Another fire blast escaped her. 'What does this have to do with getting me out of this God-forsaken chair?'

Liam's smile deflated. 'Oh, right. You don't like soccer. I forgot.'

'Let him finish, Stacey,' Hubert said. 'There may be something of value to be learnt.'

Stacey released her firestorm on the Grand Vizer. She could not believe that he was playing favourites. She wanted to protest, but a small voice at the back of her head piped up. *Hear him out one more time. If something in what he says can let you down, then what do you have to lose?*

My pride.

Stacey exhaled slowly, pressing her lips together to stop another release of flames that was building at the back of her throat. 'Fine. Please go on.'

Liam raised his hand and placed it behind his scalp. A steady stream of soccer balls flowed to the floor behind him. 'Okay then. When the other douchebag intercepted my ball, my team ran after him. So, I thought, 'what the heck', and I ran after him, too.'

Stacey did her best to control her hyperventilation as she struggled to follow his recount.

'He was a fast bugger, but I kept trailing him, and eventually, I got the ball back and gave it to my teammate Poochie, who carried the ball back down to the goal. I did my triple-eight weave and waited for him. Then there it was. Poochie passed the ball back to me and I shot it again. I scored, we won... yay me.'

A minute of dead silence passed.

Stacey glared at him, unable to prevent another storm of fireballs from raining down on the amateur soccer player. Then she directed them at the old warrior trainer. She could not believe that they could continue to insult her in such a way. The story, other than puffing up Liam's ego, did nothing to reveal how she was going to get out of the fear-binding chair.

'You think I'm some kind of imbecile?'

Liam held his hands up high and ducked. A large round ice shield saved him from the flames.

'You are missing the point,' Hubert said calmly.

'What point?'

'He accepted it and moved on.'

'Accepted what?'

'The situation. The predicament. His powers. The circumstances. He did not dwell, deny, nor try to change what had already happened. Instead, he accepted it and moved on with the flow of events. By letting go of what he could not change, it freed him to take action in the present, and get to where he wanted to be.'

Stacey searched her mind for an intelligent response but found none. Tunnels of fire escaped in sync with her open and shut jaw. She shut her eyes to process Hubert's lesson through the haze of jumbled thoughts.

'So, what you are saying, is that I need to accept these powers? That I'm trapped in this awful binding chair until then?'

'Precisely. Accept what you cannot change in order to let go and move on.'

Stacey worked to slow her breathing. It sounded preposterous, nevertheless, she took her mind back to the flame incident at the restaurant, the dragon flame in her lab, and her fire rays in the training room now. No matter how unscientific it was, in a mystic way, it would explain what she had experienced. 'Fine. I am the yellow stone bearer with fire powers. Now what?'

The chair swooped down from the ceiling and hovered a metre below it. Her chair resumed its circular path. She gripped the edge of her seat tightly until her knuckles tingled and turned white.

'Now breathe. Hear its message.' Hubert said.

'What message? Whose message?'

'Fear's message. Your fears.'

Stacey frowned. 'You make that emotion sound like a delivery person.'

'That's one way of looking at it.' Hubert rhythmically stroked his beard with a distant look. 'Every emotion is trying to tell you something.'

'What could being terrified out of my mind possibly tell me?' Stacey asked.

'Get prepared, so the outcome you fear does not eventuate.'

FOURTEEN

Callum blinked. Whether his eyes were open or shut made no difference—the tunnel he floated into was pitch black. Vomit splattered onto his face, but he couldn't tell if it was Stacey's shrieks or the rocking chair that churned his stomach.

'Get me out of here!' he screamed, echoing Stacey's cries. It disturbing to hear her but do nothing to help. At least yelling in sync made him feel closer to her, distracting him from his own predicament.

'Stacey, Callum? What's going on, where am I?' Ryan's voice grew louder until a foot hit his mouth. He leaned to the side to avoid it and ended up with a mouthful of hair. Nearly choking, he spat out the strands. When Ryan continued to thrash, Callum twisted his chair further to the side to avoid him.

'Take it easy, Ryan. I'm here.'

'What do we do now, Cal? We're trapped.'

Stacey's cries echoed through the dark tunnels, shattering Callum's already frayed nerves. He sucked in a deep breath to calm himself.

'This isn't fun anymore,' Ryan said, with a sob. 'I don't wanna die.'

Callum gritted his teeth. 'Hubert! This is no way to train them.'

'*Stay alert and connected,*' Hubert said telepathically. '*Still your mind amidst the chaos. This is your training, too.*'

'What training?'

'*You have the life amulet. It connects you to each of the life stones and their bearers.*'

A foot in his face again snapped Callum out of his conversation.

'Sorry, Cal. Why are you talking to yourself?' Ryan said.

Callum grunted and pushed Ryan off. 'Relax for a minute. I'm talking to Hubert, trying to figure something out, stop screaming.'

'I'll try. Can you get us out?'

'I'm working on it,' Callum said, doing his best to keep calm.

'*That's the spirit,*' Hubert said. '*You are vital to the stone bearers coming into their powers.*'

What a ridiculous statement, he was just an insignificant cleaner.

'*How can I train anyone, Hubert. You're the warrior trainer. Aren't you meant to do the training?*'

'*Yes, and that's exactly what I'm doing.*'

'*By scaring the living daylights out of us?*'

'*All warriors must first learn to embrace their fears in order to master them. Only then will their powers be at their command. Taking away the cause of their fear now will only disempower them.*'

Callum spat out his frustration, '*Okay, then. How do you expect someone like me, with no knowledge or powers, to train them?*'

'*The knowledge is in your amulet. Still your mind. Create an open vacuum, and the answer will come to you.*'

'Can we go yet?' Ryan whined. 'What's taking so long? I don't think I can take any more spinning in these chairs.'

'*But I don't even know what their powers can do,*' Callum said, leaning away from Ryan to focus. '*Let alone teach them how to use it.*'

There was a loud gag from Ryan and a splatter of foul-smelling content dropped onto Callum's his lap. He held his breath, desperately trying not to inhale the fumes, and fought to hold back his own vomit.

'*Trust your instincts,*' Hubert continued. '*Drop into your senses.*'

Callum grimaced. 'It's hard with everyone hysterical.' Then added for Ryan's benefit, 'and spewing.'

'*Move past that. The fear is simply projected energy. Weave through it towards the heart. Let go of your doubts. Try it.*'

Callum closed his eyes and let his mind's eye take over. Green waves of energy bombarded him. As he dodged between them, he resisted the urge to respond. Concentrating, he willed himself forward through the energy waves, then stopped abruptly when Ryan appeared. He was lit up in a bright green aura. As soon as Callum touched him, electrical energy zapped through his fingertips. A spreading blast of green imploded in his mind, it was as if a hidden compartment in his brain had snapped open.

Callum pictured the crackling training room and focused on Stacey's voice like a rope attached to a life raft. Emerald lights filled his vision, and he and Ryan floated down to land beside Stacey in her chair on the ground.

On the way down, Callum knocked into Liam's solid form. Pain lanced through him. Beams of ice shot from his eyes into the wall, followed by a wave of angry heat.

Callum's chair immediately floated up again. His head pounded with a vision of amber, blue, and green lights that sent waves of electric shocks rippling through him.

He shivered, then sweated profusely as the climate seesawed between scorching heat and icy cold.

'Hubert,' Callum called out through chattering teeth. 'Help. I can't stop it.'

'Your body is processing and memorizing their powers,' Hubert said. 'Not to worry.'

'Make it stop!' Callum shouted.

Hubert began to hum and rock in his corner. 'Transformations are never pain-free. It'll be over soon.'

'I don't think he's going to make it,' came Liam's voice from a distant space.

'Help him,' Stacey pleaded. 'It's killing him.'

As the intense heat and the violent cold returned, Callum bit into his bottom lip to contain the growing pressure.

'Oh crap, he's not holding,' Ryan called out and disappeared into another portal.

The mounting pressure inside Callum increased ten-fold and continued until he was no longer able to bear the pain and collapsed into it. Walls of ice and fire exploded from every part of his body. His fear-bound chair shattered into pieces and he crashed face-first to the floor.

He lay there, breathing heavily, every cell of his body aching. He glanced up to Hubert and the others hovering over him.

'Very good,' Hubert said with a satisfied smile. 'Now, come with me.'

Callum glared at him. 'I can barely move.'

'You'll be fine. Get up. We need to retrieve the next stone bearer. Before it's too late.'

FIFTEEN

Paige walked briskly along the six blocks from the hospital to uncle Rob's gym. She'd missed their training sessions—he'd been sick for the past month with chest pains. Although his cardiologist had cleared him, Paige was determined not to let him push too hard in the boxing ring.

After seven straight shifts covering for her pregnant colleague, she was more than ready to blow off steam with a hard circuit routine and a session on the punching bag. With two days off, she looked forward to some much-needed time off.

The gym door was slightly ajar. When pushed open, it gave a loud creak and fell off its hinges. Her hairs stood on end as she slipped inside. The gym had been trashed—metal debris littered the floor, gym equipment smashed with its electronics bare and scattered.

Nerves stretched tight, she hurried to the back room. The boxing ring was torn to shreds. Her heart hammered. 'Uncle Rob, where are you?'

She nearly jumped out of her skin when a hand touched her ankle. She turned to find her uncle trapped beneath three large metal sheets. 'Keep still and I'll get you out.' She quickly rang for an ambulance, then with muscle tearing effort, lifted off the sheets.

After checking he was breathing, she carefully rolled him into the recovery position. 'Don't move until the ambulance arrives. Are you in pain?'

'Paige,' Uncle Rob mumbled, his eyes fluttering. 'I have to tell you something.' After several attempts to speak, he weakly pointed toward the boxing ring. 'Mother's... your mother's stone.'

The ambulance arrived as he slipped into unconsciousness. The paramedics quickly loaded him onto a stretcher, attaching an oxygen mask and IV lines. Moments later, the sirens wailed as they sped toward Dabury Hospital.

***

Paige paced the private room on the cardiology ward, fighting back tears. Uncle Rob was still in the cardiac lab, and she was certain he'd suffered another heart attack. The destruction of the gym would have strained anyone's heart.

She forced herself not to give in to the despair of losing another family member. Her colleagues visited often, urging her to rest, but she couldn't sit still.

After what felt like years, the team finally wheeled him back in.

'Uncle Rob,' she murmured, gently stroking his head.

'Did he have an AMI?' she asked as the nurses transferred his chest leads from the portable monitor to the wide screen above his bed.

Dr. Ting, the cardiologist, approached her. 'Your uncle had a complete blockage in his left ascending coronary artery. We revascularized it with a stent. He should be fine now.'

The doctor gently squeezed her shoulder. 'Don't worry, he's stable and doing well. Make sure he takes his blood thinners and beta blockers every day, okay?'

Paige nodded, allowing herself to take a breath.

As soon as the medical team left, she buried her head in her uncle's side and drifted off to sleep.

***

The next morning, Paige awoke to her uncle stroking her hair. 'Sweetheart, wake up.'

'Uncle Rob,' she said, kissing him on the forehead. 'How are you feeling?'

'I'm fine, honey. But you don't look so fine,' he said with a frown.

She scanned his face, it would be just like him to downplay any pain.

'Stop being a nurse for a second and relax,' he said. 'Listen, I need to tell you something important.'

'It can wait. You need to rest. I don't want you getting agitated.'

'No, it can't wait,' Uncle Rob said, taking her hand. 'You need to know the truth before they attack again.'

'Who? I've already called the police—they're at the gym. Let them handle it—'

'No,' he interrupted more forcefully. 'You don't understand. This wasn't a random robbery. These people... they can't be stopped by guns.'

He drummed his finger on the bed as if grappling with what he was about to say. 'I should have told you this years ago.'

Paige sat back down, unnerved by the gravity in his voice. Ever since she'd come to live with him, nothing ever fazed him. Her uncle always believed there was nothing in life that couldn't be fixed with a laugh and a positive attitude. Seeing him so serious now frightened her.

'What's going on?' she asked.

'Your mother...' he began in a strained voice. 'She didn't die in a car accident. She died saving the world.'

A numbness told hold and her voice cracked. 'What do you mean?'

'Your mother came to see me ten years ago. She said if she and your father went missing, I was to look after you and keep her stone until you came of age.'

'Are you telling me my parents were murdered? Why would you keep something like that from me?'

'Your mother said the world was under threat from a force called 'Vastator-The Destroyer.' She asked me to tell you only when a threat appeared and the power of the pink stone was needed again. She wanted you to keep your innocence for as long as possible.'

Paige clutched the arms of the chair to steady herself, doing her best to keep the spinning at bay. What he said made no sense.

'The warrior stone bearers stopped a war that would have cost millions of lives,' Uncle Rob said, his eyes filled with deep sadness. 'The price of peace was your parents' lives.'

Her mind, still numb from the revelations, refused to allow her a way to understand.

'I know it sounds far-fetched; I didn't believe it at first either. But your mother made sure I was one of the few who remembered.'

'Why don't I?' Paige asked, her spinning head spun faster. 'Why doesn't anyone remember?'

'Your mother said that everyone's memory of the war would be erased to preserve order and peace. She asked me to make sure you were well-trained in combat to prepare for the next fight, should it ever come.'

'What fight?'

'The fight against the next Destroyer. Another war is coming, Paige. You need to be prepared. You are the pink stone bearer now.'

'What is a stone bearer? And why me?'

'All I know is that your mother was the pink stone bearer, and so, by blood, you are too,' Uncle Rob replied. 'Stone bearers are warriors with special powers.'

Paige blinked at her uncle, wondering if the doctors had been a little too heavy-handed with the painkillers.

'Try to suspend your disbelief,' Uncle Rob said. 'I've hidden the stone underneath the boxing ring. I think that's what the intruder was looking for. You need to go back and retrieve it.'

'I'm not leaving your side.'

'You must,' he said, his voice rising. 'Even if you don't believe me, at least retrieve your mother's stone. I would never forgive myself if it fell into the wrong hands. Can you do that for me?'

Paige stiffened, catching the urgency in his voice. She nodded.

He smiled relaxing his shoulder back into the bed. 'I'll be fine. They're not after me. I'm safe here. Now go get your pink life stone.'

***

When Paige left the hospital, she had to force herself to walk toward the gym. What her uncle told her was so surreal, she wasn't sure what to believe. The pounding headache didn't help.

If Uncle Rob lied about Mum, what else could he be lying about? Then, she reminded herself that this was the uncle she had known and loved her whole life. The heaviness in her heart made it feel like she was losing Mum all over again. It was frightening to think that she hadn't really known her mother at all. She had chosen her mission over her own daughter. How could she betray her like that?

As she turned the corner, a cold sensation spiralled chills down her spine. Was she being followed? She spun around, but the street was empty except for two women talking outside a shop. Reluctantly, she kept walking, though the feeling someone was behind her remained. She increased her pace, relaxing only when she reached the gym.

Stretches of bright police tape and orange cones blocked the entrance. Paige checked for authorities before ducking under the tape.

It was dark inside, lit only by the fading light filtering through the broken windows. The once bright and activity-filled gym now looked like a war-torn warehouse.

The cold presence grew stronger, setting her nerves on edge.

She forced herself to move toward the boxing ring at the back. The foam mat had multiple tears in the centre of it like it had been sliced open by a large kitchen knife

Rob had said the stone was hidden underneath the floorboards. She peeled back the padding and searched for a trapdoor or loose planks.

At first, she found nothing. But then, she spotted a narrow gap in the wooden floor, just large enough to slip her fingers in. She wedged it open to deeper a compartment.

Inside was a small, ornate wooden box. The box snapped open to reveal a pink gem attached to a silver chain.

When Paige reached for it, a hot pain seared her wrist, and she involuntarily flung the box across the room. She immediately dove after it and suffered a blow to her back which knocked her forward. Someone was definitely behind her. She grunted in pain as she landed but forced herself to roll to face her attacker. Aghast, a masked cloaked figure pick up her mother's stone.

'Get away. That's mine!' The cloaked figure held out the pink stone in one hand and with the other motioned for her to come forward. Paige charged at the intruder. No was allowed to touch her mother's stone but her.

She threw a strong right hook at her attacker but the purple figure leaned back and gracefully flicked her arm to the side. Paige sidestepped to keep from falling, surprised that such a small movement had so much power.

The figure kicked her in the stomach, which sent her flying back onto the boxing mat. The years of training with her uncle took over. Paige shot up and charged at the assailant again. Keeping her guard up, she stood her ground and threw rhythmic side and forward punches. She breathed in deeply between each punch, ensuring that the power came from the centre of her body. But every strike missed its mark— the intruder was too quick, dodging every blow.

Changing her tactics, Page lunged for the pink stone. The figure blasted her with a violet heat wave. She blinked; was that even possible? 'What are you?'

The figure dangled the pink stone in front of her again.

She was being baited into another fight, but had no other option. Her mother's stone was her only keepsake. She switched to her martial arts training, ran at the intruder and threw a spinning sidekick. As her attacker grabbed her foot in mid-air, the stone flew loose and rolled to the side of the ring. Using her opponent's hand to leverage her, Paige spun through the air and her free leg dug into the figure's side. The impact brought them both down hard onto the mats.

Paige dived for the stone but a sharp pull on her leg made her fall short. She slipped to stand and found herself face-to-face with her opponent again. The figure leapt, with one foot raised ready to land on her chest. She caught the assailant's foot and pushed it away. Paige alternated between a quick series of fast punches and sidekicks which, to her dismay, her opponent weaved past with ease.

The fight seemed to last hours and Paige slowed from fatigue.

When she took half a step back to catch her breath, her opponent moved towards the pink stone. In a panic, she flung herself against the figure and they both sprawled onto the ground. Her opponent attempted to wriggle out from under her, but was held fast between her knees.

Paige was just centimetres away from a beautiful set of bright blue eyes that twinkled back at her. With the black mask hanging halfway off the assailant's face, she was shocked to realise that her attacker was a young female not that much older than she was.

'Why are you attacking me?' Paige asked

The young woman curled her lips into a taunting smile.

'Answer me,' Paige demanded as she snatched her mother's necklace back.

A blinding white light appeared. Paige quickly held up her arm to shade her eyes. The young woman pushed her off, then disappeared.

When the light settled, an old man with white hair in a multi-coloured robe stood next to a familiar, gauntly looking man. 'You're Callum, right? What are you doing here?'

The old man smiled at her, as if welcoming a new disciple into his cult.

'We came to rescue you,' Callum said, the ornament on his chest glowing as pink as his cheeks.

SIXTEEN

Paige stood up and glared at the duo, her hands planted firmly on her hips. Callum yanked the glowing pink necklace from his neck, his eyes wide as he stared at her.

'How did you find me?' she demanded.

Callum's gaze dropped to the floor. The old man beside him looked like a multi-coloured wizard straight from a movie set. He stood with a shoulder-height metal staff topped with a prism in one hand, while his other hand stroked his long white beard. He smiled, his twinkling eyes studied her with an intensity that made her squirm.

'Are you supposed to be some rainbow Dumbledore heading to a costume party?' Paige asked.

The question snapped the old man out of his trance. He threw his hands up. 'Why do you youngsters keep calling me that? Who is this Dumbledore?'

'He's a wizard from a kids' series,' Callum said. 'Sorry, Hubert, you just look like him from the movies.'

Hubert snorted and scanned the gym.

'Are you okay?' Callum asked. 'Did the assassin hurt you?'

'Assassin?' Paige struggled to reconcile the shy hospital cleaner with the man who had just materialized out of thin air. For all she knew, he could have been one of the attackers too.

'Why are you here?' She readied herself for another confrontation.

'We followed the assassin... I mean, Hubert did. I followed him,' Callum stuttered, his face bright red again. 'I mean, I came to make sure that... that...'

'We came to ensure the assassin didn't harm you,' Hubert interjected

Paige forced down her annoyance. 'I didn't need your help I would've had her arrested if you hadn't shown up.'

Hubert laughed. 'That would never happen.'

'And how would you know?' Paige fought the urge to wipe the smirk off his face. Strangers appearing out of thin air and belittling her was not something she appreciated.

'You've encountered the assassin,' Hubert said. 'The Destroyer's most skilled hitman—'

'Hitwoman,' Paige corrected.

'Yes, she is,' Hubert nodded. 'She's his fiercest and best-trained disciple. Cunning, fast, lethal.'

'Why didn't you tell us any of this before?' Callum asked, frowning.

'I'm telling you now,' Hubert replied. 'She could have killed you in an instant, and you'd never have seen it coming.'

'I can't believe the assassin is a woman,' Callum said, seemingly more to himself.

'If she's as dangerous as you say, why didn't she kill me?' Paige asked.

Hubert chuckled 'You must be a novelty to her. And nice to look at, too. I think she might like you.'

Paige rolled her eyes. 'We need to inform the police. Someone that dangerous needs to be behind bars.'

'If only it were that simple. Even if you managed to capture her, how would you detain someone who can walk through walls?'

'Geez,' Callum said shaking his head. 'She's really that powerful? I'm surprised she didn't kill us all the other night.'

'How do you know her?' Paige asked, suspicion creeping into her voice. 'And you never answered my question—who are you?'

Hubert's eyes darted toward the entrance before returning to rest on her. His fingers tightened around his staff.

'I am your guide,' he said finally. 'But this isn't a safe place to talk. Come to Waltor Manor. I'll answer your questions there.'

'You mean the Waltor Manor in Maine's countryside?' Paige asked, surprised. 'The one that's been deserted for years?'

Callum handed her a piece of paper with an address. 'Yes.'

'Do you own it?'

'Waltor Manor belonged to my father.'

Paige gaped at him. How could this old man be the Waltor manor heir? Surely Hubert couldn't have aged so quickly.

She studied him, looking for signs of dishonesty, but found none. Hubert's shoulders seemed more relaxed, his grip on his staff loose.

'Then where have you been all these years?' Paige asked.

Hubert waved his hand dismissively. 'I was occupied elsewhere. Come to the manor this afternoon. I'll be waiting.'

'I know this sounds crazy,' Callum said, his tired eyes pleading. 'But we're safer together now that the assassin is targeting us.'

Paige frowned at Callum. She still couldn't grasp how a timid cleaner could be involved with this eccentric old man.

'Yes, Callum is right,' Hubert added. 'And remember to wear your mother's stone at all times. You are the pink stone bearer now.'

'Wait, how did you—'

But before Paige could finish, the duo turned and walked toward a cloud of white light.

'Why aren't we taking her with us?' Callum's voice drifted back.

'She needs to come of her own accord. Give her time.'

Seconds later, Paige was alone in the gym, clutching her mother's pink stone in one hand and Callum's paper in the other.

People don't just appear and vanish into thin air.

She resolved to forget about the morning's events when her uncle's words echoed in her mind—*you are the pink stone bearer now. War is coming. You need to be prepared.*

Oh, come on, just because Uncle Rob thinks it's real doesn't make it so, she argued with herself.

But he said your parents died for peace. Don't you want to find out what really happened to them?

An ache gripped her heart, threatening to bring on fresh waves of tears. The encounter with Hubert had raised so many questions. If anyone could give her answers, it might be him. And if there was even the slightest chance someone could tell her what really happened to her mother, then insane or not, she would risk anything to find out.

***

Waltor Manor sat deep in the countryside, where expansive blocks of land stretched for hectares. As Paige drove that afternoon, she recalled the media coverage from ten years ago about the mysterious deaths of the manor's owners. Since then, there had been numerous fake claims from supposed distant relatives trying to claim the estate. A year-long investigation had been conducted to locate the missing heir, but the Waltors' only son was never found. The manor had been abandoned ever since.

Ten years. The same time her parents died. That couldn't be a coincidence. What really happened ten years ago? Was Hubert somehow connected?

Three hours later Paige reached the old, weather-beaten gates of the manor. At the centre was the letter W embedded into an intricate floral design. She was about to lean out of her window to press the buzzer when the gates creaked open.

The double-story building, made of old sandstone, stretched deep into the green pastures. She parked her car at the entrance and approached the double front doors, where two white stone lions stood guard on either side.

As Paige drew nearer, the lions glowed bright pink. She froze in horror when they both got on all fours, roared, and then bowed their heads.

The pink stone on her necklace glowed in response, and as if on cue, the double-door entrance swung wide open.

She shook her head. It must be some kind of hologram.

The stone lions roared again, as if losing patience, beckoning her inside with their front paws.

Her heart pounded her ribcage, and her muscles tensed. Paige spun on her heels to go back but was stopped by a slicing pain in her head. She fell to her knees.

A familiar voice reverberated in her mind: '*Paige, enter the manor and walk straight past the stairwell to the west wing. We are all waiting for you here.*'

She shook her head again to get the voice out and crawled toward her car.

'*If you want answers to your questions, I am waiting inside,*' the voice said. '*The real question is, do you have the courage to seek them?*'

With another cry of pain, Paige fell face down into the gravel. It was as if her head was being split open. *Stop! I'll come in!*

She crawled to the front doors. Only able to stand when the echo in her head died down.

Inside, Paige caught her breath at the sight. She had been expecting an abandoned manor with peeling paint and broken floorboards—anything but a lobby as immaculate as a five-star hotel, complete with a high hanging chandelier and marble columns with a grand stairwell to match.

Paige made her way slowly down the hall, where faint chatter echoed out. At least there was some sign of life. Her heart raced as she walked in the direction of the voices, stopping in front of a set of glass double doors.

They swung open.

'*Come in, Paige,*' Hubert's voice echoed from a distance.

She walked down the white-marbled hallway cautiously, wary of any other inanimate objects that might come to life. The bright lights from the swinging chandelier made her squint. The sound of laughter prickled her ears as she drew closer to another set of double doors at the end of the hall.

Before she reached them, they swung open and Hubert beckoned her in. He stood patiently, stroking his white beard, giving her that same annoyingly serene smile from the gym, as if to say, *I know what you're thinking.* A part of her wanted to call out, *stop studying me; it's off-putting,* but held her tongue out of politeness.

'You were the voice in my head,' Paige said when she reached him. 'How did you do that?'

'I'm a telepath,' Hubert replied. 'You'll get used to it eventually.'

The idea of a real-life mind-reader was disconcerting. She shuddered at the memory of the searing pain in her head. 'I'd rather not,' she retorted.

Hubert was strange, too calm and difficult to interpret. She had never encountered a person or situation she couldn't understand before, and this left a queasiness in her gut.

To have a crazed pervert pry into my mind? No, thanks.

'I am not a crazed pervert trying to pry into your private thoughts,' Hubert spoke, making her jump. 'That would be exhausting. There are people for that. I believe you call them psychologists.'

'Stop that!' she snapped.

'The mind is a complex structure,' Hubert continued. 'I wouldn't be able to hear all your thoughts at once; my mind would fry, as would yours. I can only hear the most immediate thoughts you use to speak or take action in the moment.'

'You're doing it again.'

'I'm trying to help you understand.' He stepped aside and motioned her forward. 'Come. Let's go inside. We've spent too long out here.'

Behind him was a room three times the size of her living room, each wall lined with hundreds of tattered books on shelves that stretched to the ceiling. The rest of the room was empty, except for a red mahogany wooden desk that seemed oddly placed in its diagonal position.

Once Paige was standing next to him, Hubert gave the desk three rhythmic taps. It let out a burst of white light that revealed an arched opening in the wall. Bright light poured in from the adjacent room, and loud chimes from an unseen clock made her jump. She rubbed her arms, trying to calm her frayed nerves.

'There's nothing to be afraid of. Come into the living room,' Hubert said.

What he called a living room looked more like a royal lounge. The high ceiling housed another glass chandelier, and the curved, cream-colored couches hugged the sides of the room, showcasing a stylish round glass coffee table. For a mansion that had supposedly been abandoned for a decade, it was surprisingly well-kept.

Hubert stroked his beard again, and Paige had an overwhelming urge to yank it off. Being the subject of someone else's amusement was unsettling.

'Who are you exactly?' Paige asked.

Hubert sighed. 'Don't you want to eat dinner first?'

'No.' Paige folded her arms.

Hubert nodded. 'Very well. I am the Grand Vizier. I see past, present, and limited future.'

'You mean like a prophet? An oracle?'

'No. I see possible threats but cannot predict the future. No one has that power. And any attempt to do so would have dire consequences.'

'So, what do Grand Viziers do?'

'I train warriors-to-be. The stone bearers of this time are divided and weak. You are all in desperate need of training if you are to survive the Destroyer's next attack.'

Paige eyed Hubert closely, watching for signs that he was making a bad joke or in the midst of a psychotic break. But he stood still, smiled, and returned her gaze with the same glittery grey eyes.

She embraced the uneasiness in her gut. A warrior trainer who could see the future? Insane was an understatement. How could the old man appear so lucid and deliver such preposterous assertions? And that colour-blinding outfit—surely the heir to the Waltors' fortune could afford better clothes. Assuming he was even from the same country.

'You mean my robes?' Hubert asked, then laughed.

Paige deepened her frown, still perturbed by the exposure of her private thoughts to a stranger.

'They are wonderfully comfortable. The colours on my robes help me travel through any light frequency. And I do exist in this time.'

Paige turned the statement over. *Exist in this time?* What an odd thing to say. Did he mean he was a time traveller?

Hubert's eyes darted quickly toward the door before resting back on her.

She fixed her gaze on him. He was hiding something. She could feel it.

He stroked his beard again, giving her a tight smile. 'My dear, in time, you will learn to trust me. I promise. I am here to help.'

A curvy, blonde-haired girl with glasses burst through a side door, cutting their conversation short. The sweet aroma of freshly baked roast followed her into the room. Paige's stomach rumbled, reminding her that she hadn't eaten all day.

'Dinner's ready,' she said. 'Did you want to come in?'

'Ah yes, Stacey, we would love to,' Hubert said, then winked at her before disappearing into the adjacent dining room.

'Hi, I'm Paige,' Paige said, extending a hand.

Stacey stared at her for an uncomfortably long time before responding. 'You look like a nurse that saw my brother in Emergency.'

Paige's mind took her back to a blond boy being scolded by his sister in triage. 'Yes, what a small world.'

'Come on, then.' Stacey beckoned her through. 'There might not be anything left of dinner if the boys start without us.'

Paige followed Stacey through the door, surprised to find Liam Michaels sitting at the dining table.

Liam leapt toward her. 'Nurse Paige, is that you? What are you doing here?'

Callum came over and pulled out a chair, motioning for her to sit. 'Stacey is an amazing cook. You'll enjoy her food after a difficult day.'

Hubert took a seat at the head of the table and motioned for everyone to sit.

Stacey sniffed and found a seat on the opposite side of the table, looking displeased. Liam plonked himself down next to her. Paige didn't understand her reaction but was too tired to think about it, and focused on dinner instead.

The large dining table was filled with an impressive banquet of food, from roast pork, stir-fried seafood, potato bake, and grilled fish to salads, fruits, and yogurt.

'Wow, who else is coming? This all looks delicious,' Paige said.

'Yeah, Stace loves to cook in excess,' said the blond teenager next to her. 'That's why she has such a hard time losing weight.'

Stacey's cheeks reddened.

'Ryan, that's not a nice thing to say about your sister,' Callum said.

Liam wrapped his arm around Stacey. 'Aw, that's okay, I don't mind. I like you, Stacey, chubs and all.'

Stacey burst into tears and ran out of the room.

'Did I say something wrong?' Liam asked with a confused look.

Hubert shook his head and sighed. 'Youngsters.'

'Maybe I should go talk to her,' Paige said, surprised by a deep ache of embarrassment that filled her chest as she watched Stacey leave.

'No, give her some space,' Hubert said. 'She'll come back.'

Paige was about to insist that someone talk to her when Hubert's body stiffened. He gasped, beads of sweat sliding down his temples and his eyes glazed over. He collapsed to the floor, going into rigor while making incoherent sounds.

Ryan, his mouth full of food, froze mid-chew. His dropped metal cutlery made a resounding clang against his plate.

Liam sprang to the fallen elder. 'He's not moving! What do we do? Help!'

Paige knelt next to Hubert, who now began to convulse, his eyes glowing white. His lips moved, but no sound came out.

A loud cry from Stacey, who re-entered the kitchen, made Paige jump. 'Oh God, what is happening to him?'

'Call an ambulance,' Paige commanded, not knowing who would be calm enough to make the call. She swallowed the grip of panic rising from her gut and began assessing Hubert's vital signs.

SEVENTEEN

A hard object hit her head and a phone bounced into her lap. Paige glanced up to Stacey's pale face and shaking hands. Liam yelled at his phone, banging on it to turn it on. She was relieved when Callum moved to a far corner of the room to speak to an operator.

Hubert's pulse was racing, his breathing ragged. Paige did her best to wake him, but he remained unconscious.

'Maybe we should move him onto the couch,' Liam said.

'No,' she said. 'He's too unstable. I don't want to take the risk of him arresting on transfer.'

'An ambulance is coming,' Callum said. 'Don't you need to do CPR or something?'

'No, he's got a strong pulse and he's still breathing,' Paige said. 'Help me roll him into the recovery position.'

Before they could, Hubert jerked upright, throwing everyone back. 'It's him,' he hollered, 'the Destroyer. Apollyon.' His eyes turned hollow and grey and when he opened his mouth to speak again, the voice was low and menacing.

'Hubert, how good to see you again.'

Hubert gritted his teeth. His eyes glowed milk white and he crumpled to the floor shaking.

Paige rolled him onto his back and checked his vital signs again. 'Hubert, can you hear me?' she asked, rubbing his sternum. 'Can you open your eyes?'

He jerked upright again. His eyes glowed grey once more. 'Did you really think that I would not see you?' The voice laced shivers down Paige's spine. 'How dare you trail my assassin!'

Hubert drew in staggered breaths, crying out in pain each time he opened his mouth. 'Apollyon, you can stop... stop the destruction. Fight... fight the evil inside.' He reached out blindly.

'Stop?' Apollyon's voice boomed, flopping Hubert back to the floor. 'I'm just getting started.'

'You are not your father. You are stronger than this.'

'You of all people should know better than to mess with the inevitable. Your own father learnt that the hard way and paid the price.'

Hubert sat bolt upright with his arms stretched out. His fingers clawed, reaching for an invisible foe. 'We'll stop you. I'll make sure of it!'

Apollyon's menacing laugh cut through the air. 'Your naïve optimism is indeed entertaining. Whatever you do, your presence here will only serve to strengthen mine.'

Hubert collapsed again as the cackles died down. Paige made sure he was still breathing before rolling him onto his side.

'Are you all right, Hubert?'

'No ambulance needed. He's gone. I'll be all right,' Hubert said, taking a deep breath. His face pale and his wrinkles looked more pronounced.

It was peculiar, how he seemed to have aged further within minutes.

After a few attempts, Liam helped Hubert into the lounge room, onto the couch. The team hovered around him, with worried looks

'I'm fine,' Hubert said, his eyes bright, as if nothing had happened.

'Someone spoke to you telepathically, didn't they?' Stacey asked.

Hubert nodded.

'Who?' Paige said. 'I think it's time we got those answers you promised.'

Hubert motioned everyone to sit, a conflicted look sweeping across his face. 'It was Apollyon, the next Destroyer.'

'Who is this Destroyer?' Callum asked.

A gripping sensation crept into Paige's chest, coupled with a sense of amusement as Hubert responded to Callum. She could somehow sense that the warrior trainer found it ironic that Callum had asked the question.

'Hubert?' Callum asked again. 'You're not doing something telepathically again are you?'

'No.' Paige studied his face. 'He's scared. He's considering what's safe to tell us and what isn't.'

Hubert eyed Paige with a cautious look. 'I will do my best to answer your questions. I know you need answers but please understand, if I reveal too much it can have dangerous consequences for your future.'

'Wow,' Liam said. 'How did you know what Hubert was thinking?'

Paige shrugged. 'I… felt it.'

'Paige is an empath,' Hubert replied. 'She is by nature an empathic person but having the power of the pink stone has amplified this ability.'

Paige's mind spun in a haze. She had never considered empathy to be a power. She thought back to her first incident with Liam, maybe that strange connection was what Hubert was referring to. She had been struggling with jumbles of emotions ever since. At the time, she had put it down to exhaustion from work. If this was empathy power, there had to be a way to make it stop, before the exhaustion consumed her.

'Can you to turn it off?' she asked.

'There is a way to control it,' Hubert said. 'But you'll need training, especially after you've fully absorbed the stone's power.'

'So, who is this 'Apollyon-Destroyer'?' Stacey asked, pressed firmly on the couch between Callum and Ryan. 'And why is he such a threat?'

'He is a cursed, evil force of nature who will bring death and destruction to our world.' Hubert answered. 'Billions of lives will be lost.'

Stacey wrung her fingers. 'What could possess someone to do something so awful?'

'Apollyon holds the earth's ancient power and, along with it, its curse.'

'So, the more he uses his powers, the stronger the bloodlust becomes,' Callum said.

'How did you know that?' Stacey asked.

Callum shuddered. 'I saw it in one of my dreams. A king from an ancient world possessed it. He massacred millions and destroyed everything.'

'Yes,' Hubert said. 'Three thousand years ago, King Argos took the ancient power of the life stone and became the first Destroyer.'

'Is that where you're from?' Ryan asked. Stacey shushed him.

Hubert looked taken aback. 'You think I'm that old?'

'The queen,' Callum said, raising an index finger. 'She stopped him. She broke the life stone into pieces then sent them away with her warriors... The stone bearers.' His voice trailed off as he looked down at his amulet and closed his eyes.

Hubert stroked his beard and nodded. 'Yes, go on. What do you remember?'

'She bound her warriors by blood to fight for peace. And that mission was to be carried on by the warriors' descendants until peace was restored.'

Paige sucked in a deep breath. Her mind pieced together the information but refused to accept it.

'What does that have to do with us?' Liam asked. 'Why do you keep calling us stone bearers?'

'Each piece of the life stone possesses a set of powers that was absorbed by each warrior who was sent away,' Hubert said. 'They became stone bearers. Upon their deaths, these powers are passed down to their offspring to continue their parents' mission.'

'Are you trying to tell us that we are descendants of these ancient warriors?' Stacey asked in a croaky voice.

'Yes,' Hubert replied.

Everyone in the room seemed to mirror the same bulging eyes and stunned expressions. Stacey's eyes glistened with tears, while her mouth opened then closed again without making sound. Liam rubbed the back of his scalp repeatedly.

Ryan clung to his sister's arm, burying his face in her side as he cried. 'Our parents were killed by a Destroyer maniac.'

Liam hung his head and rubbed his red eyes. 'My mum and dad left me to carry out a suicide mission.'

Paige burst into uncontrollable sobs. A deep wrenching sadness washed over her like a tidal wave. Thoughts of never being happy again paralysed her. She had never been so overwhelmed.

Hubert waited patiently for everyone to compose themselves before he continued. 'Apollyon is the next Destroyer of this world. We must stop him from killing and re-enacting the ancient curse.'

'But who is he exactly?' Stacey said angrily. 'Where does he come from?'

'Apollyon has not fully revealed himself yet. But when he does, you all need to be ready.'

Paige used all her strength to push herself across the room. All she could think about was running away, but the part of her that wanted answers forced her to remain in the room. The others gave her a quizzical look as continued crawling to the farthest corner of the room. Who cared if it was the most undignified moment in her life. The slow release of the tight binds of emotions confirmed her move was the right one.

'How are we going to fight an enemy we can't even see?' Callum asked.

'You can't,' Hubert agreed. 'We must make sure that you're all prepared.'

'That's comforting,' Stacey huffed.

'It is imperative you all find your stones and embrace your powers. We need you to continue training,' Hubert said, an edge to his voice. 'I suggest you all move into the manor. As you come into your powers, you will become targets.'

'In that case, I'd prefer to go back to my own life,' Stacey said. 'I'm not going to put my brother and I in danger.'

'You're already a target,' Hubert said. 'Your encounter with the assassin proves that.'

'She could easily attack us here, too!' Stacey said with an elevated her voice.

'The manor is protected. There are layers of forcefield around it, put in place by the warrior stone bearers… your parents.'

'Stacey, maybe it'll be safer for us to stay together for a while. At least until things settle down a bit,' Liam said softly. 'We can protect each other.'

Stacey looked at Liam, then at Ryan, then buried her face in her hands, massaging her temples.

'At any time during your training, if things get out of hand or you are attacked again, you may call out to me and I will be there,' Hubert said. 'Callum and I will continue to train you.'

'What do you expect me to do with them?' Callum said. 'How would I even know how to train them?'

'Use your connection to the life amulet.' Hubert said. 'It will give you knowledge of the warriors' powers. When you were in the training room your body became tuned to the energies of the life stones. Clear your mind and the 'how to' will come.'

'But—' Callum began.

Hubert held up his hand and turned towards Paige.

She took a deep breath as her body her body tingled and went numb. Waves of fear pinned her to the floor. Her head and heart pounded with a ferocity she'd never experienced. The room spun so fast she was seeing triples. The twisting in her gut churned so severely she could no longer keep it in until finally she let out a piercing cry and vomited.

'I can't stay here anymore!' she burst out then crawled towards the door.

'But Paige, it's dangerous—' Callum started.

'I can take care of myself.' Paige shuffled on her knees as fast as she could.

'It would be unwise for you to leave without learning how to control your powers,' Hubert said, standing.

'I don't care. I'm tired. I'm overwhelmed. I need to see my uncle. Nothing else matters right now.'

Once she could stand, she ignored their pleas to stay and sprinted out the door.

***

The next morning, Paige walked into hospital in a new set of pink scrubs. She had gone home to get ready, at her uncle's insistence, and was glad she had. It gave her the sense of normalcy she needed to recover. She did her best to ignore the pink stone that glistened around her neck when she looked in the mirror. It was a disturbing reminder of recent events.

She was looking forward to being back on the wards. The demanding work and gossipy colleagues could make her forget anything. She could keep an eye on Uncle Rob during breaks, too. Work was familiar, safe.

Paige settled herself in the nurses' station and began studying the handover sheet as the social chatter of her colleagues faded into background noise. *Damn, Mr Potts fell out of his bed again. That's the third time. Didn't the night resident order restraints?*

'Right, team, let's get started,' said Beth, the unit manager, with a clap of her hands. 'First patient on the list, Mr Potts. I need one of you to page the geris team to see him. He's delirious.'

'Urgh, I had to be stuck with lazy casuals and incompetent residents all night. Now to end the shift with Bossy Beth for handover. Can life get any worse? I need another job.'

Hang on who thoughts are those?

'What a bossy bitch, why doesn't she take care of it herself.'

Streams of scathing remarks catapulted into Paige's mind while Beth continued her instructions. Crap. It was all happening again. She held her breath to block them out.

But a fire burned in her chest and her heart began to thud... Dizzy, Beth's voice sounded like cat screeches, which somehow made her furious. She tried counting backwards, tried thinking about sheep jumping over the moon, tried to think of Uncle Rob's scare, anything else. But no matter how hard she tried, the angry thoughts kept coming. Until it consumed her, shaking her entire being forcing her to shoot up from her chair. 'That ass of a resident. He should have prescribed temazepam and restraints like I asked him to. Report him. Report him!'

Oh crap.

Her colleagues stared at her, wide-eyed. The night nurse on the opposite side of the nurse's bay went white.

'Paige, please sit back down,' Beth said, with a puzzled look.

A bead of sweat rolled down the back of her neck. 'I'm sorry.' She sat back down in her chair, breathed in deeply, and looked up at the clock. Not long to go until handover was finished. All she had to do was make sure she kept her distance and limited her contact with everyone.

A sensation on her skin made her look down at her hand and she caught herself rhythmically rubbing her stomach. Her pregnant friend next to her sighed and rubbed her own protruding belly. Paige crossed her legs and pressed her thighs down tight, but downward pressure on her bladder grew stronger by the second. It was going to be the longest handover session ever.

When it was finally over, Paige dived towards the observation machine. It was disturbing to be so hyper-attuned. Any emotion within a two-metre radius, caused a stir. The more intense the emotion, the harder it was to ignore. Emotions from boredom to pain to fear to frustration came at her from every direction. It was difficult to concentrate. Thankfully, relief came with morning tea break.

Beth appeared from the nurses' station. 'Oh Paige, could you see if Dr Martin is in the common room? The family wants to talk to him.'

'Sure.'

When Paige opened the red door of the tea room around the corner, the doctor was by the kitchen bench making himself a coffee. 'Dr Martin, I'm so glad I found you.'

'Paige.' He greeted her with a warm smile. 'Would you like a coffee?'

'No, thank you. I want to let you know—'

A warm tingling sensation washed over and her most private areas heated with desire. The message she needed to give him became a haze in her mind.

'Paige, are you okay?'

No, no, please no. Run. Get out. Now!

She did her best to move towards the door, but it was too late. Her body had already locked onto his emotions. In embarrassed horror, she grabbed Dr Martin by the collar, pressing her lips against his, and stroked his tongue with hers in uncontrolled passion.

Stop. Stop now. What a disaster! You will give him the wrong idea, her mind screamed, but her body refused to disengage.

Her fingers unbuttoned his shirt and Dr Martin happily kissed her back. Paige tried to push away but he held on tightly to her waist.

A loud bang at the door caused him to loosen his grip. Paige shoved Dr Martin back and sprinted for the door where Dr Collins stood with his duffel bag slung over his shoulder.

'Hey Martin, I think Mrs Hannigan is looking for you.'

Dr Martin let out a low growl as Paige pushed past the other doctor and made her way out the door. *Thank goodness Dr Collins is happily married. What a mess.* She took a shaky breath and waited for the raging hormones inside her to die down, dreading the gossip that was likely to circulate in the coming weeks.

With barely enough time to recover, the next emotional hold took over when a sharp pain in her right hip crumpled to the floor. Two porters whizzed past with Mr Potts groaning in agony on the stretcher.

'I'm taking Mr Potts down to X-ray,' the doctor said into his mobile. 'He fell again, looks like he might've broken his hip this time. I'll call orthopaedics.'

That was the last straw. She should have listened to Hubert.

'Get me out of here, Hubert, help!'

Her cries coincided with Mr Pott's wailing down the hall. The pains subsided when he disappeared into the lift, but Paige was still shaken. Hubert was right—she needed to learn how to control her abilities.

She called Beth from the locker room. Her manager allowed her to take leave without question, assuming it had something to do with her uncle's attack. It was as good an excuse as any.

Once she'd hung up, Paige flopped onto the locker bench. She allowed her feelings of helplessness to come to the surface and began to cry. She'd do anything to return to life before Hubert and the stones. The unknown was terrifying.

'I'm sorry.'

The voice made her jump. Hubert stood behind her, concern etched all over his wrinkles, as he stroked his beard with an unwavering sympathetic gaze. 'Let's get started on your training.'

EIGHTEEN

Stacey leaned back on the couch in the manor's lounge, as Ryan bounce excitedly on the opposite side. Would he ever stop being a boy? How could he not see how dangerous this was?

She desperately wanted to return to her lab, where the variables made sense. She couldn't grasp how finding ancient stones would magically protect them from danger.

When Hubert picked up the pace in his monologue about the life stones, she stood up. She'd heard enough.

'Stacey, please sit,' Hubert said, without turning around. 'It's important for you and Ryan to hear this if you want to stay safe.'

'How do we find our stones?' Liam asked, squeezing Stacey's hand as she reluctantly sank back down.

She glanced at their joined hands. Was Liam trying to comfort her or himself?

'Have you tried asking your foster father, Liam?' Callum asked. 'That's how Paige got hers.'

'No, he's already angry enough that I'm staying there,' Liam replied.

'Why do we even need these stones if we already have our powers?' Stacey asked.

'The stones help to control and amplify your powers,' Hubert explained. 'They allow you to access the full range of abilities available to you.'

'Awesome,' Ryan piped in. 'I'll never have to worry about getting picked on again. How do we find them?'

'Look within.'

'Within where?'

'Yourself,' Hubert replied. 'You are all blood-bound to your respective stones. Only you can find them.'

Irritation rose like lava from a simmering volcano. She hated cryptic answers. 'That doesn't help. Can you be more specific?'

'Look inward. Feel your powers and the emotions connected to them, and use them to guide you to the stones.'

Stacey rolled her eyes. Was the man incapable of giving clear instructions.

Liam gave a puzzled look.

'Get in touch with your innermost self—free yourself from the judgment and limiting beliefs that are holding you back from being the stone-bearing warriors you are meant to be,' Hubert said with a smile.

Stacey buried her face in her hands to stifle a groan. It felt like that time Kate dragged her to a yoga meditation class last month. 'You want us to meditate?'

'Yes, that would be one way to do it,' Hubert said, his smile growing wider. 'I'll get the next room set up.'

'Great,' Ryan muttered, looking as if he'd swallowed a lemon.

***

Hubert's face brightened as he beckoned them into a room on the south wing. 'Come in,' he said cheerfully.

The room was dim, mostly empty, lit only by a ring of candles encompassing a larger one in the centre. Pillows were placed around the circle and each corner of the room had antique looking world globes that stood proudly on their respective display tables.

'Take a seat and close your eyes,' Hubert instructed. 'You all know how to meditate, right?'

The boys gave him blank stares but closed their eyes as instructed.

'Take slow, deep breaths... Good,' Hubert said. 'Now, focus only on your breaths as you clear your mind. Let the thoughts pass through you. Imagine letting them go. Float them down a riverbank. Ryan, let go of those sexy images of male models.'

Stacey's eyes snapped open. Ryan's turned beet red and ducked his head.

Ryan's gay? Why hadn't he told me?

'Let it all go, float it down, down the river and away,' Hubert droned in a calm voice, rocking rhythmically. 'And remember to hold hands with the person next to you.'

Stacey reached out for Callum and Ryan's hands.

'And all those images of gorgeous women in bathing suits—don't engage, don't judge, just let them go. Liam, all those Playboy magazines will still be there when you get home. Float them down the river.'

Stacey tried to focus on the meditation, but the more she tried, the faster her thoughts raced. It was like trying to tame a wild horse.

That'd be right. Typical jock. Why does he act like he likes me when he can have any girl he wants? He's a good-looking athlete. I'm just a science frump. How could a guy like that possibly want a girl like me? We have nothing in common. Did he go out with me to please Kate? Or as some kind of joke? Yes, that would explain it.

Do you remember the way he fawned over Paige the other night? He's interested in her, not me. Who wouldn't like her? With her perfect body, perfect red braided hair, perfect smile, perfect teeth, perfect everything.

But why do I like him? He's just a guy. Did I fall for him pretending to be interested in my work?

Look, forget about Liam. You have more important things to worry about. Think, Stacey, think. How am I going to keep Ryan safe through all this? We need Hubert's protection, but I don't buy all this find-the-stones crap. For all I know, Hubert is some lunatic trying to trick us into something.

And Mum and Dad weren't stone bearers either. How could they have been? They were dentists who died in a bad car accident. God, I wish you were here, Mum and Dad. I miss you both so much. I'm trying so hard. I don't know if it's enough.

The last thing I want to do is go on a mystical stone hunt. Yellow stone-bearing warrior? Me? What a ridiculous notion. Makes no scientific sense at all. And even if I were, how the hell would I even go about finding this yellow stone? Look within? What nonsense! The only thing within here is damn annoyance at having to do any of this.

'Fire!' A yelp from Ryan broke her train of thoughts.

Stacey opened her eyes to find large flames roaring from the candles, reaching the height of the ceiling. The life amulet on Callum's chest glowed bright yellow and a golden beam shot forward from his chest, knocking him back against the wall. The beam landed on the nearest world globe and spun.

Everyone stared at the spinning globe with gaping mouths. Finally, it stopped and a glowing amber light marked a spot on the globe.

Ryan rushed over. 'It's pointing to Ceresville.'

'That's four hours' drive from here,' Liam said, standing up.

'I guess that means the yellow stone is in Ceresville,' Callum said, picking himself up from the floor.

Stacey drew a sharp breath. *Did I cause that? Surely not. Yellow stone? But there's no such thing. It's all a ludicrous fantasy. Besides, my mind wasn't clear in the slightest. There has to be a logical explanation for what happened.*

Hubert placed a hand on her shoulder. 'You did well. It gets easier. Come, let's go back and discuss this.'

In the lounge room, Stacey huddled in between Ryan and Callum on the couch. Hubert came back with a tray of cookies and tea. He handed her a cup. There was at least one perk to being in the presence of a telepath. You didn't have to directly ask for what you wanted. She took a sip of her beverage, letting the infusion of warmth settle her nerves.

Ryan took out his phone and scrolled it while munching loudly on a cookie.

'So, how do we know where the yellow stone is in Ceresville?' Liam asked from the opposite side of the room.

'They have a museum,' Ryan said, reading information off his phone. 'The museum director is Professor John Chu. He's an archaeologist. Maybe he knows something.'

'Can we ask for a meeting?' Liam asked.

'Oh look, they're having an opening of their new exhibit: The Ancient City of Ceres,' Ryan said bouncing in his seat.

'It's happening tonight.'

'We should go,' Liam said, mirroring Ryan's excitement with clapped hands.

Stacey swallowed the lump at the back of her throat. Everything was happening too fast. 'Great. You boys let me know how it goes.'

Ryan continued flicking his thumb over his phone screen. 'Nuhuh, museums are boring. You go. It says here he has a background in science before switching to archaeology. You're more likely to get along with him.'

'I'll take you,' Liam said quickly. 'We don't know what this guy is like.'

Stacey would rather spend the evening pulling hair out. How could they not understand her need for alone time?

'This is a good opportunity to find the evidence you need,' Hubert said with sympathetic eyes.

Stacey leapt out of her seat and threw her hands in the air. '*Stop*, all of you. If I am to even consider going on this mad hunt, you all need to give me my space.'

She left the room to manage the conflicting jumble in her mind. She had only made it halfway up the stairs to her room on the east wing when, to her dismay, Ryan had followed.

'Rye did you hear what I just said?'

'Yeah, yeah. But can you speed up the getting mad part? 'Cos opening starts at seven. That only leaves about an hour to get ready,' he said. 'Have you not got any makeup with you?'

Her brother dashed past into her room, then rummaged through the dressing table drawers.

Stacey let out a growl and pulled the end of her ponytail. 'I don't need an hour to get ready. I need some rest.'

Ryan straightened to face her with his hands on his hips. 'You want to impress the professor, don't you?'

'No, why?'

Ryan shot out the door only to reappear with a rectangular bag that opened to reveal an extensive makeup kit.

Stacey blinked with a mixture of amazement and exasperation. 'Goodness, Rye. Why do you have all these things? Is this what you have been spending your pocket money on?'

Ryan nodded and dragged her over to the dressing table chair. 'Sit,' he commanded.

He began powdering her face with foundation. Stacey coughed as dust swirled around her. She edged away, but Ryan continued applying the next layer of makeup, oblivious, as if he was in a trance.

If she had to endure a makeup session, this would be the opportunity to ask him about his sexuality. It must've been hard for Ryan, growing up without a male role model. Her heart ached with the realisation that she had been too busy providing for him that she hadn't stopped to see what he was going through.

'When did you learn how to apply makeup?'

'When I was ten.'

'That's amazing, Rye. I had no idea.'

He shrugged. 'It's nothing. You were studying and working at the lab a lot. I picked it up as a hobby to pass the time when nothing good was on TV.'

'I'm so sorry I haven't been there for you. You know you can tell me anything, right?'

Ryan continued working on her blush, avoiding eye contact.

'I will love and support you no matter who you are or who you choose to be with,' Stacey said, looking at her brother in earnest, hoping he would open up.

'I know, Stace,' Ryan said frowning. 'I'm not ready to talk about it yet, okay?'

Twinges of disappointment spread through her chest. It hurt her to wonder whether Ryan was angry with her or didn't trust her. Nevertheless, she respected his request. 'Okay. I'm here anytime you need to talk. I love you.'

'I love you, too.' He put the final touches on her face. 'I need to work through this on my own.'

They sat in silence while Ryan styled her hair, and Stacey tried not to cry out as he painfully yanked it back into a French twist. He seemed to be in his element. Once he was done, he pulled out the only dress Stacey had brought, from the closet.

'Wear this,' he commanded.

'You've got to be kidding.' She shook her head vehemently. 'No way.' She loved the dress, but the thought of someone seeing her in it made her stomach twist.

'Then why did you bring it?'

'It's the dress Mum liked to wear. It's comforting to have it with me.'

'If you want to attract the professor's attention, you can't wear jeans and a shirt,' Ryan said, then threw other clothing options out of her closet. 'And why did you bring your lab coat? Were you planning to examine the bugs on the walls?'

'No, of course not. Hey, stop going through my closet!'

'Yup, it's official—you have nothing to wear other than the sexy black dress.' He held up Stacey's lab coat in one hand and her baggy tracksuit pants in the other.

'I don't know if I can fit into it.' Stacey hated wearing dresses. They revealed everything she wanted to hide and was a sore reminder of the svelte body she clearly did not have.

'Just squeeze into it. The flabs will work its way around.'

Stacey glared at him, snatching the dress away. *I wonder what the grounds are for justifiable homicide?*

Nineteen

After lunch, Callum lounged in the living room, flipping through a trashy magazine. Ryan burst in and flopped down beside him.

'Has Stacey left?' Callum asked, not bothering to lookup.

'Yeah, she and Liam left a while ago,' Ryan replied and glanced around the room. 'I can't believe there are no video games in this place.'

'Are you bored?' Callum asked.

'Aren't you?' Ryan shot back. 'We've been stuck here for days, doing nothing but eat, sleep, and talk.'

'That's heaven for me,' Callum said with a grin.

'If there's nothing else to do, can you help me train?' Ryan asked eagerly.

'Train for what?'

'Hubert said the stone bearers need to train to control their powers. And I can't find him anywhere.'

'He's not in the manor? Let's wait until he gets back, then.'

'Oh, c'mon, Hubert said you can channel our powers and teach us how they work.' He tugged Callum to his feet. 'Please, please, oh pretty please!'

Callum wanted to resist but knowing Ryan wouldn't take no for an answer, let himself be peeled off the couch. 'I don't think it's safe to teleport without Hubert here. You don't know where you might end up.' His stomach knotted at the thought of getting stuck in a portal again.

Callum took Ryan's hand. He closed his eyes, expecting the worst—but nothing happened. They remained exactly where they were, holding hands. Waiting.

Ryan stomped his feet. 'It's not working.'.

'Okay, maybe try thinking of a place you want to go.'

Ryan nodded and they closed their eyes again. Still, nothing happened.

'Why isn't it working?' Ryan asked, frustration creeping into his voice.

'Where did you think of?'

'The Heroes Comic Convention. You?'

'I thought about going to work.' Callum shrugged at the incredulous look on Ryan's face. 'Maybe that's the problem. We're supposed to think of the same location.'

'Okay, what's a place we both know?'

'How about your sister's apartment? If we get stuck, we can call her to drive us back.'

Ryan's face lit up again. They held hands, readying themselves for action. But once again, nothing happened.

'This is hopeless! I'm not a stone bearer,' Ryan said burying his face in his hands.

'That's not true.' Callum pulled out his glowing emerald amulet. 'See? It's glowing bright green. It only glows when I'm near a stone bearer. Be patient, it'll come.'

'You're right, the last time I was this disappointed was when I was four, and my parents took me to the zoo. I wanted to see the lions, but Stacey got sick and—'

Before Ryan could finish his sentence, a green vortex opened in front of them and began to suck him in. Frantic, Callum clutched the boy's hand to pull him back, but the force was too strong. Ryan's fingers slipped from his grasp, and the green hole closed. Callum was ejected back onto the couch. He shot upright. 'Ryan, come back now!'

He had lost Stacey's brother. Callum stared numbly at the spot where the vortex had been, praying it would open and spit Ryan back out. His head spun at the thought of Stacey being disappointed in him for betraying her trust of Ryan's safety in his care. He only had a few hours to fix his mistake. How was he going to get him back when he didn't know where he is?

'Ryan, where are you?' he shouted. 'This is not a game. Come back.'

Callum dug his phone out of his pocket, and called Ryan. It rang out to voice message. He tried again and again, but still no answer.

'Damn it, Ryan. Pick up, will you? Pick up!'

He ran his fingers through his hair as he paced. *What a mess. Think, think, think how do you bring a lost teleporter back? What was the last thing he'd said before the portal opened? Something about being disappointed. Something about his past. Oh my God, the zoo! He was disappointed about the zoo. How many zoos are there? Where did he grow up? Crap.*

'Callum!' Ryan's voice broke through his frantic thoughts. 'I'm here, I'm here.'

Callum spun, relief washed over him as Ryan's face peered through a small green opening. 'Thank goodness. Where are you?'

'I'm at the zoo.'

'Which one?'

'The Ratty-Tatty Zoo.'

'Where is that?'

'It's about an hour's drive from the manor.'

An hour's drive—he could get there and back before Stacey returned. 'Okay. I'm coming to get you. Stay where you—'

A lion's roar cut him off, making Callum jump.

Ryan looked behind him and yelped. 'I'm in the lion's pit!'

There were two distant roars as Ryan's face faded and the vortex began to close.

'Help —'

'No. Ryan, Ryan, come back!'

Callum frantically scrolled through his phone and called Stacey. No answer. He cursed himself for not thinking to get everyone's numbers. In a panic, he called a taxi.

As soon as the taxi pulled up, Callum dived into the back seat. The driver slowly draped an arm across the passenger seat next to him to face him.

'Get me to Ratty-Tatty Zoo.'

'Are you sure? It'll be fifteen minutes before closing time by the time we get there.'

'I don't care. Drive,' Callum growled.

'What about Fountain Falls? It will cost you less. They're open late, and I can take you there in about ten minutes.'

'No, I want to go to the zoo. Drive now.'

'But it's a better zoo. I have brochures… somewhere. Let me find them.'

Callum's trembled with impatience. He grabbed the driver by the collar and twisted him back. 'No, you listen. Drive this vehicle to the zoo now, or I'll kick you out and drive there myself.'

The driver narrowed his eyes and shoved Callum off.

A green portal opened, revealing an image of Ryan running toward a tree with two lions behind him.

'Cal, help. Help! They're after me. I don't want to be lion food!'

'I'm coming, Ryan. Hang in there.'

'I don't know how much longer I can last!'

Callum's heart rate sky-rocketed, as lions snapped at Ryan's heels, while the boy struggled to climb the tree.

The driver slapped a hand over his open mouth.

'Hurry, Cal!' Ryan yelped as a lion managed to grab hold of a shoe and began munching.

What now? Think, think, think, Callum. Quick. Quick.

The vortex snapped shut as Ryan let out a piercing scream.

'Ryan!' Callum swiped at the closed vortex in a futile attempt to get it to re-open.

It's no use driving to the zoo. It'll be too late by the time I get there. There's no one I can call. Except Hubert. Call Hubert. Yes, call him telepathically. Why didn't I think of it sooner?

'Hubert!' he projected urgently. '*Hubert, we need you! Ryan is in danger at the zoo!*'

There was no answer.

Except from the driver. 'OK fine, I'll drive you to the zoo.'

'Hubert, Ryan is going to be eaten by lions if you don't get him. Hubert, can you hear me?' You'd better not be ignoring me, old man. I swear, if something happens to him, I'll strangle you with your own beard.

The taxi driver started the engine. 'You'd be better off in the loony bin.'

Callum, preoccupied with his summoning, didn't notice the car was moving until they reached the front gates of the manor.

'Wait, stop. Get me back to the manor. I don't want to go to the zoo anymore.'

'Make up your bloody mind,' the driver snapped, swerving the car around. The manoeuvre sent Callum crashing toward the side door. It opened, and he rolled out of the car, landing face-down in the gravel.

'That's close enough,' spat the driver. 'Never doing business with you again, ya crazy mutt.' And with that, he drove off.

Callum coughed and climbed to his feet. He was about to call out again when a blinding white light filled his vision, and he found himself lying on the couch in the manor.

Hubert stooped over him with a concerned look. 'Hmm, those are nasty cuts. I'll get Paige to see you.'

'How did I get back here?' Callum asked, bewildered. 'Did you get Ryan?'

Hubert stroked his beard. The action sent fury through Callum's veins. He sat up and clasped Hubert's arms, forcing him to stop the incessant stroking. 'Did you get Ryan?'

'It seems you all dislike my beard. I'd like to keep it if I may.'

'All good, Cal.' Ryan stepped out from behind him.

Callum jumped up and hugged him. 'Oh my God, you're back. Are you really back?' He couldn't believe his eyes.

Ryan grinned up at him. 'You're amazing. Thanks for sticking with me.'

Hubert patted Callum on the back. 'You did well, but next time try not to holler so loud. It gives me a migraine.'

TWENTY

Stacey found Liam in the manor's car park by his red sedan. He looked sharp in his black suit and blue shirt. His eyes lit up as she approached, while she self-consciously tugged the hem of her dress closer to her knees.

'Wow, you look great,' Liam beamed, opening the passenger door for her.

Was that him impressed?

The car ride was pleasant, though she it was difficult to ignore Liam's frequent sideways glances at her. If he looked any harder, they'd be swerving off the road. She bit her lower lip, it would disrupt the mood if she barked at him to keep his eyes on the road. Liam reached for her hand. Her reflexes wanted her to pull back but she resisted somehow, the warmth and strength of his grip was strangely comforting.

'Don't worry,' he said. 'Only a few more blocks. I can drive this part with one hand.'

She blushed and looked out the window. This was not the treatment she usually got from boys like Liam. *Maybe this was just him being nice like he is with all the other girls. Don't get too excited.*

When they arrived at the Ceresville Museum, Liam jumped out of the car and opened the door for her. 'Please, allow me,' he said, offering an arm.

Stacey took it, his eyes sparkled in a way she had never seen before. 'You're quite the charmer today.'

'This is me enjoying the company of a beautiful lady,' he said with a grin.

Stacey gave him a sceptical brow as he guided her towards the museum entrance. They climbed three flights of concrete steps, with Stacey leaning on him by the last flight. She cursed Ryan for making her wear Paige's black heels. She struggled to suppress her panting when they reached the glass entrance, where she collapsed against the cool surface of the museum door and kicked off her high-heeled shoes as if they were on fire.

'You rest. I'll go get a copy of the program,' Liam said disappearing into the museum.

Stacey sighed hugging herself. Was Liam disgusted by her lack of fitness? Who would want someone they had to cart up a flight of stairs?

'Here you go,' Liam returned and handed her the program. 'It was the last one.'

Stacey flipped open the brochure to avoid eye contact.

'How are we going to find Professor Chu?' Liam asked.

'It says here, he's giving a speech in an hour.'

'Why don't we check out the Ancient Ceres exhibit while we wait?'

She reluctantly slipped her shoes back on and hobbled into the museum. 'According to the map, it's on the right, past the dinosaur exhibits.'

Her blisters stung with every step as Liam kindly offered his arm again. She wouldn't have made it past the oil paintings without it. To her relief, the Ceres exhibit was only about fifty meters away.

At the entrance, Stacey was awed by the palace-like design. Large stone lion's paws flanked a staircase leading to marble columns that held up a triangular roof decorated with an intricately carved design of a griffin.

She read the introductory sign aloud. 'The ancient city of Ceres is three thousand years old. Discovered over ten years ago by Professor John Chu and his expedition team, half the city was found underwater and the other half in the desert underground. The city was ruled by King Argos and Queen Enactra, whose only heir was Prince Calister.'

The path past the columns led to displays of straw huts with villagers standing with spears. They wore simple red and purple garments. Further along, soldiers in silver breast-plated armour and black leather pants lined both sides, some holding swords, others spears, or bows.

Closer to the throne room, statues of six generals stood on either side of a trailing red carpet. The brass-coloured statues were so lifelike it seemed they might come alive at any moment.

Stacey stopped to read every sign and studied every statue as Liam trailed behind her.

One stopped her dead in her tracks. A man in a golden chest plate and matching boots, holding a round golden helmet against a sword hanging by his belt. Beside him stood a woman wearing a wolfskin coat, a bronzed tunic breast piece, a knee-length skirt, and high boots. She held a spear in one hand and a lasso in the other.

Their armour was foreign, but their faces weren't. The male statue had familiar short hair and that crooked nose she could recognise in her sleep, while the female warrior had long hair tied in a nested bun—just like her mother's. The resemblance was so striking it brought tears to her eyes.

'Liam,' she gasped and leaned on his arm for support. 'It's my parents!'

'Your parents?' Liam asked, puzzled. 'What do you mean?'

'Those statues look exactly like my parents.'

'How is that possible? These are Queen Enactra's generals. They lived three thousand years ago. They can't be your parents.'

'But they are,' Stacey insisted, showing him a photo from her wallet. 'Those statues are of my parents.'

Liam studied the photo, then bent down to read the signs. 'Noble warriors of King Argos and Queen Enactra. General Lang, protector of the Southern Kingdom, and General Castor, protector of the East.' His eyes widened. 'Stacey, your surname is Langcastor, isn't it?'

She nodded. Liam spun to look at the other warriors on display, moving from one to the next until he found what he was looking for. He stopped in front of a general on the opposite side of the hall.

Stacey joined him and read the sign. 'General Mye-Kols. Brave defender of the Northern Kingdom of Ceres. Mye-Kols. That sounds like Michaels.'

She looked at Liam and then at the statue. The general had the same strong features as the man beside her.

'That's my dad,' Liam choked out.

'There has to be a logical explanation for all of this.'

Stacey walked back to the Lang and Castor statues, and a tear trickled down her check. It took all her self-restraint not to fling herself around the statues and beg them to come alive. 'They must be our ancestors, like Hubert explained the other day.' Liam wrapped an arm around her shoulders.

'No, I've seen photos of my grandparents. They have some of the same features, but nothing like this. That statue looks exactly like my dad.'

Of course, none of it made any sense. But her heart knew beyond doubt, that somehow, these warriors were her late parents. She reached out to touch their faces, —she would give anything to feel her father's warm hugs again.

'They're marvellous, aren't they?' A voice behind made her jump. 'Queen Enactra's generals were said to be the most loyal and fierce warriors. They are legendary in the history of Ancient Ceres.'

Stacey turned to a distinguished-looking Asian man in his early forties, dressed in a black suit and bow tie. His warm brown eyes bright with intelligence.

'You're Professor Chu,' Stacey said, recognizing him from the brochure.

'Yes, I am,' he said with a slight bow. 'And you are?'

'Stacey… just Stacey.' She didn't want to discuss her family. 'These statues… they're so lifelike.'

'Yes, I agree,' Professor Chu said. 'The craftsmanship of the ancient Ceresnians are exquisite. All the statues were found underground where their palace used to be.'

'What happened to these people?' Stacey asked, swallowing the lump in her throat.

'Some believe they died in the explosion, but their bodies were never found. Others say they were sent on a secret mission and got lost. The truth is, no one knows.'

'An explosion?'

'Yes, the translation on the stone carvings we found in the desert described a bright array of colourful lights shooting from the palace, followed by a massive explosion that split the earth and sank half the city, killing thousands.'

'Did they say what caused it?' Liam asked.

Professor Chu turned to him. 'Hello. You must be Stacey's boyfriend?'

'Yes,' Liam said.

'No,' Stacey replied.

Liam turned crimson and looked away.

'I see,' Professor Chu said. 'No one knows what caused the explosion.'

Stacey could barely contain her tremble of excitement. If there were answers to be found, this was the place, and Professor Chu was the man who could provide them. 'Is there anything you could tell us about the mission these warriors were on?'

A loud bell rang, cutting their conversation short.

'I would love to, but I must go. Can I take you on a private tour and continue our conversation, Stacey? Why don't you give me your number.'

'Yes, of course.' She recited her number while he typed it into his phone. 'I would be honoured, Professor Chu.'

'Please, it's John. I'll see you soon,' he said with a wink before leaving.

Stacey glanced at a tomato-red Liam, at a loss as to what had made him so angry. Maybe he'd feel better with a distraction. She took his arm and pulled him towards the presentation stage, but it was like dragging a ragdoll through a bumpy field.

Much to her irritation, Liam's conversation was reduced to curt, two-word utterings, accompanied by a sulky expression. He only grew surlier, heckling with rude remarks during the professor's presentation.

Stacey's cheeks burned as he was repeatedly shushed by the audience. Liam, seemingly oblivious and signalled that he wanted to leave. Eager to escape the unwanted attention, Stacey allowed herself to be pulled away.

On their way out to the front entrance, Liam blithely offered his arm. Stacey slapped it away, and ran barefoot down the steps. She got into the car and slammed the door shut.

'Why are you mad at me?' Liam said. 'That Chu guy. What a pompous know-it-all.'

Stacey folded her arms across her chest and stared out the window in silence.

'I'll make it up to you. My apartment isn't far from here. We can rest and go back in the morning.'

'No. I don't want to go back to your place.'

Why was he being such a jerk around Professor Chu?

Liam pulled out of the parking lot and geared onto the road.

When she opened her mouth to protest further, Liam turned up the music that drowned her out.

'Do you want something to eat?' Liam said, touching her shoulder. 'I know a really good Thai place nearby.'

'No,' she snapped, jerking away. 'I'm not hungry. Take me back to the manor.'

'But it's almost eleven. It's not safe to drive that far without some rest.'

Stacey sighed, too tired to argue.

'Besides, my place is just around the corner now.'

***

Liam's apartment was the typical bachelor pad— an open-plan living area, with three couches placed in a U-shaped formation, hugging the fifty-two-inch flat-screen with surround sound and game consoles. There were soccer balls and sports magazines scattered across the floor and a tall shelf on the left that showcased multiple sporting trophies.

Stacey kept her distance. She'd never had a guy bring her home before and was beginning to think she should have fought harder to get back to the manor. She studied the exit—one slide lock above the door handle that could easily be removed and the door itself looked like the one from her apartment and should be easy enough to open. She stood glued to the back of the three-seater couch closest to the door.

'Are you frightened or are you still mad at me?' Liam asked.

Stacey stared at her feet to allow her mind to formulate a coherent thought.

'You're giving me the silent treatment, aren't you?'

He approached her and she took a step back.

'Hey, I'm not going to hurt you,' he said holding up her heels. 'I'm just giving you back your shoes.'

She accepted them and looked away.

'I'm sorry about earlier. That Chu guy is sleazy. He rubs me the wrong way,' Liam said. 'I didn't like the way he flirted with you... and vice versa, for that matter.'

A niggling heat rose from her chest, making her head pound while her hands curled into involuntary fists. She had been so close to finding out more about what happened to her parents and Liam had ruined it for her.

'Well, that 'Chu guy' is one the most reputable archaeologists of his time. He knows more about our ancestors than we do. He is the best lead to finding out what happened to my parents.' Stacey fumed. 'And flirting? I wasn't flirting, you jerk. I was being nice. Something you could try—you might learn something.'

'How come you were never that nice to me on our date?' Liam flushed, his nostrils flaring.

'I was!'

Glaring, Liam pointed an index finger at her. 'No, you acted like you couldn't stand me. Oh, right. I get it. You're only nice to smart guys. I'm not smart enough for you, is that it?'

Heat swirled faster inside her, making her heart pound. 'I never said that!'

'You flirted with him but not with me.' Liam raised his voice. 'And you totally ignored me like I wasn't good enough to be your boyfriend.'

'What?' Her jaw dropped.

'You acted like a schoolgirl with a crush.'

'I did not.'

'Oh, why thank you, Professor Chu, let me give you my number,' Liam mimicked in a high-pitched voice. 'Hee-hee, you're so smart and handsome.'

Stacey clenched her teeth, doing her best to keep her fists by her side. 'Great, and I suppose making farting noises during his presentation was really mature too.'

Liam folded his arms. 'He didn't present any facts—nothing but stories about how good he thinks he is..'

'You made us leave before he could present any!'

'I wouldn't worry about that. I'm sure he'll give you everything on his flirty private tour.'

Stacey gripped the edge of the couch to steady herself. She couldn't understand why Liam was picking a fight when she was the one who should be mad. She didn't know what was more humiliating, causing a commotion right in front of Professor Chu or being accused of being a flirty bimbo.

'I've had enough. I'm going home,' she announced heading for the door.

'But that's four and a half hours' drive away. How are you going to get home?'

'That's not your concern,' Stacey said in an even tone.

'Look, I'm sorry,' Liam said trying to take Stacey's arm while she gathered her things. 'We'll call it quits, and you can sleep in the spare room.'

'No, thank you.' She pushed him out of her way.

'Come on. You can't go like that.'

Stacey's tolerance broke. She could not understand anything he was saying anymore but looked him dead in the eye. 'I'm leaving, Liam. And you will respect that.'

He let out a frustrated cry. 'Fine, go then.' He slammed his hand on the trophy shelf and the trophies fell off like dominos. A golden metal soccer trophy bounced and collided with a round glass ornament.

A look of horror crossed his face as he tried to catch it. It slipped through his fingers, fell to the floor and shattered. 'No! Jeff gave me that for my birthday!'.

His expression was quickly replaced with astonishment as he stared at the floor. Stacey followed his gaze. Glowing brightly amongst the debris was a shiny blue gem stone.

Twenty-One

Paige sat in her bedroom in the north wing of the manor. Her room was more like a hotel suite with a balcony overlooking the gardens and front entrance. It was bigger than her apartment lounge room and kitchen combined, with a queen-sized bed, ensuite, walk-in wardrobe, and a comfy beige couch. Hubert had given her a penthouse room furthest from the others to allow her space to recover with minimal distractions.

She was an early riser, used to meeting her uncle before work for training. That morning, she'd decided to go for a run and explore the manor grounds. Running was cathartic; nothing was more addictive than the fresh morning air and rush of endorphins. She did her best thinking while she ran—it always allowed her to connect with herself.

As she rummaged through the closet drawers looking for her favourite black and pink sports top and tights, her thoughts drifted to the assassin. She was intriguing and her fighting skills were superhuman. Paige replayed the fight in her mind for the hundredth time. Despite training with Uncle Rob for years, the assassin's speed and agility were beyond her comprehension.

But there was something else that nagged her, the things she felt during the fight. She remembered feelings of guilt and shame that were dull aches in her gut.

Those must have been coming from the assassin. What could have possibly happened to put her on such a callous path? She could have easily taken her life. But why didn't she?

'Paige, are you awake?' came Hubert's voice through the door.

'Yes, come in,' she replied. 'It's open.'

Hubert walked in with breakfast—scrambled eggs and bacon on toast with orange juice.

Paige happily accepted the tray, marvelling at how grandpa-like he was in that moment. 'Wow, I even get room service.'

'Of course.' Hubert sat on the couch. 'Good to see you're dressed. We have a big day ahead of us.'

Paige wolfed down her morning meal.

Hubert blinked. 'That was fast.'

'You have to be working at the hospital, in case you don't get another break.'

'I see.'

'So, in her time, how did my mother actually fight off the Destroyer with empathy powers?' she asked, putting the tray aside.

'Always straight to the point,' Hubert said with a tight smile.

Paige looked him straight in the eyes. 'Always.'

She was tired of waiting. Today was the day she would press for answers. Paige had never known anyone who was as skilled at evading questions as Hubert.

'The pink stone bears more than just empathic powers,' Hubert said slowly. 'The important thing is being able to control the powers you have now. They will grow as you do.'

'Would I be gaining any physical powers?'

'Possibly.'

'What powers did my mother have?'

'I don't know.'

Paige frowned, as her aching gut sank. She needed more. 'I thought you could see the past.'

'I can only see what's relevant to a future threat. One day you will know the whole truth. But I'm not the one to provide it. As you progress further in your journey, you'll find the answers you seek. But not today.'

Paige stared numbly at his poker face. She wanted to shake him, to squeeze out the answers he had promised. How can the wise old Grand Vizer not know?

'Why am I even here if you can't tell me anything?' she cried, pain spreading in her chest.

'All I know,' Hubert said softly, 'is that she chose, with the other parent stone bearers, to give her life to protect us all. She was the heart of the team. As are you.'

Tears welled up in Paige's eyes. Every part ached to see her mother again. She closed her eyes and breathed through the pain. It was no use being angry at Hubert, it wouldn't change anything. Mum was already gone.

'I believe you are kind, like your mother,' Hubert said, giving her shoulder a gentle squeeze. 'You need not look far to find her. She is a part of you.'

Paige wiped her eyes and looked away.

'The power of empathy, being able to understand and feel another's feelings, is one of the most powerful abilities to possess.'

'How? So far it feels more like a curse.'

'Connecting to another person emotionally is true connection. A connection of that depth gives you the insight you need to resolve any conflict. It could end the fight without the need for war.'

Paige understood the theory, but it made her stomach churn thinking about having to connect with a monster like Apollyon.

'How do I control it? Anytime I get near anyone, their emotions take over.'

'You need to create an emotional barrier. Like the one I've created to stop you from accessing my emotions,' Hubert said.

There it was. He was hiding something. No wonder she couldn't sense anything.

'But if I do, wouldn't that mean I'll end up blocking access to all emotions?'

Hubert looked pleased that the conversation had moved on. 'Yes. The first barrier you must create is the one of separation. Like a one-way mirror, where you can observe another's emotions without them affecting you.'

Paige frowned. 'But it hits me so fast.'

'Learn to be self-aware. Do an emotional sweep of yourself and know your own feelings in the moment. Then imagine placing a river and the one-way mirror around yourself to block their emotional waves.'

'Why a river?'

'To slow the emotional wave.'

Was this the start of her training? It all sounded good in theory, but how she could do what he was asking before the intense emotions took over. Did Hubert even know what he was talking about? The sceptic in her wanted to reject his method of control, but the hopeful part of her gave him the benefit of the doubt. She at least needed to try.

'What about those times I do want to feel what they're feeling but don't want to be overwhelmed?'

'Resolve your own emotions first, then create an opening. That way you can control how much you let in.'

Paige leaned her forehead into her fingers, giving him a weary look. She still had no idea how to apply his teachings.

Hubert walked over to the window and stroked his beard again— she could sense it was his self-soothing habit while he discreetly read her thoughts.

Paige concentrated on the back of his head. If she could get a backway into his emotions, maybe she could glean more information. But all she felt was calm, and amusement.

'Before you choose to let someone else in, make sure you recognise and understand the message of your own emotions in the moment first,' he said, breaking her thoughts. 'It will prevent you from having to deal with your emotions and theirs at the same time.'

A slow pounding in her head made it difficult to concentrate. She ran her fingers across her face as she struggled to grasp the concept. Emotions are emotions. They don't contain meaning... do they? She'd always found others' emotions easier to understand. Her own always carried so much pain and disappointment. Even if she was willing to identify what she was feeling, she had no idea how to interpret it.

Hubert nodded with sympathetic eyes. It was easy to forget that he was a telepath. Paige chastised herself for being careless with her thoughts in front of him.

'Why don't you give it a try,' he said gently. 'Tell me what you're feeling right now without judgement and I'll help you decipher it.'

Paige narrowed her eyes at him. It seemed unfair that he could read her when she was blocked from sensing him.

Hubert watched her in silence, rhythmically stroking his beard. Waiting.

There was nothing to lose. It would be interesting to get his take on things. So she inhaled deeply and blurted out the first thing that came to mind. 'I feel frustrated and annoyed. What message am I meant to receive from that?'

'Good. Frustration and annoyance are milder forms of anger. It means that you have a belief or value that needs protecting. Now, try to tell me why you are feeling this.'

Her fingers moved to grip the hair on the side of her head. 'I feel frustrated because I want to know what happened to my parents. I need to understand why they could leave me like that. I need to understand why they didn't love me enough to stay. Is it because I'm not good enough?'

Her response seemed to surprise her more than it did Hubert. The vice around her heart made it difficult to breathe. Years of suppressed feelings of abandonment rose to the surface like an awakened lion that she was powerless to stop.

Tears quickly turned to sobs. Hubert held her as she heaved through it all. It seemed like hours before she could breathe normally again.

Hubert nodded his approval. 'Feel better?'

Paige placed a hand on her chest and inhaled deeply. 'Lighter now. But that was awful. It felt like I was dying.'

'With any emotion, you must allow yourself to feel it before it can be released. Without going through that process, it will keep resurfacing until you do.'

Paige nodded.

'Now try to listen to the message from your emotional experience. Close your eyes.'

Paige closed her eyes and took slow deep breaths. Listening. Feeling. Connecting to her inner being. 'It's telling me I have a hole inside of me. I need to understand the past to figure out who I am.'

Hubert's eyes seemed to shine with pride as he patted her shoulder. 'And you're already here taking action towards that understanding,' he said in a reassuring tone. 'It will come. Give it time.'

***

Hubert took Paige to the local marketplace after ensuring she had anchored herself to a peaceful place in her mind. The crowd moved in and out of the entrance while her feet were grounded in apprehension.

An invisible wave hit her, followed by the sensation of knives swirling in her gut. It then vanished, replaced by hundreds butterflies fluttering in her stomach followed by an explosion inside that made her head spin.

Paige gripped Hubert's arm to steady herself. 'I don't know if I can do this. Can't we start somewhere less crowded, like a quiet coffee shop?'

'You're more capable than you realize.' Hubert gently nudged her forward by the shoulders. 'This is the fastest way for you to experience the emotional sweep and intensity range.'

'Emotional sweep?'

'Yes. Learn what each emotion feels like and recognize them. Every emotion—love, peace, joy, sadness, anger, fear—has a different signature and set of messages.'

'What's an intensity range?'

'It's a way of scoring each emotion you feel on a scale from zero to ten, with zero being no feeling and ten being highly intense and intrusive. You'll need to develop a filter for each level.'

'And if I get overwhelmed?' Paige asked, trying to wriggle out of Hubert's grip.

'Then anchor yourself back to your peaceful place.' He held firm, guiding her toward the entrance. 'It's also important to learn at what intensity people tend to take action, and which emotions drive them to act versus internalizing or reframing their thoughts.'

Paige clenched her teeth. Hubert wasn't giving her a choice to back out. 'You can do this.'

Closing her eyes, Paige centred herself in her peaceful place. But the sensation of bricks on her shoulders had already begun to take hold. 'How will I know if someone is internalizing or thought-reframing? I can't read minds like you.'

'Aren't you a keen observer of body language and micro-expressions?' Hubert said with a wink.

He guided her past the market entrance. Paige's body trembled and her mind spun faster. She couldn't separate anything; every emotion hit her like a tsunami. The frustration of a mother trying to soothe her crying baby. The fear of a young man who had lost his wallet. The sadness of a woman in black, mourning her loss. The bliss of newlyweds exploring the market. The glee of a nearby stall owner quietly counting his morning profits.

Paige turned to flee, but Hubert held her arm tightly. She was trapped. She tried to return to her peaceful place, but it was a grey, blurry spot in the distant corners of her mind.

'Hubert!' she cried, clutching her chest. 'This is too much!'

'Focus, Paige, focus. What are you feeling?'

In a panic, her mind retreated to a cube with metal walls. 'I don't know!'

'Go back to your peaceful place.'

'I can't. I can't get there. Let me go, Hubert!'

Hubert seized her shoulders and spun her around. 'Look at me,' he commanded, his face etched with concern. 'I can't help you if you shut me out, too.'

'I don't want to,' Paige uttered. 'I can't do this. It's too painful.'

'Breathe.'

Paige took deep, controlled breaths. Her mind slowed, and she stopped shaking, but in her mind's eye, she remained in her cube.

'You don't have to come out yet if you don't want to. Just tell me how you're feeling,' Hubert said, his voice a mere whisper.

'I'm afraid. No, terrified.'

'Why?'

'Because I can barely manage my own emotions, let alone others. If I keep feeling everyone else's, I'll lose myself.'

'So, what do you need?'

'To feel safe. To be seen and heard. I need to protect myself.'

'What needs to happen for you to feel safe?'

'I need... more time, to connect with myself.'

Paige opened her eyes to Hubert deep in thought, his gaze distant. 'Very well.'

A flash of white light surrounded them. When it faded, they were standing on a grassy hilltop overlooking the marketplace. Paige sat down in silence, focused her thoughts inward, and began to meditate.

TWENTY-TWO

Callum stood by his bedroom window, bathed in the morning sunlight. The green pastures outside the manor blurred as he closed his eyes and tried to banish the haunting images of bleeding body parts. He was grateful for the solitude of his room, no one needed to hear him scream every night, least of all Ryan.

A low growl pierced the silence, and Callum found himself confronted by a mummified wolf hurtling toward him. He stumbled back; his gaze locked on the creature's beady eyes as it clawed at his chest. Terror rooted him in place. But with a resolute stamp of his foot, he willed himself to move. The burst of energy that surged through him, tinted his vision red. His muscles bulged, his spine straightened, and sharp black talons extended from his fingertips. He raised them, bracing for the attack.

The wolf lunged, and Callum roared, a primal sound tearing out from his throat as he slashed at the beast's neck. The decapitation was swift, and the mummy disintegrated into thick clouds of dust. He staggered away from the choking dust to the open window for fresh air. The sunlight and clear blue skies were a welcome sight.

After the dust settled, Callum wrapped his arms around himself, unable to stop the shaking. He shook his head again and again, but the nightmarish images still took a firm stake hold in his mind. He was not that beast with talons, those creatures had no connection to him. He was not one of them.

Callum examined his fingers and let out a slow breath. *See? Normal. I have normal human hands.* He spread his fingers closer to his face, fixating on his fingernails. *Same. Normal. Human.*

Something trickled down his side. When he lifted his shirt, an oblique gash than spanned the length of his arm ran down his left side. Blood soaked his shirt. Each morning brought a new injury. Things were clearly worsening.

Callum ignored the gnawing in his stomach and headed to the bathroom, only to be confronted by the warrior's reflection in the mirror. The menacing figure taunting him, was fast turning into a morning ritual, turning mundane tasks like brushing his teeth and dressing into challenges. He shut his eyes, fighting the creature's sullen gaze and twisted grin from invading his thoughts.

With each passing day, the reflection lingered longer, mimicking his movements, perfectly. Too perfectly, almost as if it could step out of the mirror and strangle him at any moment.

He longed to seek answers from Hubert, but the others constantly demanded his attention. He was after all not as smart as Stacey, not as strong as Liam, not as charming as Paige nor as quick witted as Ryan. He was just not Hubert's priority. He might as well be living back at his old apartment. But then why did Hubert entrust him with the amulet in the first place? He could barely help himself.

A loud argument from downstairs jolted him from his thoughts. 'How could you leave like that?' Liam's voice drifted up.

Callum hurried down the white marble stairs to the lounge room in time to see Liam storm through the doors. A shiny blue object dangling from the sports boy's his neck.

When he entered the room, Callum found Liam and Stacey in a heated confrontation. Liam's blue stone swung wildly as he gesticulated, while Ryan sat on the couch, clearly amused by the unfolding drama.

'Good morning to you, too,' Stacey said curtly, hands on her hips.

'I was worried sick,' Liam said. 'You could've been in a car accident, attacked, or kidnapped. How could you be so careless? You should've waited for me!'

The water glasses on the coffee table levitated with his gestures.

'Right, because I'm so helpless,' Stacey shot back sarcastically.

'You're twisting my words,' Liam snapped. 'All you need to do is apologize. Are you always this difficult? Maybe it's good I'm learning this early in our relationship.'

Stacey rolled her eyes. 'We've barely dated.'

Liam took a step back, releasing a frustrated cry.

Callum swallowed, as images of a drunken Dad slapping Mum came flooding back. He gripped the padding of the couch, grounding himself, fighting the urge to flee.

Instead, he turned towards Ryan and motioned to the door, 'Let's give them some privacy.'

'Nope,' Ryan said with a playful grin. 'This is better than midday soaps.'

Stacey's phone rang. 'Hello?' she answered sharply, her tone softened as she continued. 'Oh, Professor Chu, what a pleasant surprise.'

Her face brightened, and she twirled her ponytail between her fingers. 'Yes, I'd be delighted to have dinner with you.'

Liam turned crimson, his growls of disapproval growing louder.

'Yes, I know where Le Chateau is. I'll see you tonight at seven. I'm looking forward to it as well.'

'You're not thinking of going, are you?' Liam burst out as soon as Stacey hung up. 'It's too dangerous. You don't know him.'

Stacey folded her arms. 'I fail to see how you have a say in this.'

'It's better if I come with you—for your protection.'

'Thanks, but no thanks.'

'What if he tries something shady?' Liam said.

As their argument continued, the walls shook, and the vibrating rushes of water grew louder.

Ryan looked around the room and paled. 'Uh, guys, you might want to dial it back a bit,' his face mirrored Callum's unease. Liam's powers were being amplified by the blue stone and it was about to lose control.

Callum readied himself to intervene when memories of his father's violence flashed back again. The childhood images shrank him back into the couch, freezing him in place. In that moment, he was his powerless five-year-old self again.

'Guys, calm down, okay?' Ryan said, his voice trembling.

'Can't you see he's just a sleazy professor trying to hit on you?' Liam said loudly. 'Your crush on him is clouding your judgment.'

Stacey let out an exasperated cry. Her face flushed, matching the red of her ears and neck.

'Let me be clear,' she said, her voice icy. 'I will come and go as I please, and who I go out with is none of your concern.'

'Are you pushing me away?' Liam asked in a pained voice. 'Is that what you're doing?'

'What?'

'Tell me why you're so hot and cold with me.'

Stacey threw her hands up. 'I don't want to have this conversation.'

'Why do you hate me?'

Stacey closed her eyes. 'I don't know if I can handle you anymore.'

Liam's voice broke. 'Why, Stacey? What have I done to make you want to leave me all the time?'

The walls burst open with a florid of water, soaking everyone in the room. When the wave receded, Liam stormed off, leaving Stacey staring after him.

TWENTY-THREE

Stacey stood alone in the manor lounge, reeling from her encounter with Liam. She stared at the spot where he had been moments ago. Callum and Ryan had gone to find tools to fix the pipes. She waded through water to get to the only place that could give her sanctuary- the kitchen. The kitchen was constant, a place she could process challenges in her life. She collapsed against the bench by the sink and buried her face in her hands.

Stacey had seen so many sides of Liam that she no longer knew which one was real. The hurt expression on Liam's face haunted her. She wanted to cry but also wanted to yell too. It was like they were speaking different languages, with no interpreter to help her understand. Liam seemed to be in a different headspace. A part of her was attracted to him, but his behaviour baffled her. She had never been so confused.

A scraping sound drew her from her thoughts. Hubert stood at the other end of the dining table stroking his long white beard. 'Hello, Stacey.'

'I thought you were with Paige.'

'She requested some time alone.'

'We girls are alike in that way.' She hoped Hubert would take the hint.

'You had quite an experience,' he said, and as usual, stroked his beard rhythmically with a bemused smile.

'Is there something I can do for you?' She tried to keep the edge out of her voice at his irritating mannerisms

Hubert leaned against the table, the corners of his eyes crinkling. 'Let's chat.'

'I really don't want to.' Stacey hated when people tried to talk to her while she was upset. She preferred to process and analyse in private.

Hubert smiled serenely. 'It might do you good to step out of your comfort zone. Who knows? You might find what you're looking for on the other side.'

'I'm not looking for anything other than peace.'

Hubert stood and paced. 'I understand it can be hard to let someone new in and risk getting hurt. It's far easier to push them away.'

Stacey sighed, if only she were back at work, she wouldn't have to endure any of this. Perhaps silence would drive him away. But to her dismay, he took a seat closer to her and clasped his hands on the table.

'You don't have to talk,' he said. 'I like hearing the sound of my voice. You can listen… or not.'

She glared at him, determined to maintain her stony silence, while Hubert seemed determined to remain oblivious.

'The loss of your parents affected you deeply. It's made you unwilling to connect with anyone who tries to get close to you. You fear you may lose them as you lost your parents. Instead, you bury yourself in work and caring for your brother.'

'I didn't ask for a therapy session.'

'I like to impose,' Hubert said a little firmer. 'You shut people out to feel safe, especially those you find difficult to understand.'

She gritted her teeth. What would he know anyway? But his words pierced her chest like a hundred needles. Was he right?

'What if I have?' Stacey chewed on her bottom lip. 'It's worked fine so far. It's kept us safe.'

'So far, yes. But it's also a very lonely path.'

'Lonely is fine with me.' Stacey was fed up with his telepathic games. The unwanted counselling session fanned her irritation to new heights. She dashed toward the door, her tolerance for fake pleasantries had reached its limit.

'Does it really keep you safe?' Hubert called after her. 'That might have worked in the past, but it will not work for you now as the yellow stone bearer.'

Stacey spun on her heels; her vision tinged with yellow. 'Well, I refuse to be a stone-bearing anything,' she snapped.

Hubert walked over and placed a hand on her shoulder at the door. 'You can, but it will not prevent the attacks on you or your brother. Your survival will depend on the strength of your connection to others and your own emotions.'

'I didn't choose this, and I certainly don't want it.' Stacey shook her head vehemently, willing the heat in her chest to subside. She shrugged his hand off her shoulder and turned to face him.

Worry knitted his brow and he took a step back, but kept his eyes locked on her.

'I know,' he said softly. 'We cannot choose the hand we are dealt, but we can choose our response to it. Yes, you can deny the power of the yellow stone. But can you live with the loss of billions of lives, knowing you possessed the power that could have prevented it?'

Great, emotional blackmail.

Hubert had put her mind in a blender, nothing was clear anymore. Keeping Ryan safe was the only thought that pierced through. 'I don't want Ryan and I to die like our parents.'

That was the heart of it, after all. It wasn't so much about her. She had already lost her parents; she couldn't bear to think of her brother, dead, lost to her forever too.

'I understand, but the outcome you fear is less likely, Stacey, if you strengthen your powers through connection with others.'

She ran her fingers down her face to soothe herself. She didn't know how to connect, even if she wanted to.

'We can help you.' Hubert gently patted her arm. 'First, learn to take down the armour that shuts people out. It has protected you, but continuing to wear it now may cost you your life.'

Her mind flashed to thoughts of her high school classmates who had used her for their homework assignments, and her university lab partner who had stolen her work to win the chancellor's science award. But the most painful of all, the trust she had put in her parents' friends who turned out to be neglectful and manipulative foster parents. They had only been interested in gaining control of their inheritance trust.

'What if Ryan and I get hurt?'

Hubert closed his eyes as if reliving her pain with her. 'Yes, that's always a possibility,' he murmured. 'But by cutting off the possibility of connection to everyone, you assume that all people are like those you've encountered in your past.'

Stacey's mind was so heavy, all she could do was stare at him through misty eyes.

'Is the avoidance of pain worth the cost?' Hubert asked.

'Cost?' Stacey echoed, bewildered.

'A limited life, with so little connection to your emotions or anyone else other than your brother. Weren't you looking for love at one point?'

Hubert's words were like a noose tightening around her heart. To have a stranger dig into her most private thoughts, was mortifying.

She wanted to push him out and run, but an unforeseen avalanche of sobs froze her in place. Hubert gave her a tight, fatherly hug that only made her miss her own father more.

Once the dull ache inside subsided, she wiped her tears and allowed a space inside her to open. 'How do you propose I make these so-called connections?'

'By allowing yourself to be vulnerable once in a while. Embrace it as a strength. It's a way for others to really see and hear you.'

Stacey closed her eyes. It all seemed impossible.

'Remember, the key to surviving is to connect, now more than ever. Let go of the past, accept the present, to create your future.'

'Fine, so strength in numbers,' Stacey said, working hard to understand Hubert's reasoning. 'Then how would I bring out the power of the yellow stone? Assuming I can find it.'

'Your powers come from your emotions. Learn to connect with them. Let go of doubts, judgment, and expectations. Let go of who you think you should be and start embracing who you really are. That is where real power lies.'

TWENTY-FOUR

Paige sat at a coffee shop with Hubert, who was sipping his cappuccino. Dozens of patrons lined up for their drink, their caffeine deprived state engulfing her in continuous waves of fatigue.

'Now, find your peaceful place, Paige, and separate yourself from them,' Hubert said calmly.

Paige leaned forward to inhale the coffee's aroma. She desperately needed her hit of caffeine; every whiff of coffee pulled her head toward each passerby.

'Focus,' Hubert barked.

'Easy for you to say,' Paige rubbed her eyes. 'If you let me have my morning coffee, I could focus better.'

'No coffee,' Hubert said sternly. 'I don't want your powers affected by drugs.'

Paige narrowed her eyes at him, so close to yanking off his beard. 'Caffeine isn't a drug,' she muttered, her forehead centimetres from the table.

'Put up that one-way mirror now.' His loud, crisp voice sliced through her.

She pushed hard on the edge of the table to keep her head from dropping onto it. Through a sleepy haze, she did as she was told. The image appeared in black and white, wavering as she struggled to focus.

'Put your focus on one object first before moving on to the whole scene,' Hubert said loudly.

Paige concentrated on the large tree by the riverbank, first adding colour to its trunk, then to its leaves until the tree sprang to life. The river began to flow in vivid blue-green, washing over the rocks by the bank. The mirror appeared by the river's edge, and through it, she watched the coffee shop patrons hustle around, waiting for their orders. The fog in her mind gradually lifted, and she began to feel more alert.

For the next two hours, Hubert made her repeat the exercise, moving closer table by table to the crowd at the counter. Paige endured waves of sleepiness and sudden bursts of alertness as she sharpened the barricade in her mind. Growing bored, she asked to go to the marketplace.

Paige stood at the gates of the marketplace once more with Hubert and his silver staff. Maines Market was a quaint country place with wooden stalls lining both sides of a central gravel track. It was packed with young families with children stopped at the stuffed toys and games stalls, while older ladies stood at another buying fruits and nuts. The younger men browsed tools and utilities, with a few ladies at the clothes and accessories stand.

Paige began to regret her request. She was a meter from the entrance when emotional waves crashed down on her. She couldn't distinguish individual emotions but rated them as medium intensity. As she stood in the middle of the crowd, a queasiness rose from her winding gut.

Hubert gave her shoulder a light squeeze and nudged her forward. Paige took a deep breath, gritted her teeth, and stepped toward the crowd.

Her chest burned, her arms went numb, and her head pounded. She turned to see a white-haired lady waving her walking stick at a grey-haired man behind the nuts stand. 'This is too expensive for peanuts!' she said stridently. 'That's a crime!'

'It's fifty dollars a kilo for hybrid peanuts,' the stall owner snapped back. 'You've opened the pack. Now you pay.'

The burn in Paige's chest intensified as the hammering of her heart made her dizzy. The anger from the nut stand was more than she expected. The stall owner blew his whistle, likely calling for marketplace security. The old woman banged her walking stick repeatedly on the baskets of nuts on display in response.

Paige's mind started to collapse under the intensity. She was about to lose control again, and turned to run, but Hubert grabbed her by the shoulders. 'Focus, Paige, focus.'

'I can't. They're too intense. I can't think.'

'Remember what we practiced?'

Paige took a deep breath, forcing herself to inhale for four counts and exhale for six.

These are not my emotions. They're theirs. I know they're theirs. I feel... I feel what my own feelings are. I feel neutral. This anger isn't mine, it's theirs.

She clutched Hubert's arms, closing her eyes as she continued to breathe deeply, slowing her heart rate.

'That's good, Paige.' Hubert said soothingly.

In her mind's eye, she returned to the riverbank, leaning against the large tree while birds chirped melodically above her. The blue water glistened brightly under the sunlight. She worked to build the one-way mirror on the other side of the river.

'Get your hands off me!' the old woman shrieked.

The one-way mirror shattered, and Paige crashed to the ground. She opened her eyes to find two security guards escorting the old lady away.

The stand was empty—all the baskets and nuts scattered on the ground. The stall owner, red with fury, continued shaking his fist at her. 'I'm pressing charges for the damage you've done!'

'The one-way mirror didn't work.' Paige shook with disappointment, close to tears.

'It did work,' Hubert said gently. 'You're not behaving like that old lady or the stallholder, are you?'

'No, but—'

'Give it time. As with any new skill, it requires practice and patience.'

Hubert was right. She would never achieve anything by running away. She needed to get back up and try again. She took a deep breath and returned to the riverbank in her mind. She recreated the one-way mirror. Through it, she saw the grey image of the stallholder bending over to recover his straw basket.

'Stupid old hag,' he muttered.

She kept her mind frozen by the riverbank, and the burning in her chest subsided. She wasn't sure whether the regression of anger was due to her mirror or if the man was beginning to calm down.

Feeling braver, she let go of Hubert and approached the nut stand. She crouched down and helped him clear the mess. 'Hey, I saw what happened. I'm sorry.'

'Thank you.' The stall owner looked up at her.

Paige was about to leave when he launched into an angry recount of the event. 'I cannot believe I have to put up with that mad woman. They should ban people like that. See now, who pays for damages? It's me, you see. Me!'

The burning waves in her chest returned. She took deep breaths and brightened the image of the riverbank. The one-way mirror trembled violently in her mind as she worked to steady it.

When the mess was cleared, the man returned to his stall. Paige staggered away and collapsed again. She leaned heavily on Hubert as he helped her up.

'You did well,' Hubert said with an encouraging smile.

'Then why do I feel so weak?'

'You're not used to separating yourself from others' emotions. This process takes time. It is crucial as an empath that you learn how to, otherwise, the emotions could consume and kill you.'

'How do I keep the mirror from breaking?'

'You must reinforce it. It must go all the way around the riverbank, not just one section.'

Paige balked at the suggestion. Creating one section of the mirror was already so draining she wasn't sure she had the strength for one that stretched all the way around. 'How?'

'By imagining the strongest glass and adjusting its thickness accordingly.'

She stared at Hubert as if he was speaking German, who gave instructions as if the task were as simple as breathing.

'The stronger the emotion, the thicker the glass needs to be.'

Paige closed her eyes and rubbed her temples to ease the pounding in her head. A part of her wanted to cry, stamp her feet, and demand that Hubert take her home. Another part of her berated herself for wanting to give up so easily. Her nerves were so frayed that she wasn't sure how much more she could take without going mad. Was it even possible to control her powers? Maybe she could escape to a rural area, far away from people.

'Do you really want to live like a hermit?' Hubert asked.

Paige sighed. *Running isn't the answer, it never is.* 'But all their emotions come at me so fast. How do I know which level of thickness to use?'

'Practice.'

'I can't put up a level-ten glass all day. It's too exhausting—I won't be able to function.'

'You may need to put up a lower-level glass that is easy for you to maintain and thicken as necessary. Remember, you will still feel their emotions. The glass helps you gain control over them. It allows you to observe without engaging.'

Paige closed her eyes and focused on her mirror again. She decided that level five was a good baseline. The tempered glass began to thicken and stayed still.

Her tight shoulders dropped and her chest lightened. She was standing in the middle of a crowded market, yet a sense of peace had returned to her. Out of the corner of her eye, a young boy tugging on his mother's pants, begging for a toy bird. When she yanked him away from the stand, he burst into tears. Paige noted the boy's disappointment and was delighted to remain in full command of her body.

Hubert clapped beside her. 'Very good, Paige.'

Moments later, loud explosions erupted further down in the market, cutting her victory short. People screamed as fruit, toys, pots, clothes, and tools flew in all directions. A few patrons ducked for cover, while the rest stampeded toward the exit.

Blurred images of terrified patrons scrambling for safety shattered Paige's internal mirror. Her chest tightened in an iron grip and she collapsed, unable to stop herself from being trampled on.

Hubert dragged her to her feet. Above her the assassin in a purple cloak was suspended in mid-air, hurling violet energy blasts.

Hubert fired from his staff, but the assassin dodged, continuing to rain crackling energy balls on them. Paige dove for cover under the stands. Her hands touched something metal—a staff from one of the vendors. She snatched it up as a blast obliterated her cover.

Exposed, Paige stood to find herself alone in a face-off with the assassin who fired immediately. It gave her no time to ponder Hubert's disappearance. She held the staff out, batting away the blasts. One hit her shoulder, sending her flying back into a stuffed toy stand.

A cloud of white light blinded her. Paige crawled to her feet, stunned to see a bewildered Callum in front of her.

'I must go,' came Hubert's telepathic voice. 'Protect each other.'

'Wait!' Paige and Callum called out in unison. 'Where are you going?'

'I must catch all the civilians to erase their memories of what they saw here. It's imperative they remain unaware of our world.'

Another blast from the assassin sent the duo tumbling into the next stand. Before Paige could ask why Hubert had brought Callum to the market, Callum's eyes and amulet glowed pink. He doubled over, crying out in pain.

Paige took his arm quickly, pulling him away from the oncoming blast.

'My chest... I can't breathe,' Callum gasped, clutching his chest. 'So much fear.'

Paige wanted to cry. She had no idea how to help Callum other than to yell at him to put up a one-way mirror in his mind. He looked at her as if her face was melting off.

'Your powers are horrible!' he cried.

Yeah, tell me about it.

As the assassin continued her barrage, Paige and Callum kept running. They dodged flying debris, wood, toys, and food in their headlong flight. Their cover never lasted more than a minute, which forced them to continue moving until they hit a wall at the end of the market. Callum was still wheezing in pain as Paige turned to face their attacker.

The masked assassin stared coldly at them, firebolts crackled in her hands. The bolts hurtled toward them and Paige was about to push Callum out of the way, when he grasped her hand.

'Jump!' he called out.

Paige pushed off the ground hard, amazed at how high they soared as the purple bolts obliterated the wall meters beneath them. When the assassin fired again, Callum levitated them out of the way. In midair, Paige used a nearby metal staff to bat some blasts back at their enemy.

As they began to descend, panic gripped her. They were tiring, while the assassin showed no signs of stopping.

'Callum, we can't keep dodging forever. Do you have any other powers we can use?' Paige asked.

Callum gave her a helpless shrug. 'All I can sense is your empathy and levitation powers.'

I have levitation powers! Wouldn't flying powers be more useful? Paige silently asked her mother's stone.

'That's it?'

'Sorry.'

Her heart sank. She would have to face the assassin in one-on-one combat again.

Once they landed, Paige pushed Callum aside. 'Go find Hubert and the others. I'll cover your escape.'

'No,' Callum said firmly. 'Hubert brought me here to help you. I'm not going anywhere.'

The assassin landed and moved toward them, eyes gleaming with anticipation.

Paige readied her weapon, preparing to retaliate. 'Go, I've got this.'

Callum pulled her back. 'Look, Paige, Stacey and the others are busy with Professor Chu in Ceresville right now. I wouldn't go to them even if I could. If I die fighting next to you, then so be it.'

The assassin smirked. 'Thank you,' she said then disappeared into a cloud of purple smoke.

Callum and Paige looked at each other, their faces mirroring dread. 'Hubert!' they shouted at the top of their lungs.

Twenty-Five

Stacey went to Kate's apartment to get ready for her date with John Chu. She was happy to see her best friend—until Kate insisted on squeezing her into a skin-tight, strapless aqua-blue dress and black stilettos. Her regret deepened when the fats of her arm were exposed as she got into her car. Gripping the steering wheel, she longed for the comfort of her lab coat.

Le Chateau was only six blocks away, but she had to circle it six times before finding a parking space. She had forgotten to account for parking time and silently cursed Kate for making her try on so many dresses. She eventually found a spot three streets away. Determined not to be late, she hurried up the hill to the restaurant, ignoring how the high heels pinched her feet.

Her mind drifted back to her conversation with Hubert earlier. She still couldn't fathom how he had extracted so much information about her in a single sitting. A wave of unease swept over her. She knew he was a telepath, but his full-blown psychoanalysis of her life was unsettling.

How dare he tell me how to live my life? How dare he accuse me of shutting people out? He knows nothing about me. I don't push people away; they just aren't compatible. Why should I waste my time? Connect? I connect fine with Kate and Callum. I don't need to be Madam Butterfly to survive. What a ridiculous notion.

But a niggle deep down, told her Hubert was right. She needed to connect with the others to survive all the magical attacks, but part of her resisted, because doing so would mean dismantling every strategy she had devised to protect herself. It kept the variables in her life constant; routine and predictability were safe. And safe was so much better than hurt and disappointment.

The apocalyptic crisis Hubert talked about was a ridiculous, especially without concrete evidence. The scientist in her refused to accept it. If she had time to examine everyone's blood samples, she was sure she could find a scientific explanation for what they'd seen.

By the time she reached the restaurant, her feet were numb, and she stumbled in when the maître d' opened the door. Had it not been for his quick reflexes, she would have fallen over.

'Mademoiselle will be at table thirty-eight,' the young maître d' said in a thick French accent after she gave him the reservation name.

Stacey gradually peeled herself off the maître d' and regained her balance before thanking him. She hobbled toward her table, surprised to find the young professor already there, reading a book. She wasn't used to her dates being on time.

John jumped to his feet when he saw her and pulled out her chair. 'It's so lovely to see you again, Stacey.' He gave her a light peck on the cheek.

'Thank you,' Stacey replied, a flush rushed to her cheeks.

Professor John Chu was the perfect gentleman, charming both in manner and attire. She was impressed by his grey suit and red tie. His black hair was neatly combed back, and his face was clean-shaven, highlighting his handsome features.

'I hope you didn't have too much trouble finding this place,' he said, smiling.

'The drive was easy, but parking was a bit of a challenge.'

'Yes, it can be. I hope you didn't have to walk too far.'

Stacey discreetly slid off her heels under the table. 'A fair way.'

'I'm sorry. I didn't even think about that when I suggested this place,' John said. 'Your feet must be killing you.'

Stacey chuckled. She had never had a man so concerned about her feet before. 'As long as you don't step on them, I'll be fine.'

John lifted the tablecloth and glanced under the table. 'Your feet are very red. But they're lovely.'

'My feet or the shoes?'

John laughed. 'Both, I guess.'

'Here I was thinking a gentleman like yourself would comply with social etiquette and compliment my eyes or my dress.' She smiled. 'But I guess I'll take what I can get.'

John's eyes brightened. 'I thought I'd start from the bottom and work my way up.'

The waiter came to take their drink orders. After he left, John's gaze returned to her. 'So, what do you do, Stacey?'

'I'm a scientist. A microbiologist at Advanced Microlabs.'

'What are you currently working on?'

'A bacterium called Cytoplon with Professor Leanne Hamilton.'

'Cytoplon. That sounds familiar,' John said. 'I think I remember reading an article about it in *New Scientist*. Wait… you're not Stacey Langcastor, are you?'

Stacey was taken aback. 'Yes, I am.'

'I thought your idea of harnessing Cytoplon's rapid mutative properties and coding repair sequences into it was brilliant. A challenging feat, but brilliant nevertheless.'

A surge of excitement rose within her. 'Thank you. I didn't know a prominent archaeology professor like yourself would be interested in reading about science.'

'Before studying archaeology, I did three years of medical science in my early twenties.'

'What made you switch to archaeology?'

'Adventure. Discovering truths. Exploring the unknown. I found that I had more of a passion for the outdoors.'

'Why do you still read science journals?'

'There's always a part of me that will be fascinated by the sciences,' John said, 'but I love exploring too much.'

Stacey stared into John's warm eyes that crinkled when he smiled. She was amazed at how at ease she felt in his presence. There was none of the awkward small talk or forced pleasantries she was used to. Everything with John seemed to flow naturally. Perhaps his recognition had broken the ice. No, it was more than that. For the first time, she was seen the way she wanted to be seen. She would have been happy to keep getting to know John, but reminded herself to stay focused.

'So, how did you come to work on the ancient city of Ceres?'

John's smile widened. 'Ah, Ceres is the best of my works. Do you remember that earthquake ten years ago?'

'Earthquake?' Stacey frowned, caught off guard. 'No, I don't remember there being one.'

'Exactly. See, I do, but no one else does.'

Stacey took a sharp breath. Was her good night about to take a strange turn? But he's a professor, she should at least hear him out. 'How is that possible?'

John leaned closer, his voice barely above a whisper. 'That's what I thought too. So I went digging into every media archive I could find from that year. But there was nothing. No reports, no media coverage on the earthquake.'

She was taken aback. How could he believe such a catastrophic event occurred without any record or evidence? Was she wasting her time with a delusional professor?

'Do you think... maybe—I mean, if you were the only one who experienced it—that it was a dream or something?'

John furrowed his brows and looked her dead in the eyes. 'No, definitely not.' His voice unwavering. 'I remember standing at the university entrance that day when buildings were collapsing all around me. People were coming out from every direction, screaming. There were rays of bright multi-coloured lights everywhere. It was like some sort of battle was happening.'

Stacey leaned back to put some distance between them and ease the intensity. If she ignored the lack of evidence and simply listened to the conviction in his voice, it was hard, not to at least in part, be swayed by his story.

'You don't forget something like that,' John said, his gaze steady and intense. 'But you don't believe me, do you?'

She shifted in her chair. 'I'm a scientist. I believe in what I can see and measure.'

'Okay then, let me show you after dinner.'

Stacey's curiosity was piqued. 'Show me what?'

'The stone carvings at the museum. The history recorded by the historians of ancient Ceres. They talk of a life stone that contains all of Earth's power within it. A stone so powerful it can defeat armies, manipulate minds, and bend time.'

Stacey jolted at the mention of the life stone. This was what she had been waiting to hear about all night. Her analytical mind tried to piece together the information, but there were too many missing facts for a logical conclusion. Her irritation grew like vines in her chest. She needed more.

'But all that shows is that an ancient city and its relics existed. What does that have to do with an earthquake that supposedly happening ten years ago?'

John lifted his glass. 'We know from the Ceres historians that the king of their time was so desperate for power that he released the life stone to fight his enemies,'

She leaned forward drumming her fingers on the table while she waited for him to finish sipping his wine.

'But then the King of Ceres became too powerful, too bloodthirsty,' John said. 'He went to a dark place and lost control. So, the Queen or her warriors took the stone and hid it. The people must have seen the danger coming, because the historians noted it all over their stone carvings.'

'But how does that relate to the earthquake you speak of?'

'What if...' John paused, looking around, then leaned in closer. 'What if the life stone wasn't sealed away? What if it survived and was passed down through the generations?'

Stacey's heart raced. 'You think the stone is still here?'

'Yes. I think it was released ten years ago.'

Stacey's eyes widened. 'How, by whom?'

'I believe, it was rediscovered by a force which caused the destruction and wiped everyone's memories,' John whispered, 'What I saw that day wasn't just an earthquake; it was something far more powerful.'

Her mind spun, trying to reconcile what John was saying with her scientific understanding. It was a struggle to reconcile the lack of hard evidence and the compelling mystery John was presenting. 'What proof do you have to support your theory?'

'The hard evidence is still in the part of Ceres that is underwater. I can feel it.'

The talk of 'feeling' without supportive evidence was irksome and foreign. How could such a prominent professor spend so much time and energy on a feeling? It seemed risky and unsafe. But she did her best to keep an open mind.

'Why would you be the only one to remember?'

John gave her a hopeless shrug. 'Destiny, I guess.'

Stacey exhaled forcefully, trying hard not to roll her eyes. He sounded as cryptic as Hubert. 'And what evidence do you have that these stones even exist?'

John's eyes lit up. 'Ahh, now that, I can prove to you... because I have one of them.'

TWENTY-SIX

Stacey stared at John, unsure if she had heard correctly. Did he just say he possessed one of the life stones?

John leaned forward to touch her arm. 'I can show it to you if you're interested.'

She nodded slightly, trying not to seem too eager, but her heart sang. John had proof that her parents' stones are real.

Stacey's fork froze mid-air and her jaw hung when wine sprayed from glasses on a passing waiter's tray. The sudden splash of red wine startled John out of his chair. Staff behind the bar shrieked and ducked for cover as bottles shattered and taps burst to life. Drinks at every table shot into the air, splashing down on unsuspecting patrons.

Stacey helped John to his feet, wiping wine from his face and suit. Her eyes darted around the room, searching for the only person with the power to cause such chaos. She spotted his tall, muscular frame at a table in the far corner. It took all her strength not to set Liam on fire with her gaze. Her fury rose as when she caught Ryan beside him, diving under the table.

She took a step towards them, ready to confront them, but John grabbed her arm. 'Let's get out of here. They're ushering us out.'

Stacey shot one last glare at Liam and her brother before hooking her arm through John's and letting him lead her toward the exit.

John walked slowly, recounting his expedition adventures, seemingly oblivious to the clomping footsteps behind them. Stacey waved her arm, signalling for the duo to leave, but they continued to follow.

Since the museum was only a block away, they arrived quickly. John unlocked the door and led her inside. The museum was creepy without the usual bright lights and crowds. Stacey flinched when the doors banged shut behind them. Now she was relieved to hear the footsteps still following.

'I see your friends are keen to join us,' John said, tilting his head toward the entrance.

Stacey gave a sheepish smile. 'Sorry, is that okay? They're a bit overprotective.'

A faint snort came from behind.

'No problem. I'll reset the alarm to reactivate in ten minutes after the door closes,' John said, moving to a set of controls behind the reception desk. 'Shall we ask them to join us?'

Liam and Ryan dove behind a display cabinet.

'No, they can hang back and make themselves invisible,' she called out loudly.

John led her deeper into the museum, past the exhibits of fossilised dinosaurs and scenic oils paintings, into a large dusty room at the back filled with stone slabs of various sizes lined up in rows. 'I want to show you what my team and I have been working on. This won't be on public display until next year.'

Stacey ran her fingers over the irregular markings on the knee-high slabs. The shapes seemed scattered in rows, with no clear pattern.

'What are these red markings?' she asked. 'Are they ancient writings?'

'These are stone carvings we retrieved from the underground desert, carved by Ceres historians three thousand years ago. They used earth powder to record their history,' John explained.

He walked to a desk in the far corner and retrieved a book and a small box. 'This book contains my ten years of work on ancient Ceres—translations, myths, prophecies, everything.'

The book looked more like a hand-sized dictionary than a journal. John opened it and guided Stacey to the first stone. 'I want to share this story with you.'

He began reading aloud. 'King Argos and Queen Enactra of Ceres were beloved rulers, always putting their people first. For years, they chose peace over war, even as surrounding cities attacked. But when King Argos could no longer afford the ransoms, the other kings sent their armies. Tens of thousands of Ceresnians died. In desperation, the king sought the ancient life stone, to possess its powers to retaliate. But all power comes with a price, and King Argos paid it by enacting the ancient curse.'

Stacey fixated on the ancient scribbles. The story sounded like a myth, yet a part of her was intrigued. If the life stone was the same one Hubert mentioned, no wonder the assassin was after it. Throughout history, who wouldn't want such power—to never fear anyone or anything again?

She entertained the thought for a moment. If she were the yellow stone bearer, she might not need to fear anyone either. But then there was the curse. Would using her powers bring a similar fate?

'What did enacting the curse cost him?' she asked.

John looked up from the journal. 'His humanity. The more the stone is used for death and destruction, the more humanity that person loses.'

'The map you have outside of Ceres covers a large part of the earth. Are you saying King Argos became so bloodthirsty he invaded all the kingdoms of his time?'

'Yes,' John said. He guided Stacey to the next row of stones. 'The death and destruction became so immense that King Argos couldn't bear the cost alone—his descendants would be affected too.'

John turned to the next section of his journal. 'Queen Enactra stole the stone from King Argos and broke it into pieces. She sent each piece away with her warriors, beyond the king's reach. In the final battle, both the king and queen died, and Ceres knew peace again.'

Stacey's breath caught as the pieces came together in her mind. Could her parents actually be these ancient warriors? She shook her head. It couldn't be. She made a mental note to research genetic traits and phenotypical expressions later.

A light shake on her shoulder brought her back to John's intense gaze. 'Are you okay? You look confused.'

'Uh, yes. What a terrible story,' she said, stepping back. 'But if Queen Enactra broke the life stone and gave the pieces to her warriors, wouldn't they be cursed too?'

John frowned and flipped through his diary. 'One historian wrote that the palace guards said the queen used the Handaan protection spell. Theoretically, the curse was limited to King Argos's bloodline. As long as the warriors used their powers for good, they were protected.'

John turned a page and raised a finger. 'Ah, but the warriors and their descendants are still bound by the queen's spell to continue the quest to restore peace. Only then will their powers fade.'

Stacey wasn't thrilled about this 'quest,' but at least the queen had tried to protect the warriors she sent on a death mission.

John waved his hand to recapture her attention. 'Enough of that. What I really want to show you is in this box. It's magnificent.' He held out a small black box and opened it.

Stacey held her breath. A bright yellow stone glowed inside. The yellow life stone.

Mesmerized, she reached out to touch it. The stone emitted a bright yellow flash that filled the room. She withdrew her hand, looking at John, hoping the light would fade. But it only grew brighter, as if sensing her presence.

John's eyes widened. 'I've had this stone for years, and it's never done that before. Who are you, Stacey?'

A dark figure swooped down from the ceiling, knocking them both to the ground. Liam and Ryan appeared instantly, but a blast at their feet sent them sprawling.

John pushed Stacey away from the attacker, and she shuddered, recognizing the assassin from her apartment. The intruder launched a blast that shattered John's worktable.

Then she flipped through the air, searching the room, blasting every direction until a small, shiny white object appeared. She darted toward it.

'No!' John shouted, charging at her.

With a flick of her wrist, she knocked him aside. John took the hit square in the chest, crashed to the ground, skidding across the room.

Stacey and the boys rushed to his side. John's chest was burnt, and he struggled to move.

'St-Stacey... need... to tell you...' he gasped.

Stacey knelt beside him, heart aching as she gazed down at his twitching body. She took his shoulder to steady him.

'We're calling for help. It's okay,' she said, more to herself than to him. 'Just breathe, John. Concentrate on breathing.'

With a trembling hand he dropped the box with the glowing yellow stone into her palm. 'Yours,' he said, barely audible. 'My journal... take it.' He closed his eyes, drawing a rasping breath.

Stacey's blood ran cold, her body trembling harder. 'John? John!' she cried, stroking his cheek. 'Please stay with me.' Tears blurred her vision.

His eyes fluttered open. He looked as if something was pulling him away. 'Trans... transcription stone. Need... get it back... you must.'

Stacey gripped his limp hand falling at her side. 'John, please. Stay with me.'

He gave her a sad smile and closed his eyes for the last time.

An electric ray sizzled overhead, but Stacey barely noticed as she collapsed onto John's chest, crying.

TWENTY-SEVEN

With Hubert and Paige by his side, Callum walked through a white cloud into a large room littered with stony debris. He spotted Stacey crying over an injured man on the floor, with Liam and Ryan looking down at them.

The purple-cloaked assassin hovered above the floor, turned quickly toward them and launched a pair of rays at them. Hubert adroitly deflected them with his staff. The blasts landed on the wall metres above Stacey's head, she looked up dazed, but otherwise seemed oblivious.

Paige charged at the assassin and tackled her to the wall. A small rectangular object the size of a business card dropped out of the intruder's hand and slid across the floor. The assassin pushed herself free and dove for the fallen object but Paige blocked her path.

Callum ran across the room to the trio, trying to make sense of what had happened, while Paige was pinned to the ground by the assassin.

Callum tugged on Liam's arm. 'Copy what I do. Think about sending out ice spears towards her.'

A two-metre-long ice spear materialised in Callum's palm. He sent it flying towards the assailant. Liam tried but could only form a puddle of water at his feet.

The assassin jumped high into the air and the spear flew between her legs, smashing into the wall. Hubert sent a blast of light at her which she dissipated with her own energy beam.

Paige charged at her from the side, throwing a side hook with her left arm. Then, balancing on her left leg, she sent a spinning sidekick with her right. The assassin blocked the hook with one palm and deflected Paige's kick with the other.

Paige regained her balance, then attacked with a forward punch. Their enemy bent over backwards, and with her hands on the ground, kicked Paige in the stomach. Paige flew back, landing hard on her side.

'More ice spears, now!' Callum shouted, looking at Liam.

Callum kept his palm and arm postured as if holding a spear, and threw them as rapidly as they formed in his hand. Liam finally managed to add golf-ball-sized ice balls to the ice storm.

The assassin stood her ground. She held up both arms and created a wall of electrical energy that melted every icy object as they hit.

Callum backed up when a purple blast advanced towards him. Hubert stepped in front of them, his shield neutralising the blast. Waves of violet energy quickly followed.

The waves progressed despite Hubert's blockade and his shield wavered. Callum bent down and grasped Stacey's hand. He dragged her away from the body while still holding on to Liam's arm. 'Stacey, we need you to get up and fight. The others need you.'

Stacey gazed at him, like she'd just woken up.

'C'mon Stace,' Ryan pulled his sister to her feet. 'They need your firepower.'

'Hold onto my arms,' Callum commanded as Stacey stood up beside him.

The assassin sent out another wall of energy towards Hubert. He held out his staff, ready to send out another blast as the team locked arms behind him and took a step forward. Callum held his arms in front of him and held Hubert's shoulder as he fired. Hubert's shield of white energy was interspersed with blue, yellow, and green rays. It engulfed the assassin, sending her crashing into the wall.

Callum watched in disbelief as their opponent landed in a crouch on the ground, unscathed.

In a flash, the assassin picked up the white rectangular object and disappeared.

***

Two days later, back at the manor, Callum stood outside Stacey's bedroom door on the east wing. He didn't understand why Paige suggested that he talk to her when she had already turned Hubert and Ryan away. He was mystified—talking to grief-stricken girls—or even girls in general—was not his forte.

'You'll be fine. Listen and ask her how she's feeling,' Paige had said. 'She'll talk to you, trust me. You have the best chance out of any of us.'

'How do you even know that?'

'Just a feeling.'

Callum had doubts about even getting past the door, let alone getting Stacey to talk to him. Stacey was a caring person, but in the weeks he had spent with them, he'd seen how angry she could get when provoked. He knew well enough to keep away and give her space at those times.

But despite his reluctance, a part of him was worried. Stacey had not left her room or eaten since coming back from the museum. He had to be sure she was okay. Being fired upon was a risk he'd have to take.

With a deep breath, he rapped on the door.

'I told you I don't want to talk,' came Stacey's voice.

'Uh, it's Callum. I wanted to see how you're doing.'

There was a long pause.

He was about to leave when the door opened and Stacey stood there in her yellow and white bunny pyjamas. Her messy blonde hair stuck out wildly in all directions. Without her glasses, she looked sixteen.

'You've seen me. Are you happy now?' she barked, with a small brown book clutched tightly in her hand.

'Uh, how are you thinking... I mean feeling?' *Feeling. Ask her how she's feeling. Damn it.*

'Was it Paige or Hubert who put you up to this?' she asked with narrowed eyes.

Callum gulped and stared at his shuffling feet. *Crap, she's way too smart for her own good.* 'Uh, me. I wanted to see if you were doing okay. So, are you okay?'

'I'm doing fine.'

You don't look so fine. He pressed his lips together to keep his thoughts from slipping out.

'You can go back downstairs and tell the others I'm fine,' she snapped, closing the door.

He stuck his foot in the door frame and pressed his hand against the door.

'What are you doing?'

Callum could just imagine himself disintegrating under the flames of her blazing eyes.

Think, damn it, think—say something. Dig deep. Say something nice. Something genuine. Quick, before she closes the door again. 'Um, I'm not going to take no for an answer. I want to talk. You didn't give up on me when we first met, so I'm not giving up on you.'

Her expression softened but she shook her head, trying to close the door. 'I just want to be by myself, Cal. I'm sorry.'

'Wait.' Callum pushed harder against the door to keep it open. 'I know... I know what it's like to shut people out when you're scared. It helps in the moment, but then you end up alone. And I don't think that's what you want. Please, Stacey, let me in.'

A conflicted look crossed her eyes. 'You really care about me?'

Phew.

'Yes, of course,' Callum said, knowing in his heart he meant it. 'You're like the sister I never had.'

She wiped away a tear, pulled the door open and went back to her bed.

Callum found a chair and carried it close to the bed. He sat with her in silence as she wept, then handed her a box of tissues.

He remembered what Paige had advised. *'If she cries or is expressing an emotion, don't say anything, remain quiet and allow her to work through it. Give her a hug if she wants one, otherwise don't do anything until she speaks first.'*

Callum wriggled in his chair, tugged at his fingers. Seeing a friend in pain and not being able to do anything was like having his teeth drilled into. He desperately wanted to fix it and make her pain stop. But he pressed his lips together, remembering Paige's instructions.

Paige's words seemed to go against everything he was itching to do, but being an empath, she was probably better at handling people than he was. So, he settled himself into silence once again.

'Thanks for being here with me. You're great,' Stacey said in a hoarse voice and pulled him in for a big hug as she continued to cry.

Geez, is this girl made of tears, when is she ever going to stop crying? Okay, to hell with the not speaking thing.

'Stacey, what happened?' Callum asked pulling away.

When she was finally able to let go, she sniffed and stared out the window. It took another long pause before she answered. 'Maybe you should read it for yourself.' Her voice cracked as she handed him the journal.

'Does this belong to the late professor?'

Stacey nodded, her eyes filling with tears again. Callum was tongue-tied, his mind garbled with incoherent thoughts. Nothing he could think of was worth saying out loud for fear of upsetting her.

He hadn't realised that he was flipping the pages of the journal back and forth, until Stacey

took his hands. 'Careful. Don't rip it. Just read.'

Callum carefully turned the pages back to the front of the book and began reading.

I start my journey on this day, the 26th day of June.

It was meant to be the day I made my mark at the young archaeologists' summit at Garlands University. But instead, it was the day I almost lost my life. The day when the earth trembled so violently it enveloped dozens of ten-storey buildings as if they were models. The ground quaked so violently I lost my balance and fell, along with hundreds of others. I hung on to the edge of the open earth and endured the screams of my colleagues behind me. My only thought at the time was to hang on.

When my arms tired and my fingers slipped, a strong pair of hands pulled me up.

I remember a flash of bright yellow light and I was thrown onto the grass. The earth was no longer shaking. I looked up at the man that towered over me. He was dressed in golden-breasted armour, honeycomb-leather pants, and boots. There was a sword hanging from his belt. He looked like a warrior painted in yellow. I tried to look at his face, but his blond hair glowed so brightly under the sun I had to squint.

The golden warrior yanked the name badge from my suit jacket. His deep, commanding voice read out my name and title as he looked down and spoke to me as if ordering a soldier. 'The ancient city of Ceres. I want you to find it and bring it to the surface.'

I must have looked like I thought he was crazy because he went on to say, 'You will understand everything once you start your expedition.'

'Why me?' I asked him.

'Chance—maybe fate,' he replied. 'I will make sure you will be one of the few who remember.'

'Remember what?'

'My yellow stone will be embedded in my armour and buried where I rescued you. Guard it with your life. My descendants will come and find you.'

All I could think of at the time was how wild it all sounded. I wanted to ask him more. I needed to understand. Nothing he said made any sense. He sounded like he was tasking me with something important, but I was confused—why would he entrust such a valuable keepsake to me, a stranger?

But he held up a hand, silencing me. 'We are in desperate times. I must go. Make ancient Ceres known, guard my stone. The future depends on it.'

At the time I did not know what he meant by 'one of few who will remember', not until I went back later that afternoon to Garlands and found that all the buildings were intact. The world carried on as if nothing had happened. I grabbed everyone I could find to ask them about the earthquake, but they all shrugged me off, telling me I was insane.

Something happened today with the magical, golden warrior. The world is asleep, but I am not. I shall find the truth or die trying.

Stacey blew her nose quietly into her tissue. 'That golden warrior was my dad. I'm sure of it. He and my mum died protecting us from that earthquake ten years ago.'

'How do you know?'

'The statues at the Ceres Museum showed a warrior who wore the outfit John described. Warriors Lang and Castor were my parents.'

Callum found the whole thing ludicrous but reminded himself it was no more surreal than seeing bony, grey creatures in his reflection. He did not remember anything from ten years ago, other than hiding in large industrial bins to keep warm. He couldn't help shake the odd feeling that it was all related to him somehow. It was frustrating to have the pieces, but not the full picture. He must call for Hubert, again, and get answers out of him, even if he had to hold him down by his beard.

'Did your parents die ten years ago in the battle, too?' Stacey asked.

Her words cut as images of his mother came flooding back.

'Uh, no.' Callum coughed. 'My father left when I was five and my mother died twelve years ago on her way to work.'

'That's odd. We all seem to have lost our parents ten years ago.'

'Yes, you're all stone bearers. I'm not. I seem to be... the amulet bearer.'

He took out the amulet from under his shirt. It emanated an amber glow. Brighter than he had ever seen it glow. 'Professor Chu gave you the yellow life stone, didn't he?'

Stacey nodded, pulling out her stone on a silver chain hidden under her nightwear. She looked away, her eyes glistening.

'I'm sorry this is so hard for you,' Callum said, the way his mother had spoken whenever he'd been upset.

'This is exactly why I don't like getting close. They all leave.'

Callum reached out and placed his thin hand on Stacey's. 'I'm still here, and I'm not going anywhere.'

'What do I do now, Cal?'

'What do you want to do?'

'I want this all to go away. I want my parents back. I want Ryan safe and as far away from all this as possible.' She sounded childlike.

'If you want to run, I'll come with you and make sure you're both safe,' Callum said.

Stacey covered her face with her hands and shook it. 'I am so tempted. But I can't. We're no safer out there than we are in here together.'

Callum squeezed Stacey's hand. 'Since my mother died, no one has shown me any kindness, until I met you and your brother. Tell me what you need and I'll do it.'

Another tear rolled down Stacey's cheek. 'Can you train me? I'm more comfortable with you. I know nothing about being a warrior or how to use my powers. That seems to be our best protection right now.'

'You don't have to do this. You can walk away. You don't owe anyone anything.'

'I know.' Stacey raised her chin and clenched fists by her sides. Her voice and gaze were sharp and unwavering, 'I want to honour the memory of my father and John. I can't let them die in vain. I wouldn't be able to live with myself.'

A tightness gripped Callum's chest. He did not want to lose the Langcastors but did not know what to say to change her mind. It was too dangerous, and he did not fully understand what they were up against.

'I have to try,' she said with pleading eyes.

Callum wanted to respect her decision but Stacey was not physically skilled like Paige and Liam. How could he tell her that he feared horrible grey monsters would rip her to pieces? He couldn't let that happen. He wouldn't.

'It's too dangerous. You could die.'

Stacey pulled him into a tight hug. 'I won't if we all stick together as a family. It's all we have right now.'

TWENTY-EIGHT

At lunch in the manor dining room, Stacey was famished. She wasn't sure if it was nerves over training or the fact she hadn't eaten in a couple of days. Across the table, Callum pushed his plate aside and quietly waited. Ordinarily, it would have been embarrassing to eat in front of another person, and even at work, she made sure she ate alone. But with Callum, she was completely at ease. He had seen her cry and hadn't disparaged her in any way. He seemed to accept her in whatever state she was in, without the need to tell her what to do. The only other person who had been able to do that was her father.

After lunch, Callum led her out to the courtyard behind the manor. The yard was lined with maple trees, carpeted with their orange-red leaves. In the middle of the yard stood a fountain with two cherubs back-to-back, tipping water from vases.

Stacey's heart ached with regret when she caught sight of Liam in a far corner of the yard. Her eyes lingered on his rippling muscles under a soccer jersey and shorts that seemed a size too small for him. A warm flush spread across her cheeks as the breeze ruffled his short, brown hair, revealing his chiselled facial features and strong jawline. Should she go over and make amends?

'Don't worry about him. Hubert and I were working with him this morning. He's practicing making ice spears,' Callum said. 'He won't bother you.'

There was a part of Stacey that hoped he would. It would at least give her an idea of what their fight was really about.

Callum took her arm and turned her to face him. 'I think it would be good to start with some fireballs.' His voice was a distant garble of sounds and random hand gestures.

Her mind drifted to Liam and their confusing arguments. It was difficult to have him just on the other side of the yard and not being able to ask him why he got so worked up. Her best guess was that he was anxious and needed someone to be with him all the time.

'Stacey, did you hear what I just said?' Callum asked, frowning.

'Yes. Fireballs. Let's do it.'

'Can you make one?'

'I don't know how.'

Callum tossed his hands up, grunting. 'Stacey, I've spent the last half hour explaining and demonstrating. Were you not listening at all?'

'Sorry,' she muttered.

'Stop looking at Liam and focus on what I'm telling you.'

Her cheeks burned as she searched for a reasonable excuse.

'So, what you do is hold your hands palm up. Close your eyes and focus, like this,' Callum said. Two fireballs immediately appeared in his palms.

Stacey cried out and staggered back.

'It's okay. The fire won't burn you if you're the one creating it. Give it a try.'

'What do I focus on?'

'The heat. Concentrate on drawing heat from your blood to the surface, then channel it through your palms.'

Callum held out both fists again, then opened them. His eyes glowed yellow, and flames the size of tennis balls appeared in his hands. Stacey did her best to mimic the demonstration, but nothing happened. She tried again as he instructed. Still nothing.

You can't create fire out of thin air. Even a chemistry student knows that. You need fuel, an ignitor, and oxygen to create fire. You can't just magically create it from blood flow.

But it happened the other day. How do you explain that, Miss 'I'm-so-smart'? Maybe, something broke off at an atomic level, releasing a high level of energy. Bah! And you call yourself a scientist? What kind of baseless hypothesis is that?

Stacey's mind spun with theories on generating energy at the subatomic level. She searched her memory for textbooks and papers she had read on the topic but drew a blank. Her inner critic went rampant.

You're terrible. You have the memory of a fish. How do you expect your colleagues to take you seriously when you can't even come up with a plausible explanation for what you've seen? They'll disprove your work on Cytoplons and laugh you right out of the international micro-biology conference. They'll see what you've known all along—you're not good enough.

An agonizing burn filled her chest. She wanted to shut her inner critic out, to tell her it was wrong. But Stacey's attempts were feeble against the storm of self-doubt.

The burn inside her chest intensified, spreading to her face and body. All she could see was orange. Within seconds, a heatwave blasted her face, knocking her back a few steps. She opened her eyes, aghast to find beams of fire shooting up toward the sky.

She let out a scream and shook her hands, trying to extinguish the fire. But the flames kept coming in a never-ending stream of energy. They set Callum's shoes alight, he yelped and hopped, trying to kick the flames off.

'Make it stop!' she shrieked, her body trembling.

'Stop moving your hands. Put them in the fountain!' Callum threw in his sneakers.

Stacey lunged at the fountain and plunged her hands into the water. She kept them there, too afraid to move.

'It's okay. The fire's out. You can take your hands out now,' Callum said.

Stacey refused to move her hands until he gently pulled them out of the water. She tried to dive them back in, but he blocked her.

'Look, we'll stand close to the fountain in case you need it, okay? Let's try again.'

Stacey glanced at Liam. The dull ache in her chest returned. All the commotion should have caught his attention, but he seemed oblivious, instead he focused on the ice blocks forming in his hands.

She turned back to Callum to make another attempt. He was trying so hard to train her; the least she could do was be a willing participant.

She copied his every movement down to his breathing, but her mind still floated to the amateur athlete. She had messed things up, and now he hated her. The ache weighed inside her like sandbags.

Another heatwave blasted against her. She opened her eyes to basketball-sized flames hovering above her hands.

'Don't shake your hands,' Callum called out. 'Keep them still.'

With a scream, Stacey sprang back, and flicked the flaming balls away from her. They struck the side of Callum's head and set his hair on fire before creeping down his back. He howled, dropped to the ground, and rolled.

'Keep still!' Liam appeared next to Callum. With a quick movement of his hand, the fountain water arched onto the flaming clothes.

Unable to move, Stacey stared at Liam, then at Callum. She had almost killed him. Her body shook. She should have listened, should have paid more attention.

Liam pulled her in for a hug while Callum scrambled to his feet. Having a body to lean on was a welcomed change.

'I'm so sorry, Cal.'

'You should get Paige to take a look at you,' Liam said. 'That looks serious, man.'

'I'm fine,' Callum said. He gingerly touched the burnt patch on his head. 'I need to lie down for a bit. Can you get Paige to train her with some self-defence exercises once she's settled down?'

Paige to train her? *No! How embarrassing.* But she nodded to Callum, reluctantly, then stared after him when he left.

Great, he was leaving, too. Anyone who gets close to her ended up leaving. It was only a matter of time before she drove him away for good.

Guilt weighed heavily in the pit of her stomach.

Liam put an arm around her shoulder. 'It would be good for you, Stace. Paige can help you with upper-body strength and aim, too,'

Stacey shrugged him off and stalked inside without looking back. She blinked repeatedly to push back tears. Her vision was blanketed in a yellow veil as her hands transformed into flames. She couldn't imagine anything more embarrassing than a training session with Miss 'Perfect'. How could Liam be so insensitive, comparing her to Paige as he did? She fumed in silence as she made her way to the kitchen and shoved her hands under running water. Her heart rate slowed as her hands returned to normal. Once she was sure it was safe, she dried them, then opened the cupboards for the biggest bag of chips and cookies she could find and began to eat.

TWENTY-NINE

When the kitchen door swung open, Stacey shoved the bag of snacks under the table. Her tight shoulders dropped when her brother walked through the door. If anyone else had caught her binge eating it would have been mortifying.

'Yo, Stace. Whatcha doin'?' Ryan asked.

But as he sat down next to her, his face turned to a look of concern. 'What happened? You're stress-eating again, aren't you?'

'No, I'm not.' Stacey swallowed her mouthful of cookies.

'C'mon, I've known you my whole life. I'm fourteen now, not that kid you need to look after anymore.'

She avoided eye contact as she wiped crumbs from her mouth. 'And you're still that kid under my protection.'

'Let's talk about it. Get it off your chest.'

Why did everyone assume she needed to talk about things to feel better? Any hope of alone processing time was being diminished by her brother's earnest stare. Her mind drew a blank for an escape plan, especially knowing how sensitive Ryan can be.

'It really bites when you shut me out, Stace. It's like you don't trust me.'

Stacey stifled a groan. 'That's not true. I do trust you,' she said, hoping that would suffice as reassurance.

'Then tell me why you're bawling and stuffing your face.'

She suppressed another groan. He clearly had no intention of leaving. She regretted not hiding in her room— at least there she could lock the door and pretend to be asleep.

'Have you found your green stone yet?' she asked, anything to shift his attention away from her.

Ryan made a sour face. 'No. I don't want it anymore.'

'It's our parents' legacy.'

Ryan reached under the table and took the bag of chips from her hands and began to eat.

'Hey, that's mine. I don't feel better unless I finish the whole packet.'

'You have a quota? That's silly. Do you really feel better after?'

Stacey gritted her teeth. Unpacking her emotional eating habits was the last thing she wanted to do. She was the older sibling—if anything, she should be the one giving support and making sure he ate right, not the other way around.

'Well, no. It makes me sick, but that's beside the point. Give me back my food.' She snatched back the bag. 'And these are terribly unhealthy. I'll make you a healthier snack. How about some carrot sticks?'

Ryan scowled. 'I'm not a rabbit. You do realise you're being a humongous hypocrite right now?'

Stacey suppressed a smile. Ryan always had a way of making a good point yet sounding immature at the same time. It was often hard to take him seriously. Nevertheless, she ignored his assertions. It was time to help him overcome his fears, as any good sister would.

'So why are you not looking for your green stone?' she asked.

Ryan raised an eyebrow. 'I thought you didn't want us to be stone bearers. What changed?'

'I don't, but I realise now it might be our best protection against whatever threat is out there.'

He wound his arms tightly around his chest 'I'm done. Someone else can go play hero.'

'I don't think we have a choice, Rye.'

Stacey was taken aback when Ryan pounded his fists on the table. 'I don't care. I'm not getting sucked into a hole again.'

Stacey didn't argue with him. She hadn't realised his teleporting experience had rattled him so much. Part of her didn't want him to be a stone bearer either. She wanted to keep him home. But even home wasn't safe anymore. There were too many unknowns, too many threats she didn't understand.

Though she didn't fully trust Hubert and the others either, being at the manor training with them was their best chance of survival.

She sighed. 'I'm scared, too. But I think it's better we learn to control our powers rather than let them control us. Would it help if you trained with Hubert?'

Ryan went to the cupboard, pulled out a bag of corn chips, and tore into it. 'You're right. This does feel good. No wonder you keep doing it.'

She wasn't sure if he was copying her out of spite or fear, but she decided to leave it. Her brother was right—he was older now and could make his own decisions. He needed to embrace his powers in his own time.

'Whatever you decide, Rye, I'll support you.'

***

Later that afternoon, Stacey decided to explore the manor to clear her head. Having been living in one section, it was bigger than she'd imagined. There were four wings—east, south, west, and north. Each one had a large hallway with rows of rooms on either side. The walls were lined with paintings of men and women which she assumed were Hubert's ancestors.

A loud punching came from a room in the middle of the north wing. 'Hi-ya!' came Paige's voice, followed by a thud.

Curious and a little apprehensive, Stacey approached the room stopping at the doorway. The concert-hall-sized room had mirrors for walls and weights of all sizes lined up against it. On one side, two boxing bags hung from the ceiling, while a stationary bike, rowing machine, and treadmill were stored on the other.

Paige powered through her exercises. Her braided hair swung methodically behind her as she dropped to the floor, then it shot back up when she pulled heavy weights towards her abdomen for ten counts. Her toned muscles rippled behind her pink crop top and leggings with every movement, much like a professional athlete.

Stacey couldn't believe anyone could look so pretty doing a gym workout. Paige was the perfect woman, good at everything. She hated how every strand of hair on her head was in place and how graceful she looked.

A glance down at her body caused her to reflexively suck in her own tummy and pull the 'science is the bomb' shirt that Ryan had gotten her for Christmas past her protruding waist.

'Oh. Hey, Stacey,' Paige said, waving at her. 'Sorry, I didn't see you there. Come in.'

Stacey had not meant to draw any attention to herself. She had not seen Paige since the museum fight. Ever since Paige came to stay at the manor, Hubert had instructed them to keep their contact to a minimum. Surely being an empath couldn't be that bad—at least not as bad as setting people on fire. Paige looked perfectly fine. Nevertheless, Stacey made a mental note to keep things short and leave. She was not much for girl bonding anyway.

'Aren't I meant to stay away until your powers are under control?'

'I'm getting better. It's okay, come in.' Paige motioned her into the room, wiped her face with a towel then drank from her bottle,

Stacey shuffled in. 'I didn't know the manor had a gym.'

'It didn't. Hubert let me set one up. How are you today?'

'Good.' Stacey stared at her feet with folded her arms, doing her best not to look at her reflection. But the mirrors still reflected every of bit of imperfection that fanned her insecurities.

'How are you coping with everything?' Paige asked and ushered her to sit on the floor with her.

'Not coping.'

'It's a lot to take in, isn't it?'

Stacey sat as far from Paige as she could without appearing rude. She continued to hug herself. Could Paige be any more perfect or nice?

Paige tilted her head to one side to look at her, as if she couldn't quite understand her. 'I get the feeling that exercise puts you off. When I went to live with my uncle I hated it, too. I used to find ways to sneak off or pretend to complete the reps. I mainly did it to stop him nagging. Then eventually, it got easier. I can show you a few simple moves if you like. We can go at your pace.'

Every part of Stacey told her to run. But the image of Callum on fire grounded her. She thought of Ryan and how fearful he'd looked. She needed to improve her strength and coordination if she had any hope of protecting him.

'How do I get better at aiming and throwing fireballs?'

Paige smiled. 'It would require a strong core, upper-body strength, balance, and good coordination. My uncle owns a gym and trains amateur athletes. I used to help him train them before I got into nursing. Can I show you? The exercises are simple.'

The 'simple exercises' consisted of push-ups, bicep curls, and chest presses with a bar. After ten minutes, Stacey wanted to hurl. Despite Paige's encouragement, her muscles burned and every fibre of her being screamed for her to stop.

'You're doing great, keep going. Count with me now. Just five more reps.'

Stacey didn't think she could last another round, let alone five. She wished Paige would stop talking—nothing made sense about form and technique. It was infuriating jargon to her.

The burn in her muscles intensified. She hated exercise, hated how incompetent it made her feel, hated how easy Paige made it look, and hated how her own arms wobbled and how could barely breathe.

She was about to tell her that she had had enough when Paige screamed. Her arms blazed with fire, and she dropped to the floor and rolled. It took a moment for Stacey to spring into action. She grabbed her towel, and smacked Paige's flaming arms to put out the fire.

'My water bottle,' Paige gasped.

Stacey emptied its contents onto her. To their relief, the fire sizzled out.

Paige looked at her, bewildered. She shuddered, clutched her arms and shrunk away. 'Wow, that's some serious anger you've got going on there.' She straightened, breathing heavily. 'Maybe we should talk about it.'

And there it was again.

Stacey examined the burns on Paige's arm. 'That's really red.'

Paige narrowed her glazed eyes at her. She drew in sharp breaths as beads of sweat rolled down the side of her face. Her whole body tensed as if she was restraining herself in some way. 'What you went through was awful.'

Paige headed down the hallway and beckoned her to follow. 'The washroom is down the end. I need to put this burn under running water. Come and help me.'

Stacey blinked. What could she possibly need help with?

Paige laughed as if sensing her thoughts. 'I need you to help me wrap the bandage around my arms, once I'm done.'

Stacey tugged at the edges of her shirt and trudged behind her. She should have made an excuse to leave early.

Paige's arm was getting redder by the minute and it was all her fault. With a hung head she examined the stitch patterns on her shirt that were now more interesting to look at. First Callum, now Paige. Her powers weren't protecting anyone, they were hurting people. The guilt inside her turned into gripping shame.

She was a fool to think she could train to become good enough to fight anybody. She had a sudden craving for chocolate cake and turned for the stairs.

'Stacey, are you leaving?' Paige sounded disappointed. 'I was hoping to have you keep me company for a bit longer.'

No, this was the time to leave. Stacey opened her mouth, but her mind froze with no plausible excuse to offer.

Paige's eyes widened as if sensing something again. She hung her head briefly then straightened to give her a light squeeze on the shoulder. 'You are way too hard on yourself. Accidents happen. It's not your fault.'

Stacey stared at the ceiling. Being in the presence of an empath and a telepath was mind boggling. If only she could wrap herself in the comfort of her oversized coat and go back to her lab.

She swallowed the despair. A part of her was relieved at having someone understand how she felt without having to explain. Another was perturbed by the vulnerability of such an exposure. Her thoughts and feelings were private, and she wanted to keep it that way.

Paige nodded and gave her a sympathetic smile. When they reached the bathroom, Paige eased her arms under the running water.

Stacey hovered by the doorway, not knowing what to do with herself.

'You know, I failed biology during my training,' Paige said.

Stacey was taken aback. This seemed to be coming out of nowhere. 'Really?'

'For you, maybe. I had to re-sit it three times in my first year of nursing. I almost quit.'

Paige must be using her empath powers again to make her feel better. 'Why are you telling me this?'

'To show you that we all have our strengths and weaknesses. The work you're doing on the Cytoplon bacteria is nothing short of amazing. I can barely understand the terminology, let alone research it.'

Stacey straightened startled by the compliment. How did Paige know about her research? Damn, she was so hard to hate.

'I heard about it at the hospital grand rounds, months ago. I didn't realise you were one of the ground-breaking scientists until recently.'

'Hospital grand rounds?'

'It's where the doctors present new medical science research to all medical staff. It's a monthly meeting for us.'

Stacey was floored. She'd had no idea her paper would be so widely received. It was difficult to comprehend that the medical community would place any value on her work when she had not completed her research other than publish progress findings, nor was she a prominent professor in microbiology.

'I was thinking we could slow down and work on your balance and core strength,' Paige said, handing her a set of bandages.

Stacey began wrapping bandages around Paige's wounds. 'What does that involve?'

'I'll show you if you don't set me on fire again.'

THIRTY

Callum hobbled into the manor lounge to look for Hubert. He tried not to scratch at the bandage wrapped around the new injuries on his leg, not sure how much more he could endure. He had a sinking feeling the old trainer was avoiding him. This time, he would not accept any more excuses.

'Hubert, we need to talk. You owe me answers!' he called into the empty room, determined no longer to take silence for an answer. 'If you don't appear, I'll keep shouting your name until you do. Hubert!'

A blanket of white light shimmered, and Hubert stepped through. 'Yes.'

'I want to know what's happening to me. Why do I wake up with wounds on my body?' Callum demanded.

Hubert slowly stroked his long white beard. 'Young people are so impatient. No small talk? No pleasantries?'

Callum's irritation rose as he fought the urge to shake the old trainer. He had tolerated this treatment all through his teenage years, and wasn't about to let it continue. 'I want answers.'

'I know.' Hubert continued stroking his beard as he paced the room.

'And?' Callum asked through gritted teeth.

'I am thinking.'

'About?'

'Your question.'

'Do you even know what's happening to me?'

Hubert's eyes glazed over, and his face became expressionless. Callum's impatience grew with every stroke of Hubert's beard.

'You're not even really here, are you?' Callum's vision flickered red. 'You're doing something else.'

'I'm here,' Hubert said blankly. 'What's happening is... disturbing. Interesting.'

Callum fought hard to keep his anger in check, not wanting to say or do anything that might jeopardize his chance of getting answers. He pushed back the impulse to lunge at the old man.

Suddenly, Hubert's eyes widened, his wrinkles stretched as he bared his teeth, then his face went pale, and he screamed. Panicked, Callum took Hubert's shoulders and shook him, but Hubert was trapped in his trance.

'Snap out of it. What's going on?'

'No, he is here. I cannot. I will not,' Hubert yelled. 'Let me out. Let me out!'

'Get a grip!' Callum shouted, his vision now a blood-red haze. His nails elongated into talons. 'Tell me what I'm becoming! Is this some freakish power or am I sick?'

'No!' Hubert yelled, his eyes blank. 'I cannot. I will not. Let me go. We will defeat you.'

Callum shook him harder. 'Wake up. It's me!'

A loud crash echoed from the door. Hubert shook his head, dazed. Callum turned to see Ryan in the doorway, a plate of cookies and a glass of milk spilled at his feet.

'What are you guys doing?' Ryan asked, his eyes wide. 'What's with all the noise?'

Callum dug his hands into his armpits, blinking rapidly to will his vision back to normal.

'Ah, Ryan, dear boy, just the person I wanted to see. Come in, come in.' Hubert beckoned him with open arms as if nothing had happened. He then ushered Ryan to the grandfather clock on the other side of the room, not looking at Callum.

A burn crept into Callum's chest. He couldn't believe Hubert was ignoring him again. 'Hey, what about helping with my dreams?'

'Yes, yes, come over here,' Hubert said. He stood in front of the clock and motioned Callum to join them. 'This will benefit you too.'

'What happened just then?' Callum asked. 'You looked like you were possessed.'

Hubert chuckled, patting him on the back. 'Nonsense. Let's focus on Ryan, shall we? We'll talk later.'

Callum's body trembled as an energy surge tightened his muscles. He was sick and tired of being brushed aside. He had done nothing to deserve it, and he was going to give Hubert a piece of his mind.

'Tonight, be patient. Meet me in the kitchen when the others are asleep,' Hubert said to him telepathically. *'Ryan needs his training now.'*

Callum slowed his breathing and focused on the grandfather clock in front of him. *Get a grip. Ryan's here, you don't want to scare him.*

Though far from happy with Hubert's response, Callum decided he could wait a few more hours and shoved the burn of anger back down. Ryan was his friend after all.

Hubert put an arm around the boy. 'Tell me, young man, what's holding you back?'

'Er, back from what?' Ryan asked, rubbing the back of his neck.

'From following your destiny.'

'Dude, you are making no sense,' Ryan said.

'I think he means your stone. Why haven't you found it yet?' Callum replied with a sigh.

'You're afraid,' Hubert said.

'No, I'm not,' Ryan pouted, folding his arms across his chest.

'You don't want to be a stone bearer.'

'Hey, stop reading my mind. That's an invasion of privacy,' Ryan scowled.

'Indeed.' Hubert chuckled, offering no apology.

The boy hung his head. 'So, what if I am? I want no part in your stupid 'save the world' mission. I'm just a kid. I'm no hero.'

Hubert hummed softly, with a dreamy expression and distant eyes. He must be communicating telepathically with Ryan.

'Is there a way Ryan can get the green stone?' Callum asked.

'Being a hero is not the absence of fear, quite the contrary. But I can sense you're not just afraid of the power of the green stone. You resent it and your mission.'

Callum walked over to Ryan, when tears filled the boy's eyes.

'Your mission and your powers are your birthright—' Hubert began.

'I don't want it!' Ryan exploded, flicking Callum's arm away. 'Why do I have to be part of saving the world? What has it ever done for me or my sister other than get my parents killed?'

Baffled by his outburst, Callum tried to take Ryan's shoulders to calm him. That only seemed to anger him more—Ryan shoved him back hard.

'I am not a child. I am not a hero. I am not the green stone bearer, and I don't want to be,' Ryan spat out with clenched fists. 'I don't want to talk about it.'

Not wanting to talk seemed to be a Langcastor trait. Callum tried to think of something comforting to say but settled for silence. The only sound in the room was Ryan's raspy breathing and the ticking of the grandfather clock.

Hubert stroked his beard rhythmically, leaving Callum to wonder if this was his go-to move whenever he tapped into his telepathic powers. 'Well, you certainly have a choice,' Hubert said slowly. 'I'm sure your sister would rather you stay away from danger.'

Ryan zoned his glare to the clock against the wall.

'No one could ever blame you for walking away,' Hubert continued. 'But think about the team you'd be leaving behind. Are you going to let your sister fend off the next threat on her own?'

Ryan's stony expression shifted to one of apprehension.

'Would you be okay if something happened to her or the others, knowing you had the power to prevent it?'

'I'm not good at protecting anything. I'm just a burden to my sister.' Ryan protested, rubbing his eyes.

'That's not true,' Callum said and draped a gentle arm around Ryan's shoulders. 'I've seen you think fast on your feet.'

Ryan continued to rub his eyes, his face a mix of frustration and uncertainty.

'Stacey loves you,' Callum added. 'I've seen you make her laugh. You're her comfort.'

'Yes, indeed,' Hubert said and pushed a button on the side of the clock. When the glass cover creaked open, he tapped the big hand. The clock face swung to the side to reveal a multitude of brass cogwheels.

'Why are you showing us this?' Ryan asked.

'Do you see how the cogwheels turn?' Hubert asked.

'Yeah, so?'

'What do you notice?'

'Uh, they're turning,' Ryan replied, giving Callum a look that clearly said, *this guy is nuts.*

'In what way?' Hubert pressed.

'Together?' Ryan ventured.

'Exactly. Very good, Ryan. What else?'

'They're all different sizes,' Ryan observed. 'What does this have to do with anything?'

Hubert's face lit up with a knowing smile. 'What happens if I were to remove a cogwheel?'

'It would stop working,' Ryan answered.

Hubert clapped his hands. 'Precisely! Now you understand.'

'Understand what?' Ryan and Callum asked in unison.

'For this clock to function, every cog must turn in unison with the others. If you remove even the smallest wheel, it all stops. Every piece, no matter how big or small, has an important part to play.'

Callum found himself nodding along. But Ryan seemed unconvinced.

'What are you saying? That I'm one of those cogwheels?' Ryan asked.

'Yes, everybody is,' Hubert replied. 'And on this team, you definitely are.'

'I think what he's trying to say is that the team needs you,' Callum said.

Hubert beamed. 'All you need to do is figure out where you want to be and how you want to play your part. So, what will it be, young man?'

Ryan closed his eyes, his shoulders slumped as if burdened by invisible weights.

'What if embracing the power of the green stone meant you could protect your sister?' Hubert suggested.

Ryan perked up, his eyes now more alert.

Callum caught on at last. 'If you can master the art of teleporting, you can pull her away from danger before it even escalates.'

Ryan's face lit up as it dawned on him too. 'I never thought about it that way.' He closed his eyes again and stretched out an open palm.

A light breeze brushed Callum's hair aside as a plate-sized vortex opened behind him.

'I want to find the green stone,' Ryan whispered.

With his eyes still closed, Ryan reached a hand over the vortex's opening. When his eyes opened, they glowed bright green. 'I don't know which part I'm going to play, but I want to protect my sister like she has protected me my whole life.'

Callum could not close his jaw as an emerald gem flew out of the vortex into Ryan's open palm. 'How did you know how to do that?'

The green glow faded from Ryan's eyes as he stared at the glowing stone in his hand.

'Cal, Hubert. Oh my God!' He bounced with excitement. 'Is this my green stone?'

Hubert nodded.

'How did it magically appear in my hand?'

'Things happen when you trust your instincts,' Hubert replied.

Ryan tilted his head, looking puzzled. 'I thought you said I had teleporting powers.'

'You didn't think teleporting was the only power you have, did you?' Hubert said with a sparkle in his eye.

THIRTY-ONE

That night, in his room on the south wing of the manor, Callum floated back into his dream world to a dank cave with a shadowy figure. As it moved closer, Callum recognized the masked face of the assassin.

'My Lord Apollyon,' she said, bowing her head. 'The warriors have each acquired their life stones, but are still too weak to control their powers. Their stones are ripe for the taking.'

'Excellent,' Apollyon's booming voice echoed through the cave. 'Send my order. Prepare to attack.'

The assassin bowed and raised her hand. It crackled with energy, as if relaying the command to someone unseen.

'And what of the amulet bearer?'

'He has begun transformation but is resisting completion,' the assassin replied.

Callum thrashed in his bed. *Transformation? Are they doing this to me?*

'He will need a stronger motivator,' Apollyon said. 'Send for the general to set the next phase in motion. We need the amulet bearer active in his more instinctual form.'

The assassin placed one arm across her chest and bowed her head again. 'It will be done. Success is assured, my lord.'

The scene shifted, then blurred until it stilled on the image of the manor's front entrance. The ground shook violently. The assassin appeared, hovering in mid-air, her cloak billowed around her. Her eyes glowed violet, and when she gestured with her hands, the earth cracked open. Creatures erupted from the ground, clawed their way out and charged forward.

To Callum's horror, Stacey and Ryan were nearby with their arms outstretched. Stacey threw a fireball, but it fizzled at her feet. She tried again, but the fireball only rolled a few centimetres. The siblings turned to run with the creatures closing in. Their tongues hung out and the drool that leaked from it sizzled as it hit the ground.

With a shriek, Ryan waved his arm in a desperate circular motion. Small green portals opened and snapped shut, though each one failed to stop the advancing creatures.

Callum willed himself forward but his legs remained fixed. He tried to call out to Ryan to focus, but his throat tightened, and no sound emerged. It was as if an invisible force held him back.

Stacey screamed as a creature lunged at her and dragged its claws down her back. She collapsed with Ryan by her side. Holding her palm up, she unleashed a fire blast that pushed two creatures aside. 'Run!' she yelled.

Instead, Ryan kicked the creature attacking Stacey and tried to pull her free. Blood poured from her gaping wound, and she fainted. Dozens of creatures opened their jaws and pounced, burying the siblings beneath them.

Ryan's high-pitched cries sent surges of pain through Callum. He tried to turn away but a force compelled him to watch his friends suffer.

Loud beeping yanked Callum from his nightmare. He jerked upright from the floor, and pain lanced through his abdomen. His nightshirt was soaked with blood. He lifted it to find a gaping wound the length of his hand. He stifled a scream and began to feel lightheaded. Callum took the shirt draped over a chair and pressed it hard against his wound.

His vision blurred as the phone alarm blared relentlessly, reminding him of his midnight meeting with Hubert. It took a half hour before Callum was able to sit up. He lifted his blood-soaked shirt and dread piled down like a mountain rocks. An oblique laceration that spanned his sides, tracked blood down to his pants. Things kept getting worse.

He managed to open the bedside table drawer with his foot to retrieve the first-aid kit. After quickly bandaging the wounds, he stumbled downstairs, hoping Hubert was still waiting.

He was relieved to find Hubert hovering above the lounge room floor in a lotus position, eyes closed. Callum leaned against the doorway, panting, while sharp pains jutted his sides.

'Bad dreams again?' Hubert asked without opening his eyes.

Callum folded his arms. 'Sorry to interrupt. Actually, no, I'm not sorry. I've waited for answers long enough. Am I turning into those creatures? Is what I'm seeing really going to happen?'

He shuddered when images of the flesh gouging creatures came to mind again.

Hubert opened his eyes, floated down, and headed to the kitchen. 'Let's get a drink, shall we?'

Callum gritted his teeth but followed, determined not to let Hubert stall. Whatever happened he wanted answers. The team was in desperate need of training.

'Yes, I agree. The team needs to be ready for the fight,' Hubert said. He walked to the fridge for a jug of water, then filled two glasses slowly as if buying time.

'It always feels like I'm there, but I can never move or speak. Then I wake up with new gashes, like this.' Callum fought back panic as he lifted his shirt to show the old warrior trainer.

'That looks nasty. You should see Paige about it in the morning,' Hubert said, handing him a glass of water. 'Drink. You need to replace all that blood you've lost.'

'Stop stalling and give me some real answers,' Callum demanded. 'I'm sick of your roundabout replies. You're not leaving my sight until I get them.'

'Very well.' Hubert leaned back against the kitchen counter and took a long sip from his glass. 'I cannot say for sure, as nothing is set in stone. It may be real, or it may not be.'

A burn rose in Callum's chest, his vision turned red. The energy surge trembled through him, straightening his back muscles. The wound by his side shrank and he welcomed the muscular bulge in his arms. The pain in his side subsided, but he barely noticed, as he zeroed in on Hubert, so close their noses almost touched. 'Give me a clear answer. Yes or no.'

'Yes,' Hubert replied without a flinch. 'But it's not so simple.'

'What do you mean?'

'The future changes with every decision you make. By believing what you see is inevitable, you may make it so.'

Callum's head ached; the spinning words made no sense. 'So, I can change what I saw?'

'Yes. You always have a choice, Callum. There will come a time when you can stop all this with a single decision.'

'How? What decision?'

'You will know when the time is right.'

Talons grew from Callum's fingers. 'What do I do?'

Hubert stroked his beard with a distant gaze. 'Our best defence against the future you see is to strengthen your connection with the others. Help them fully embrace their powers.'

The inferno from Callum's gut rose, getting answers from Hubert was harder than drawing blood from stone. He wanted to bang his head—or Hubert's—against the table to make sense of it.

Hubert's eyes glowed white as he placed a hand on Callum's chest. Callum's vision and pulse steadied by whatever the warrior trainer infused into him. The claws on his hands retracted. He exhaled with relief, leaning back against the kitchen counter.

'Why me?' Callum asked quietly as the fog cleared from his mind. 'Why must I be the one who trains them?'

'You possess the life amulet. And, as I've said, the stronger your connection to the stone bearers, the more likely you are all able to stop Apollyon's apocalypse.'

Callum opened his mouth to protest.

'Calm your mind, let go of doubts, and trust the knowledge that flows from your blood's connection to the life amulet,' Hubert continued.

'Blood connection?'

Hubert raised a hand. 'I've said too much already. Know that you are exactly where you're meant to be.'

The fire inside Callum ignited again. These were not the answers he sought. He'd spent the entire week chasing Hubert, only to be given more questions.

He tugged Hubert's beard. 'Who are you really, Hubert? And why aren't you telling me what you know?'

Hubert pried back his beard. 'You will know when the time is right. Be patient.'

'How can we trust you when we don't know who you really are?'

Hubert maintained his calm expression. 'Faith. I hope my actions speak louder than words. I am here to help. That is my promise to you.'

Callum slammed both fists on the kitchen bench. He was within a hands breadth from strangling the old man. 'I can't work on blind faith. I need more.'

'If I could tell you more, I would,' Hubert replied, his tone calm but firm. 'But right now, your efforts must be centred on training the stone bearers. That is the only way we will all survive.'

'But—'

Hubert held up his hand. 'That is enough for now. I need to focus my efforts on finding the transcription stone.'

With that, he disappeared in a flash of white light.

Callum let out a roar from deep in his chest and hurled his water glass at the wall. His body thickened as the beast inside rose to the surface. The pain by his side diminished, his fingers brushed against the closed wound, now replaced by a silver scar.

***

The following morning, Callum waited for Ryan in the lounge room, a set of plastic silver handcuffs in his hands. He had found them on his bedside table and couldn't imagine where they'd come from. A practical joke? Something Hubert left? It was difficult to imagine the girls leaving him something like that by his bedside. As he pondered, drifts of last night's conversation only re-amplified his frustrations. He still didn't have any answers.

Maybe training the stone bearers was the best way to keep his mind off his predicament. If being closer to them meant preventing himself from turning—or worse, contributing to a future massacre—then he'd resign himself to becoming the tutor they needed. Especially if it meant helping the Langcastors.

Lost in thought, he barely noticed when Ryan burst through the door, his green stone dangling around his neck on a silver chain.

Of all the stone bearers, Callum was most nervous about Ryan. The kid was reckless, unpredictable. If he got lost in a vortex again, how would he ever find him? Then the reflection of the ceiling lights off the handcuffs struck him with an idea.

'What are we doing today, Cal?' Ryan asked, bouncing on the balls of his feet.

Without a word, Callum locked one loop of the handcuffs around Ryan's wrist, then his own.

Ryan tugged at the plastic cuff. 'Hey! What did you do that for?'

'So I don't lose you again during training,' Callum replied.

'Ow, did you have to put it on so tight?'

'You'll get used to it.'

Ryan shot him a surly look. 'I didn't know you played with kinky toys. How long have you had these?'

Ignoring the comment, Callum took Ryan's hands, closed his eyes, and pictured reappearing next to the couch. A green hole opened, and after they moved through it, they emerged exactly where Callum had imagined.

Ryan's eyes bulged, and he doubled over. 'Whoa! What happened to an intro pep talk?'

'I thought we might start with short-distance teleporting,' Callum said.

Composed now, Ryan pressed his arms across his chest. 'You're kidding, right? That's so boring.'

'Baby steps. Now you try. Close your eyes and picture us moving next to the grandfather clock.'

'Why can't we go to the markets or the park?' Ryan asked with a grimace.

'Let's master this first, okay? I don't want you getting stuck with the lions again. Come on, close your eyes and show me you can do this.'

Ryan nodded. 'Fine. Easy-peasy. Grandfather clock it is.'

'Remember,' Callum said, 'you need a clear picture in your mind and think of nothing else.'

'Yeah, yeah, got it,' Ryan said, waving his free hand dismissively. 'It's only a couple of meters away. Jeez.'

Seconds later, Callum was yanked up towards the green portal. Beside him, Ryan cried out as they banged their heads on the ceiling and then crashed back down on the couch.

Callum frowned. 'You were saying?'

Ryan rubbed his head. 'That was just bad luck. I'll try again.'

Another green portal opened, and a swirling wind sucked them into the dark hole. Before Callum could brace himself, his face smashed into the glass cabinet encasing the grandfather clock. The glass shattered.

They fell to the floor, groaning. Callum nursed his bleeding lip and throbbing face, while Ryan stared at the blood on his hands from his forehead. Callum's heart missed a beat when Ryan's eyes rolled back in his head and passed out.

'Ryan!' Callum cried. He shook him, but there was no response. He shouted for help, but no one came. He called with his mind for Hubert, but there was no answer.

'Hey, stop yelling,' Ryan said. Awake now, he pushed himself up, looking dazed. 'I'm okay.'

Callum breathed a sigh of relief. 'Don't scare me like that.'

Ryan grinned. 'I got us to the clock. Let's go again.'

Callum wiped the blood from his chin and looked at the cuts on Ryan's forehead. He handed him a handkerchief. 'Keep pressure on that. Let's get cleaned up and find Paige. If she's still in the manor.'

'Oh, she is. She's always in her gym, training.' Ryan jumped up and struck a fake karate pose. Callum staggered to his feet with Ryan's help. 'Paige is like a super ninja.'

'How do you know?'

'I've seen her in the gym upstairs. She's with Stacey now. I can get us up there. I know where it is.'

'Wait, no—'

But Ryan had already closed his eyes and made a circular motion with his arms. A green portal opened from the ceiling, and they were pulled up into another dark void. Callum's body jerked twice to the right before being pulled up again, the vortex pitch-black around them.

He bit his tongue to keep from crying out as a sharp left turn sent pain shooting through the tender scar on his abdomen. It felt like being dragged through a pipeline. Frustration gnawed at him—Ryan's impulsiveness was dangerous. Callum would have to rethink how to train him; Ryan was a hazard to himself. The stairs would have been much safer. Callum cursed himself for not being more forceful.

Seconds later, bright lights hit his eyes as they burst up through the floor of Paige's gym. Across the room, Paige and Stacey balanced on one leg in what looked like a tree pose.

Stacey's eyes flew open, and she toppled over when she saw them.

Paige opened her eyes and gracefully lowered her leg. 'Why are you guys in the floor?'

Ryan screamed as he tried to pull himself free. Callum involuntarily did the same, realising he could see only half his body. The other half dangled elsewhere, unknown.

'My legs!' Ryan shrieked. 'I can't see my legs!'

Callum took a deep breath, trying not to mirror Ryan's hysteria. He closed his eyes and focused on finding his legs. They moved beneath him as he kicked one up, then the other.

Stacey rushed over and began pulling on Ryan's arms. 'Damnit, what happened? How did you get like this?'

'I've lost my legs,' Ryan cried, his voice breaking. 'Stacey, help! I'm sorry I messed up.'

Paige joined in, pulling Callum's arms. She glanced at Stacey.

'Okay, we'll do it together on the count of three.' She took a breath. 'Ready? One, two, three—pull!'

Paige was stronger than Callum expected. He could have sworn she'd pulled his arm out of its socket. He retracted it from her grip, dismayed to find himself still embedded in the floor.

'Sorry,' Paige said. 'Let me check your shoulder.'

To Callum's relief, Paige reported that his joints were intact. His feet brushed against a hard object. Up and down and to the side, there were many of them, all stacked atop each other. Goodness, they were stairs.

His feet were on stairs. That's why they were stuck—Ryan had been thinking about getting upstairs, and he thought about using the steps. They were connected, so their thought signals must've crossed.

Callum didn't want to imagine how his upper and lower body could be so far apart without tearing him in half.

Ryan continued his hysterics. 'It didn't work! Get me out! Get me out!'

Stacey looked close to tears. 'It's okay, Rye, I will. Give me a moment to figure this out.'

'I know what to do,' Callum said. 'Ryan listen.'

With eyes like saucers, Ryan sucked in a breath and nodded.

'Focus on opening the portal again. Picture us standing in this room. It has to be clear, and we both need to think it at the same time. Ready?'

Ryan nodded.

'Okay, on my count. After three. One, two, three.'

As soon as the words left his mouth, Callum lurched forward and landed on Paige, while Ryan fell on his sister.

The girls laughed and helped them up.

'I did say standing in the room,' Callum said, a flush rose to his cheeks. 'Sorry, Paige.'

He massaged his legs. He had never been so happy to see them again. Beside him, Ryan bounced around and hugged his sister.

'Thank you,' Stacey mouthed.

'That was awesome. Scary, but awesome. I teleported us upstairs!' Ryan exclaimed. 'Let's go again—to the park this time!'

'No, Ryan,' Stacey said sternly with her hands on her hips. 'I am confiscating your green stone.'

THIRTY-TWO

Callum spent lunch with Stacey discussing her brother's training. They both agreed that Ryan needed more visual input to guide his teleporting. Stacey ordered her brother to walk around the entire manor ten times, a task Ryan undertook with continuous complaints that echoed through the hallways.

Callum waited on the lounge room couch with Stacey's laptop, surfing sites of famous tourist destinations.

After his final round, Ryan collapsed next to him. 'That was so dull. I don't want to see another room or hallway. All those paintings looked like they were following me with their eyes. It's creepy.'

'Now you can look at all these places,' Callum said, handing him the laptop.

Ryan clicked on a few sites. 'Ugh, no. I hate geography.'

'If you're going to teleport, you need to know where you can go so you can find your way back,' Callum said, trying to mimic Stacey's stern tone.

With a shrug, Ryan clicked on a random picture. 'I don't see how learning about Fervens Desert is useful.'

'It might be.'

'Really? Fervens Desert is in the middle of the Alcoltaren Continent,' Ryan read aloud. 'Temperatures can reach over sixty degrees Celsius, and is inhospitable to life. The nearest village is twelve hundred kilometres away. Why would I need to know about a place I'm never going to?'

'Keep surfing and studying,' Callum ordered. 'You never know what's going to be useful.'

Ryan grumbled but pulled the laptop closer.

'And don't even think about teleporting while I'm training your sister. Without your green stone, your powers are unstable.'

'Fine. But I know where she keeps it,' Ryan muttered.

Callum left Ryan with his 'homework,' hoping he had the good sense to comply. He turned his thoughts to Stacey, and tucked the target boards he'd prepared the previous night under one arm. With the other, he lifted the heavy water bucket and stumbled into the training yard, where Stacey waited by the fountain.

She hurried to him. 'You really shouldn't have. I've already set up the equipment.'

Half a dozen red cylinders were lined up on a bench by the tree. 'That's a lot of fire extinguishers.'

'I found you a firefighter outfit, too.'

He wanted to protest, but seeing the you'd-better-wear-it-or-else look on Stacey's face, he slid into the orange fire suit.

'Where did you get this?'

'I borrowed it from Kate's friend. He had a spare.'

Callum waited patiently for Stacey to master the fireball and long-range fire formations before setting up six target stations around the courtyard. Each had a fire extinguisher beside it. Her training with Paige must be working as Stacey seemed more enthused.

Stacey planted her feet firmly apart to steady herself and stretched from side to side. Her eyes glowed yellow as she rubbed her hands together. 'I can do this,' she whispered to herself. 'Rotate and extend.'

A large fireball formed in her right palm. She took a step back and turned her upper body. 'Hi-ya!' She let out a battle cry and launched the flames forward.

The fireball whizzed past Callum, grazing his arm before it struck the corner of the nearest target board. The flames spread across the cardboard, and collapsed. Callum hurried over to put the flames out, before he rearranged the targets to bring them closer.

Stacey stood with a deflated expression. 'I thought I did that exactly as Paige said.'

'It's fine. Try again. That's why we're practicing, right?'

She nodded; her eyes glowing yellow again as she prepared for another attempt. This time, she showered the courtyard with fireballs and rays.

Callum stood well away, he didn't know whether to be amazed or give in to despair. The flames ignited trees, flowers, the bench, and even his jacket. Stacey's aim, was the worst he had ever seen. Nearly everything in the courtyard that could catch fire was alight—everything except the target boards.

'Sorry, Callum. Drop and roll. I'm so sorry,' she called out.

Callum didn't feel the burn but rolled. Once the fire was out, they hurried to extinguish the rest. When the last flame died out, Ryan appeared, grinning, a thick set of papers under his arm.

He was about to order Ryan back inside, but curiosity got the better of him. Part of him welcomed the distraction, uncertain of how to proceed with Stacey. 'What are those?'

'I thought Stace could use some extra motivation for her firepower,' Ryan said with a cheeky grin. He hung a picture at each target location.

Stacey's mouth hung open as she stared at the targets.

Callum burst out laughing. The pictures were all of Liam. 'Where did you get these?'

'From his dad's sports site,' Ryan replied.

'You want Stacey to use his picture as a target?'

'Yeah.'

Stacey reddened. 'That's madness!'

'Oh, come on, Stace. I know he annoys you. Now's your chance to get back at him. Let it all out.'

'Ryan, that's asinine. I'm not doing it,' she said with folded arms.

'Just do it,' Callum said, suppressing another laugh.

'Or I can get Liam to come out here himself,' Ryan threatened.

'Fine,' Stacey snapped and tossed another fireball. 'But it won't work.'

Callum's jaw dropped in awe as the fireball shot through the air in a perfect arc. It hit the picture square on the nose and the paper ignited.

'Yay!' Ryan pumped his fist in the air. 'You were saying?'

'All right then,' Stacey said, her eyes a bright yellow glow. 'I'll let it all out. Don't blame me if you catch fire.'

Ryan gripped Callum's shoulder and ducked behind him as the glow in Stacey's eyes spread across her face and down her body until she was a blinding yellow hue. Fire rays shot from her palms and eyes, striking each picture three times, along with every leaf and tree branch in the courtyard.

'Uh, Stacey, you can stop now. There's nothing left to hit,' Callum said, too afraid to face her.

'Wow, yeah, sis. Cool down. You got it.'

Stacey took a deep breath. The light from her body dimmed, and the fire in her palms dissipated. 'What now?' she asked.

When she spun round to face him, Callum sprang back and held out his palms.

Her eyes sparkled with amusement. 'Take it easy. I've stopped.'

Callum was relieved to see her blue eyes again. Now that she had obliterated all his target stands, he needed a new training strategy. At the other end of the courtyard Ryan darted between fires with an extinguisher. He was so light and agile, every time Callum blinked, he seemed to be in a different location. The boy's green stone swung wildly around his neck. It took a moment to realize he wasn't running, but teleporting.

'Ryan,' Stacey barked, 'did you go through my bag? I thought I confiscated your stone.'

'I don't think it's fair to treat me like a child,' Ryan shot back. 'You get to keep your stone; why can't I keep mine?'

'Rye, that was for your own safety. I thought I said no more teleporting.'

Ryan stuck out his tongue at her. 'You're such a hypocrite.'

Callum grabbed a thick branch from nearby and held it up. 'Ryan, do you have any more pictures of Liam?'

'Yup,' Ryan said, disappearing then reappearing with another stack.

'What are you planning, Cal?' Stacey asked with narrowed eyes.

Callum stuck Liam's picture on the end of the charred stick and walked toward her. 'I want to see if you can hit a moving target.'

Ryan beamed and yanked the stick from his hand. 'I can teleport in and out of the courtyard with the picture.'

Stacey looked between Callum, the picture, and Ryan. Her face darkened. 'You want me to try and hit the picture with my fire while Ryan teleports with it?'

Callum grinned. 'Precisely.'

'No,' Stacey shook her head. 'It's too dangerous. I might hit him.'

Ryan formed his hands in prayer. 'Oh, come on, Stacey. Puh-lease? I can't stand looking at another geographical map. Please, please, please.'

'Don't worry. I'll handcuff myself to him again,' Callum said. 'And he can wear the fire suit.'

'What about you?'

'I'll be fine,' Callum said, sounding more confident than he felt. 'I trust you.'

'I'm not sure about this.'

'It's fine.' Callum stepped out of the fire suit as Ryan reappeared through a vortex with the handcuffs. He waited for Ryan to get into the suit before cuffing them together again. 'Let's get started.'

Callum cringed every time he saw a fireball form, but to his relief, the balls consistently hit the picture. As Ryan teleported back and forth across the yard, Callum became dizzy.

Had it not been for his growing urge to vomit, he would have been proud of Stacey's improved aim. Ryan cleverly varied his distance and timing, but Stacey's skill had advanced too, as she anticipated his moves.

'Oh, come on, Rye. Don't play games like little Madeline Rowe now,' Stacey called from a distance.

The churning in Callum's stomach became unbearable. He doubled over as darkness surrounded him, all he could think about was collapsing onto his knees in the courtyard.

He heard a snap at his wrist as he flopped out of the portal. Stacey rushed to his side, and he vomited on her shoes.

'Where's Ryan?' she asked in a high-pitched voice, looking around frantically.

The handcuffs on Callum's wrist were broken, and Ryan was nowhere to be seen. Even though his stomach had settled, Callum's head continued to spin. He dreaded the possibility that twisted his insides twice over.

'Ryan?' they called in unison.

Stacey's eyes darted wildly as she moved across the yard, shouting his name. They called out repeatedly, but there was no answer.

Callum pulled the glowing green amulet from under his shirt, his gut crunched as the light slowly dimmed and faded.

Ryan was gone.

THIRTY-THREE

Paige began her usual morning routine— a quick jog, followed by a martial arts workout, weights, yoga balance then warm-down. She couldn't return to work and risk being out of control, or worse, losing her mother's pink stone. So, she settled on remaining at the manor to focus on her training, but missed the hustle of the wards and even the social gossip she usually disliked.

She kept her contact times with the others controlled and limited as Hubert had instructed, focusing on strengthening her mental and emotional filters. Though she longed for more connection, she made up for it with long conversations with her uncle on the phone. Everything was so monotonous at the manor that training Stacey had become the highlight of her stay, although many times she was relieved when it ended.

Paige stared at the punching bag; her workouts were beginning to bore her. She decided to practise her spinning kicks again—it wouldn't hurt to strengthen her legs more.

When she rotated and slammed her powerful leg into the hanging boxing bag, her legs lifted off the ground. Paige floated, lighter than air, over a meter off the ground. Was this a physical power she was coming into? Levitation powers. Yes!

Still hovering mid-air, she raised and rotated her other leg into the bag, then allowed gravity to lower her to the ground.

A few loud claps turned her towards Liam by the doorway.

'Bravo,' he said, continuing to clap. 'Now that looked awesome.'

She wiped her sweat away with a towel and beckoned him in. 'Hey, it's been a while. How've you been?'

'Yeah, not too bad,' he said in a less cheerful tone than she'd expected.

'What's wrong? Weren't you meant to be training with Hubert this morning?'

'He's off looking for the transcription stone. Says we can't unite our powers without it.'

'You mean the object the assassin fought me for at the museum?'

'I think so.'

Paige thought back to their fight at the Ceresville Museum. The assassin had seemed very persistent in gaining the small relic. Through all the chaos of that night, it had not occurred to her that it was important. Now Hubert had left the team to get it back. How could that rectangular piece be used to combine anything? It was irresponsible of their trainer to leave without a clear explanation.

'Did he train you at all?'

Liam hunched his shoulders. 'Hubert said you can help me with my powers.'

Paige raised an eyebrow. 'Sure. But how can I help?'

Liam shrugged. 'I don't know. He says I have an emotional block.'

Hubert kept saying their powers came from their emotions. She guessed he wanted her to use her empathic abilities to help Liam remove his block. Given all the commotion and pipe repairs from the previous week, she speculated that his emotional block had something to do with Stacey.

'Tell me what's going on.' She beckoned him to sit beside her against the mirrors.

'OK, so I was standing in front of the waves, and I could cause some movements in the water, but when he asked me to move the waves apart, I couldn't.'

'What happened when you tried?'

He flinched and shrank back against the mirrors next to her. 'I dunno. My heart got heavy. Then all I could produce was this.' He turned both his palms up to show a small ice sculpture of Stacey's face. He put the miniature sculpture down then opened his palm again. Another sculpture of Stacey's face appeared almost immediately. 'See? I can't do anything with my powers now but this.'

Paige bit her bottom lip to stifle a laugh. Liam was like a lovesick puppy. 'Have you tried talking to her again?'

Liam hung his head. 'No, I think she's avoiding me.'

Paige closed her eyes and mentally thinned out her one-way mirror. She aimed to get her filter down to a three. A pain immediately gripped her heart; there was something else hidden under the sadness.

In her mind's eye, she stood by the riverbank and watched Liam put his head in his hands. She pulled down her internal mirror. Alarm bells went off in her mind, but she ignored them. Liam was burying a deeper emotion and this was the only was to connect with it.

Then it hit her. A giant wave of emotion knotted her stomach to her throat. Beads of sweat rolled down her neck as she sort a way to escape.

Paige brightened the image of the flowing riverbank and resurrected the one-way mirror at level five and her mind and body began to still. She was in control of herself again.

'You're frightened.'

'Is that even a question?' Liam wrinkled his nose. 'I'm not.'

'You really like her, but you're afraid she'll hurt you again,' she said instinctively.

Liam's face became sullen. 'Humph. No!'

Paige thought back to conversations that had echoed up from downstairs in the past week, making associations with the feelings she sensed. She decided to test her suspicions.

'She hurt you when she left you to come back to the manor alone and again when she chose to go on that date with the professor. But after everything that has happened, you're even more terrified of losing her in the next attack.'

He smacked a small tear away. 'No. Stop that. What does this have to do with my powers?'

'Everything.'

Liam was more sensitive than she realised, less able to compartmentalise like the other men she had encountered in her life. The only way for Liam to gain control over his power was for him to get in flow with his feelings. All of which seemed to be related to Stacey.

The best way to help him was to bring it all to the surface to help him process it, no matter how much he resisted. 'You clearly have strong feelings for Stacey. What do you like about her?'

'Do I really have to answer?'

'If you want to learn to control your powers, yes.'

Liam looked up at the ceiling and rubbed his chin. 'She's caring, even though she doesn't let on that she is. I like that she's smart. I struggled to finish high school. What she can store in her brain is amazing.'

'Caring and intelligent, huh?'

'Yeah, but I feel really dumb next to her.'

Paige gave him a reassuring hug. 'No, you're just a different kind of smart.'

Liam laughed and leaned in, but his eyes quickly saddened again. 'I don't get her. She can be nice one minute then be annoyed with me the next and I have no idea why.'

Paige wondered if this was the first time Liam liked a girl who wasn't as forthcoming in reciprocating her feelings for him. 'Have you tried telling her how you feel?'

Liam ran his hand along the back of his neck. 'But she doesn't like me.'

'Have you asked her?'

'Well... no. We had such a big fight.'

'So? Couples fight and make up all the time; you learn more about each other that way. Maybe try apologising and keep yourself open to an honest conversation.'

'You think a talk would help?'

'Absolutely. Don't assume anything, you never know what's really happening unless you ask.'

Liam's face brightened and he jumped to his feet. The ice sculpture on the floor melted into a puddle, then merged into an icy bouquet of flowers in his hands.

Paige raised an eyebrow. 'How did you do that?'

'I dunno. That's what I feel like giving her, so I guess it appeared. You're right,' he said, smiling. 'I'll go find her. Maybe if I can sort things out with her, I can get my flow back.' Liam opened his opposite palm and another bouquet of ice flowers appeared. 'Thanks, Paige.'

THIRTY-FOUR

Callum and Stacey were still in the courtyard, taking turns shouting Ryan and Hubert's names, when Stacey's phone rang. She answered it, pressing the phone so tightly against her ear that her knuckles turned white. Her face paled as she listened. Her free hand flew to her open mouth.

Callum grabbed her shoulder, the sinking pit in his gut expanding. 'What is it? Who is that?'

Stacey wriggled out of his grip and turned away. 'No, it's fine, Kate. Whatever it takes. I'm on my way right now.' She power-walked towards the manor without another word.

Callum had to run to keep up. Finally, he took her arm and spun her around to face him. 'What's happening?'

Stacey slapped his arm away. 'I need to get to Dabury Police Station now.' She turned and ran toward the manor car park.

Callum sprinted after her. She was shaking so badly he had to snatch the keys from her. 'I'll drive.'

He eased the car onto the road, while Stacey rambled hysterically. All he could make out was, Ryan had been arrested in a girl's bedroom.

The drive did little to calm her. She bit her lips and picked at the handle of her bag. Callum was surprised it hadn't ripped apart. At the traffic lights, she dropped her bag into the footwell and started to pick at her cuticles. Callum reached out and clasped her hands.

'It'll be all right. You said your friend Kate is a really good lawyer, right?'

Stacey nodded; her eyes still wide with panic. 'The best. But why would he even be there, Cal? I don't understand.'

Her phone rang again. She fumbled to fish it out of her bag. 'Kate, how is he? Is he okay? Were they rough with him? Can you get him out?'

Callum stepped on the accelerator, glancing at Stacey out of the corner of his eye. 'Just breathe.'

'Ryan's fine,' Kate's voice came through the speaker. 'Maddison's parents filed a charge for breaking and entering, but we managed to convince them to drop it since it was a first-time offense. He was let off with a small fine.'

'Oh, thank goodness,' Stacey exhaled. 'Kate, thank you so much. I owe you. You're a godsend.'

Kate chuckled. 'Everything will be fine. I'll put him on for you.'

'Ryan!' Stacey bellowed. 'Don't you ever do that to me again, do you hear me?'

'I'm sorry,' Ryan replied. 'I don't know what happened. One minute I was in the vortex, planning to come out and surprise you. Then I heard you say, 'Stop playing games like Maddison Rowe,' and ended up in her bedroom.'

'Oh, goodness.' Stacey covered her face with her hands. 'This is all my fault. I'm so sorry, Rye.'

'What does the girl have to do with Ryan disappearing?'

'She was in Ryan's class when he was eight,' Stacey said. 'She used to tease and hide from him. I think she had a crush on him.'

'What happened after you teleported into her room?' Callum asked.

'She screamed, then I screamed, then her parents called the police,' Ryan continued. 'The police came, cuffed me, and took me to the station, so I called Kate. I was hoping to get out and get back to the manor without worrying you. I'm sorry, Stace.'

'It's okay. We're coming to get you.'

Callum pulled up in front of the police station. Stacey shot out through the passenger door before he had a chance to tell her he'd wait in the car. He was glad they'd found Ryan. The invisible weights lifted from his shoulders and he closed his eyes.

A loud rap on the window startled him. Two police officers in blue and white uniforms were peering in. He must be parked in a no-parking zone.

Callum rolled down his window and started to apologise.

'Get out of the car now,' one officer barked.

'Sorry, officer. I'll move the car right away.'

'I said, get out now.'

Taken aback by the officer's abruptness, he held up open palms. 'Sir, did I do something wrong?'

'Out now,' the other officer echoed.

Confused, Callum clambered out of the car. He straightened up to face the first officer, but to his horror, the man's eyes hollowed out and turned black, his face ashen and skeletal. The second officer's beady black eyes glared as he pulled out his baton.

Callum's heart hammered. He pushed the first officer aside and ran. He hadn't taken more than a few steps when a sharp blow to his side made him crumple. A strong hand grasped his neck, yanked him back up and slammed his body onto the car's bonnet.

Behind the officer, he glimpsed a man in a black suit and wide-brimmed hat standing on the street corner—the same man he'd seen in the alleyway the night he first met Ryan.

The man tipped his hat and vanished in a cloud of black smoke.

Callum thrashed, making futile attempts to free himself. The iron hands that pinned him, forced his wrists together, then clamped on a set of handcuffs. A surge of fury washed over him.

'Why are you doing this? What have I done wrong?'

'Quiet!' the tallest officer bellowed. 'You are under arrest for the assault of Mitchell Buchannan, Tate Roth, and Brian Summers.'

Thirty-Five

As the officers dragged Callum through the police station doors, a haze of black smoke swirled around him. He gagged. Through the smoke, he glimpsed Stacey and Ryan on the opposite side of the station, talking to a woman in a suit. He called out to them repeatedly, but neither of them acknowledged him or even glanced his way. It was as if he were invisible to them.

Callum thrashed, trying to break free from his captors, but their grip were ironclad. 'Where are you taking me?' Callum tried to dig his heels into the floor. 'You've got the wrong guy!'

'Do we?' came a voice from the shadows.

'Who said that?' Callum demanded, as he was hauled past the precinct doors.

A man in a black suit and top hat stepped through the smoke. 'I did say we'd be seeing each other again. I've been waiting.'

Callum glared at the figure in disbelief. 'Why did you bring me here?'

'I'm bringing you home,' the man said with a snigger. 'You need help.'

'Help?' He spat.

'Surrender to the source of infinite power and let the beast rise within.'

'What are you talking about?' Callum said through clenched teeth. He took a deep breath and willed the beast's pulsating energy at bay.

'You're still resisting, I see,' the man said. 'No matter. In time, our friends at the watch house will help you become your true self.'

'No!'

'Enjoy your stay, ta-ta.' The man gave a small wave and vanished into the dark smoke.

His captors flung him down the hallway. A burning pain exploded in his chest, and his vision turned red. He swung his body forcefully to the side and kicked wildly. Their grip loosened, and he broke into a run.

Loud sirens blared, and officers charged toward him, batons raised. Callum turned back, only to be confronted with another group closing in on him. He was trapped.

His heart pounded as the thinning bodies of the officers became skeletons floating in police uniforms. Every part of him shook the longer he stared at their bony faces and hollow eyes that flashed red then black.

In half a breath, the grey skeletons struck. Callum curled into a ball as searing pain shot through him from every direction. No matter where he turned, he was met with bone-shattering blows from the batons.

He screamed, hoping someone would come to his aid, but the storm was relentless. The pain was unbearable, and he closed his eyes, speaking to Death. 'Take me, damn you. Just make it stop.'

***

Callum opened his eyes and blinked. A hard, cold surface was pressed against his side, with a series of metal bars shadowing over him. He tried to get up, but the tearing pains forced him back down onto the concrete floor cell floor.

He gingerly lifted his shirt and touched the bruises running down his ribs and abdomen. He winced as sharp pains stabbed into his sides each time he inhaled. His ribs were probably broken.

Callum shuddered as he recalled the beating. There had been nowhere to run. He had never been so helpless. What had he done for them to beat him unconscious?

'Suck it up, loser,' a voice floated over from the other side of the cell. 'Congratulations, you passed, newbie. Sleep. You'll need your strength for the next round.'

Next round? He'd barely survived the last one. Is this what happens in these places? Why the hell was he even here? He hadn't committed a crime. What kind of screwed-up mistake was this?

His head hammered in sync with his heart as he searched for answers. If he'd had the strength, he would've hollered at the top of his lungs and banged on the bars until someone let him out.

Callum didn't know which was worse: lying awake and struggling to breathe or risking another nightmare. He placed his hand on his neck, searching for his amulet, but it was gone. The life amulet he had once refused had come to symbolize his connection to the Langcastors and the other stone bearers. It gave him power and purpose. Now, he was lost without it.

A dull ache crept into his chest as he remembered his room at the manor and the smiling faces of Ryan and Stacey, the only real friends he'd ever had. He found himself wishing he'd never met them. Having family again and then having it ripped away hurt more than his physical pains.

Loud snoring made it difficult to sleep. In his mind, he called for Hubert for the hundredth time. The thought of Hubert ignoring him filled his chest with a deep burn that spread to his head, intensifying the pounding. His breathing became shallower, and the image of the dark cell blurred with a red veil. The burn spread throughout his body as his muscles tensed. Callum was ready to explode. Images of officers, whose necks he wanted to wring and whose arms he wanted to break, flashed through his mind.

Then Hubert's face appeared. Callum lunged forward, wanting to hurt him the most for not helping as he'd promised. He landed painfully on the cold concrete floor.

Get a grip. He drew a painful breath and pushed his anger aside, but his breathing quickened, and his body convulsed. This time from fear of the intensity of his rage. Controlling himself was becoming harder—the feelings took longer to suppress.

What if Hubert wasn't answering because something happened to him on his quest for the transcription stone? Maybe he was killed by the assassin.

The thought made him break out in a cold sweat. He immediately banished it, remembering how Hubert had previously fended off the assassin. Callum needed to hold on to the belief that Hubert was still out there; he was his only chance of getting out. He closed his eyes and calmed himself with the thought that he would call Stacey tomorrow with his one phone call to find out what was going on.

***

The next morning, a loud clanging on the cell bars woke him.

'Peterson, off the floor and on your feet,' a bald, overweight prison guard barked. 'You have a visitor.'

Callum's heart leapt as he jumped up. It must be Hubert, or maybe Stacey, coming to get him out.

Sharp pains travelled through his sides, and he flopped forward onto the bars. The prison guard entered the cell, slapped a set of chains on his wrists, and jerked him through the doorway.

The guard led him down a hallway of cells where other inmates jeered at him. Some threw food scraps, while others hurled abuse. This seemed to be the usual prison greeting.

They made a left turn before the guard opened a grey metal door and shoved him inside.

'Knock when you're done. I'll be waiting outside,' he said before the door shut slammed shut.

The room was almost empty, except for a wooden desk in the middle and two bolted-down chairs on either side. One of the chairs was occupied by a woman dressed in a wine-colored suit and white blouse. Callum's heart sank. It was neither Stacey nor Hubert.

The woman's wavy hair bounced across her shoulders as she shook her head at the pile of papers in front of her. She shuffled them to the side and looked up. A warm smile spread across her full lips, and Callum found himself hypnotised by her blue-green eyes. His heart skipped a few beats—she was stunning.

She stood up and extended a hand. 'Hi, I'm Kate Henshaw. I hope you don't mind me assigning myself as your defence attorney.'

Callum hesitantly took her hand, not wanting to dirty it. 'How…? Stacey's friend?'

'Yes, I was with Stacey when they took you in at the precinct the other day.'

Callum's throat went dry. 'Er, thank you.'

Kate Henshaw looked like she'd stepped off a modelling catalogue. He'd never thought about what she looked like but assumed she was something like Stacey. It was difficult to look straight at her without blushing. He tried to control the flip-flops in his stomach, but they ignored his commands. What was most shocking, was why such a smart and beautiful woman would want to waste her time on him.

'Callum, are you okay?' Kate asked. 'You seem surprised. Were you expecting someone else?'

'Uh, n-no,' he stuttered.

Kate frowned as she eyed his bruises. 'Did you get hurt in here?'

'Just a few bruises. It's nothing,' Callum puffed out his chest before recoiling at the sharp pain in his ribs.

Kate sighed and held up a piece of paper. 'I'll file a report. Maybe we can get you out on bail.'

'Why am I here?' Callum asked when they were both seated.

'They didn't tell you?'

'No.'

While Kate made several notes in her diary' Callum admired her graceful movements and neat writing from across the table. She opened another file on her desk and pulled out a sheet of paper.

'Callum, you have been charged with the battery and assault of three teenage boys. Two of them are currently in intensive care on ventilators. Your hospital ID badge was found at the crime scene. The DA will be pushing for the maximum sentence.'

'What?' A cold shiver ran down his spine.

'Boys by the names of Mitchell Buchannan, Tate Roth and Brian Summers. One stated that you were the one that assaulted them before he went into a seizure and became unconscious. The other two are still too ill to speak.'

Kate's words sent his head spinning. He tried to think back to the last time he was in a fight. 'You mean Ryan's bullies? They were still able to walk away!'

'Then you were in a fight with them?'

'Yes, but it wouldn't have been enough to put them in hospital.'

'Tell me exactly what happened that night. Don't leave out any details,' Kate said, her pen poised. 'We need to make sure your story is consistent.'

Callum nodded. 'I'd just finished work at the hospital and was on my way to the station. I was walking past the alleyway when I heard a scream and loud banging. I walked over to the entrance and saw three bigger boys throwing Ryan against the industrial bins. The leader of the gang they called Butch.'

Kate glanced down at her notes. 'Mitchell Buchannan.'

'Yes. He was pinning Ryan to the bins and spitting on him, while the other two were on either side throwing punches at him. That's when I ran and pulled them off him. I punched one in the face and kicked the other two in the stomach, but then they all ran off together. They were still able to walk after the fight. None of them were seriously injured the last time I saw them.'

'Was there anyone else there?' Kate asked, frowning. 'Anyone else who might have been there in the alley with you boys?'

The demonic man in the black suit had appeared after Ryan opened a portal, but Callum couldn't mention him. Kate would think he was psychotic, she'd never understand.

'I don't remember anyone else.' Callum averted his gaze to the floor. 'Ryan and I left after that to go to the hospital.'

'What time was that? Which hospital?'

'Right before midnight. We went to Dabury Hospital.'

'I'll look into it. Do you have anyone who would be willing to give you a character reference? Anyone who has known you for more than a year?'

Callum sighed in despair. 'No. I don't connect easily with people. Just Ryan and Stacey.'

'It's going to be hard to use them, but I'll talk to the judge. I'll call Ryan to get more information.' She leaned across the table and eyed him intensely. 'Are you hiding something from me?'

'No,' he said taken aback, avoiding Kate's scrutinising stare.

'Callum, you have some really damning evidence against you. Only your DNA was found on those boys. If there is no one else, then you are the only suspect. You need to tell me everything if I'm to have a shot at defending you.'

THIRTY-SIX

Paige sat at the dining table eating Stacey's lamb roast. It was the best she'd ever tasted, though no one in the room seemed to notice. The Langcastor siblings played with their food while Liam fidgeted next to her in silence, all wearing the same glum expression. The despair coming from them were so strong she had to put her emotional barrier up to level eight to keep from bursting into tears.

It had been days since Callum's imprisonment and Stacey had spent every day on the phone to her friend Kate. The usual excited chatter from Ryan had died down and he spent most of his time in the lounge room with a laptop.

Paige had called for Hubert endlessly, but he was gone, too. No one wanted to talk about his disappearance or the transcription stone. The team had lost the only two people who could help them control their powers.

'Why aren't you speaking to me?' Liam sliced through the silence making her jump. His forlorn expression fixated on Stacey. 'It's been over two weeks since our fight. I'm sorry I went berserk, but I really—'

'Liam, I can't do this with you now. I can't think of anything else but getting Callum out of gaol. I need to call Kate again.' Stacey whipped out her phone furiously pressing the screen. 'I don't even know if I can afford the bail money.'

Liam reached for Stacey's hand. 'If it's a money thing, I can give you some.'

'No.' Stacey pulled back in her chair. 'I don't need your help. I just need time to think.'

'Why do you keep doing that?' Liam cried, his eyes glistening.

Stacey let out a sound that was between a groan and a growl. 'Oh God, you're yelling now. Please stop.'

'You always push me away when I try to get close to you.'

'What are you talking about?' Stacey let out an exasperated cry. 'I just need some space to figure out how I'm going to help Callum.'

'Is it because you like Callum more than me?' Liam furrowed his brow and folded his arms. 'I mean, the professor I can understand, but scrawny Callum, really? You can do better than that.'

Stacey's nostrils flared and her eyes emanated a yellow glow. 'Don't talk about him that way. Callum is a beautiful man that doesn't deserve any of this.'

'So that's it then. You choose him.'

A blazing fire spread across Paige's chest, cutting air to her lungs. The tingle in her head spread and her world became hazy. She jammed her eyes shut, forced herself to inhale deeply, and immediately thickened her mirror, trying to push it beyond a level ten.

A blurred grey image of Liam and Stacey came into view. Stacey stood up to leave but Liam followed, clutching at her arm. Waves of intense emotion wavered her protective mirror.

Stacey spun around, twisting herself free. A fire ray shot from her palm, setting Liam's blue soccer jersey alight.

Liam yelped, pulled a handful of water from the air and dowsed his upper arm. 'That was uncalled for.' He flicked his wrist. The tap by the kitchen sink spouted water onto Stacey, while her body emanated a yellow glow.

Ryan ducked under the table as the squabbling duo stepped away from the dinner table to find a free space in the room to continue their spat.

Paige's head reverberated from the ping-pong of insults and hurls of fire and water. The mirror in her mind shook wildly and began to crack. She clutched her aching head to keep it from bursting open. She had to stop the fight, and soon.

She sprang across and wedged herself in between them then immediately regretted it. Bites of flames licked her sides, followed by showers of icy water.

'Stop!' she commanded. 'You're both acting like children. We're a team. We need to work together and be prepared for the next attack.'

'Oh, now you sound like Hubert,' Ryan said from under the table.

'Great. Little Miss Perfect to the rescue,' Stacey muttered under her breath.

'Do you always have to be so snarky?' Liam said. 'Look at what you did to Paige.'

'What I did?' Stacey said, her eyes blazing.

Stacey and Liam's eyes glowered brighter. They side-stepped to avoid her, their hands poised, ready to blast at each other again.

Paige closed her eyes to steady the rocking in her mind. The duo ignored her and continued their loud bickering. Anger swelled inside her. She clutched her sides to keep the building pressure under control, but even with her emotional blockade beyond a level ten, it was all too much. She was helpless. A scream escaped, as an explosion of pink energy radiated from her body.

The pink blast sent the duo flying into separate walls.

Liam gasped and looked at her with wide eyes. 'What was that?'

Stacey whimpered, retreating further against the side wall like a frightened child.

'Sorry, I told you to stop,' Paige said. Had it really been her powers that had forced them to stop?

'Awesome, Paige. That was wicked. What power is that?' Ryan asked, peering out.

Paige stared at her hands dumfounded. 'I-I'm not sure.'

'What happened right before you blasted us?' Stacey asked, edging closer with baby steps.

Paige tilted her head and thought back. 'I guess I was sensing so much emotion from the two of you, I got overwhelmed and wanted it all to stop. I'm not sure what happened.'

Stacey rubbed her chin. 'Interesting.'

'What is?'

'You're an empath, right? You sense and take in other people's emotions.'

'Right.'

'Maybe being an empath also means you can project out emotions, too.'

Paige stared at Stacey in awe. She seemed to have a knack for assessing situations and bringing logical conclusions to them. Paige took her mind back to the rising energy inside before the explosive blast. It was definitely anger she'd been sensing from Stacey and Liam, combined with her own frustration. Could empaths really project out emotions at will?

Exhaustion flooded her, and this time it was her own. If she didn't retreat, fast, she'd collapse again. Taking her plate and cutlery to the sink, she was about to excuse herself when a thunderous blast from the lobby caused the plate to slip from her fingers.

Liam shot out through the doors. Ready to confront their intruder, no doubt. She sprinted after him, not wanting him to be alone if there was an attack.

They found the assassin cloaked in her usual lilac attire, hovering mid-air in the lobby. 'I want your teleporter.'

Stacey and Ryan ran out into the hallway and fled upstairs. The assassin flew to them and grabbed the boy. Stacey shrieked and pried her fingers from his throat. 'Let him go, witch!'

Paige charged at the assassin, barely noticing that her feet were off the ground. She threw a punch, which the intruder caught, then pushed her to the floor.

Liam ran up to Stacey as their attacker floated away, Ryan still in her grip. He opened his palms and threw ice spears at her. Stacey, following Liam's lead, sent blasts as if she were holding a machine gun. The lobby was filled with rays of fire and ice.

The assassin weaved through each attack unscathed. Liam held up both hands and sent a shower of ice daggers towards her. Stacey's eyes glowed bright yellow as her body emanated waves of fire. The assassin laughed and dissipated it all with her energy shield.

Paige sprang back up and charged at her full speed. Her feet lifted into the air as her legs continued to move. She planted a foot on the assassin's stomach, shattering her shield. Ryan dropped to the floor.

She fell back down as their assailant crashed against the opposite wall.

Paige rolled to her side, groaning as her muscles spasmed from the shooting pains in her back. She tried to sit up, but the pain kept her glued to the floor. The assassin, light on her feet, bent over and seized Ryan's throat again.

'Open a portal,' she commanded. Ryan's legs dangled high in the air, kicking wildly. His face reddened as he choked and clawed at his throat.

Stacey threw large fireballs at her. 'Let him go!'

'Stacey, no!' Liam called out. He tried to pull her back, but she pushed him aside and dove straight for the intruder in a flurry of fireballs.

The assassin dodged them and floated to the ground. She waited for Stacey to get closer before tripping her, then slammed one foot on her chest.

'Open a portal now,' the assassin growled, turning to Ryan, 'or I'll crush her.'

Ryan looked down at his sister and did as he was told. 'To where?'

'Just open it.' The assassin's eyes glowed bright purple and her lips moved in a foreign chant.

'No, Ryan don't!' Stacey screamed.

A portal opened beside them and strong winds swept across the room.

'Stacey!' Liam barrelled towards their attacker, attempting to run her down.

The assassin side-stepped and sent a blast with a flick of her wrist that knocked him into the portal. Stacey rolled and lunged forward; her arms outstretched. The glow in the assassin's eyes intensified. Paige froze in horror as the green portal opened wider and engulfed both Stacey and Liam in seconds. She pushed through the pain to stand. This was her last chance to get to Ryan.

The assassin's eyes gleamed as she moved closer. Paige held out her hand, ready to jump and grab her youngest teammate, but the assassin tossed Ryan into the portal as if he were a discarded toy.

'No!' Paige leapt for him, but he was gone. She ran and levitated through the air, landing a spin kick on the assassin's ribs. Paige repeated her attack, kicking her in the stomach.

The glow in the assassin's eyes disappeared and the portal snapped shut.

'Bring my friends back!' Paige demanded, her fists held high. 'Where have you sent them?'

The assassin retreated into a cloud of smoke and winked. 'Try not to follow me.'

Paige ran full speed into the haze, swiping her hands blindly through the smoke to pull her back. Her fingertips finally grabbed the back of her cloak. Seconds later, she fell face-first onto grass.

When the haze cleared, the assassin leaned leisurely in front of a large oak tree. Her eyes bright with a bemused smile. 'You can't stay away, can you?'

Paige climbed to her feet. 'Where are we?'

The assassin gave her another wink, then disappeared.

The ground quaked and split open. Paige clawed for something to hold onto but found nothing except air. The earth beneath her feet gave way and she fell, wrapped in a blanket of darkness.

THIRTY-SEVEN

Stacey held her breath as she was ejected from a dark tunnel and plunged into ice-cold water. Bright sunlight hit her eyes. She squinted against the glare, reminding herself to keep moving to generate body heat. She bobbed up and down, getting used to the shock of the ocean. The sky was a cloudless blue, and the water so clear she could see the coral. If it weren't for the terrifying uncertainty of not knowing where she was, she might have thought it was a perfect place for a swim.

Taking a deep breath, she scanned the horizon for a boat or an island to find refuge, but there was nothing. She kicked harder, pushing herself higher above the water's surface to get a better view, but all she could see in every direction was water.

Panic numbed her mind. 'Help! Help! Anyone, please!' She prayed for a miracle, forcing herself to continue kicking, not letting fear paralyse her. She had to get back to Ryan.

'Aarrrghhh!'

Something yanked her underwater. She kicked furiously and swung her arms, striking a large, moving body. Water filled her nose and mouth, choking her, as she fought her way back to the surface. She did a double take, the mop of brown hair on that white chiselled face was Liam.

Before she could say anything, Liam gasped, clasped her shoulders and shoved her under again. His tight grip maimed her in place despite her wild kicks. Her lungs burned for air. She tried to pry his hands loose, but he clung to her like a lifeline. Her vision blurred. She was seconds away from drowning.

With a final burst of strength, she tucked her legs up and kicked him hard in the chest Once free of him, she propellered herself back up to the surface, then sucked as much air as her lungs could hold.

'Where…? Help!' Liam thrashed frantically, a few meters away.

'Kick your legs,' Stacey called out, edging cautiously toward him.

He floundered helplessly. 'Can't… can't!'

How can he not swim? Wasn't he supposed to be the athlete? She couldn't risk getting closer in case he pulled her under again, but she couldn't leave him to drown either. The safest way was to approach him from behind.

'Liam, I'm coming. Stay still and lean back when I hold you, okay? Otherwise, we'll both go under.'

'Okay,' he sputtered as his head dipped below the water again.

Stacey swam toward him, just avoiding being smacked across the face as he surfaced. She maneuvered around his flailing arms and hooked one arm around his neck, then leaned back as hard as she could.

'Stop thrashing! I've got you. Just stop.'

She kicked her legs hard to keep them afloat. It took several firm instructions before Liam finally calmed down and let himself float.

'See? All you needed to do was lean back.'

'Don't let me go,' he whimpered.

'Never. We're in this together.'

'Does that mean we're back together?'

An unexpected laugh escaped her. At least he was feeling calmer. 'We'll talk about that when we get back home.'

'How do we get back home?' he asked, fear still evident in his voice.

'I'm thinking. Got any ideas, Mr. Blue Stone Bearer?'

'Hubert?'

'I don't think he's coming.' Stacey scowled. They wouldn't be in this mess if Hubert hadn't abandoned them. He'd promised they'd be safe together. Now they were anything but safe.

'Some warrior trainer he turned out to be,' Liam muttered.

Stacey knew she had to keep control, to stay calm and focused to find a way out. 'Kick your legs gently. So, why can't you swim?'

The tensing in her shoulders eased as they kicked in sync. She held his shirt and stretched out her other arm for balance. She shivered ignoring the condensation of her exhales. Despite everything, Liam's presence still filled her chest with warmth.

'My dad... I was five,' he said through chattering teeth. 'Took me to the lake. Told me to come back, but I didn't listen. I drowned, and he revived me.'

'You were too afraid to get back in the water after that?'

'Yeah. But I like water, though.'

'What do you like about it?'

'The splash. The softness, the movement.'

His teeth chattered louder, his lips turning blue. They had to get out of the water before they froze. Her powers were useless in water.

'You could get us to land,' she said.

Liam raised his arms. 'Can't.'

She thought about the properties of water and mentally flipped through her chemistry knowledge. 'But you have hydrokinetic powers.'

Liam slapped the water repeatedly. 'Useless.'

He began to sink. Panicking, she splashed water on his face and slapped him across the cheek.

Liam grunted and lifted his head. 'Hey!'

'Stay awake. I need you to focus.'

'Mean.'

'Listen, you can control water. Water molecules can take the form of gas, liquid, or solid—ice. Try to create some kind of solid raft for us.'

Liam grunted again but raised his arms. She watched with bated breath. Within seconds, small icy objects sprouted from his palms. She picked one up and tightened her lips in a grimace. They were tiny figurines of her.

'Why are you making these?' she demanded.

Liam turned away, coughing, his hands sinking underwater. 'Sorry.'

'Then stop it!'

'Trying. I can only make what's on my mind.'

Stacey shook her head, pushing away the implication. They had to focus on surviving. 'Pull yourself together. We'll die if you don't make that raft.'

'Fine.' Liam closed his eyes, pressing his palms together. He exhaled, then separated his hands, pushing forward as if shoving something away. To Stacey's amazement, icy beams shot from his palms, forming a small boat just a meter away.

'There. Happy now?'

'Yes. Swim to it.' Stacey kicked her legs strenuously and pulled Liam forward to the boat.

They clambered on board, and collapsed. Shivering violently, Liam rolled onto his back beside her. After one look at her, he sat up, raised his arm and waved it through the air in a circular motion. The boat rocked wildly, then sliced through the water.

'Which way?' he asked.

Stacey took hold of the side of the boat and pulled herself up. In every direction, there was nothing but sea.

She licked her finger and held it up. 'That way.' She pointed in the direction of the wind.

'Which way is that?'

'Where the wind takes us.'

'Really? That is the vaguest answer you have ever given.'

'I'm a scientist, not some seaman. I don't know which direction that is, but it's as good as any.'

'I can't see anything there. I hope you're making the right decision.'

Stacey swallowed. She hoped so, too.

Liam kept his arms stretched out with his palms down. The rocking of the boat eased, propelling them forward at a steadier pace. As they stared silently at the sea ahead, Stacey prayed that they would see a landmark soon.

Before long, grey clouds cloaked the skies, and thunder rumbled. While Liam continued to propel the ice boat forward with his arms. Dread twisted her gut.

'Wait,' Stacey said, clasping Liam's arm. 'Maybe we should change course.'

'To where?'

A loud whistle blasted her ears. Finally, a rescue boat. Eager to see where it was coming from, she turned trembling with excitement, but dull aches of disappointment quickly settled in. It was just the howling wind.

Minutes later, the sea became rougher, the rolling waves tilted their boat alarmingly.

Stacey gripped the sides of the vessel and fought to remain calm. She took Liam's hand—whatever was about to happen, she didn't want to endure it alone. Liam pulled her against him and held her tightly with one hand and gripped the boat's side with the other.

Rain poured down as the skies crackled and blackened. The choppy waves flung the boat wildly about threatening to capsize it.

When the grumble of the sea turned into a ferocious howl, Stacey buried her face in Liam's chest. Her stomach churned as the ice boat pitched and lurched. Not able to hold it in any longer, she vomited over the side of the boat.

When she looked up, her terror escalated to the next level—they were metres away from something much worse than the storm. 'Whirlpool! Get us away. Now!'

Liam's eyes widened and he immediately sprang into action. He threw himself to the front of the boat and made wild pushing motions with his arms. The boat swayed under his icy command but continued to edge closer to the maelstrom.

Stacey linked arms with him and attempted to use her fire rays to increase their momentum, but the flaming rays snuffed out in the water as quickly as she could form them.

The whirlpool sucked them further and further down into a swirling pit of cold darkness. The rapid circular motion jostled her stomach, and she spewed again until she was dry retching.

When the swirling finally ended, Stacey found herself hurled through a dark opening where she landed face down on hard stone ground. She moved her hands across the wet, irregular surface then held them up to her face. Nothing but pitch darkness. The sound of gushing water was in the distance. The sucking maelstrom must've taken them to an underwater cave. If they were surrounded by sea, where was the oxygen coming from? Why hadn't the cave collapsed under the water pressure by now? Something must be holding the space open.

Seconds later, Liam landed, spluttering nearby. A frighteningly loud bang followed.

Stacey crawled through the darkness. If there was some monster ahead, she didn't want to fight it alone. 'Liam, tell me where you are.'

'Over... here,' Liam called between coughs.

She found him three crawls away and leaned on him to stand.

'I can't see a damn thing,' he muttered. 'Where are we?'

'An underwater cave is my guess,' Stacey replied.

She held up her palms to conjure up fireballs, ignoring the scientific fact that fire couldn't be produced without an ignition stimulus. When nothing happened, she let out a frustrated cry.

'Are you trying to create fire?' Liam asked

Stacey sidestepped away as his waving hand smacked her in the side of the head. 'Ow. Careful. I am, but it's not coming. Maybe I'm too soaked.'

'Let's keep moving. We might find something up ahead.'

Stacey blew out a sharp breath. 'That's what I'm afraid of. Finding that 'something ahead'. I'm not moving until we can at least see where we're going.'

'Then hurry up,' Liam said. He tapped his sloshing foot with increased frequency while it took several more attempts for Stacey to form fireballs in her palms.

'Patience is a virtue.' Stacey sniffed, then pushed past him.

Liam shuffled after her.

A crack beneath her foot froze her in place. Smoke filled the air, as acidic gas tickled her nose and lungs. Something sharp sliced her arm a second before Liam slammed her to the ground.

'Get down. Those are arrows,' he yelled.

Arrows whizzed above them, while Stacey covered her face to avoid inhaling more smoke. But in seconds, she became lightheaded and drowsy. No longer in command of her body, Liam dragged her forward.

'Just a few more metres,' he said in a strained voice. 'I can see light up ahead.'

Seconds later, a blast of fresh, cold air woke her from her stupor. She gulped in the smoke-free air with relief.

'Hello, Stacey. Hello, Liam. I'm so glad to see you,' called a familiar old voice. 'Though I would have preferred it to be under better circumstances.'

Thirty-Eight

Despite her efforts to stay calm, Paige resisted the urge to curl into a ball and cry. She did not want to fight or be alone in some dank stony dungeon with walls of overgrown fungi.

'Not afraid now, are you?' came the assassin's sultry taunt.

The voice snapped Paige from her thoughts. 'Show yourself!'

'I will, if you can survive the gauntlet.'

'Gauntlet?' Paige yelled into the empty air. 'Why are you doing this?'

Her heart raced, and a surge of adrenaline propelled her toward the fire-lit cobble stoned walkway that appeared. She took a torch from the wall and swung it continuously, trying to anticipate the assassin's next attack.

One hallway led to another, each as monotonous as the last. Paige fidgeted, waiting for the ambush that never came.

She kept walking until a hard object brushed her leg and tripped her. Smoke filled the air, and the acidic fumes burned deep in her lungs. Her eyes watered from the gaseous burn, as she covered her mouth and nose with her sleeve.

In the smoky haze, she coughed incessantly, and became light-headed. A fast flow of air moved past her ear with a loud whizzing sound. She didn't dare open her eyes, fearing the burning smoke would melt her corneas off.

Another whizzing sound came towards her, followed by a razor-sharp object embedding itself in her arm. Paige ducked as the next one clipped the tip of her ear. She pressed herself to the ground to avoid the shower of arrows. Releasing her sleeve from her face caused fresh bouts of coughing from the smoke.

Paige broke off the arrow's tail from her left arm, leaving the head until she could remove it properly. Careful not to aggravate her wound, she reached out with both hands and inched forward as more arrows continued to whiz above her head. Her lungs burned for air, but she gritted her teeth and willed herself forward.

A sudden blast of cold air hit her. She hungrily breathed it in, allowing the oxygen rush to clear her hazy mind. She lay still, breathing heavily, not opening her eyes until she was sure the smoke had vanished.

Paige's respite lasted only minutes before flaming spears started raining around her, and she sprang back into action. She leaned to the side and ducked the next spear. Dozens more zoomed towards her as she dived behind a boulder meters away. Terror gripped her as the spears hit the boulder, shattering it into shards. She leapt forward and somersaulted out of the flying rocks' trajectory. The momentum caused her to crash onto another hard surface.

Surrounded by darkness again, she groped her way forward until she found the nearest wall. Not knowing how long before the next attack, she tended to her wounds. Tears of pain rolled down her cheeks as she dug her fingers into her deltoid to pull out the remaining arrowhead. Using the sharp end of the arrow, Paige tore what she could from her clothing in the darkness and tightly bound her wounds.

She closed her eyes and called for Hubert. When he didn't answer, she prayed for divine intervention to free her from this dungeon.

A low growl filled the room, and a set of red eyes appeared. Invisible fingers of terror wrapped themselves around her throat, suffocating her. She could just make out the silhouette of a towering, four-legged animal approaching.

Tamping down her fear, Paige rose to her feet—if she was going to be eaten alive, she would at least put up a decent fight. She kept her back to the wall, sliding along, delaying contact for as long as possible.

The black-coated animal sniffed and panted rapidly, its glowing eyes lighting up a section of the chamber as it moved toward her. It looked like a large, furry dog.

It stopped a meter in front of her, sat back on its hind legs, tilted its head, and barked. Paige stumbled, crying out in pain as it jolted her wounds. The dog leaned forward and sniffed her as she edged to the side. She frantically searched for an escape, but the dog was so large she couldn't see past it.

It licked her feet and barked again. A wave of excitement from the canine broke through her terror. It expanded inside her, and she was overwhelmed with a sense of joy.

Paige held her breath as the dog nuzzled its huge head affectionately into her chest. Its tongue slapped her face, washing her cheeks with saliva. She let out a long, slow breath, and with a shaking hand, patted the creature on its head.

The dog moved its head back and forth against her fingers, encouraging her to continue. She took another slow breath and decided to trust her powers. 'My name is Paige. What's yours?' When there was no response, she said, 'How about I call you Blackie?'

The dog barked, jumping to reveal a brass ornament around his neck. Paige picked it up and squinted. The round metal tag had cramped, engraved rows of wavy lines and odd-shaped stars on it.

'That's some strange writing. How long have you been trapped here?'

Blackie barked and licked her face again.

'Do you know a way out? We can escape together.'

The dog leapt on all fours, nipped the edge of her shirt, and pulled her to the opposite end of the chamber. He nudged her closer to the wall, and his eyes glowed brighter until the darkness receded.

Paige made her way to the opposite wall, running her fingers along its rectangular frame. Her heart surged with hope. There was a distinct door carved into the wall, with carvings covering its surface. The symbols seemed to match those on Blackie's collar.

He barked, then licked, slobbering on her hand.

'Down, boy,' Paige said, looking for a hidden latch that might open the door.

Blackie barked again louder and jumped, almost crushing her.

'What is it, boy?'

He bobbed and lifted his head to reveal his collar, then turned and pressed his front paws onto the wall. Paige held his collar and then looked back at the wall.

Maybe the collar contained the sequence code that opened the door. With trembling fingers, she pressed the shapes on the wall in the order they appeared on his collar.

The door rumbled in response, and two opposite stone walls slid open to reveal another space. Meters beyond, her eyes caught bright rays of sunlight and grass beyond the furthest open wall.

Blackie bounced past her to the opening.

Paige stepped cautiously into the next chamber, closer to the outside wall. A loud swooping sound alerted her to a large net flying toward the dog. She dived toward Blackie, pushing him out of the way. He rolled out of the chamber opening onto the grass outside, while the net swooped across the room and scooped her up, dragging her toward the ceiling.

Blackie barked incessantly, trying to claw his way back in. But it was as if an invisible force field blocked his entry. The outer wall dropped with a resounding thud, taking her sinking heart along with it. The net released her, and she sprawled across the ground, alone again.

She lay still, letting tears fall freely, wondering how, in just a few short weeks, life had become so dark and chaotic. She hated that she wasn't skilled enough to fight her way out and that she wasn't able to prevent her friends from being sent away. She hated how her powers had changed her life. She wasn't the warrior her mother must've been.

'Poor baby needs a rest,' came the assassin's echoing voice. 'Right when the fun was just getting started.'

Paige sprang up. 'Show yourself now! I've had enough of your games. Come face me and fight, coward.'

A soft chuckle filled the air. 'That's the spirit.'

A rumbling sound drew her attention toward a piece of wall that retracted high into the ceiling to reveal yet another hallway.

Paige's rapid breathing clouded her head. Her body trembled with anger as she stumbled into the pitch-black hallway. She banged against its walls, called out profanities at her enemy to provoke her into appearing, but the only response was silence.

Exhausted, she fell backward into a wall. It gave way and she dropped to the ground. As she rolled to her side, groaning, the opening in the wall began to close. She lunged toward it, but it snapped shut and she slammed against it.

Paige numbly turned to see where she was. Another chamber, this one cold and dimly lit. On the far side was a single bed with neatly folded sheets and a bedside table with a dark green book on it. The walls displayed every handheld weapon she had ever heard of, and some she hadn't—swords, daggers of all shapes and sizes, guns, and metal weaponry. The owner of the room was obviously a keen collector—it could have easily been a display in a weapons' museum.

Who would live like this?

Possessed by a bout of curiosity Paige rummaged the closet. Inside were multiple purple leather tops, pants, and lilac cloaks. At the bottom were more weapons piled in a wooden box.

She held up the purple cloak. It looked exactly like the one the assassin wore. Paige drew a sharp breath as her muscles tensed, her senses sharp again. This must be the assassin's room. She gripped the nearest dagger and sword, then spun on her heels. With her weapons poised, she edged closer to the other side of the room, ready for a confrontation.

When everything remained quiet, Paige made her way to the bed and sat to survey the room again. Was there anything else in the assassin's life other than darkness and destruction?

Her eyes wandered to a green book on the bedside table, but when she tried to lift it, it remained fixed in place. The book had a leather covering with the same shapes etched on the wall. Paige could only guess it was some kind of ancient writing.

She opened the book. It had dusty, thick pages and more ancient symbols written vertically in a rusty colour that looked like dried blood. Paige flicked through, surprised when her fingers brushed a firm object in the middle of the book.

She pulled it out. It was white and rectangular, no bigger than a business card. She examined the golden carvings and could hardly believe her eyes.

It was the transcription stone.

THIRTY-NINE

In the underwater cave, on the opposite side of a rocky cliff, Stacey looked up aghast to find the voice belonged to Hubert, suspended in chains against a bolder. Fire pits nestled in metal baskets that lined the rocky wall behind him.

'Can you get us out of here?' Stacey called while Liam waved.

'I'm afraid these chains are quite limiting,' Hubert replied.

'How did you get stuck there?' Liam asked.

'I followed a trail to this underground cave where I thought the transcription stone was hidden. I was tricked.'

Stacey raised an eyebrow 'The old, wise, all-knowing warrior trainer, tricked?'

Hubert chuckled. 'I am still human. Perhaps in my haste to get back to you all I was careless. A good lesson for you youngsters, too.'

As Stacey made her way to the cliff's edge, a flimsy bridge of broken planks and worn ropes made her stomach lurch. The bubbling lava below it, leapt up and licked the bottom of the bridge, as if giving her a welcome wave.

She retracted into Liam's muscular frame.

'We need to free him,' Liam said, and nudged her forward.

Her mind took her back to the shuddering memory of her six-year-old self, falling off a rope bridge at summer camp. She winced, re-living the cracking pains in her shins she had landed on. 'I can't.'

Liam side-stepped to face her. 'What do mean, you can't? We must cross that bridge to get to Hubert.'

The tentacles of panic gripped her chest. 'That bridge is unstable. It won't hold. We'll fall.'

'It's fine.' Liam clasped her hand and slowly pulled her forward. 'We'll cross together.'

Stacey retracted her hand away and stepped back. 'No. By my calculations, you and I are over a hundred and eighty kilos combined. The ropes are frayed and held by half-hitch knots to those metal anchors. It'll snap as soon as we step on it.'

As if in response, the spurting lava engulfed a wooden plank from the middle of the bridge.

Liam peered over the edge. 'How did you know that?'

Stacey tugged at her ponytail and moved further back. 'Girl scout. Never mind. It's not safe.'

Hubert's eyes glowed white. 'Warriors, you talk amongst yourselves and decide whether you want to cross. There is no threat for the moment. I'll tell you if there is.'

'Maybe if we run quickly and jump over the gap we can get to the other side,' Liam said.

Stacey let out a frustrated cry. 'Have you not been hearing anything I just said? The bridge will collapse. It's unsound.'

To Stacey's dismay, Liam burst out laughing. 'Oh, c'mon. It's only a couple of metres. Hubert needs rescuing. Time to be a hero.'

Hero. Stacey hated that word. It was like being forced to swallow three bitter melons at once. She hated everything it embodied. Courage, fearlessness, strength, sacrifice—everything she was not and everything she balked at.

Why was she now expected to magically use her powers to save the world as if it was her birth legacy? There was no choice, no negotiations, and no compromise. Just expectations. It made her want to beat her chest and set the world on fire. If there was an antidote to remove her powers, she would gladly take it and return to her lab and the Cytoplon colonies.

'Hey,' Liam said, giving her a light shake. 'If we can free Hubert, he can take us home and this will all be over.'

Cross the bridge, jump the gap? What about the rising lava that will burn us to a crisp? What about the trap that might be waiting for us on the other side?

She resented him for making it all sound so simple. A wave of lava licked up and swallowed another wooden board as if saluting its agreement with her.

Stacey pulled him back. 'Liam. If there is a force that can maim someone as powerful as Hubert, what makes you think we can defeat it? We can barely control our powers.'

Liam gripped her by the shoulders, his jawline square and his gaze steady. When he spoke, his voice was firm, clearer than she had ever heard it. 'All I know, is across that bridge is our best chance of going home. We'll never be free unless we try.' He gave her shoulders a tight squeeze and moved her forward again. 'Let's go.'

Stacey suppressed the urge to clobber him. How could he not see that she would never be the hero he is?

'Stacey, focus on your strengths,' Hubert said. 'Use them to move through your fears.'

His words fuelled the bubbling inferno growing inside. She glared at their mentor, rays of fire shooting from her eyes. Waves of lava by the rocky side lapped up to match.

'Stop. Stop. Stop. I can't hear it anymore,' Stacey spewed. 'I am not your hero, and I am not my father. He lied to us, Hubert, he lied. They both did.'

Thinking of her father's abandonment turned Stacey's world yellow. An unrecognisable tirade burst open. It gathered speed like a boulder down a steep hill, that no amount of mental logic could suppress. 'I'm just trying to take care of my brother in peace. I'm not the hero my parents were. They made their choice and left us. I won't die on some pointless mission.

Ryan's right—what has the world ever done for us except tear our family apart? You're asking us to fight a battle we can't win. We keep losing to the assassin. There are six of us and one of her, and we still lose, every time. What if there's an army like her? What chance do we have?

You can't expect me— chubby, uncoordinated me—to beat a trained assassin. To suddenly find courage after a motivational speech when everything in me is screaming to run. I just can't.'

Hubert rustled his chains and coughed.

'Hey,' Liam said. 'Calm down. You're getting worked up over nothing.'

His words ignited another wave of fury that overpowered her. Lava surged up, and her world turned blinding yellow. A heat wave exploded from her, and formed a two-meter-tall dragon.

'Don't tell me to calm down!' she thundered as flames disintegrated the remainder of the bridge.

The red dragon breathed fire onto Liam. He screamed and rolled to the side, then raised his hands to form an ice shield.

'Stacey, let's talk about this,' he pleaded.

'I. Don't. Want. To. Talk,' Stacey bellowed, each word punctuated by a blast of flames from the dragon.

Liam darted around the cave to avoid the fire. He threw swords and daggers with one hand while reforming his ice shield with the other. All were consumed by the dragon as fast as he created them.

'Hubert, help! Do something. She's too powerful. I can't keep this shield up.'

'Build a snowman,' Hubert called out. 'Now, before she attacks again.'

'What?'

Stacey cowered back on her bottom as her dragon continued to breathe flames onto Liam. He rolled and jumped in a flurry. There was a mix of satisfaction and horror as she watched with a sense of detachment, powerless to stop it.

'You'd better do it now,' she whimpered, 'before the dragon sucks all the water from the air.'

Liam ducked away as the dragon stomped after him. 'I don't know how to build a snowman!'

'Tap into your fear,' Hubert hollered. 'Bring it to the surface with an image. Be clear about what you want it to do.'

Liam squeezed his eyes shut, held out his palms, and with a grunt, summoned a whirling blizzard. Awestruck, she could not take her eyes off the pot-bellied snowman that matched the height of her dragon.

Liam swung his right arm, and the snowman mirrored the motion, knocking the dragon sideways. It screeched and breathed fire at it. The snowman threw a shield into the dragon's mouth which neutralized the flames.

Lava spurted from the pit and severed one of the snowman's arms. In a final effort it hurled itself against the dragon and both were reduced to a puddle.

Stacey collapsed, her energy drained. Liam guided her into a sitting position as she buried her face in his chest. 'I'm so sorry.'

Hubert rustled his chains and gave a sympathetic smile. 'Stacey, no one expects you to be someone you're not. Your passion for finding new treatments comes from your desire to ease suffering. Remember, courage isn't the absence of fear but the ability to act in spite of it. You've shown great strength in raising and protecting your brother. You just need to extend from what's already there.'

Stacey leaned back into Liam's arms. She wanted to say she was ready, that she would brave whatever came next. But fear of failure held her in place.

She didn't know how to bridge the gap in her combat skills or know how to protect Ryan if they continued on this path. Ryan was the only family she had left, losing him was unthinkable, but ignoring her father's legacy would be like losing him all over again. Her head pounded with conflicting thoughts.

'I know it's a lot to ask,' Hubert continued, 'but sometimes, in taking that journey, we find our true selves.'

'I don't know what you expect me to be. I'm just a scientist,' Stacey said.

'Heroes come in many forms. It's not just about powers or physical strength. It's about heart and finding the hero within you. Stacey, you're more powerful than you realize. We don't need another version of your father or Liam or Paige.'

'Really?'

'What we need is your mental strength, your ability to analyse and reason. Your voice of reason will be crucial for the team's success. Remember that,' Hubert said.

Stacey closed her eyes, processing the conflict between her heart and mind. She needed more time, but at least she was beginning to open up to the journey ahead.

Liam tightened his arms around her. 'Let's get home first and figure the rest out later.'

Stacey snuggled closer. 'I do want to make the world a better place, but I need to find my own way. I can't think beyond getting Ryan and Callum back. I will help you, Hubert. That's all I can manage right now.'

The warrior trainer nodded. 'Then I'm grateful for that.'

A green portal opened, revealing Ryan's pale face. 'Stacey. Stace, listen to me. You are a hero. You're my hero. I wouldn't have survived without you. You're the best sister in the world. So, stop doubting yourself, okay? I need you.'

Every part of Stacey jolted awake. She rushed to the portal. 'Ryan! Tell me where you are. I'll find a way to get to you. Or can you teleport to us?'

Ryan shushed a creature beside him, sounding out of breath. Behind him was a large tree trunk he was trying to climb, with a small, furry creature snapping at his heels. 'Some jungle. Sh-shush. Soft kitty. Hush, cubby bubby, sleep, bubby kitty. Don't wake your mama and papa, okay?'

Stacey held her breath as the cub swiped at Ryan's sneakers and began chewing. With a yelp, he hoisted himself onto a branch. 'Which jungle, Ryan? Where?'

'Shush, shush, pretty kitty, sleepy kitty, happy cubby,' Ryan sang.

Liam came up behind her. 'What is that awful song you're singing?'

'The lions go to sleep when I sing to them.'

Liam stuck his fingers in his ears. 'Wow, lions must be tone-deaf.'

Stacey smacked Liam across the chest and ushered him aside. 'Hubert, please get him out! Or maybe you can guide him here?' The portal crackled and began to close. 'No, Ryan!'

'We are underground in a cloaking spell,' Hubert said. 'It would be difficult for Ryan to teleport through. He has done well to open a communication channel; the bond between you two must be strong.'

'It's okay, sis. Breathe. I know you'll find a way; you always do. I'll keep trying, too,' Ryan said right before the portal snapped shut.

Stacey swiped at the air and willed it to open. 'Bring him back. Please.'

'There may be a way for me to get to him if we can break this underground barrier.'

Stacey stared at the missing bridge and the gap separating them. Waves of guilt twisted her gut. 'But the bridge is gone, and the gap is too wide to even consider jumping.'

Hubert smiled widely. 'Ah, when you burn one bridge, all you need to do is build a new one.'

'What do you mean?' Stacey cried shrilly. 'There are no materials or tools here!'

Liam placed a hand on her shoulder. 'Relax, take a breath. I got this.'

Stacey glared, contemplating showering him with flaming daggers. 'Don't patronize me.'

Liam held out an open hand. 'I'm not. Watch this.' He pointed his palms towards the cliff's edge. Rays of ice clumped together to form a walkway that closed the gap. 'Like Hubert said—'when you burn one bridge, build a new one."

Stacey's jaw dropped. How had she missed such a simple solution? She smiled at Liam with newfound respect. Perhaps she hadn't given him enough of a chance. 'You're right.'

With a grin, Liam laced his free hand into hers. 'Can you repeat that? I didn't hear you.'

And there goes that chance.

'Now, I know what you're thinking,' Liam said, tugging her toward the ice bridge. 'I'll reinforce the bridge as we walk across so it's not melted by the heat below.'

'What if—'

Liam gave her a quizzical look. 'For a smart girl, you let your fears hold you back a lot.'

Stacey huffed and averted her gaze.

'Have you thought instead about what if we do make it? What if we focus on freeing Hubert so he can get to Ryan? Then we can all go home. Isn't that worth the risk?'

Stacey opened and closed her mouth, trying to come up with a counter argument. For the first time, she found herself agreeing, grudgingly.

They made it across the bridge without a hitch. Liam tugged at Hubert's binding chains on one side while Stacey bent low to examine the cuffs. They looked like ordinary iron-clad chains.

'Maybe a key, or pick the lock?' Liam mused.

'Can you pick a lock?'

'No,' Liam said with a sheepish grin. 'I thought you might know.'

The ground below them shook violently. She stumbled then fell onto her back as flames from the boiling lava shot high into the air.

'That wasn't me,' Stacey said, her pounding heart picking up speed.

More flames licked the edge of the cliff.

'Okay, maybe that was me,' Stacey yelped. 'What's happening?'

'I believe this volcano is about to erupt,' Hubert said in an eerily calm voice.

'How can you be so calm about this?' she shrieked.

'How would you prefer I be?' the old man replied with a bemused glow in his eye.

'I don't know. Do something!'

'I'm afraid I cannot; these chains are rather binding.'

Liam, who had his back against the rising lava, ignored their new threat. He clicked his fingers. 'Hammer and chisel.'

When he opened his hands, there was one in each palm.

Stacey swallowed as a splash of lava oozed past the ledge towards her feet. She sprinted to Liam as he continued to hammer at the chains. 'Hurry.'

With every lick of flames, more lava poured over the edge near their heels.

She looked up at Hubert for guidance. But to her frustration, all his crinkled eyes seemed to say was 'be the truest hero you are meant to be.'

Think, Stacey. What do you normally do when there's a difficult problem?

But she was just a scientist. Then it came to her—any metal, no matter how hard, has a melting point.

'*Very good, Stacey,*' Hubert said telepathically, his eyes closed. '*Now focus your mind on the solution. Use your fears and doubts to charge your powers.*'

Ha, sounds like another training session.

Stacey summoned her abundant supply of terror and brought it to the surface. Her vision turned yellow again. 'Make sure you reinforce that hammer and chisel with the hardest ice formation you can make.'

'What are you going to do?' Liam asked, not breaking focus.

'I'm going to melt these chains.'

Hubert's eyes flung open. 'Oh, but try not to burn me.'

Chuckling, Stacey gripped the chain. 'Tough luck, old man.'

She allowed the heat to spread up inside her and through her palms, doing her best not to pull back as her hands turned to flames. The metal in her grip glowed red-hot. She ignored the rumbling beneath her feet and her rising panic and widened her stance to maintain balance.

To her relief, a snap and a clang released Hubert's ankle. They continued to work on the other chains while Stacey stifled her cries as the lava melted her rubber heels. At least it helped her channel more fear through her hands.

When the chains finally broke Hubert collapsed to the ground on all fours.

The ground shook again; this time they were propelled high into the air.

Liam pushed the tower of lava beneath them back with his ice wall, right before they were encased in a protective bubble.

It floated them upwards, and in a blinding flash of white light, they found themselves sprawled on a beach. The volcano erupted in a horrifying yet magnificent sight.

Hubert curled in a ball by the water's edge. 'I am sorry, warriors. Breaking that forcefield took away all my strength. I'm afraid in this weakened state I cannot get to your brother.'

Stacey's heart leapt to her throat and she averted her gaze, unable to watch Hubert's writhing form, dashing all hope of getting her brother back.

The sandy ground shook in sync with the grumble of the erupting volcano. A flow of lava rolled down the volcano's rocky side at a terrifying pace.

'We need to get out of here,' Liam said and turned towards the sea. 'I can make the boat again.'

Stacey pushed aching thoughts of Ryan aside. They had to survive if they had any chance of getting to him. With all her strength she heaved Hubert onto his feet.

When an explosion sounded, they dove into the sea as hot gas and rocks rained down on them.

Liam bobbed in the water, scrambling to reform the ice boat.

A hissing rumble turned her to a river of lava fast approaching. 'Hurry!'

This was it, all was lost, then a voice echoed above them. Ryan appeared in a flash of green and dragged them into his tunnel. 'I gotcha, Sis. My turn to rescue you now.'

FORTY

Stacey sat in the manor lounge, sipping her chamomile tea as Hubert paced across the room. His eyes flashed milky white then returned to their normal grey. In that moment he looked more like a frail elder than a powerful warrior trainer. He sank back into the couch, his expression shifted from confusion to exhaustion to despair.

Ryan, on the other hand, returned to his bubbly, immature self. 'I teleported everyone back. It was so awesome. My powers are growing, right Hubert? That's what you said when you gave me a headache and spoke to me. So cool. I'm so very, very cool. I can lock onto people and poof, there I go. So bloody unreal, right?'

Stacey glared at him, willing him to stop. They had only been back at the manor for a few hours and she was already sick of Ryan's continuous recounts of how he had saved everyone. Liam clapped and laughed next to her. She shot him a 'stop encouraging him' look.

The room seemed bigger without Callum and Paige. She stared at the door, hoping they would burst through and tell them everything was fine. She wanted to shake Hubert and get him to bring them back. She resented him for letting Callum get arrested. But what she hated most was her inability to help him as he had Ryan.

Liam squeezed her hand, then looked towards Hubert. 'Any news of Paige and Callum?'

'No,' Hubert said in a mechanical tone.

Stacey drew in a breath. It seemed like Hubert was doing something far away, and it was not going well.

'Can't you go get them like you usually do?'

'No, I cannot.'

'Why not?' Liam asked.

The doorbell chimed. Hubert's eyes flung open and he shot to his feet. He paced across the room again, sprinkling strands of white hair on the floor as he stroked his beard.

'What is it, Hubert?'

'Stacey, please let our visitor in,' he said with an edge in his voice.

Stacey had never seen Hubert so jittery. The person at the door must be someone of importance or very dangerous. She wasn't sure whether he was excited or afraid.

She opened the manor door, shocked to find Kate on the threshold.

'Kate, what are you doing here?' she asked, hugging her.

'Callum wanted me to check up on you,' she said, frowning. 'He was very insistent. But you seem fine.'

'How is he?'

'Not good. I'm working as fast I can,' Kate said. 'I need to speak with Ryan again.'

Stacey ushered her into the lounge room and introduced her. Ryan came over and embraced Kate. Liam gave their mutual friend a brief hug, but Hubert's eyes flashed and he continued to fixate on Kate, as if she were an omen.

'Is everything all right?' Stacey asked.

Hubert extended a hand, an unnatural lop-sided smile plastered on his face. 'Where did you grow up?'

Kate looked taken aback as if debating with herself on how to respond. 'I grew up in Southern Calypso. Why?'

'Ahh, that makes sense,' Hubert said. 'The blanket city.'

'Excuse me?' Kate frowned and pried her hand away.

Hubert's eyes glowed and he began to shake and sway. Liam caught him before he fell and eased him to the couch. 'No, no, it can't be.'

Kate's hand flew to her face. 'Oh my God. Is your friend okay?'

'Uh no, he... has a condition,' Stacey muttered, as bewildered as Kate. 'He's incredibly old. He'll stop on his own.'

Kate deepened her frown. 'That must be some condition. His eyes went all white. I think we should call a doctor.'

'Yes—an eye seizure condition thing.' Stacey sounded ridiculous even to herself. 'He'll be fine, don't worry.'

Kate narrowed her eyes, fingers hovering above her phone. Stacey knew she was not fooling her best friend for a second.

She was about to usher Kate out of the room when Hubert sat up. Smiling as if nothing had happened, he continued his unblinking stare at Kate.

Stacey was at a loss. She had never had to deal with anything like this before and was relieved when Kate asked to speak with Ryan in private. Kate gave her a 'this isn't over' look, before following her brother into a room across the hall.

Stacey went over to Hubert, with hands on her hips, now able to freely air her annoyance. 'What was all that about?'

'What was what about?' Hubert asked, his eyes wide with childlike innocence.

'Why were you being so rude to Kate?' Stacey said. 'Did you see something while you were reading her?'

'Hmm... see something.' Hubert gazed into the distance.

'You acted like she was a dangerous criminal.'

Hubert looked at her with a serene smile. 'Did I? That is not true. Your friend is... special. Very special.'

'Special in what way?' Stacey asked.

'In every way. Now is not the time.'

'Then when is?' Stacey demanded.

To her frustration, Hubert stood up and walked to the door. 'Please excuse me. I need to find Paige.'

FORTY-ONE

Paige tucked the transcription stone deeply in her pocket, then set about finding a way out of the assassin's room. She ran her hands along the walls, searching for a lever, hidden button, or handle. She pushed against the spot where she'd entered, but the opening was sealed shut as if it had never existed. Twisting and pulling on the weapons mounted on the wall yielded nothing. Paige took a deep breath through the despair.

How did the assassin get in and out without an opening? With a sinking feeling, she remembered Hubert's words: she could move through walls.

Paige's chest caved in as she slumped onto the bed, taking shallow breaths. How was she going to get the stone back to the others? She scanned the room again and her eyes landed on the green book. She opened it, flipping all the way to the end, on instinct. At the bottom was a rectangular hole with a black button at its centre she hadn't noticed before. Her fingers hovered above it, ready to press. But a voice in the back of her mind halted her index finger mid-air. *This wasn't here before.* What if it triggered another trap?

Paige closed her eyes, weighing the risks of pressing the button versus doing nothing. Her head ached, and she was no closer to deciding.

Life was about taking chances. If she didn't take the risk, she could be stuck here forever. Taking the risk had to be better than remaining idle. Before she could change her mind, she slammed her fingers on the button and held her breath. A door near the foot of the bed rumbled open.

She hurried through the opening and broke into a hobbling run. The path led into a dark passageway which she prayed would lead to an exit.

What if she was running in the wrong direction? She slammed the thought aside. She was too far in to turn back now. She raced to outrun the doubt creeping in. To cling to the hope that this was the way out.

She kept running until bright lights blinded her. She squinted, barely making out two silhouettes on the other side of the room. When her eyes adjusted, there was only one figure dressed in a grey cloak.

Before she could comprehend what was happening, Paige's head was forcefully jerked back and a blindfold tightened around her eyes. She tried to pull it off, strong, but a set of bony hands wrenched her wrists down and bound them. A sharp blow to her stomach doubled her over in pain.

The crack from a whip sent searing pain across her arms and chest. She staggered back, colliding with a body. Another whip strike kicked her forward. She crashed to the ground in agony.

When a boot dug into her, she rolled away as best she could. Footsteps approached. With a concentrated effort, she managed to stand and run. She hadn't taken more than two steps when a whip lash knocked her down again. She let out a shriek and fought through the pain to keep moving.

She pushed herself to levitate out of the way just as another crack sounded.

'Get back down,' someone growled.

Paige landed softly. Two sets of heavy boots approached from opposite directions. She waited for them to get closer, then somersaulted high into the air. She was pleased to hear them collide.

They charged again. She tried to levitate away, but her aching muscles failed her. The increasing sound of grating swords made her gulp. She had no choice but to stand and fight, even with her hands tied.

She listened for their footsteps and the swoosh of their swords. She managed to duck one attack, but her arm caught the blade of the other. She kicked one attacker in the gut and delivered a spinning kick to the other's legs.

Both fell with a thud, groaning. She pushed up, levitating as far as she could above them. They were on their feet again as she landed.

'Stop!' she hollered. 'Why are you doing this?'

They hissed and clanged their swords together. She tried to focus on their footsteps, but two sharp kicks to her chest sent her crashing into the wall.

Paige cried out as intense pain wracked her body, rendering her immobile. Fear seeped through her veins like poison. If she had to die, she would face her attackers head-on. But despite her efforts, she succumbed to the pain and exhaustion, closing her eyes, bracing for the next blow.

Her mind drifted back to her riverbank by the tree, next to the one-way mirror. Through it, two grey-cloaked figures charged, swords raised to strike.

Trusting her instincts, Paige destroyed the one-way mirror, dulling the serene image in her mind. She summoned all her fear—the fear of losing her uncle, breaking her leg in the boxing ring and enduring the underground gauntlet. Terror rose within her like a tsunami, which she blasted onto her attackers. Their shrieks filled the room, followed by two heavy thuds.

'Stop!' they both yelled.

Paige continued to send waves of fear, watching through her mind's eye as they writhed and jerked their limbs on the floor like electrocuted snakes.

'Stop, make it stop!' they shouted. 'We'll show you the way out.'

'I don't believe you,' she said.

One figure rolled towards her and cut the binds on her wrists. Paige pulled off her blindfold and levitated to the opposite side of the room while her attackers groaned in pain.

'How do I know you're telling the truth?' she demanded.

'Through those brass doors.' They pointed to the centre of the wall. 'Behind you.'

Satisfied they'd had enough, Paige took a deep breath and returned to her place of peace. She inhaled slowly, making the image in her mind brighter, louder, more tangible.

'How do I open them?' she asked.

'Walk through it.'

Paige turned to examine the golden doors behind her. They appeared solid. She placed a hand on one, and her hand disappeared. She jerked back, and faced the cloaked figures. 'This better not be a trap. 'What's behind those doors?'

'We don't know. We are only the keepers of this room,' they said, then faded into the walls.

Paige studied the arched double doors and the iron walls of the room. Everything was solid metal, except for the arched passageway. There was no other choice but to step through.

She moved cautiously through the halls until she entered another empty chamber with stone walls. Sunlight streamed in from an opening above. It's warmth filled her with hope, But her relief was short-lived when she realised the opening was at least five meters above her and there was nothing to stand on.

Her muscles tenses as she fixated on the opening. She would have to push down to levitate out. Hard. She took a step back, preparing to jump, when a loud snap sounded beneath her feet. *Shit! Another trigger.* Her throat tightened but her legs refused to move. Metal-spiked walls on both ends of the hall now free from their holding place, rumbled steadily toward her.

Paige smacked her leadened thighs repeatedly, willing them to come alive. Her legs shook and throbbed in protest, carrying her no further than a meter off the ground before she crashed back down. With her jaws clenched, she staggered back up. There was no way she would stay down when freedom was just meters away.

Eyes closed in concentration, Paige dug deep and levitated higher, but the fall this time sent shooting pains relaying through her back. Her muscles spasmed, glueing her to the cold stony ground. Terror wound it's iron vice around her chest sucking the air from her. Her hammering heart sky-rocketed to new heights as the enclosing walls grated towards her, now just a couple meters away.

Flashes of Mum and Dad, Uncle Rob, and her friends flooded her mind. If she had to go, she would hang onto them as her last thoughts.

No, wake up. A voice piped up from the back of her mind. *Not like this.*

'Be strong, you're my little warrior,' came Mum's voice. Something she used to say to her every time she fell over. Mum always stood nearby but never held out a hand to help. 'Learn to stand back up on your own.'

The wall approached, slower, but the spikes now a couple of meters away.

Paige jerked up. She can't die like this. She won't. The team needed her. And she needed Mum to know that she could do this. Limping back up, Paige gulped in a breath that renewed her adrenaline surge and readied for another jump. The ends of the metal wall protrusions were sharp but the metal rods attached to it weren't. They were just wide enough for her to step up on. With a concentrated effort she levitated onto the nearest foot hold as the opposing walls groaned towards her. With gritted teeth, she leapt on to the first foot hold, then hopped up to the next, steeling herself against the pains, until a final surge of energy propelled her out into fresh air, colliding into a body dressed in a multi-coloured robe.

'Hubert, is that you?'

His eyes twinkled with what seemed like fatherly pride, as he helped her up. 'Well done, Paige.'

The walls came together with a resounding thud beneath them. All the tension in her muscles dissipated, her legs gave way and she landed on the warrior trainer again, gripping him tight, as he dragged her through a white portal back to the manor.

FORTY-TWO

At the Dabury City Gaol House, Callum fought to keep his drooping eyelids from closing. He stared at the dripping tap in the far corner of his cell, not knowing which was worst, slipping back into nightmares or facing the return of the skeletal guards with their batons. But the overwhelming need for sleep eventually won out and the peeling paint on the ceiling morphed into a dark, wet rocky tunnel. In his mind's eye, he followed a slender figure gliding gracefully through it. In one hand, she held a wooden flame, with the other, she cradled a sleeping infant.

She entered a dimly lit chamber where a warrior with shoulder-length hair and a bushy moustache waited. His lilac tunic draped across one shoulder, doing very little to cover the tattooed eagle that spanned his chest, and wings that extended to meet his leather arm brace. The tunic brushed his knee-high boots as he knelt upon the queen's arrival. 'Majesty, I urge you to reconsider. This is too dangerous.'

The queen gestured for him to rise. 'General Rose, dear cousin, you are my most noble warrior and family. You have been with me from the beginning. Now, I must beg of you one last service.' Her voice cracked as she stroked the sleeping infant's face. The baby snuggled deeper into her arms.

General Rose bowed his head. 'I would die for you, my queen, but this… this is too much of a risk for the last heir of the royal bloodline. There must be another way.'

The queen's eyes hardened. 'There is no other way. Please, Jacob. Promise me you'll protect him.'

With tears streaming down her face, she pushed the baby into the general's arms.

The warrior held the infant awkwardly, his eyes filled with sorrow. 'I have sworn a blood oath to protect Prince Calister, and so will my descendants.'

The queen nodded and steadied the baby in his arms. She placed a white rectangular object with gold writing in his free hand. 'This transcription stone contains the reversal spell that will recombine the pieces of the life stone. Use it only if a threat ever arises again.'

Queen Enactra faltered back. The colour drained from her face as she blinked away the tears. 'Go, now,' she said urgently. 'Get him as far away from the curse as possible. I will do everything I can to repay the debt his father incurred. But you must go, Jacob, before Argos learns of your betrayal.'

General Rose reached out to steady the queen. 'Come with us. It doesn't have to be this way. All we need to do is get Calister away from his father, and the curse won't affect him. I can protect you both.'

'No, Jacob, I can't.' Her voice broke as she shoved him away. With glowing eyes, she raised her arm and began a chant. A swirling portal opened before them. 'Go now. Argos is coming. I must hold him off.'

A roar shook the caves. Rocks tumbled down— King Argos had arrived. An empty brown ornament swung wildly across his chest with every step. His eyes glowed red, and his face twisted in a feral snarl.

'Go, now!' Queen Enactra shouted. 'Or all is lost.'

The warrior, his expression pained, gave his cousin one last look before disappearing through the portal.

King Argos lunged forward, his hand tightening around Enactra's neck. 'How dare you take my son away from me?'

The queen gasped for air. 'Argos, please. Let's live in peace and repay the debt of the curse together.'

The wind swirled around them, shaking the cave rocks as the portal began to close.

Argos's face turned skeletal, his snarl deepening with demonic rage. 'Fool. I repent nothing.'

'Calister and the stones are gone. You'll never find them. Let go, please.'

Argos let out a guttural roar, threw her over his shoulder, and entered the portal. 'The curse of the life stone binds me by blood. I will find them all, no matter which lifetime they're in.'

His laugh echoed as the cave collapsed around them.

***

Callum woke to a brightly lit room and a loud rapping by his ear. A voice called his name with increasing urgency. His eyes fluttered, adjusting to the light. He wiped the sweat from his brow and took a deep breath to steady his breathing.

Through blurred vision, he saw Stacey, her silver-rimmed glasses bouncing on her nose as she banged her palm against the Perspex divider.

'Callum, wake up!' she called. 'What's happening? Guard, help him!'

Callum held up his hand to stop her. 'I'm okay. You're here. Where are we?'

Stacey picked up the phone on her side and leaned closer. She motioned for him to do the same, her worried eyes narrowing. 'We're in the visitor's booth. You blacked out as soon as you sat down. What's going on?'

Callum shook his head, trying to clear the fog in his mind, but images of King Argos surged back to the forefront. He pressed his forehead against the glass, his head pounded with Argos's words in his mind *I will find them all... no matter what lifetime they're in.*

Stacey's eyes shimmered with concern. She placed her hand against the glass panel as if wanting to touch his face. 'You look terrified. Are they mistreating you? Those wounds look awful.'

'I'm fine,' Callum said, waving her off. 'Stacey, listen, you're all in danger—'

'Who did this to you?' Stacey asked. 'You don't deserve this. I'll talk to Kate and—'

'Stop worrying about that and listen!' Callum said sharply

Stacey drew back but nodded. 'You need to tell Hubert and the others to find the transcription stone. I think the Destroyer—Apollyon—is really King Argos, sent to our time. He's going to attack to get his life stones back.'

She shook her head, then pressed her lips together. 'He's connected to the stones, and he's coming. You have to find the transcription stone and warn the others.'

'Why is finding this transcription stone so important?'

'Queen Enactra said it can be used to combine all of your powers if the enemy becomes too strong.'

'You mean Enactra, Queen of ancient Ceres?' Stacey asked with knitted brows. 'How do you know for sure that Apollyon is King Argos?'

'I saw it in my dreams,' Callum said while he strummed his fingers on the table continuously. 'Find the transcription stone. It'll help you fend off Apollyon's next attack.'

Stacey hands flew to her mouth. 'But now that you're here, who's going to lead us?'

'One of you will need to step up.'

'Paige,' Stacey said without hesitation. 'She's balanced, with all the attributes of an effective leader. But she's still missing.'

Callum nodded slowly. 'Find her, fast. You all need to come together to survive. The others will need your clear head and analytical mind. Apollyon is powerful. Remember—together is the key.'

The back door swung open, and a big-bellied guard with short hair appeared. 'Peterson, time's up.'

'But I just got here,' Callum protested. 'One more minute, please.'

The guard yanked him up by the arm and dragged him away.

Stacey's eyes brimmed with tears again as Callum called out, 'Transcription stone!' repeatedly, his voice echoing down the prison hallway.

FORTY-THREE

Stacey power-walked through the manor looking for Hubert, determined to make him get Callum out of prison. She had insisted on following Kate back to the city to visit Callum despite her objections. After seeing him, she understood why.

Stacey fought back tears as the image of his sunken cheeks and bruised face lingered in her mind. It had broken her heart to see his cuffed wrists at the visitor's booth. He'd spoken to her like a madman about the next attack with a certainty that frightened her.

She called incessantly for Hubert until she found him in the lounge room hovering over the couch. The boys sat opposite them, eating dinner in silence. Their faces brightened when they saw her.

Hubert placed a finger to his mouth. '*Shush. Later,*' he said telepathically.

How can he quieten her like that? She let out a forced breath through her nostrils. Her matter was just as pressing. She opened her mouth to protest when Hubert moved aside to reveal Paige asleep on the couch, with bruises tracking across her forehead and bandages covering almost all of her limbs. Paige was back! Barely.

While her face relaxed into a smile, she still could not forget about poor Callum still trapped in prison.

'Hey sis, how's Callum?' Ryan asked quietly.

She sat at Paige's feet. 'Not good,' she whispered back.

'But why? He's innocent.'

Stacey rubbed her temples. 'I know. We have to work through legal proceedings to get him out. Let's trust Kate on this, okay?'

Stacey gave him a hard stare to discourage anymore protests, then turned her attention to Paige 'You look like you've been to hell and back.'

Paige's eyes fluttered open. 'It sure feels like it.'

Stacey placed a hand under Paige's shoulder and helped her up. 'Sorry, I didn't mean to wake you.'

'Glad to see you're back, too.'

'Where did you disappear to?' Stacey asked. 'Why couldn't Hubert sense you?'

'I'm not sure exactly.'

'I believe Paige was trapped underground in the lost city of Ceres,' Hubert said, his eyes distant. 'It is sealed by magic.'

'Then how did you find me?' Paige asked.

'The dog you befriended, Big Santa, was very helpful,' Hubert replied.

Paige laughed. 'His name is Big Santa?'

'Yes, he kept barking your name. I was able to pick up his telepathic signal and follow it to the cave's entrance.'

'Wow, that is so super cool. You can talk to animals too, Hubert?' Ryan said.

'So how is Callum?' Paige asked. 'Why is he still in gaol?'

Stacey shook her head. She did not want to burst into tears—or flames—in front of everyone. She had to be composed for Ryan's sake, but it was hard thinking of Callum beaten in gaol for a crime he didn't commit. The pit in her stomach ached as she tried to push the image of Callum's thin, tortured frame from her mind.

Hubert let out a weary sigh. 'It seems that Callum has been wrongfully accused. For some reason, I cannot connect to him, nor open a portal to his location. I'm afraid I cannot get him out.'

Stacey's heart sank.

'Why would someone do that?' Ryan clenched his fists. 'He's just a nice guy who was trying to help.'

Liam wrapped an arm around him to keep him from bouncing up. 'Easy, buddy. We'll figure something out to help him.'

'Kate is looking into a lead,' Stacey said, biting her lower lip. She wanted to brainstorm ways of rescuing Callum but knew the team needed to focus on the imminent threat ahead. If she couldn't get him out, then at least she could take his warnings to the team. 'Cal says the next threat is coming very soon and that we need to find the transcription stone to combine our powers.'

'How does he know that?' Liam asked.

'He's right,' Hubert said in a grave tone. 'We don't have much time.'

'How the hell would we go about finding this transcript thingy?' Ryan asked.

Paige reached into her pocket and pulled out a white, rectangular object marked with rows of gold carvings. 'You mean this transcription stone?'

Hubert's eyes widened. 'Yes. Where did you find it?'

'In the assassin's bedroom.'

'Wow, she took you to her bedroom?' Ryan asked with bright eyes. 'She must really like you.'

Paige's cheek flushed. 'No, geez, no. She didn't take me there. I… fell in.'

It was odd to have the transcription stone suddenly reappear and that the assassin would let go of it so willingly. They must be missing something. 'Right, you just fell in,' Stacey repeated doing little to hide the scepticism dripping in her tone.

'To her bedroom,' Ryan added.

'Where you conveniently found the transcription stone.'

'Wait, what are you saying?' Paige asked looking puzzled. 'That I'm making this up?'

'That's mean, Stacey, especially after everything she's been through,' Liam said.

Stacey glared at him, a twinge of jealousy piercing her chest. It hurt that Liam was so ready to jump to Miss Perfect's defence. Would he ever defend her that way?

'It all just sounds too easy,' she said, keeping her voice steady.

'Easy?' Paige's jaw dropped as if she wanted to slap her.

'Look, it makes no sense. Why would the assassin hand over a relic that we could use against her in battle?'

Liam's confused expression relaxed, and he began to nod.

'She didn't give it to me, I was bound and blindfolded by two guards who tried to stop me from leaving,' Paige retorted.

'But did the assassin herself ever appear?'

'No,' Paige admitted.

'Something doesn't add up here.' Stacey tried to piece the events together in her mind, but the mystery had too many missing pieces for any clear picture to form.

'Do you think Paige was led to a fake stone?' Liam asked.

'Possibly, to throw us off track, like she did Hubert. Or maybe to sabotage our training.'

'Don't you have the professor's diary?' Paige asked. 'Maybe we could see if there's something there that could tell us if it's real.'

***

After dinner, Hubert excused himself, retiring for the night. The rest of the team returned to the lounge room; no one wanted to be alone that evening.

Stacey brought down John Chu's diary. She ran her fingers down its spine, wishing she'd had the chance to thank him. She clutched his life's work tightly in her hands, vowing to make his sacrifice worthwhile. The thick feel of the diary pushed back against her fingers, giving her a sense of calm, as if John was still present in its pages.

She found the others huddled over the transcription stone, trying to make sense of the writing. Stacey squeezed into a spot next to Ryan and sat down cross-legged, the journal resting in her lap.

'Is there anything in there that tells us what this is?' Liam asked as he ran his fingers along the carvings.

Stacey flipped through the journal until she found the section on the transcription stone. Clearing her throat, she read aloud, 'The transcription stone, created by Queen Enactra, is said by historians to contain the reversal spell that can recombine the forces of the life stone. The writings on the stone are in a language I can only partly decipher: 'Evil arise... stones combine... to evil defeat. One chant spell.''

'Does it say how to combine our powers?' Paige asked.

Stacey flipped through a few more pages until she found it. 'John's interpretation is that the stone bearers must recite the eternal life spell together and combine their powers through a singular thought.'

'Huh?' Ryan said.

'So we have to all be thinking the same thing while reciting the spell?' Paige asked.

Stacey nodded.

'Good luck with that,' Ryan huffed out. 'We can barely agree on the same TV channel.'

'Whose fault is that?' Liam retorted.

'We'll have to try,' Paige said. 'If Apollyon and his assassin attack again, this may be our best defence.'

Stacey nodded again. 'The spell we have to recite is: Kahhrarg tethman gool, persey ra chee ma, bum cha bum cha na.'

'What the...? I'm not going to remember that,' Ryan said.

Liam laughed. 'I think you're pronouncing it wrong.'

'You should write it down for us,' Paige suggested.

'Maybe we can ask Hubert. He'll know,' Liam said, calling for Hubert and frowning when there was no answer. 'Hm, he must be asleep.'

Stacey wrote the spell down on separate sheets of paper and handed everyone a copy. Ryan read it aloud and laughed with Liam.

'Is it really that funny?' Stacey's patience was wearing thin. 'Come on, be serious now.'

'Okay, okay, I'll stop,' Ryan wheezed.

'It really isn't that funny.' Stacey read the spell again, 'Kahhrarg tethman gool, persey ra chee ma, bum cha bum cha na.'

To Stacey's dismay, this only caused fresh bouts of laughter from the boys. She folded her arms and glared at them, waiting for them to stop. It irritated her that they found it all a joke when the danger they faced was so serious. It made her wonder what she liked about Liam, given he was as immature as Ryan.

'Is there anything else the professor says about what the real transcription stone looks like?' Paige asked.

Stacey flicked through the pages again. 'No, nothing more.'

'There's only one way to find out, then,' Paige said.

Stacey did her best to curb her annoyance at the boys. 'How are we going to learn to combine our powers when you're all laughing like hyenas? Ryan, stop being so childish.'

Liam was the first to get control of himself. Ryan gave her a sour look before doing the same.

'I'm sorry, Stacey,' Liam said. 'We'll try and learn the spell properly.'

Despite their best efforts, it took them nearly an hour to learn it by heart. Stacey couldn't believe a twelve-word sentence could take so long to remember. Even Paige struggled.

'We're new at this,' Paige said gently. 'We'll get there with a bit more time. What does Professor Chu say to do next?'

Stacey reminded herself to be patient. She was not used to waiting for others to complete tasks; anything she had to do, she did alone. 'Teamwork' was a foreign concept.

'Now we have to stand in a circle, holding hands, and focus on combining our powers,' she said.

The team gathered in a circle, held hands, recited the spell, and waited.

'Is something meant to happen right about now?' Ryan asked, one eye open.

'Damn, the stone's not real, then,' Liam said.

'Let's chant the spell again, but at the same time,' Paige suggested. 'Maybe we have to keep repeating it.'

'Right. On three,' Stacey said. 'Together, continuously.'

The team held hands again and chanted in unison. Their stones glowed, and beams of light projected forward, meeting in the centre of the circle.

Ryan's eyes widened. 'That is so cool. It almost looks like a rainbow.'

The beams of light vanished.

'Ryan, you broke concentration,' Stacey growled. 'You need to focus.'

'Sorry,' Ryan muttered. 'You don't have to be so mean about it.'

'Let's try again. We're still training,' Paige said. 'I'm sure it'll take us a few goes to get it right. We're making progress.'

'Yes, Paige is right,' Liam said. 'That was only our second attempt.'

Stacey tried not to look at Liam as she pushed aside the burning vexation in her chest. They held hands again and repeated the chant. The stones glowed and shot forward beams once more.

'Right, now please focus, everyone,' Stacey commanded. 'One single thought of combining our powers.'

The beams of light projected from their stones again, merging in the centre.

I would love chocolate cake right about now, came Ryan's voice. *My stomach is growling.*

A plate of chocolate cake appeared in the centre of the circle.

Did I change my underwear? This itch is really annoying. This time it was Liam. *What if Stacey hates my red boxers?*

You know we can hear your thoughts, Paige projected.

Oh crap, really? Ryan thought. *You didn't hear about me going out to the gay bar too, did you?*

Yes, Paige and Liam replied in unison.

Try and stay focused, everyone, Paige thought. *I can feel our powers fragmenting.*

Oh no, crap. Stace, I can explain, Ryan began.

Oh well, now that you know, Stacey, do you like red? Liam thought. *You know, seeing as you're so fiery and all.*

Stacey's head pounded, and the burning in her chest intensified. She fought to keep her vision from turning yellow. *Don't think you're getting away with anything, Ryan. You are so grounded.*

I wonder if Stacey owns any black lingerie. Damn, she's so sexy when she's mad, Liam projected again.

Paige's chuckle could be heard from across the room. Stacey shifted on her feet, struggling to maintain focus. The heat rising inside made it feel as though her face was on fire. She couldn't understand why the boys couldn't take things more seriously, especially after everything they'd been through. How were she and Ryan supposed to stay safe working with such clowns?

A small explosion of light burst from the centre of the beam, and an attractive woman in a bikini appeared. She smiled and blew kisses in their direction before making her way around the circle, giving everyone seductive hugs.

Make it stop, Stacey cringed as the woman started her round again, this time smooching them on the lips.

Think about something else, Paige suggested telepathically. *Anything else!*

A series of dead puppies appeared, scattered in the middle of the circle.

No, who thought that? Ryan's voice came through. *That's so cruel.*

Sorry, Paige replied.

Damn, the half-naked lady is still here, Ryan thought, turning away from another kiss. *Video games, video games, video games.*

A pile of game consoles and CDs appeared on top of the puppies. The woman, unfazed, sauntered her way toward Liam.

Crap, she's still here, Ryan thought.

Oh, what's the harm? Liam laughed as the woman ran her fingers through his hair.

Is there a way to send her back? Paige asked. *To reverse it?*

Stacey clenched her teeth, as the woman draped herself over Liam. Her mind was clouded by intense heat.

What about saying the spell in reverse? Liam suggested, his laugh becoming nervous as he glanced at Stacey. He wriggled to stop the woman from unbuttoning his shirt.

Stacey did her best to keep herself under control, bursting into flames would ruin their progress.

It's worth a try, Paige shrugged.

Ryan nodded enthusiastically. *Spell in reverse, let's go.*

Liam, Ryan, and Paige began chanting the spell backward, while Stacey struggled to recall the words. The woman turned, her eyes widening as if sensing she was about to be sent away. She flung herself onto Liam and pulled him into a passionate kiss.

The heat inside Stacey shot to boiling point. She couldn't take it anymore and threw her hands up. The seductive woman vanished, replaced by a firework like explosion that knocked them all onto their backs.

'You guys are impossible to work with!' Stacey shouted, getting up to jab her finger into Liam's chest. 'Especially you!'

'Hey, I wasn't the one who thought of bikini lady,' Liam protested. 'Relax already.'

'Really?' Stacey retorted. 'Who else could it have been? Ryan's into boys.'

How could Liam lie so blatantly? He was obviously the one responsible for conjuring the half-naked woman. Stacey spun on her heels and stormed out the door.

'Stacey, wait. Please,' Paige called out. 'Let's calm down and try again.'

'So, does that mean the transcription stone is real?' Ryan asked.

A sharp pain sliced through Stacey's head. She turned to the others who clutched their heads the same way she was.

'Yes, it is real. Now go to sleep,' Hubert snapped telepathically. *'Or I will put you all in a coma for a month.'*

FORTY-FOUR

Paige leaned her elbows on the railing of the balcony outside her room and breathed in the crisp morning air. She loved the rolling carpets of grass on the hills that stretched to meet the dazzling sun, a gentle caress of the breeze against her cheeks, and the rustle of leaves that swirled in its embrace. The chirping of birds, nested high above, was a soothing, melodic piece of heaven she desperately needed.

After days of listening to Stacey and Liam's constant bickering over the transcription stone, Paige was relieved to connect with her own emotions and thoughts again. She was beginning to understand why Hubert had to continually excuse himself from the group. After many attempts at playing peacemaker, she had finally given up and done the same. Stacey was like a simmering volcano, and Liam a raging tidal wave. Paige was exhausted from having to maintain a constant emotional blockade.

The only silver lining to the group spending so much time together was that they had confirmed the transcription stone was real. But getting four different personalities to maintain one singular thought was much harder than she had anticipated.

A loud crack drew her attention to the manor's front entrance, and the edge of a billowing purple cloak caught her eye. Paige moved to the far end of the balcony for a better look.

She drew in a sharp breath as the familiar athletic form of the assassin came into view. A heaviness washed over her like a wave of liquid concrete. Despite the team's intense training over the past week, they were far from ready—and even further from being able to unite.

The assassin lifted her masked face to the sky, her arms outstretched. Her long, braided hair shone in the morning light, as a peaceful smile spread across her face. She looked almost approachable.

The clouds moved, and the sunlight dimmed. The purple cloak snapped in the gusty wind. The assassin shook her head as if coming out of a trance and slowly raised her arm. Purple rays shot from her palm, and a thunderous blast reverberated throughout the manor as the front doors splintered apart.

Paige grabbed the railing as the balcony shook. She stumbled back into her room to get the metal staff she had kept from the markets. She hurried toward the entrance and prayed she was strong enough to fend off the attacker before the others woke.

'What do you want?' Paige asked when the assassin appeared.

The assassin's blue eyes brightened. 'You survived. It's a shame it won't be for long.'

'Take off your mask,' Paige demanded, holding the staff out in front. 'I want to see the face of the coward who plays such sick games.'

The assassin's unblinking eyes shone with amusement. She flew back toward the fountain, bowed her head, and beckoned Paige into the fight circle. 'Come, let's start.'

Paige couldn't help but admire her confidence. There wasn't a quiver in her voice nor a flinch of hesitation. 'You're very self-assured, aren't you? What's your name?'

The assassin took a step forward, her head cocked to the side, eyes gleaming with mischievous excitement. 'I'll tell you... if you can knock me off my feet.'

Paige charged at her, then pulled back at the last minute. In her mind, she was ready to do everything in her power to protect her friends, but at heart, she was a nurse, not a warrior. She was tired of fighting. There had to be a better way.

'What can we do to end this madness?' Paige asked. 'All this fighting is so senseless.'

The assassin threw an energy ray at her. 'Hand over the life stones, and you won't have to.'

Paige ducked, and the ray shattered what remained of the doors behind her. The assassin clearly had no intention of negotiating. With a deep breath, Paige launched a series of front punches and knee kicks at her opponent. Her nemesis leaned to the side, raising an elbow to block the attack. Her lower body planted solidly on the ground and she deflected two further rounds of sidekicks.

Crack.

Paige took a step back, ignoring the throbbing in her right foot. Landing kicks on the assassin was like kicking a statue.

The assassin placed one hand behind her back and beckoned her back into the circle with the other. 'Would you like to try again?'

Paige picked up her staff, crouched low and delivered a sweeping kick to the assassin's ankles.

To Paige's surprise, her opponent fell forward, landing on one knee. She couldn't believe the oldest trick in the book had worked. Swiftly, she yanked the black mask off the attacker's face.

The sight stunned her. She had been expecting a crooked nose, unsightly scars, or an ugly deformity—nothing like what she saw. Paige's heart stopped as the woman's pale, oval-shaped face and high cheekbones stretched into a mesmerizing smile.

'Why are you Apollyon's assassin?' Paige asked, turning to hide her blush.

'I don't have a choice,' the woman replied.

'There is always a choice.'

The assassin gave her a rueful look. In a blink, she took a step forward and beckoned Paige once more.

Taking another breath, Paige sprang through the air, extending her leg in a spin kick. The assassin raised her knee to block it. Paige swung a half-hearted left hook at her, but the assassin dodged as expected. An intense warmth spread across Paige's chest as the assassin gazed at her with admiration.

'I don't want to fight you,' Paige said, meeting her gaze. 'Let's talk this through. There's good inside you. I can feel it.'

The assassin's eyes flickered with sorrow before closing. When they reopened, a cold, glassy stare replaced them. Her soft facial features hardened, and her warmth evaporated. 'Your emotions are a weakness that will cost you your life.'

Paige stepped closer and looked her straight in the eyes. 'You're wrong. My emotions guide me, make me feel alive. They're my greatest strength.'

A conflicted look crossed the assassin's face. Dark clouds moved above—a warning, or perhaps a reminder. She snapped back into action with another energy ray at Paige.

Paige dropped, rolled, then held up her staff to deflect the blast. But another struck her shoulder, which sent her sprawling across the ground. A heavy weight on her belly pinned her in place. She was wedged between the assassin's knees. Paige lifted her arms to push her off, but the assassin held her wrists to the ground.

Her breath brushed Paige's cheeks like a set of slender fingers. Paige's pulse quickened, and a hot flush rushed through her. She wasn't sure if she was excited or fearful of being forced into submission.

'My name is Ahndra Rose,' she whispered in her ear.

Paige stared into Ahndra's sky-blue eyes, searching. Searching for the real person beneath the darkness. Searching for what she wanted to believe was goodness behind the beauty.

Ahndra returned her gaze, amusement still twinkled in her eyes. 'Now that you've unmasked me, when are you going to take off yours?'

'Get off her!' A loud battle cry from Liam, made Ahndra sit upright and release her grip.

Paige watched, dazed, as he charged toward them. Stacey hurled tennis-sized fireballs, but Ahndra laughed and somersaulted away. Liam and Stacey stood in front of Paige like a barricade, ready to fend off their attacker. Hubert held Ryan by his side. Paige rolled to her feet, ready to rejoin the fight when Hubert pulled her back.

'Reserve your strength. Let them handle it.'

Stacey and Liam attacked together., They launched a storm of fireballs and ice spears from every direction. Ahndra stood her ground and, with a flick of her hands, sent the attacks back. Stacey ducked for cover while Liam created a shield.

'I need to help my sister!' Ryan jerked his arm free from Hubert's hold and teleported away.

He reappeared behind Ahndra and charged at her. Paige held her breath. It was like watching a train wreck. The assassin cackled, the wave of energy emanating from her knocked Ryan onto his back. He disappeared through his vortex. Moments later, he returned with an armful of rocks. He hurled them at her then had to dive behind the fountain as the rocks came flying back.

Liam attacked again with two newly formed ice spears. They shattered in his hands as Ahndra sidestepped. Losing balance, Liam fell forward. Stacey rose, unleashing a long-range fire ray. Liam steadied himself and formed a shield and sword. Ahndra grabbed his wrist, took control of his shield, and used it to meet Stacey's fire ray.

'Liam, get out of the way!' Stacey yelled. 'Ryan, stay down. Don't even think about attacking again.'

Ryan vanished through his vortex while Liam moved to the side and Stacey dominated the frontline. Liam's eyes glowed blue as a continuous shower of ice daggers flew from his palms. Ahndra held out both hands to fend off their strikes. The fight was a spectacular display of bright yellow, blue, and purple lights.

Out of the corner of her eye, a small green light appear. A vortex opened, and Ryan barrelled through, swinging a large tree branch. With a laugh, the assassin sent out waves of energy that knocked everyone down. She turned her attention to Ryan. Stacey shrieked as Liam leaped up. He threw himself in front of Ryan and pushed him out of Ahndra's trajectory.

Her rays caught Liam's upper arm and turned it charcoal black. He crashed to the ground, clutching his arm as Stacey ran to his aid.

Paige saw her cue. She sprang into action and returned to the fight circle. 'Stop! Right now. Your fight is with me.'

Ahndra winked, blew her a kiss, then flew back and hovered.

A clap of thunder sounded. Hubert materialized beside them and threw bolts of lightning at their intruder. Ahndra deflected them easily. With a flick of her wrist, she pushed Hubert back. Her eyes glowed, and a chant escaped her lips. Hubert writhed in pain, engulfed in a halo of purple light.

'Hubert!' They ran toward him.

'You'll have to defeat me if you want to free him,' the assassin said.

The soft-faced Ahndra was gone, replaced by an ominous, violaceous presence. Paige turned to Stacey, who stood in front of Ryan, holding tightly onto his arm. A leaden weight tightened around Paige's chest as she felt Stacey's fear weave through her.

Paige forced herself to take command before fear froze her. 'Stacey, Liam, blast her with your powers, now.'

Stacey gave her a despairing look while Liam sprang into action. He launched ice rays at their enemy.

'Keep him safe.' Stacey pushed Ryan toward Paige and ran to Liam's side. She mimicked him with fire rays.

His face pale, Ryan clung to Paige with shaking arms. She held his shoulders to steady him.

Meters away, Ahndra's purple rays met Liam and Stacey's energy beams. The coloured rays interlocked, but Ahndra slowly advanced.

Paige replayed all her fights with Ahndra in her mind. Then it hit her, the assassin had a blind spot—the place where Paige had landed the most strikes in their previous encounters.

'I need you to get me to the assassin's left, thirty degrees back from her horizontal eye line,' Paige instructed.

'That's really specific,' Ryan said. 'I'll try.'

Paige took Ryan's hand. There was no time for hesitation. 'Now!' she shouted.

To her relief, they landed precisely where she intended. Paige unleashed a flurry of Muay Thai kicks to Ahndra's ribs. The assailant fell to the ground. Her eyes rolled back, and her head struck the concrete with a loud crack.

Ahndra lay motionless as the team regrouped around Hubert. The halo broke, and he stretched himself free.

'Oh my God. Did we do it?' Ryan breathed.

'Stay alert,' Hubert commanded.

Paige stared at their fallen enemy, a dull ache of remorse spread through her. It quickly vanished when Ahndra climbed to her feet. Paige's jaw slackened and sweat rolled off her temples. Ahndra's eyes glowed demonically, her entire body wrapped in a violet blaze. With open arms, she floated to the sky. Her lips parted, and a song emerged. The words seemed to shake the heavens as lightning thundered down.

The ground rumbled and dropped them all. Ahndra caught two lightning bolts in her hands and, in one swift motion, split the earth open.

'Team, on your feet! Now!' Hubert shouted through the howling winds.

Gruesome four-legged creatures crawled out from the fissure— mummified wolves and lions with long fangs and black claws the size of daggers. Each creature more terrifying than the last.

The mummies charged. They snapped their razor-sharp teeth and fixed their beady red eyes hungrily on them. Stacey screamed, retreating with Ryan behind Hubert. Paige gulped down her terror and followed Liam to the frontline as he charged forward with his ice spears.

Paige swung her bo staff in a continuous circle, some turned to ash while others clung to the ends of their weapons.

Out of nowhere, a sharp pain gripped her shoulder. A long, wet tongue slapped her head, and the weight of a creature knocked her to the ground. Its claws dug into her. Another creature trampled her abdomen and legs.

Paige lifted her head, frozen in horror as the creature opened its mouth wide to bite. She tried to push it off, but it only dug its claws in deeper. She screamed as another set of claws tore at her legs.

She coughed and choked when the weight suddenly disappeared into a pile of ash.

Stacey with her firelit eyes and flaming hands, must've blasted the creatures off her. A swarm of dragons extricated out from her hands, engulfed the oncoming sea of creatures.

Liam unleashed ice figures that tackled a line of mummies, while Ryan weaved in and out of his vortexes, running the creatures into each other.

Paige grabbed her bo staff, relieved to find it still at her feet, and charged toward the creatures. Adrenaline pumping, she swung methodically, energizing herself with the strength of her team.

'Where's Hubert?'

'By the gates,' Liam replied. 'He's trying to stop the animals from getting past the manor walls.'

A piercing scream and roars from the gates reverberated through her. A wave of mummified animals flew at Hubert. Her blood iced over when they sank their claws into him and tossed him high into the air.

'I need to get to the gates now!' Paige hollered.

Ryan pulled her into a vortex, and in a blink, Paige found herself next to their fallen mentor. Creatures snapped at the staff as she fended them off, and with a strong, wide arc, she swept them back.

'I need to put up a shield to stop them from escaping,' Hubert gasped, clutching his abdominal wound.

Quickly, Paige tore off part of his robe and wrapped it around his stomach. She slammed her bo staff at the nearest creature with one arm and held Hubert up with the other. 'We need to get you back to the manor. You're in no condition to fight.'

She didn't take her eyes off the swarming creatures and batted two into the air.

'They'll escape and attack civilians,' Hubert wheezed. 'I need you to hold them off for two minutes.'

Hubert stepped behind her, his body emanating a heating glow. He drew the thunder towards the prism on his staff. White energy waves emerged from it, cloaking the manor walls and disintegrating the nearest mummies.

Paige created a protective arc around him. She clenched her teeth against her burning muscles and swung furiously at the creatures. One latched onto her arm, sinking its teeth deep. She levitated, throwing it off onto the advancing army.

'We need to retreat. There are too many of them,' Paige yelled, catching Hubert, who was already on his knees. She kicked away the nearest creature.

'Another minute.'

'Hubert, get us back to the team now, while you still can. I can't hold them off much longer.' She slammed her staff on one creature's back, kicking another that charged from the side.

'Almost done.'

Hubert pushed Paige aside, scrambling to his feet, only to lean against her again. His eyes glowed brighter and the crackling energy wall closed in, just meters away from completing the full circle.

Three mummified wolves howled and leapt toward them. Paige knocked two out of the air while Hubert blasted the other. A mummified lion tackled Paige and lunged at Hubert, tearing its claws into his shoulders. Light shot from his eyes as he completed the seal around the horde. Paige thrust her weapon into the lion's heart, turning it to dust.

Hubert went limp, his eyes rolled back as his head hit the ground. Paige screamed his name, holding her weapon ready for the next wave.

A portal opened, and Ryan dragged them through just before hundreds of creatures crashed down.

FORTY-FIVE

Stacey grinded her heels into the ground and pushed her back against Liam's for strength. She hailed fire balls on to the next line of advancing creatures but they continued to screech, climbing over each other to crawl towards them.

'Ryan,' she called. It didn't matter where he was, as long as he was safe, and preferably able to teleport them away from the army of mummified beasts.

Two bodies flanked her sides.

'Yes, I'm here,' Ryan replied.

'Where's Hubert?' Liam asked leaving a trail of ice as he moved sideways to meet the next onslaught of creatures.

'We took him back to the manor.' Paige batted the flying ones out of the air. 'He's badly injured.'

It was her turn, Stacey fired machete blasts at the next advancement in her direction. But despite their efforts, an endless sea of creatures flowed up from the ground, seemingly multiplying. They circled them and pushed closer until they were all squashed together. Stacey's arms dropped as more fire blast fell at her feet. Liam's ice wall melted, and he could only manage ice cubes. The creatures clawed and gnawed at Paige's staff as she tried to fight them off.

'We need to combine our powers,' Paige said. 'Think of creating a protective dome.'

They grasped each other's wrists, and chanted loudly. The creatures licked their lips then pounced. Stacey turned away, shut her eyes, and prayed. A wet tongue slapped her face, and she gagged on a gust of sulfuric breath.

Loud bangs and screeches filled her ears. She opened her eyes as the creatures rammed into a protective forcefield and slid off. Enraged, they bit, climbed, and clawed over one another.

Her vision darkened. All she saw was the underbelly of hundreds of creatures as they hurled themselves at the dome. The cacophony was deafening.

The team chanted until their voices became hoarse. Stacey swallowed her terror as the dome buckled and shrank under the weight, forcing them to their knees.

'It's not going to hold,' Liam telepathed. 'We need another plan.'

'What if we sent them away?' Ryan replied. 'I can open a portal.'

The dome pressed them down further, and they raised their hands high to keep it intact.

'To where?' Liam asked.

'Fervens Desert. I think I can create a portal to suck them back underground there. The nearest city is over a thousand kilometers away. Even if they escape, the heat would get them before they could reach civilization.'

'That's perfect, Ryan,' Stacey projected. 'But I don't know where that is.'

'Keep your minds blank and back me up. I'll do the rest.'

Light poured into the dome from an opening above as a portal sucked in the nearest creatures. A group of mummies charged together, and part of the dome shattered. Paige swung her staff in an arc while Liam blasted them with a flurry of frozen daggers. Ryan kept his arms forward and spun them to open the vortex. Stacey gathered all her terror into a wave of heat and pushed it onto the nearest mummies. Some ignited, others disintegrated, and countless more were pulled into the vortex.

'Keep it going, buddy. It's working!' Liam shouted.

Once Stacey was satisfied with the distance between the creatures and her brother, she joined Liam, using her fire to drive the creatures into the portal. They screeched and clawed at the ground as they were sucked in.

Thunder clapped in the distance. A tilting dizziness made her stop. She lifted her shirt, a gaping wound appeared on her side dripping blood down to her waist line. The ground rocked her vision blurred, and she collapsed.

She called out to Paige, but she was already flying toward the assassin. The boys had their backs to her. Ryan kept the portal open, his arms visibly shaking, while Liam drove the creatures toward it with his ice bat.

A searing pain spread through her as a set of teeth sank into her arm.

Her world went black, and everything stopped.

FORTY-SIX

Paige charged towards Ahndra, who hovered mid-air, her eyes a blinding purple. Ryan's portal weakened as creatures began to crawl back out.

The team was tiring, yet the mummies still came in ferocious waves. If she could just stop the assassin's summoning, the flow of creatures would stop. Paige swung her bo staff with determined precision that knocked her enemy out of the air mid-chant.

Crashing to the ground, the glow in the assassin's eyes faded and the earth began to close. But Ahndra flipped away in a flash and flew up again. Paige struck again but Ahndra blocked it, and they both landed heavily onto the ground.

The assassin bounced back delivering a sharp blow to her back. Paige crumpled and took ragged breaths through the pains. Ahndra charged at her, she rolled away in time, levitating up to retaliate with a series of spinning sidekicks, which knocked the assassin away.

Behind them, Ryan's green portal snapped shut. Liam appeared with an unconscious Stacey in his arms.

When Ahndra tried to rise again, Paige pinned her down with the staff pressed against her neck. Ahndra blasted her away with a burst of energy and shot up into the sky.

'Ryan, we need that portal again!' Liam called. He swept an arm across which sent dozens of knives slicing into the oncoming creatures.

The ground cracked open once more. Paige bolted upright, then dropped to a cross-legged position. With her eyes closed, she channelled the most intense terror and anger from her memories. They merged into a rising pink force that she hurled at her airborne nemesis.

Ahndra gave an anguished cry, crashed to the ground, and writhed frantically as the earth rumbled shut.

'Paige, we need you back!' Liam called out.

In an instant Paige leapt to her feet and sprinted toward them. The trio joined hands, supporting a half-conscious Stacey and began to chant.

A sharp tug at her feet sent Paige tumbling face-down. She kicked hard to shake off Ahndra's steel grip, but the assassin continued to claw her way forward. Paige closed her eyes and sent another wave of anguish. Ahndra cried out, but held on tight.

Gale-force winds knocked them sideways as a portal, the size of a dinner plate, flickered open.

'Paige, hurry!' Liam pushed himself up further to support Stacey's limp frame. 'She's too weak!'

Paige dropped her staff, pushed herself off the ground, and dove into the circle with Ahndra still clinging to her ankle. She grasped Liam's hand and joined the transcription chant.

The portal widened, and the winds intensified, drawing the mummified creatures high into the air.

An inexplicable impulse surged through Paige's mind—an instinct she couldn't fully understand but chose to trust. She pulled Ahndra into the chant circle.

Liam, take Ahndra's hand to complete the circle, Paige urged.

Are you crazy? Liam thought back. *Why?*

Trust me.

Ahndra's eyes widened. 'No!'

The portal expanded, crackling with energy as it spread across the sky. Turbocharged, the vortex sucked in the mummified animals at lightning speed. The creatures clawed wildly as they were swept upward.

Keep going! Stacey's thoughts were faint as she slumped forward, eyes closed.

Ryan and Liam flinched.

Stacey would want us to stay focused, Paige thought. *Just a little longer.*

How many more left? Ryan asked.

About a hundred. We're almost there, Liam replied.

Ahndra howled, struggling to break free, but Paige tightened her grip. 'If you don't cooperate, I'll make sure your chest explodes from the worst heartache you've ever felt.'

The assassin glared at her but remained still.

The screeches of hundreds of mummies filled the air as they flew past in a relentless stream.

Paige watched with relief as the last one vanished. But her joy was short-lived. The portal continued to suck in trees around the manor, and everyone began to lift off the ground.

Ryan, reverse the vacuum! Close the portal! Paige projected.

'I'm trying! It won't close!' Ryan cried, his voice high-pitched with panic.

'Stacey has fainted. We'll have to break formation,' Liam projected.

'But that might pull us in further,' Ryan thought. 'We've never broken formation without her before.'

As the team pulled closer to the portal's opening, Paige's mind raced through a series of options.

'We could try reciting the transcription spell in reverse again,' Liam suggested. 'Then focus on closing the portal.'

'We've never done that before,' Ryan thought.

Precious seconds passed as they edged closer to the sucking portal.

'Do you have a better option?' Ahndra projected.

Ryan shook his head.

'Let's try it,' Paige telepathed, narrowing her eyes at the assassin. 'Don't you dare mess this up.'

Ahndra gave her a wry smile.

'*Okay, on three, everyone,*' Paige commanded.

The team chanted the spell in reverse, their voices merging into a single rhythm. Slowly, the vacuum's force diminished. They descended, and the portal began to close. When it finally snapped shut, a loud thunderclap sent them all hurtling across the yard.

Dazed, Paige opened her eyes. The creatures were gone, the earth sealed.

And Ahndra was nowhere to be seen.

FORTY-SEVEN

At Dabury Gaol House, Callum hid his shaking hands below the table in the interview room. He did his best to focus on what Kate was saying but couldn't comprehend it. Her voice sounded distant and garbled even though she was sitting right in front of him.

The pounding in his ears grew louder and the words on the pages did a jagged dance. They were nothing but lies wrapped in fancy forensic jargon.

He wanted to tear the pages apart and keep tearing at them until they all disappeared. How could they not see that he was innocent?

Callum fought hard to slow his rapid breathing. The red veil that covered his vision flickered and was getting harder to push away.

Kate's slender neck was an arm's length away. The walls inside him began to buckle like a cracking dam. If he could reach out and tighten his fingers around that beautiful long neck, then maybe he could get her to stop talking and convince himself that none of it was true.

No, stop! he screamed in silence. *What are you thinking? You've gone mad. Get away from her, now! We are not a monster.*

The beast inside banged harder on his walls of restraint. *Just one squeeze and we are free. The pretty girl is useless. You know we have the power. No door or chains can hold us. They are fools and you know it.*

Callum grimaced as the muscles of his arms wasted into a bony limb wrapped in wrinkled grey skin. Black talons grew from his nail beds and the beast inside him roared, commanding him to satisfy an insatiable appetite to dig in and take a bite.

'Callum, did you hear what I said?' Kate asked as she leaned forward and placed a gentle hand on his arm. 'Are you all right?'

He stared into her warm eyes and reminded himself of her kindness. He took a deep breath and pushed back in his chair, then closed his eyes and willed the beast back into its cage. When he opened them again, he was relieved to see only Kate's oval-shaped face.

'Did something happen?' she asked.

'No.'

Kate sighed. 'I really need you to be honest with me.'

'I'm trying.'

'Do you understand the situation we are in now?'

'Yes. I'm up for physical assault charges and they want to keep me in gaol for it.'

'It's more than that now,' Kate said solemnly.

The blood in Callum's face dropped to the floor and the numbness engulfed him as he remembered.

'Mitchell Buchannan died this morning. You are now on trial for murder.'

The beast inside him shook its cage and roared.

FORTY-EIGHT

That evening, Stacey hoisted a tub of food under her arm as she walked beside Liam, who wheeled the mobile barbecue into the manor's courtyard. Ryan happily chattered as he helped Paige set up the outdoor dining table and chairs.

Liam set up the grill and utensils while Stacey took out the butter and marinated food, placing them beside him on foiled plates. Liam seemed fixated on getting the dials correct.

Stacey waited as Liam struggled with the controls until the barbecue turned on.

'I can do the cooking.' Liam picked up the tongs. 'You rest. How's your wound?'

'Good,' Stacey mumbled and lightly touched the bandage that Paige had slapped on for her. The tablets she gave her worked wonders. She could barely feel the pain anymore.

Stacey shuffled on the spot looking over at Paige and her brother who were doing a good job setting the cutlery and drinks. She'd be redundant with them. A niggle urged her to speak, but the tongue tie prevented her from making any sounds. She took a breath, not quite sure how best to talk to Liam and too jittery to sit.

The meat sizzled and popped as Liam threw the steak and seafood on the grill.

'Uh, you'll need to flip the steak now otherwise it'll burn,' Stacey said quietly.

Liam rubbed the back of his neck and frowned but flipped the meat as instructed. He turned and looked at her.

'I'm sorry,' they both said together.

Liam laughed. 'I can't believe how awkward this is, despite everything we've been through.'

Stacey let out a sigh, at least it wasn't just her that was finding their conversation uncomfortable. She hadn't wanted to connect and make amends with someone she was attracted to before, until now. She swallowed and opted to wait for more courage to arrive but cursed herself at the same time.

'I'm um, sorry for the times I was a jerk to you,' Liam said as he turned the prawns on the grill. 'I didn't mean to get all jealous-y on you. I'm sorry about the professor.'

'You were jealous of Professor Chu?' Stacey gave him an incredulous stare. 'Why?'

Liam placed the utensils aside, laced his finger behind his neck and looked up at the star-lit skies. 'You seemed to connect to him better than you did with me. I could never be as smart as he is, or as you are.'

Stacey gently moved his hands down from his neck, holding them tightly in hers. She let herself bask in the warmth of his gaze. 'I may be good at remembering facts. But you are smart in a way that I can only imagine. I like that you can see things from a different perspective.'

Liam beamed. 'Yeah, you think?'

'Yes.'

'Are you trying to make me feel better?' Liam narrowed his eyes but grinned.

'I'm being honest,' Stacey replied. 'I'm sorry, too, for all those times I shut you out.'

'Why did you? Was it because of something I did?'

Stacey returned Liam's earnest look. 'No, it boils down to...' She shut her eyes to reduce the intensity. 'I... I'm not used to...'

'Used to what?'

Stacey shook her head, willing the words to come. She wanted so much to articulate how she felt.

'To connecting, um. I get overwhelmed.'

'By me?'

'By people in general. By things I don't understand. It takes me longer to process... to understand.'

'Understand what?'

'How I'm feeling, how others are feeling. I don't think my insecurities help, either.'

Liam cocked his head to the side and gave her a puzzled look. 'What do you have to be insecure about? You're super cute and super smart.'

Stacey couldn't help laughing. 'Thanks.' A giddiness filled her chest and she was grateful to Liam for seeing her that way. She loved how the breeze lightly tossed his hair aside to reveal more of his handsome features. 'I'm glad you were with me through all this. I'm braver when I'm with you.'

His grin widened. 'Right back at you. And I'll try and give you more space in future, to process.'

'Thank you.'

Stacey cleared her throat. She needed to take the plunge or her mind would find an excuse not to. It would be stupid to let such a good guy go. Maybe he was exactly what she needed—her blessing in disguise.

'Liam, will you go out with me?' she blurted, then held her breath.

Liam's eyes brightened and his mouth stretched into the widest grin. He wrapped his arms around her, lifting her off the ground. 'What took you so long?'

'So that's a yes?'

Liam twirled her around, planting a kiss on her lips. 'Yeah, absolutely!'

FORTY-NINE

Later that evening, Paige sat back in the portable chair by the foldable dining table and observed the boys happily sipping their hot drinks and wolfing down their dinner. Stacey, like a mother hen, was quick to refill everyone's plates with lamb roast and steamed vegetables. A chunk of meat and gravy landed on her empty plate before Paige had a chance to decline.

'Wait, you're a health buff, right?' Stacey said and scurried back with a bowl of yoghurt, berries, and melons filled to the brim. 'I think this will help balance the meat.'

Stacey was so commanding in her insistence that she eat more that Paige didn't dare refuse her third helping of food. Instead, she thanked her, having no idea how she was going to fit dessert in after such a big dinner.

'Oh, it just moves and fits in around the sides,' Stacey said, sitting back down next to Liam. 'Eat. It'll give you more energy to train.'

Paige stirred her bowl, nibbling at the melon on her fork, doing her best to show Stacey she was still eating. Stacey nodded in satisfaction then turned her attention to Ryan and Liam.

Relieved, Paige placed her fork and bowl down. Her mind drifted back to Ahndra Rose as she replayed their last encounter. Hubert had said the manor was cloaked under the stone bearer's protection spell, so how on earth was Ahndra able to break through the barrier twice?

Where had Ahndra disappeared to? Would she be punished by Apollyon for failing in her mission. Or were they planning something else more gruesome?

But there was something about Ahndra that didn't fit the typical profile of a cold-hearted killer. There was a warmth that came from her that didn't make sense. Her opponent had had ample opportunity to deliver the death strike but never did. She mainly blocked and deflected. Was she teasing them? Or were they part of an elaborate game?

A light touch on her arm made her jump. She turned to Stacey who was now sitting beside her.

'It doesn't add up, does it?' Stacey said. 'Why would the assassin wreak havoc and then help us in the end?'

'We did force her hand,' Liam said.

'Yes, but someone that powerful could have easily killed us or thrown us into the vortex again. Nothing about the assassin seems to happen by accident.' Stacey folded one arm across her chest and rested her head on the other palm, deep in thought.

'I agree.' Paige wrung her hands. 'It almost feels like we're pawns in a larger game here.'

Ryan shuddered. 'That's disturbing.'

'Do you think they were involved in Callum's arrest?' Stacey asked.

'Maybe we should ask Hubert about it,' Ryan said.

'Yeah, how is he?' Liam asked. 'His wounds looked really bad.'

'The bleeding's stopped. He's resting upstairs. I'll go check on him.' Paige rose and made her way inside. She couldn't let the team see how rattled she was. Even though, they may have won the fight, but still, there was a queasiness that gnawed at her. A niggle deep within her gut, told her the fight was far from over. If Hubert was awake, she would press him for answers.

'Ask him if he wants any dinner,' Stacey called after her.

Paige nodded and ascended the marble staircase to a corridor on the west wing.

Hubert's door was ajar with light pouring into the dimly lit corridor. She stiffened as voices floated from his room, sending cold flushes through her core.

'They're not ready. They need more training.'

'Paige got through your training gauntlet did she not?' came Hubert's voice.

She shuffled closer, her heart skipping beats. The other voice was familiar. So familiar it quickened her pulse.

'Your stone bearers did a bang-up job of rescuing you,' came the female voice.

Hubert chuckled. 'They got there in the end.'

'They are still not ready,' the woman retorted.

'If together they cannot defeat you, then, I agree, they are not.' Hubert drawled. 'But remember, they have not been through what you have.'

Light footsteps moved across the room as Paige reached the open door and found Hubert staring out the window with his back to her.

'What do you propose we do now?' the woman asked.

'I'm sure you'll think of something,' Hubert replied in a bright tone. 'But perhaps a more motivating challenge this time.'

When the door swung open, she was right up against the breath-taking face of Ahndra Rose. The shock of it all cemented her legs in place. The assassin's hauntingly beautiful eyes bored into hers as they shimmered bright purple, seizing every corner of her mind. Paige fought to stay awake, but her consciousness slipped further and further away, like sliding down a steep metal slope on grease.

Ahndra smiled and brushed her fingers lightly across her cheek. 'Fine. We'll start with the empath.'